Spell Bound

Kristen McDonald

Black Rose Writing

www.blackrosewriting.com

ISBN: 978-1-61296-081-4

PUBLISHED BY BLACK ROSE WRITING

www.blackrosewriting.com

Printed in the United States of America

Spell Bound is printed in Angsana New

To Grace for brilliant ideas and hilarious times, to my loving Turtle (you'll know who you are... I hope), and to my family for keeping me up to my nose in books. And for all of you keeping me spell bound in a thick, fuzzy sweater of love.

Spell Bound

Chapter One

The Beginning

I

The room was an obscurity of darkness. Along the walls, baleful shadows licked fervently at the chipping bricks. They patiently swayed, watching their master, waiting with him. Drapes of eccentric, sheer fabric hung around the study while a young man with dark blond, curly hair paced zealously, waiting for his sister. His cloak was ankle-length and striking, yet it blended in with his background. He wore a look of furrowed bereavement on his face. His patience was wearing thin when footsteps began to echo along the high-ceilinged halls. His heart leapt feebly. The show was about to begin.

"Scarlet." It wasn't a question; he could tell it was her from three miles away.

"I'm here," the young woman announced. Her brother turned his head and smiled a smile that was something less and something more than painful to look at. Her stomach twisted in ways it shouldn't. *Why can't he have someone else do his work? Doesn't he enjoy to inflict the pain himself?* Her stance quickly deflated from confident to weary.

"I wouldn't start if I were you," Colon warned softly, picking thoughts up from her mind. "We have better things to argue about."

Scarlet's eyes flashed to meet his. Their eyes met together and, while his glare was stronger, she refused to break the connection first. Finally, he looked away.

She took this moment to her advantage.

"Keep your head out of my thoughts," she snapped, the slightest hint of remorse flickering inside of her. *Stupid necklaces… they allow him to read my thoughts. Then again so can I, to his.* She thought these secretly, holding them in tightly, refusing his sight on them.

"Only if you do this one thing for me," Colon compromised, voice calmer. More controlled. He had heard the thoughts she had struggled to keep secret easily. He had always been stronger.

But his focus turned away from her. He handed her a woven scroll tattered with edges held loosely together in a feeble gold strand. When his hand touched hers, she withstood the chills. His fingers were like hot iron. A side affect. That was worth it? She still hadn't figured that out herself. She fought and won control over her emotion-filled face.

Peering up from her blazing red hair, she took the scroll. In this room every moment felt like hours. She was already feeling drained.

Scarlet didn't need to peak into his mind or open the tattered parchment. She knew what it was all too well. They had been preparing for this moment. He had found out where the girl was going to be... Nevertheless, thoughts and questions danced around in her brown eyes. *I don't trust you,* was shimmering delicately.

He almost slapped her face.

She noticed his blurred thoughts drain away to one clear one, and she was both interested and annoyed. She was *older*. This was supposed to be *her* job. Yet he was the one who had become obsessed with revenge. She thirsted for it too, but she'd settle for anyone. Even him…

"It's a simple task I know you can complete. But if you fail, let's just say it will hurt much more than the pain our father went through. I will ensure that."

Scarlet cast a dark look at him, but nodded. She walked towards the large fastened window in her brother's lavish room. Opening the hatch, she thrust her head out and called out a shrill whistle. The sound of flapping came near. She leapt out the window, and landed squarely on the black hide of her scaly familiar. She cast a look behind her to see she was closely followed by her watchman. Scarlet eyed him, watching him bob and weave past the air currents on his own, probably untrained, dragon. She was used to him having her back since she had become a person people feared. And there would be more coming. Someone to back her up.

I'm ready, she thought. *How long has it been since I was able to touch the skies? To constrict fear into our enemies' hearts? It's time for us to rise again. This time, we won't lose.*

A note was tucked under one of the over-reflective scales of her dragon, Téashi. Scarlet peeled it out gently enough to not hurt the monster. There in bright red letterings, recognizable as her brother's decorative penmanship, were the sentences,

Remember, he killed us, and he's still alive.

She's born and will finish us, but we can kill her.

It will kill him. And we will be victorious.

Once again.

She sped Téashi, adrenaline pulsing through her veins like sparks of electricity. The air flipped her hair wildly, and her eyes narrowed.

As if I could forget, Scarlet thought.

II

It was raining. A tiny hospital that lay near a village was still surprised that a couple had come to them to deliver their baby. There is a fancier, better hospital up the road, they tried to argue. They had no expertise and people who were qualified for baby delivery here. This was a hospital for minor things such as picking up over-the-counter and prescription medications. They could barely call their small cabin-like building a hospital. Although somehow, they had pulled it off.

The soon-to-be parents however, insisted.

Now, the parents watched their baby, healthy and born beautiful, trying not to laugh when the doctors didn't believe how she didn't cry when she was born. The gullibility of human doctors... The couple talked quietly to each other, and when the doctor asked if the mother wanted to see her child she said yes enthusiastically, but she never took the child from the doctor's hands. She claimed it was a part of a family tradition. However, something else was being hidden behind her words. The doctors didn't say anything though, only asking what the girl's name would be. "Nicole. Nicole Colon." *Nikki,* the man and woman thought at the same time. They had had this planned for a while now.

The parents couldn't touch their child. At least for now. They would have a moment. Only a few seconds, but they had been warned from a person whom they trusted severely. To not touch her. All was well however, because the doctor wanted to check the newborn child out, still fearing something wasn't quite right since she hadn't cried.

They were the only people in the hospital, as it was pouring out, and was a slow day. The man whispered something to his wife, his accent clearly reflecting where he lived. England: far from the city life. The parents looked from behind a thick glass window at the doctor and nurses.

The man rubbed his hands together and blue flames sparked in-between his fingers and palm. He was ready. The woman looked at him nervously, but he had a look of sheer confidence on his face. It was against all the rules that they lived by to do this, yet the person who would punish them were the people they were doing this against.

The man lifted his hand to the glass that separated him from his child and the doctors. At the moment they were just looking at the baby girl. He could risk it. He pressed his palm against the cold frame and a silver substance seemed to leak from his fingers and through the thick glass. He watched as the doctor turned stiff. The nurses' eyes turned slightly misty. They placed the child down, and looked at each other. Together, they walked out the back door of the room.

The man nodded as if approving, but his wife bit her lip and shook her head slightly to herself.

"We have little time before—"

"I know," the woman interrupted gently. "Trust me, I know."

He placed his hand gently in his wife's. She sighed quietly at his warm hands from his fire magic, as he whispered, "She will be okay. You know that. You *saw* it."

"The future can change easily. What I saw could be different as we stand here in this moment."

The husband looked down and then back at his child, who was sitting still, as if waiting for them to come in. "Come on," he pressed slightly.

He walked to the door of the room and opened it, closely followed by his wife.

The man sauntered to his child and picked her up, careful not to touch her skin. He could hold her now, as it wouldn't matter in a second. Touching her skin however, would still put them all in jeopardy.

"What about Jake?" the woman started to ask.

"He will be waiting for us when we get home. He's small but bright. The Berlidge family are watching him. When Nikki gets older and Jake grows and learns the skills at Primrose, he will be able to protect her better than any of us can."

"Are you sure it was the right thing to put the **curse** on him?"

"My brother insisted before they..." the man's thoughts trailed from his brother to his death. "They knew the risk. Besides, Jacob's a part of our family, he'll have the courage and strength to take almost anything."

5

The door flew open then.

The man clutched his child closely with one arm, and with the other, he outstretched it. His blue flames spread about an inch from his palm, read to attack if needed.

When two, mystical figures appear quite suddenly out of nowhere in a hospital, a normal pair of parents' instincts would be to scream and shout, "How in the world, did those insane freaks appear out of nowhere?! Get them out of this nursery!" And the doctors would have come back in. The two figures would have done one of two things: let themselves get captured, or disappear as quickly as they had come.

Yet the father put his outstretched arm down. "You're here. Finally."

"Yes," the first figure said, his voice low and well used. He was an older man with rich wrinkles tracing his face. "Are you ready for this?"

"No," the woman said just as her husband answered yes.

The second figure smiled warmly. She was easily identified as the elder's apprentice. The older man spoke again, "Remember to put on a good show. If you believe it, we'll have more of a chance of passing this off."

The couple nodded.

The hearts in this room were all beating abnormally fast except for the child, who was still in her father's hands.

"The doctors are gone?" the elder man asked.

The mother nodded. "For now."

"We mustn't wait much longer," the apprentice whispered. "The longer we wait, the more of a risk we have."

"It's true," the elder confirmed.

The father looked at him with sudden realizing eyes.

"Scarlet is coming. Her brother's pinpointed Nicole's location." The elder looked discouraged as he said this.

The mother didn't want to know how her daughter was found.

"Take her. Keep her safe." The father reluctantly but trustingly handed over his daughter.

"We will," the elder man said.

"Thirteen years will go by fast," the apprentice assured.

"Let's hope she stays a secret for that long." The mother brushed a long strand of auburn hair back behind her ear. Her worries would not remain unspoken.

"Trust me, where she is going, no one would think to look," the apprentice almost laughed. A smile had spread across her face despite the contrasting emotion that filled the room.

"Where exactly?" the father asked.

The apprentice was about to answer, but the older man stopped her. "Maybe it's best to keep it a secret for now. Scarlet has a way with the mind remember."

"Yes," the mother answered back, recounting this comment from past experiences.

"We must go now. The exchange will need to be complete as soon as possible."

The couple nodded together.

They watched as the apprentice and her master disappeared instantly from their sight with only a spark and a small sound that had the reminisce of a breeze drifting over the ocean. The figures were gone. So was their daughter.

III

"Are you kidding me?" a doctor groaned loudly. People were rushing in like there was no tomorrow. At this point, it seemed like there wasn't going to be. The world was in chaos as if the apocalypse was this very night. The patients were on needles, the nerves of every worker were on the edge, and there was a feeling in the air, quite unlike anything ever felt in this small town.

"It's raining violently Doctor, and people are coming in injured from traffic jams and accidents," a nurse tried to explain calmly, while taking a thick strip of gauze and rushing it over to a person whose head was slit open.

"This is nuts." He shook his head, chugging down the rest of his coffee. "Ok, take the workers from the nursery—there's isn't a baby in there needing intensive care. They'll be fine for the moment. We need more help out here." He felt a twinge of remorse; if anything happened to those babies now, there was only one person to blame.

"Yes Doctor," the nurse said with a smile.

She went into the nursery and spoke to the employees, telling them to care for the people who were coming in. They hesitated, but she scolded them, saying in a rushed tone, "Hurry! Doctor's orders!" They left the room then, stepping up to help people who needed them more.

The nurse slipped off her apron and her thin hospital hat, brushing her nausea-colored nurse-dress with her hand gently, turning it back to a slightly weathered cape and emerald dress. A spark of golden light cast off the walls. A breeze shifted through the room like a warm spring draft.

The young woman, not older than sixteen, watched her master wave away the last yellowish threads of a magical transportation **enchantment**, as if he were waving off smoke. *Indiana, the United States,* the woman thought almost satisfied. It made sense to her. She hadn't even heard of the small city they were in. The name didn't make any sense on her elfin-influenced tongue. It didn't happen by coincidence that it was one of the busiest nights in the history of hospitals. And later all of the doctors and nurses would slouch in the chairs and throw their heads back in anguished crying, "We don't get paid enough to do this job!" As if it mattered that their feet hurt. But it was all for Nikki. Yet they didn't even know it. The thought almost made her smile. They would never know.

Nothing is a mere accident anymore, even the flood that happens to be causing havoc to everyone, thought the woman pulling out her hair from under her heavy cloak to reveal bleach-blond elfin curls held with a large, elaborate brown comb. The memory of Garden and her conjuring and enhancing the should-have-been small rainstorm, ran alongside her many other thoughts. She loved to influence the weather. Garden usually suggested to stray away from doing so. In this case however, he claimed it was a necessary risk for executing their plan flawlessly. She always laughed at his over-explained theories, this being no exception. She wasn't surprised that she was scolded once again, being told this was a matter that needed to be taken serious in order for everything to succeed. Alex, however, knew something was bound to mess up everything. *Humans are so predictable.* "Their incompatible ways have always neglected the philosophy of our existence," Garden always told her. However, she believed there were a rare few who actually believed in the magic that surrounded her on a daily basis.

Catching her eye, the rusty man twinkled his eyes at her to tell her to share her speechless thoughts. She was entranced by the amount of gray flakes that seemed to have sprinkled rather recently unto his coarse black hair. He always wore it in a slicked-back style.

"When will you tell me your plans for her?" she asked curtly. Her lips twitched down in dissatisfaction. *Why does he always smile and twinkle his eyes when his "enchanting" voice could say it all in one word? If only his mind were as easily penetrated, as the rest of the world is.*

He only smiled at her rage. "Alexandria, when we know that one of these babies is safe, and preferably the one we are sworn to protect, and that we ourselves are safe from..." He trailed off. It was unlike him to do so, but it would have been odder to hear him say a vague word such as "things" to replace the word he was forbidden to talk about aloud. His wise eyes still burned with the kindness his mouth refused to display. "Even though you are very young and are still learning, you should understand enough to not underestimate the dangers of our mission. Needless to say, the explanation I gave to you beforehand about our plan should be enough for now."

Alexandria sighed, feeling like a stubborn three year old. *Does the man always have to talk in riddles? What would my ailing mother think of me now if she knew her elfin daughter was a witch with a master who was out of his mind—whatever is left of it. She wanted me to stay at Blaire Hills, but I was losing* my *wits there...as if this is much better.* A sharp pang echoed through her as she realized what she had just thought. *It's awful of me to think this way. I am a failure as an apprentice.* She hadn't gotten much sleep, and without thinking of the consequences, she began to ask a dangerous question. "Garden, would Col—" she started with new warm eyes but her words faded as the look on Garden's face grew graver. She always had a bad taste on her tongue after she finished saying his name anyway.

"You know they're on our tail. He knows our voices, specifically mine. We must be wise in the words we speak. Besides, we are cutting it close as it is, and we don't need to be caught at the moment we thought we were safe. Best to get business going now."

Alexandria nodded and returned to rocking the England baby softy. The baby wasn't even moving though, rather she looked at Alex with still, wide eyes and a broad expression. She saw through the baby's sweet green-speckled brown eyes, strangely reminding Alex of fall and amber fire, to find not scrambled thoughts, but pure strands, stringing themselves together to form questions. Alex continued to examine the baby's mind, intrigued to the point where it felt like she was reading pages of a book. She hugged the girl tight to her, wordlessly growing more attached to her and promising her that she wouldn't let anything happen to her. *If only I could read your future. Maybe your thoughts would silently become what you will be when you get older like me. I can't wait 'till I can actually see you again.*

Garden summoned Alexandria to follow him as he walked around baby cribs, watching the few scarlet-faced, fist-pounding babies in their current plastic homes. There were also the small amount of sleeping babies with tear stained faces. There were no more than five babies in the room, but none of them as calm as the baby they held in their arms. They traveled until they stopped at a baby whose sign had rushed handwriting scribbled carelessly. This irritated Alex. Was everything rushed mayhem in this state? Nothing was marked with magic as far as she could tell. Maybe it was her elfin skepticism that brought her to disdain this place. Maybe it was the haunting deeds they themselves were doing. Magic couldn't be transferred, couldn't be deported. Yet here they were. She looked at the sign in anguish.

Chrystan Nicole Richard

They both peered into the pink-lined crib, to find the single loudest baby of the bunch. Alex handed Garden her silent baby, "You'd think that one's dead already."

Garden shook his head at her naïve nature, but gave into a small, disconcerting smile all the same. They both knew that the screaming baby wouldn't last more than a month due to a sickness that none of the doctors had recognized yet. Yet the irony that a child so silent could be taking an extremely loud, soon-to-be-dead child's place in order to escape death herself, was extraordinary. Especially since the England child was as silent as death already. Alex, making a sour face, regretfully gave the quiet baby to Garden and picked up the thrashing baby. She sang her elfin hymns. She rocked and swayed her. The baby *would not stop crying*. "You can easily tell which one is one of us," Alex said rolling her eyes. While the corners of Garden's mouth twitched ever so slightly, Alex was given a headache from the baby's useless thoughts.

She was an average baby human. Not a speck of magic flowed in her blood. While the silent child was a different story...

Garden placed the baby from England to this new plastic prison. Quickly, she handed him the Indiana child. Alex sent a skeptical look at him as she eyed the pink linings. Taking a small breath, she stretched her hand and laid it on the lining. The pink scurried away and was replaced with a glossy red fabric that had the sparkle of sequins.

The lining turned to drapes, elaborate and rich in detail.

Garden chortled. "That's a magnificent way to make her stand out, even though it's quite beautiful."

"She deserves it!" Alex argued. "You know what her parents would have given her if they had the choice."

Garden nodded. "Indeed I do. Perhaps for now though," he placed his hand on the lining and it instantly turned back to the pastel pink and plastic, "it would be best to stay as nonchalant as possible."

Alex bit her lip, and ran a hand through the tuft of auburn hair that the silent baby girl had sticking up. "How is it possible that she and her cousin will accomplish this?"

"They aren't going to be alone. You know this."

"Even so...it's just hard to imagine considering Jake's two right now, and that he will be training her someday soon."

"He's already had a lot of training for himself. His magic is showing through quite obviously."

"Are you sure he's safe where he is?"

"Right now, we should be worrying more about Nicole."

Alex nodded.

Garden continued in a voice that felt to her, like the final words of their conversation, "Those with minuscule faith have little to reach for, for you have to reach for something, or you'll fall for anything." With that, he gave her a wink and he carried the Indiana baby off, disappearing for the third time in a dusty cloud of gold, leaving the hospital and Alex once again in a place where they knew no one would ever think to look to find this girl who they depended on living.

Alex took a breath. As she did, her emerald cloak turned back into the sea-foam green skirt and top of the nurse outfit. Magic was becoming more complicated than she had hoped.

IV

Two Days Later: England

The doors of the hospital flew open and crashed into the crumbly bricks of the building. The short, slender woman with rich brown hair, bounded forward with her husband. She was severely shaking, despite the unnaturally warm temperature for this area. Her hands had a firm grasp on a sleeping baby, whose unfamiliar red, puffy cheeks almost irritated her. Her heart was sore. *How am I suppose to know if this will work? I'll admit switching the two babies was an... interesting plan, but it doesn't seem to have that flawless touch that Garden always has.* She didn't want to remind herself that it was *her* who had the vision and told Garden about it, to switch the children. She knew which baby was going to die an early death. She refused it to be her own.

Despite the immense amount of scorn this woman thought a person would need to have to perform such a task as switching a child and then taking her back when it was safe again, she didn't regret it. *Her* child needed to live. If she didn't, so many things would be torn apart. Lives worn to shreds, futures forgotten. Not that the world relied on her girl. There were no prophecies about her child; there were no ancient tales, no legends, no expectations. There were only thin-lined whispers spoken in the **shack**, rumors flurrying in the air like a snow fall that refuses to touch ground. Sometimes, rumors are worse than prophecies...

It was an uncommon thing for this family to fear. It *was* a common thing however, for them to be put in the spotlight of danger. Through generations they had always been ready to die on the spot. It was the sort of attitude you had to live with when you were a **Je Ne Sais Quoi**. Especially when you were a part of a family with a history like theirs. *Why does Colon have to be after Nikki anyway?* But she knew the answer to that question. Revenge.

Trotting beside the worried mother was a lanky, auburn haired man who kept glancing up every other second. If someone hadn't known him, they would have thought he had a nervous twitch. He limped slightly, and the woman looked at him in concern. Would he survive the attack they both knew was coming? He had barely come out of the last one alive... He wasn't sure he'd be so lucky next time. The atmosphere was dead silent, as if something were going sneak up on them from behind. The man worried about his wife Ruby, he worried for this innocent blood being spilt—after all it was just a harmless baby, and he didn't even know who the parents were— and most of all, he worried about his own daughter. All the way in North America. He didn't know exactly where. It would have been too dangerous to know. *I promise no matter what happens to me today I will find you and keep you safe,* he vowed to her.

She has the most beautiful name, after her grandfather, yet it will be thirteen long years before she gets to use it again. He caught some irony in his tone to himself, and was surprised he could still use humor. Tomas's thoughts were more calm than Ruby's. He had complete confidence in Garden and Alexandria. That was his problem.

They could feel the safe spot impending. The spot they had specifically designed to be able to get out of reach of the eyes of the town and escape, the same way Garden had done so with their daughter. Quickly, they composed themselves. They put on masks of their former, worried selves, just in case their fears became veracity. They were exactly thirteen inches from the invisible border for magic, when the air became something that was no longer air.

It was as though you were being shoved by the neck into deep water. The air was cold and clammy, sticking to your skin. The air had jaws; it clamped down and tore at them every which way. Forcing them to stand completely still, in fear they would lose all sense of direction. Yet they did anyways. If you were cut off from the world: your sights, your smells, your hearing, *that* was what it felt like in this darkness. Wind flew in all directions. Ruby's hair fluttered like pages of a book. She closed her eyes. Tomas wrapped his arms around her. His eyes were wide, searching for a point where their attackers would emerge.

As if the sky were releasing toxic gas, a thick, smoky fog swirled around the shoes and waists of the parents. It wrapped around the foreign girl in their arms. The fog had fingers, and they wrapped themselves around her, claiming her to the darkness. The mother Ruby held her securely.

Tomas lit a spark from his hand. A great blue flame leapt from the top of his fingers,

The fog shuttered off, as if repulsed by the match within his fingertips. It strayed away from them for a moment, bitten by the strength of his fire. The fog seemed to come alive. It knew how to move by itself. It was commanded by no one but whom it had been created by. Tomas knew this. His magic would not hold off the darkness. Not when the smoke could figure out how to stop them. By the look of how the smog edged closer, it wouldn't be long.

He killed his own flame, as the fog had created a tunnel around them, cutting off most of the oxygen. He didn't want to waste precious air. If they could reach out, they would stroke the fabric-like velvet atmosphere. If the air wasn't so dense and didn't clamp their mouths shut, they could suck in something that resembled exhaust fumes.

Then, it stopped.

Everything stopped.

It became clear they were in the eye of the storm. Only, the real danger was inside of it with them.

Bursting out of the smog, came two mangled creatures. They blended in so tremendously with the darkness, that all the parents could make out was some sort of mass with red eyes and black-slit irises. One of the two creatures let out a smothered growl. The black mist swirled in the air around them with its echo. Breaking through the thick air, it opened its mouth, showcasing gleaming white teeth overlapping the bottom rim of its gums. They shone like headlights—

fat and round—except the tip was a dagger-like edge. As their translucent red wings beat, the misty air swirled like a demonic child shaking a morbid snow globe.

So much for going as planned, Thomas thought grimly to himself. But it *was* according to plan. To one of them at least.

Across the dragons' backs, two separate knee-high boots appeared. Two bodies came from that, and soon it was easy to recognize a woman and a man. When their hands finally left the saddles, that was strapped tightly around the beasts' ridged backs, they turned to gaze at the unsightly parents whom their duty had sent them to. By now, Ruby's face displayed a look of pure horrorstricken worry, and her delicate features seemed a bit twisted. She was grateful that the fog slightly hid her expressions. Her own doubting thoughts chimed in her head so loud that she longed to just drop the baby and cover herself. To protect her ears from her own head. It wasn't her child, and her own was safe. So maybe...

No, I have to make this convincing. He is not easily fooled and we need to make sure that this performance will not be our last. For our daughter's sake. For a moment, the parents believed that Colon had actually come down and met them himself. If that had been so, they could have forgotten all hopes of surviving. They both breathed a sigh of relief. The only man who had come was stockier than Colon and wore thick gray-tinged clothing that Colon would never be found in.

The woman had on tan boots with such lavish designs that there wasn't a single question that she was royalty. An elaborate wine-colored cloak pooled on the foggy pavement, and her hood concealed her facial features all except the leaking of her blazing red hair.

The guard stepped beside the perfect-postured red head and looked uncomfortable, as he seemed to disappear in the blackness because if his suit of onyx. His leather belt cradled a dazzling bright sword that glinted, even though there was nothing for it to reflect off of, as if to inflict threats. And just as that sword longed for that certain feeling, so it was that the two parents felt.

A smile that didn't bring the least bit of comfort, flurried around the atmosphere, radiating from the young woman, while she snapped out a golden scroll. As soon as the girl started out preaching, "By the order of King Colon III, ...," Ruby had tuned out the whole declaration by the soft sound of her pounding heart. "Child...," *Boom, Boom.* "Die." *Boom, Boom, Boom.* Would Garden's plan really work, or would it flop like the never ending beatings of the dragon's wings?

Not a moment was wasted, and the dreaded moment came when the young lady finished her train of words. She pushed down her dark hood, to reveal the ripe-strawberry pool of hair that covered her head. Then brushed it all back in the single, sweeping motion of her hand. She was not smiling, The woman Scarlet stood completely blank, while she spoke the first words of her own in a mocking tone, "So, what shall your choice be?"

I have to put up a good act, Ruby thought to herself. She knew that Tomas was thinking the same thing. Even though she didn't have the slightest idea what the document *really* said, besides the few words that she had heard, she knew. It was in her heart, causing her thoughts to become unstable. It was about a choice. Both ending in death.

Ruby made it convincing enough as she clutched the sleeping baby tightly in her hands. Tomas and herself stayed as silent as death itself.

"I figured that would be your choice," Scarlet responded with her lavish accent, a wide-spread grin creeping up on her lips. She whipped out a silver and black wand, and pointed it directly at the baby and Ruby. "Hmm... Who to kill first? The baby whom I'm after, or the mother who loves it dearly, or the father who will suffer the most?"

Right when she was about to attack the baby, she had a change in thoughts. A bright purple and black swirling cloud of light exploded from the stick of wood. Before anybody could do anything, change anything, or even react, the hex had found its target, which spun backwards uncontrollably and finally fell with a thud to the black pavement.

Tomas did not move.

Ruby couldn't contain her fear now. A ripple of scream flew from her lips. She didn't care if she was in the protective magic field, she pulled out her own brown stick, and sent a blue shield over herself and the baby. Another purple flame shot forward, shattered the feeble shield like a baseball viciously to glass. Ruby dashed forward and at that instant, the child awoke. A last **enchantment** followed Ruby as she frantically skittered away, but she could not escape it. The hex hit its target, the baby, directly in the heart. Suddenly, Ruby felt it spreading through her entire body. Thoughts clicked in her mind. The child was too small for an **enchantment** that big.

Since it hit its target, Ruby knew that she would receive the effects that occur when you survive the nearly unstoppable spell. Her thoughts became scrambled. Things were forgotten. Important things. The effects were never simple. They were never the same. This time, they chose to steal valuable memories and common sense from the mind of the young mother.

At that moment, not only was she incredibly confused, but she had totally forgotten that the baby that was dead wasn't her baby. Tears welled in her eyes. She could barely control the grief flustering inside of her body. A thickness spread in her throat, despairingly. Ruby swept her wand once over herself, and disappeared into the new night sky whispering the words, "I have failed you."

Scarlet ran over to the discarded baby in shock and surprise. Her plan was that the **enchantment** would hit Ruby, killing her too. It hadn't happened, but Ruby's reaction wasn't what she had expected if she survived. *How could she just leave the baby there? After all she'd been through, after that sacrifice she gave to try and save her daughter,* this *is what happens. Oh, I'm unimpressed. Very unimpressed.*

Scarlet bent over the pink blanket and unwrapped it from the little infant's face. Still half in shock and half in the process of crying, an unfamiliar baby was held in Scarlet's arms like a chunk of hard, dead-cold piece of rock. Scarlet's mock-smile returned, but her eyes were hard as they examined.

This isn't the baby that Colon saw, that he saw me see. How could my vision not come true? They always have... She stroked the babies cold cheek and felt its still-warm tears.

She blew breaths of wind in-between her own paling lips. They turned into a line so thin they were nonexistent. If she returned empty handed and without news for celebration, Colon wouldn't forgive her. Let alone let her live. Trying to calm her heart beat, her mind fluttered to all that had happened in the last twenty-four hours. Something about the way the parents looked when they came out. Sure, defiant, unafraid...

Where did Tomas go? She could barely breathe as her feet led her to where the body of Tomas should have been. Yet he wasn't.

She spun frantically. By now, Scarlet's heart was racing but her mind had finally clicked. *It's not the girl. She's still alive.*

Scarlet ground her teeth. *Some way, some how... You won't be what those idiot parents want you to become. I will find you. You will die.*

V

North America: Mishawaka, Indiana

It was a clear day in the hospital near the tip of Indiana. in a city where no oddness had ever occurred. No strange figures had been spotted. No dragons lurking around the corner. No revenge seeking princes would take their wrath out. It was quiet and still. Quite boring. Excitement was found in small things. Tiny events were considered extraordinary. If a child was hidden in the city (if you could call it a city) no one would think to look. Because everyone always overlooked this city. Which is why Nikki was hidden there.

Right when a skeptical, crinkly nurse named Karen popped into the nursery to retrieve the baby, she was immediately overwhelmed by the headache all the crying and screaming gave her. She was working in overtime, hadn't gotten sleep in the last week, and her stepmother was driving her crazy. Tiny things that were exciting.

She had never touched magic. Never been around it. Never *wanted* to feel it. However suddenly, she was overwhelmed by an intense urge to feel something different than what she had been feeling for the last forty years.

She was just about to give up both of her searches. The parents had described their baby as a plump, red faced girl that was the loudest in the room (and she had described her urge to feel something different as ridiculous and worthy of a ten-year-old). Although together all of the babies made one deplorable noise, there was not a single child who made a particular cry that could definitely be classified as the loudest. Karen ran two finger across her temple, trying to remember why she hadn't retired yet.

 The irritated nurse was not in the mood for parents that couldn't even identify their own child. *Hair like an angel. Dimples the size of moon craters. Any information like that would have surely been more useful.* Her sarcastic thoughts brought a slight smile to her face. *Maybe I'll start my own comedy show, be on live TV, and actually make some money instead of the trash I get here.*

A crib caught Karen's eyes. The lighting seemed different around it. The atmosphere seemed perplexed at how to handle itself around the crib. Karen walked over to the side of it without realizing what she was doing. A certain feeling was filling her that she couldn't explain. It wasn't the sight of the child, who was, although cute, quite like any other baby. Except for one thing. The baby girl was wrapped soundly in her pink blanket and was just starring at the ceiling. Not moving. Not gurgling. And her eyes seemed to be stirring—the green into the browns.

Is that child actually not crying? What a miracle. Something became unsettled in her as she thought that, as if it wasn't right to talk about a child when they couldn't understand anything you were saying. Karen's thoughts continued however, for a while as she found herself staring at the queer child.

She couldn't figure out how, but this would be a child she would remember. In forty more years if she lived that long.

"I wonder whose parents are lucky to have you," she said softly to the baby girl. The tone of her voice surprised even her. She couldn't remember the last time she talked like that.

The girl looked up and stared sideways from her bed. Straight into Karen's eyes. They met hers. Karen almost fell backwards in shocked. Although she couldn't understand why until she realized how odd this behavior was for an infant. *Does she actually know I'm right here? It's as if she understands and is trying to answer... How strange.* Karen slowly walked to the end of the crib where the baby's name was boldly printed on pink paper: Chrystan Nicole Richard.

I think that was the name of the baby I was sent to get. Karen sprinted over to the sign out sheet and saw that the Richards and their new baby Chrystan were indeed checking out. *Humph. Puffy faced, screaming baby I'll say. She's the quietest baby I've ever seen in my entire life. Actually, it seems so abnormal for a baby of this age to act this way.* It had only been two days since she was born.

In a quick motion, Karen swooped up the calm thing and rushed her over to the room where the parents would be eagerly waiting. She stopped when she got to room 130B. Cradling the baby for probably the last time, she peeked in the pink blanket. The girl was fast asleep! The hospital was bustling with machine growls and doctor yells. *Karen* would have never fallen asleep in all of this chaos. *Goodness!* Karen thought to herself. She quietly peeked in the room where both parents sat staring off in different directions. *They don't look a thing like her! The baby's cheek bones are round and circular, but both parents have slim long ones. Their hair are both a color near black, but the baby's is unmistakably auburn. Am I sure this is the right baby?*

Her thoughts were coming together to create an oddly-pieced

puzzle. By now, Karen had serious doubts about whether all of her marbles were in the glass bowl or not. *Ah well,* she thought, *it is not my problem nor my duty to try and explain why this is.*

Karen walked into the hospital bedroom.

"Here's your baby," Karen said as if reading from a script. She sounded *delighted.* As always when she was in front of people.

The woman took the baby lovingly from Karen's arms and Karen quickly walked away. She couldn't be blamed, she had to remind herself. It would have been the doctor's or nurses' faults if a child was mixed up.

Karen went on her way through the hall but stopped dead. Standing in the middle of a deserted hallway was a creature. It stood at least three and a half feet tall and had the resemblance of a wolf. Without breathing, Karen examined it within the second she had stopped, gathering details as quickly as she could. It was white, and its fur was gathering in large pellets on its chest. And its nails were like a birds'.

Karen blinked. The creature was gone.

Karen collapsed, unconscious, on the ground.

VI

Charlotte held the baby in her arms as if something was erroneous in her heart but her mind couldn't process what. She quickly unveiled the soft, pink shield because unlike most moms, she had not yet seen an up-close of her baby yet. The baby had been taken straight from her. Doctors had claimed that were some signs of brain damage. Although when they tested they found nothing, they still kept the child under watch. Charlotte and her husband Ted were forced to look at their baby through a thick piece of glass.

The baby that she saw now was nothing less than a stranger, and not a single thing like she remembered from the finger-smudged, glass pane. She had taken pride in the fact that her baby was the most red-faced and the loudest of the bunch, taking it as a sign of early dominance. What she didn't know was it was a sign of the foreign disease.

"Does she have your eyes, dear?" Charlotte asked as the baby girls eyes opened and her tiny lips made an "o" of a yawn. The girl's eyes where deep muddy brown but had speckles of green and gold splattered here and there like a muddy pile of autumn leaves.

"It doesn't appear so," her husband Ted responded searching their girl's eyes.

"She has your fingers though." Charlotte tried again, this time holding up the frail baby's long fingers.

"I'm not sure if she looks like us in any way I can see!" Ted said with anguish. *I swear it looked just like us the last time we saw her!* he thought. It was strange to Charlotte and Ted.

Immediately panic swept through them. What if someone had gotten their child mixed up with another? Then again, the odds were against that weren't they? Wasn't it nearly impossible, since their child's name was on her crib? They shook away the thoughts, refusing to accept that there was any chance of a mix-up.

On the way to their home that afternoon, the sky clouded over. Rain fell in silent drops. The world seemed still and solemn. Almost as if the sky was in morn. The parents grew into an argument. One that shook the whole car, and rattled the window panes in the house. The walls of the home soaked in the hatred. The child Nikki was silent the whole time.

Chapter Two

Magic

I

"BEEP-BEEP! BEEP-BEEP! BEEP-BEEP!" an alarm clock screamed to a dazed girl. Her eyes flew open in a sudden realization, and Nikki sprang up with urgency, her long hair flying out like dandelion fluff. Something was wrong. She felt her forehead and pulled it back with a wince. *My head is dead hot. Of course, I'm going to get sick right before my birthday. Yep. This is the sort of luck I live with.* She turned her head to see what time it was. Instantly, some sense was knocked into her like a fat, brick wall. With a panic rising through her throat, Nikki registered what the clock was giving a final warning of.

"Nooo..." she uttered, falling for a moment back into the cool sheets. Nikki no longer cared about the short spikes of heat that ran through her body. This would be the forth time this month she was going to be late to school. There was no use trying to rely on her parents waking her up anymore. Not since... She pushed it aside with a heavy heart. *I don't need to think about it this early in the morning. It consumes enough of my time already.* Reluctantly, she flew out of her bed and threw on the nicest clothes she could come up with within a three second time period. Which ended up being a red t-shirt and dark jeans.

Before anything or anyone could stop her, Nikki had grabbed her bag, raced down the stairs, and was outside of the door in a flash. The bright sunlight met her eyes in a reflective glare they had not anticipated. Although instead of feeling overheated, it felt nice. *Got a couple minutes until there's not a chance that I'll be on time. I have to make it, somehow. I know that if I just make it to school...* A hope stirred inside of her as her gut told her that everything would end up fine today. She almost laughed out loud. School was *never* fine.

Why does middle school have to be so far away? Nikki whined to herself. She hated whining, but this seemed legitimate enough. She was a runner in disguise, a fact never to be known by anyone but close friends, and she pumped her legs heartily in a rhythmic pattern.

The air was crisp, silent, and sweet. No cars traced the streets. Animals and insects were hushed. It was almost edgy, as if the world waited for a sound. Nikki loved it. For a second, she closed her eyes and took a deep breath, trying to forget everything...

"Oomph!" Nikki gasped as she ran straight into a tall, thin girl, that she recognized almost immediately with a friendly smile. It brought her back to the reality of life. "Kay!" Nikki cried in her surprise. The blond girl looked at her still in the trance of being run into, but then smiled warmly. Her slim body posed naturally, in a striking way.

Kay twirled a strand of shoulder length hair nonchalantly. It was a regular pattern for Nikki to meet up with her once she had passed Kay's street, two blocks from where they were now. It didn't surprise Nikki that Kay had started the thirty minute journey without her.

"Hey Chrystan, late this morning? I was afraid you were sick or something..." Kay responded, although she knew differently. There was an awkward pause where they looked at each other, silently reading eyes. Kay studied Nikki's face, which was slightly saddened. Nikki saw something she couldn't describe. As quickly as she had seen it though, it was gone.

They started walking again.

"Last night's homework sure was brutal," Kay continued, as if nothing had happened.

"Yeah, I hate Mr. Shiner so much, he doesn't teach the lessons in a way we can understand. It's like he thinks we're teachers too and he just needs to refresh our memories of it."

"Totally! It makes me so mad…."

The air thickened as Nikki no longer listened. It wasn't Kay, whose conversation she was always happy to partake in. It was something else. Her eyes were drawn to across the street. Nikki stared at the bushes and trees that lined the sidewalk in heavy army-lines. For a moment, nothing *looked* off, but deep inside of her, she could feel it. Her eyes widened when the oddity became a reality.

There, halfway hidden by the bushes, was a very white, shaggy creature. Nikki stared closer and saw that the creature's paws were scaly and ended in long bird-like talons. It's head and body however was covered in thick fur and it was shaped like a wolf. It was so breathtakingly beautiful, Nikki couldn't help but look.

What the heck? Nikki thought. A squeak slipped through her mouth. As Nikki opened her mouth and stretched her vocal chords to form choked words to Kay, two pale skinny hands reached out of the bushes and grabbed the wolf creature back in the shadows. In the quiet air, Nikki swore she heard a soft voice scold, "Arola, no, you have to be back here!"

"Oomph," Nikki gasped for the second time that day when she stopped and this time Kay, who had set a pace behind Nikki, ran into her.

"Okay, what is your problem, Chrystan? Are you having some distraction problems today or are you just having off-and-on stopping issues?" There was a hint of laughter in Kay's voice that allowed Nikki to know she was joking, even thought most of her tone was annoyed.

However, Nikki was too dazed to laugh. Her heart was pounding in her ears. This event had nothing to do with her. It was probably just some child whose dog had gotten loose. His scaly wolf-dog got loose... She must have imagined *some* part of it. Her mind wasn't processing words fast enough to make sense.

"Neither," Nikki finally answered Kay. "Come on, we have to look behind those bushes. There—there's someone... or something...!" Nikki stuttered out.

She had started walking absentmindedly towards the spot where she thought the scene had taken place, but Kay grabbed her arm.

"Look, if we go and look now we're going to be twice as late for school as we were going to be originally."

"If we wait until *later*, whatever was there isn't going to be," Nikki reminded her.

"Do you really want to be late for school?" Kay asked with pleading eyes.

Nikki sighed. "No... Let's just check real quick, then we'll make a run for it."

"Fine." Kay reluctantly let Nikki go so they could take a look.

Nikki and Kay crossed the street as hastily as possible then sprinted towards the bushes. *It's not going to be there, it's not going to be there,* kept repeating in the rhythm of her heart and in Nikki's head as if what lie behind the bushes was trying to convince her it was true.

They reached the other side of the street.

Nikki pulled back the surprisingly thin brambles, the thorn catching on her skin. Was it this thin before? How could a person....or animal hide back here? To her, none of that mattered. All that mattered was seeing behind...

It wasn't there.

Great waste of time, she thought sullenly. Her heart sank, unexpectedly.

"Are we going to go to school or not?" Kay urgently asked. "There obviously isn't anything here; we're getting later by the second."

"Yeah, I guess we'd better get there."

They took off. The wind whipped through both of their long hair, and as they ran, Nikki tried to make sense of what had just happened.

I don't understand it. How could it just disappear? I swear that wolf creature-thing was there, and I wouldn't imagine something like that. Well at least I haven't imagined anything like that until now...

"What did you think you saw anyways?" Kay asked. Her breath was slightly taken, but the sentence was strong.

Nikki was surprised at her tone. It was curious, not doubting. "Er... It's sort of hard to explain. I mean, are there such things as wolves with bird claws?"

Kay stared at her with wide, secret eyes. "I can't say I've seen one before, but that doesn't mean one doesn't exist."

The ran a bit faster, staying silent for a moment to catch up with their lost time.

Kay broke the silence after a while.

"Chrystan, I don't think you should worry about it. It was probably nothing," she gasped through their running.

This was what Nikki had been expecting to hear all along. "I just don't think I would imagine something like that. Even if I did, I didn't think my imagination was *that* wild."

"You know what I call things that I can't explain?" Kay asked, as she slowed down in front the white granite steps of Simber Middle School.

"What?" Nikki enquired back. She looked at Kay with her heart pounding loudly. Not because she was slightly out of breath, but because she was nervous. *What will she say, that it's strange that I saw something that wasn't there? That I'm weird? Or that I actually might have seen something that wasn't just my imagination?*

"Magic."

Nikki stopped halfway up one stair. "Are you serious? Do you honestly believe in that sort of thing?" She looked suspiciously at Kay as if she thought this was just to mess with her.

This time it was Kay who turned grave. "Of course I do. Don't you?"

While Nikki stared right into her eyes. She was forced to bite her tongue from what her mind begged her to say, and managing to mutter, "Yeah... I suppose...maybe."

In her thoughts, Nikki was immediately roused with the feelings of betrayal. She just couldn't figure out why.

II

A cold autumn whisper echoed through the white stone of Simber Middle School. No one was outside, but Nikki knew that if they went in the school, they could arrive to their class just in time for the final morning bell. Although it was obvious that they had made it at the right time, Nikki's brain was scrambling to make sense of how that had happened. It felt like she had just crossed a time zone.

Appearing just at the moment where Nikki would have least expected it, her friend Breannen popped out of nowhere from behind them. She was always good at sneaking up without a sound. Nikki swirled around as the flash of her friend's light brown-blond hair passed her. She was about to speak when another girl raced up the steps vigorously. The girl flew towards Breannen.

Jasmine. Of course, to make my day feel so *much better.* A deep pang crossed Nikki. This was about to get interesting.

The girl with raven colored streams of hair, and icy blue eyes, froze where she stood. She took a step towards Breannen, but was too focused at that moment on Nikki. Nikki could still feel the soft sting of where Jasmine had brushed past her t-shirt. Their eyes met and each of them were locked into one, adverse glare. Breannen hollered behind Nikki, waving her tan arms, her wavy short hair flowing wild in the breeze, "Hey, I've got something that I think you forgot!"

Jasmine broke the challenge of glaring back, and her eyes grew wide as Breannen's fist flew through the air. From where Breannen was standing, Nikki was still in front of Jasmine. Nikki cringed, wondering why the heck Breannen would throw a punch when there was not a chance that she would hit Jasmine at all. In a matter of milliseconds, frantic thoughts flickered through her head of trying to move out of the way. Before anything could move, Nikki felt as though her body were shifting, slowly but steadily, to the right without her control. As if someone had given her a hard shove to the side.

In a sudden clear shot, Jasmine got smacked in the face. In shock and total disbelief, Jasmine shot off into the school building, long onyx hair fluttering behind her. Breannen shot at her, "I hope that's the last time I ever see your face." They all knew it wouldn't be.

Breannen turned to Nikki and Kay. Whereas Kay was frail-looking and perky enough without being a cheerleader, Breannen was built thicker and was one of the rebels of the school, never tolerating much of anything.

"Uh... What just happened?" Nikki asked, directing her question towards Breannen.

"Nothing happened, besides a brat getting smacked with what she deserved," Breannen answered, satisfied grin shining on her face.

"Breannen, you can't just take out every single person who barely even insults you!" Kay was always against violence that she qualified as unnecessary.

Breannen rolled her eyes. "It's Jasmine. What *doesn't* she do to insult people?"

Nikki rolled her eyes as well but for a different reason. "I *know* that she just got smacked in the face, and she probably deserved it, but I meant with me moving... I was in the way... and somehow I moved...?" Seeing no response whatsoever from her blank, innocent-eyed friends, Nikki died down. "Never mind," she whispered quietly. Deciding to change the subject, Nikki sighed and said, "We are going to be *so* late,"

"No we're not, it's ten minutes 'till." Breannen looked down at her watch and then showed Nikki.

On the clock was the exact time it had been from what seemed like an hour ago. "That's impossible," she whispered to herself.

"It doesn't matter if it's possible, we have to go *now*," Kay inquired. She gave them a small smile then pranced up the rest of the steps.

Breannen gave Nikki a playful punch in the arm, and they made their way up the stone stairs themselves. Kay's hand was opening the door when the second dilemma of the day came running up to them. *School hasn't even started and I know it's going to be a loong day,* Nikki thought remorsefully.

A stocky, but thin, boy came out of the building, stopping right before he would have crashed into Breannen. Luckily, they knew each other well.

James pushed back his brown hair and muttered, "Sorry," then scampered away again as fast as he could. As always, Nikki's head buzzed with questions to where he was going. He was always running somewhere, always in a rush. She managed to receive a smile and a wave as he fled the school doorways, but otherwise, he was unresponsive. She had known him for as long as she could remember, but only through Breannen.

"It's okay," Breannen sighed, only half annoyed.

Nikki and Kay gave each other similar looks of irritation. It was a nonstop talk of either James or Jasmine around the clock when you were around Breannen. For the most part, they had come to a point where they were used to it. There was only so much they could handle of both though, and they were still trying to figure out which was worse.

The three entered the building where the bustle of students jumbled through the hallways. Nikki stuffed her unwanted homework for later classes away into her locker. This day was turning out more eccentric than she had hoped. She enjoyed a break from the regular routine, but it was starting to make her uneasy.

James came scurrying back a few seconds later; Nikki could see through the black glass of the doors that he nearly tripped on one of the steps. She stifled a laugh.

He looked around, a slight distracted glance of confusion and being lost sweeping through his eyes. He seemed to see someone and hastily went over to them. Nikki followed his path to see it was Breannen. Nikki wasn't one to eavesdrop, but she was too curious to not try to listen over the shouts of other students.

"Breannen," he started, "... bark of the trees ... wood," he whispered in her ear as his eyes flickered to a direction, that looked like it was near Nikki, constantly. The rest of the conversation was drowned out in the last roar of students going in different directions. *Did I just hear what I think I just heard?* Nikki contemplated. *Did he honestly just say something about* wood? *No, he couldn't have... He wouldn't have, would he?* James wasn't into building or much of a nature loving-guy. He was more into video games than anything except a few girls here and there. Breannen wouldn't have had anything, that Nikki would know about, to do with wood either.

Nikki looked over at the next locker over, but Kay was intently staring off into space. Nikki waited patiently for Breannen's conversation to be over. Then as James left, and Breannen was left with a smug smile, Nikki brought her confused look to Breannen instead. Breannen met her gaze.

"What in the world was that all about?" Nikki thought aloud, coming alongside her.

"Oh nothing, just a question on homework." Breannen shrugged it off as if it were nothing but what she said it was. For a moment, Nikki believed her.

Don't trust what she's saying, her mind begged her. *Why not?* she wanted to ask back. Except she had learned to trust her instincts. Nikki crossed her arms skeptically, looking ahead with frustration.

Breannen only shrugged again.

"So....class?" Kay asked, nervously eyeing Nikki's face.

"Yes," Nikki and Breannen said in unison, except Nikki sighed it in anguish and Breannen sighed in relief.

"Then, let's go." Kay edged them both on.

For several yards, the three walked together. It was a quiet and hostile walk, one of the very few that they had had that way. Eventually, they had to branch off into their separate ways. All of them split up. Kay left, Breannen right, and Nikki remained going straight on. For once, Nikki was glad.

Alone in her own thoughts again, Nikki couldn't help but thinking simple thoughts of being left out of some huge enigma. *It's like they're all in on it. And they've been acting like this for days. Whenever I get around them, they shut down, and don't say a word. I wonder if they're going to plan a party or something.* At this, Nikki bit her lips, hating the idea of a party. Keeping her friends was as much of a gift as she wanted. *That just doesn't explain it though, and it would be so stupid. Unless the wolf thing was just a fluke or something. Not to mention the wood.*

The strange mention of wood in her thoughts brought a tiny, quirky smile to her face. She took a deep breath as she gained a closer distance to a doorway with a familiar number on it. With thoughts mingling inside of her head, Nikki stepped into her first class.

III

Her thoughts were swarming around in her head, causing her eyes to blur and fuzz. A tiredness swept over her, yet through all of her classes, her heart was pounding. It wasn't the classes themselves. Nikki was barely paying any attention to those. There was a constant nagging from within her that told her that something was extremely wrong.

She got away from getting in trouble with her daydreaming. She doodled on the margins of all her papers. Twists and twirls spun wondrously through the lined tablets. Until in one of her last classes,

Mr. Phillips caught her in a process of being lost in a thought of some far-off subject. Which was a subject very far away from math.

"And would Miss Richards like to tell us what the answer to the question is?" Mr. Phillips smiled in an I-know-you-weren't-paying-attention way. Nikki's eyes flickered to the board and saw the subject: area of a circle. It was a familiar field of study, but without the problem written down, completely useless.

Nikki's lips twitched sheepishly.

"Um, no I can't. Sorry."

"Come on guys, this is a simple review! Right, well, can anybody else tell me what the area of a circle is with the diameter of 3.22 centimeters, rounded to the nearest tenth of a centimeter?"

Nikki blushed a deep crimson, as about ten hands immediately flew up.

"Yes—James?"

James...? Oh, yeah, he's in this class with me. Gosh Chrystan, what's wrong with you today? She put her hand to her temple and pressed lightly, closing her eyes. Again, Nikki went off into her own world for just a moment. Until James acknowledged Mr. Phillips's call, Nikki was trapped in her own thoughts. It was odd. This time she hadn't done it willingly...

"8.1 centimeters squared," James announced proudly. Turning to Nikki, he caught her eye for the first time that day. At first, she thought his expression would be smug. She wished it were smug when she saw what his face actually displayed. His face had a troubled look on it. *Are you okay?* his eyes bled.

She turned away with frustration. She wished her expressions were as easy to read as his. It might have made it obvious that she was so annoyed by his and everyone elses' mysterious classified information.

"RINGGGGGGGGG!"

Startled by the bell, Nikki nearly flew from her chair.

James's expression changed from concern to one eyebrow raised in confusion. Looking away again, Nikki felt sick to her stomach. A sudden heat wave spread over her. She felt as though she had just been locked in a small room with heavily heated lights pressing down on her, although the room was quite large the lights were dim. It passed as soon as it had come, and left her with a sudden numb feeling. She rubbed her hands together for friction. *Ice cold.*

Along with the strange temperature of her skin, Nikki shivered.

By now, almost half the class had left for their last period. James was lingering by the door, waiting for her, but as Nikki gathered her books and pencils, Mr. Phillips appeared beside her. Realizing Nikki was about to be talked to, he left. *What a great friend,* Nikki thought.

"Hello," Nikki greeted as friendly as she could manage. She avoided Mr. Phillips's eyes.

He was staring her down making it impossible for her not to look up. Nikki grabbed her bag off the side of her chair. "Chrystan, are you okay today? You seem kind of distracted with something."

Nikki looked up at the tall teacher and stared straight into his black eyes. "Um, nothing is wrong; besides the fact that I might be late for P.E."

"I'll let you go, just... If there is anything wrong, you can always come to me and tell me about it."

Never, Nikki thought, but aloud Nikki stated matter-of-factly, "Of course I know that. Nothing's going on."

She brushed by him to get to the door, and went out, filled with dread.

IV

The hallways were dark and shadowed where Nikki strode quickly. She hadn't planned on being late to her last class of the day, but nothing seemed to be going right anyways. She was so consumed with determination to get to the class on time, that Nikki didn't see a mahogany crimson blob running straight at her.

"Chrystan! There you are! We're going to be late for P.E.!" Michelle nearly made Nikki jump out of her skin.

"Calm down Michelle, we have a lot of time still." She couldn't figure out why she said that, considering they only had a minute left until the bell, but she figured it was just because she was annoyed at Michelle's cheeriness. *Is she in on the big secret too?* Nikki wondered.

Michelle, being slightly hefty, was quite out of breath. Running from one end of the school to the other just to meet up with her friend was a burden after a while. Michelle did have a small number of friends though, so she was always happy when she was around Nikki, who cared about her deeply. She brushed her red hair behind her ear.

Michelle's furrowed brow changed to a wide smile in less than an instant. "Well, let's go on then."

As they turned the corner, the darkness that had been crawling on the walls of the last hallway faded into a bright, white one. "So, have you been doing anything interesting lately?" Nikki asked, as innocently as she could. If there was one of her friends she could pry information out of, it would be Michelle, who couldn't keep a secret to save her life.

Michelle nodded.

Nikki's hope rose.

"Oh yeah, my brother came home this weekend and we've been spending a lot of time together."

"That's cool," Nikki said earnestly. She tried again. "So Breannen and Kay seem to be planning something..."

"Really? I hope it's something fun." Michelle gave Nikki an honest smile.

It was the first time in Nikki's life that she wished Michelle hadn't told the truth.

V

Relief was flooding through her like a cool rainfall. *Last period and the best one too.* Nikki was smiling to herself, almost conceitedly. Last period P.E. was the only class where Nikki could meet up with her complete clan of friends. As with every class, there were people she couldn't stand there, but she could deal with that as long as she was with her friends. Walking out of the door to the school building and onto the Simber Middle football field, Nikki slung her backpack over her shoulder. They were allowed to bring their things to leave outside and onto the fields.

"Chrystan, over here!" Breannen called, waving her arms.

Sprinting, Nikki raced over to her group of friends. Her awkward gym uniform clung to her.

They all threw their backpacks and other books onto the steel bleachers. The twenty students lined up in a row, eagerly awaiting their gym teacher. *Deep breathing Chrystan, maybe it hasn't been that bad today. It's just been you worrying, like always.* She looked between her friends. A great wave of heat fluttered through her body. Nearly falling, she caught herself with a step forward. Maybe lying to herself was a bad idea.

A stocky man, heavily built, came from inside the school. He wasn't their regular gym teacher, yet he substituted for them so often he knew most of them by name.

"All right then, today," he pulled out a familiar object, "We'll play football. Everyone get into a line and I'll pick two people to pick teams."

No! Not football! Why is he doing this to me? The look on Nikki's face was nothing short of terrified. She was overly clumsy, couldn't catch and thing, and everyone knew it. Nevertheless, she swept herself along the row of people. Sweat was beading on her brow from the burning sun above.

"Let's see, Jasmine, Emily, come up to the front and start picking your teams."

Nikki tried to cover up her "O" shaped lips. *Why is he* doing *this? The two people who hate me the most in this school are going to pick teams?* Emily and Jasmine were two of the best... everything. The picking began.

Soon, only Michelle and Nikki were left. They sent each other a grimace of I-can't-believe-this-happened. Nikki wasn't bad at sports. She ran as fast as lightning when necessary. It was simple the fact that neither of the captains wanted her on their team that kept her from being picked. It was Emily's choice. *I'm sorry Michelle, but I hope don't I get picked last. If I'm on Jasmine's team...*

"Michelle," Emily sighed. She sent a smile bleeding a mock at Jasmine, which turned quickly to sympathy.

Jasmine froze in her place. Her eyes slid over to where Nikki was standing, but this time, Nikki forced herself to look her straight in the eye, and feel the loathing.

So much for the heat wave.

Nikki got a long stretch of chills when those icy pair of blues stabbed themselves full in her face.

"Chrystan." Jasmine pulled each letter into one pile of messed up hate and dread. Only few people could accomplish something like that.

Well Chrystan, you get what you deserve. She's never going to forgive you and you're never going to fully forgive her for what she did. This is the way it has to be. Forever in a constant duel to the death.

Jasmine and Nikki had been the rivals since each of them had first saw a glimpse of the other. Through elementary school it had always been a bloody battle. They were complete opposites, too far apart to become friends. They were both competitive, but Jasmine always had the upper hand. She always had the people and the naturally ability. While Nikki had to work hard for everything in life.

Once, Nikki had gotten a victory in a small, enjoyable art show award. Jasmine had worked day and night for that prize. In her spite, she had told everyone that Nikki's "parents" were going to get a divorce because neither one could decide which one hated Nikki and loved Adriana more.

It had been known to the neighborhood, that Charlotte and Ted could be heard screaming at Nikki almost every night. The day before the art showing, Nikki had showed up, covered with bruises, leaving everyone to think that her parents had beat her. In truth, it had been her sister Adriana. She was born five years after Nikki, an actual blood-related child to their family.

Adriana fought blood-drawing wars with Nikki daily as well. To avoid it, Adriana was constantly over at Jasmine's house, as Charlotte once did to see Jasmine's mother. Jasmine treated Adriana like her own sister, which just brought on more wars. It was humorous to Nikki how her sister could be so in love with her enemy and that her enemy loved her sister so much.

What Jasmine said hadn't been true, not a single word. It was the principle of the matter, that had screwed with Nikki's mind. Nikki could never forget that day and now neither could Jasmine. Nikki had made sure that Jasmine had paid for every last word. There had been a fight, and Nikki *had* punched Jasmine several times, but *Nikki* had gotten nasty cuts in a number of places plus over ten *more* bruises, and a black eye. Jasmine had sprained her wrist from tripping over the sidewalk as she tried to run away.

In all honesty, Jasmine had thrown the first punch.

Nikki just knew how to hit.

It was said to be an accident throughout the school; that both of them had merely tripped over the fields and paved track, and into the track equipment (which to Nikki seemed more than an outlandish excuse). This was to defend and protect them both from being suspended or even expelled. Besides, no adult would have believed that Jasmine had said those things anyway, except for those few who were close to Nikki. People who weren't on Jasmine's bad side were constantly dazzled by her beauty and her fake amiability.

Everyone thought their fighting was over and done with. They were highly mistaken.

Now Nikki and Jasmine had unending spiteful, hostility towards each other. It would never be mended, or even tried to be fixed in any way. The fact was done and over with. They were severe foes. Even if Nikki forgave her, Jasmine wasn't looking for forgiveness. She was looking for revenge.

Irony hit Nikki hard. Her parents *did* get a divorce then.

Leaving Nikki unable to not think of the words Jasmine had said.

Like Kay, Jasmine acted as peppy as a cheerleader, and had made the squad easily this year, She always wore a bright blue bow that matched not only the school color, but her own eyes. Unlike Kay, Jasmine didn't have a sense for what really mattered in life.

VI

Silence rang throughout the field. Nikki could feel the hostility thicken the clear air.

The P.E. teacher could tell something wasn't right. He had substituted for these kids more often than not, but he still didn't have the main position. He probably knew their names better than their real teacher. Yet, he didn't want to figure out what was wrong with this moment. He figured, kids shall be kids, whether they embrace or punch in the face.

Clearing his throat, he sighed. "Okay, Chrystan, head on over to Jasmine's side."

Nikki's feet obeyed but her mind was screaming. *No! This can't be happening! Do something you blind teacher. I know you're a substitute, but anyone can figure out from Jasmine's face, that what awaits couldn't be anything but torture and hate. Are you* daft? It would have been funnier to her at any other point in time that she had used the word "daft" when she didn't mean to. Laughing was incomprehensible at the moment.

Uncomfortable, she fiddled with the ends of her blue, gym t-shirt. She found her way next to James. It occurred to her in satire that she was on enemy fields, yet she was part of the enemy's team. How had her luck depleted as it had?

"I knew she'd pick me first," James garbled.

Nikki nodded subconsciously.

However, what he had said brought her to thinking. It didn't quite click to her at first, but then she remembered a few years ago when James had liked Jasmine. Apparently, Jasmine still had powerful feelings towards him too. Nikki shuttered at the thought, heat draining away. The sun was searing but Nikki was to the point where she was shivering. *What's wrong with me? I* must *be sick.*

Their "daft" instructor handed the football to Jasmine. Nikki backed farther away from her, in fear the first thing Jasmine would do would be to throw it at her head.

"You don't have to exactly play football with it. Just toss it back and forth between your team mates and the other sides'. I don't know... Do whatever you want." He ran a hand through his thinning hair.

Nikki rolled her eyes. He obviously did not know a single thing about teaching middle school football. With that in mind, she knew why the school didn't ask him to be their permanent teacher.

She turned to James.

He was toeing the land with his foot.

Out of the corner of her eye, Nikki saw the football, spiraling out of control and racing towards him. She didn't have time to warn him.

"Smack!"

"Ouch!"

The football hit James square in the head.

While James rubbed his face tenderly, Nikki was not only flaring and igniting with immediate guilt and embarrassment for him, but also anger. It only figured that the next thing Jasmine said brought wider feelings and even something more.

"Oh I'm so sorry! I didn't see you! I was just throwing the football and you got in the way." Jasmine grinned from ear to ear fake innocence leaking through her teeth.

"Oh yes, you just *happened* to throw the ball right at James's face," Nikki spat before she could stop herself. Immediately after saying these words, Nikki regretted them dearly. She didn't want a fight. James was barely her friend anyways. Why did she care so much?

Jasmine turned straight towards her, eyes ablaze. "Excuse me? Was I even talking to you? I didn't purposely throw the ball at James!"

Nikki ignored her questions, biting back with all the venom that had been building up that day. "Well it didn't just magically fly over there and hit him perfectly in the face by accident did it? You threw it at him because you knew he wasn't going to catch it. You just want him to look at you!"

"Why don't you bite your tongue before someone comes along and cuts it off." Jasmine looked like she would be more than willing to do the job. Her tone had gotten softer, yet somehow that made it all the more vicious.

"My mouth is nothing compared to yours! It takes up more than half your face!" Nikki couldn't believe she was saying this. She didn't fight like this, and she didn't say things to people like this, even if it was Jasmine.

By now their substitute teacher had definitely noticed some aggression tensing the air and saw who it was radiating from. With more mild annoyance than anger, he called out, "Come on girls, don't fight."

Both Nikki and Jasmine had stopped listening.

"Why don't you throw the ball yourself to James. Let's see if you can throw it any better than I can, since I'm such *a terrible thrower,*" Jasmine spat threw her teeth. There was a crowd of people around them now. They were mostly silent, waiting.

"Fine I will!"

Nikki's skin felt red hot. Her heart was pounding in her ears. All she could see was Jasmine and large red streaks that filled out the rest of her vision. Jasmine pranced over and picked up the fallen ball, roughly throwing it to Nikki. Again, the ball flew haywire and landed a yard away from Nikki's feet.

"Nice throw," Nikki muttered, her feet flying as she went to pick it up.

As ball and hand met, A sudden gasp from somewhere around her made her swirl around. The sound brought perspective back to Nikki, if only for the moment. *Was that Kay? It sounded like her. What's the matter?*

A flame laced through her body, red hot. Nothing mattered right now though, except to throw that ball at James. It had to be perfect from start to end. She had thrown a football many times, but with this rage lancing her body, she wasn't sure how this was going to turn out. It was hard to think straight.

As the ball left her hand it started its spin. It was a perfect spiral, a most fortunate event especially since Nikki wasn't considered athletic, even though she was. Nikki was about to grin, exultant to herself.

Then it all went wrong.

VII

It seemed like the ball was slowed in midair, but Nikki's mind was thinking at a rapid pace.

With the contrasting actions, the world seemed to spin. Nikki felt for the second time today, sick to her stomach. The ten seconds of the ball flying through the air became three minutes.

The ball was beautiful, its oval body spun rapidly.

Nikki's head started to pound. She could feel it before it happened. Something building.

Half way into its arch, the ball burst into flames.

It was like a gas bomb had been unleashed within the football, but with flames that were bright red and purple. The normal everyday football the ball once was, was now a flaming torture device heading straight towards James, in its still-perfect spin.

There was no chance of anyone moving.

For although the time seemed frozen, the ball kept traveling. The people were still-life paintings. All that Nikki could hear was the rippling of the ball's flames (a phrase she had never thought she would see) as it passed through the air, and the thunderous panging of her heart.

Everything exploded back to life.

It was as though time had to catch up with the last minute it had spent on pause.

As the ball sped up to fast action, Nikki heard the feeble murmur of the substitute teacher, "In all my days..."

She could imagine that was what everyone was thinking.

James hadn't seemed so far away, but the ball still hadn't made it to him.

Was this all just an illusion? As the ball was about to make contact, Nikki panicked.

Suddenly not caring what happened, Nikki backed up towards the bleachers.

She grabbed her bag and ran.

Although she didn't stay and watch, she heard the motion of fire hitting flesh. The scream James let off, as the moment came to a final, absolute fast-forward sent her heart racing.

And the one thing that haunted her the most as she ran home.

The smell of something burning.

Chapter Three

Secrets Unveiled

I

No one was laughing. James hadn't even noticed his blistered hands and the scorched sleeves of his sweater. Kay was the only one that didn't have a look of shock displayed on her face. She sprinted over to Breannen and whispered something into her ear. Breannen nodded then turned to look at Jasmine. Although there was still hints of confusion and astonish blending in with her perfect features, Jasmine had an almost smug, "I-knew-it" look.

Breannen looked away, disgusted at Jasmine.

The gym teacher was probably the only one who felt like he was going to be sick. *In all my days. How in the world...? She just left... I have to... What should I do?*

"Stay here," he told everyone. School was going to end in a few minutes, and he trusted them to not kill each other for that long. Bringing his wits together, he marched towards the school doors, preparing to talk to the office.

Everyone on the field stood silent for a long period of time, not sure what to do. Finally, James rushed towards the building muttering incoherently about the nurse. Breannen and Kay stood by each other and began talking rapidly. Jasmine stood quietly to herself.

Almost every other person began to gather their things as the last bell rang. They mumbled among themselves, each trying to convince each other that what they had seen couldn't have happened.

Substitute Gym Teacher Williams strolled at an uneven pace down the hallways. His mind was scrambled, and he feared for his sanity. Trying to be logical, he focused on recalling what he would do when he got to the office. What he would say would be more important…

I'm going to have to call her parents. She did *leave the school grounds. I'm going to have to tell why…flaming football… No, I can't say that. It was… embarrassment. That will work. One of the kids were making fun of her so she just ran. No flaming footballs should be mentioned. What was her name?*

Gym teacher Williams racked his brains, until his memory overcame the force that made him forget what students had called her. Finally, the name stuck like a thistle inside his thoughts. *Chrystan.*

Well, Chrystan, you're about to get a nasty shock of a phone call for leaving school. And no flaming football flying in the air—whether real or illusion—can change that.

II

Her thoughts were plain and simple. *What just happened?* Tears glazed her eyes as she ran. She had heard her friend Michelle call out to her, right before she was out of earshot. "Chrystan come back!" An almost humorous yelp came soon after that, "Please?" It sounded more exasperated than begging. They all knew something… Everyone around her seemed to be keeping a secret so big that it leaked onto their faces.

But they don't get it. I can't go back after that. I don't even know what just happened. How could *it happen? It's not possible for that to happen. That kind of thing just* doesn't *happen. I don't want to know what happened. To know how James is.* Nikki shuddered. Out of all her thoughts and questions, the last one was the one she knew. Forever would she smell that pungent odor of burning skin. *Why couldn't it have been Jasmine?* She was suddenly shocked at her own malice.

All of this is stacking up to be just one confusing mess. Are they all *in on it?*

There was nothing left for her to do. So she ran. Running meant hiding herself from all of the people who saw what she thought she did, and couldn't make much more of it than she could. That was just what she wanted. More than anything. The world was nothing but a slight flash as she sprinted, hyper on adrenaline. It seemed to take an eternity to make it to the dusk blue house she called home.

Angrily pushing in the security number into a tiny black box attached near the garage door, Nikki prayed that no one was going to be home. The clanking and clonking of the metal rang in her ears just like Jasmine's unforgettable words. *She changed everything. Just because of a stupid football and a crush on James.* How could the words of someone cause such a thing to happen though?

Nikki shook her head, trying to make the heat radiating from her body go away. *I'm getting sick, and I can feel a dangerous fever coming on, if it hasn't already. What's wrong with the world today?*

Luckily, one thing had finally gone right that day. There wasn't a car in the garage.

Thank goodness. This is what relief felt like?…It seemed like it had been so long since she had felt it.

She heatedly walked to the garage door and into the house. The house was a barren, lonely place. Too many sad memories filled tension into the walls and floors. Today, Nikki ignored the fact that she was surrounded by bitterness. She flew up the stairs and into a bedroom overstuffed with many various items. However, most of her room was covered in notepads, as she found herself writing many stories to escape her world. Nikki pulled several off her bed and clambered into it, exhausted.

There's nothing left you can do about school. It's over and you might as well not worry about it until later. It's not your fault. Jasmine probably messed with the ball so it would do that anyway. You should be happy. You've always written about stories of magic. Now you've finally gotten your wish. There was a sweet resentment with her bitter joke to herself. Yet, with those thoughts, a brief smile flickered across her lips. Tuckered out from the strange and crazy things that had happened that day, Nikki drifted in a shallow sleep.

The air around her was sharp and bitter. A slicing sound came from behind her. *What is this?* Nikki pondered as she stared around in the dreamland. Drapes of fabric hung everywhere. The sound came again. Swirling around, Nikki caught a glimpse of Jasmine hurling a huge blade towards her.

III

Nikki hurled herself up with a jolt that traced itself all the way down her spine. *Seemed so real... Am I still in my bedroom?* The covers were on the floor. It was so. She was still in her room. She felt her forehead. *Is it possible to fell colder on the outside than the inside if you're sick? Why did that dream feel so real? I could taste the air...* Unfortunately, she thought as the trace of acidity lingered on her tongue.

A loud yell rang through the hallway.

"Chrystan! Come down here!"

Nikki jumped, as startling message wafted through her mind. *Oh no,* was all she could think. *I think Dad got a little phone call from the school.*

Fully awake, Nikki slid off her bed. Her thoughts strangled her like a murderous man. *Could it all have been a dream? For the sake of my sanity I hope it was!*

A shadow stretched across the hallway. Nikki hardly noticed the looming figure as she stared down at the ground. until the shadow became a person and pounced.

Nikki flew down the stairs with a rattling, "Bump, bump, bump."

"Ha hah ha hah ha!" The figure laughed in a song-like voice, as Nikki pulled herself up, clutching her ribs.

"Adriana." Nikki said. Her amusement was low. Revenge flickered through her mind as she stood.

There at the top of the stairs, Nikki's sibling nearly fell on the ground laughing so hard. She had thin bleach-blond hair and crystal blue eyes just like Jasmine's. Was that why they hated each other so much? The comparison to Jasmine and Adriana were strikingly similar. Or was it the fact that everything was the complete opposite of Nikki and Adriana; one liked one thing and the other hated it? It was like a forest mage against an ice witch. They could never get along.

"What was that noise?" Ted asked while walking toward the stairs.

Adriana's smile flittered quickly then she practically flew down the staircase. She flung herself down and started to cry. She rubbed her knee as if she was in pain.

It wouldn't have been convincing until the tears were real when a thunderous roar draped the house in a steady shake. Then came the hard sound in rhythms like "pitter-patter, tick-tack" against the flat roof of the house. Rain had begun to pour outside. It *was* the only thing Adriana was afraid of. Nikki's eyes flickered to the window just in time to spot a streak of light fall from the sky. It was a complimentary way to end a disaster of a day.

Ted had come up to her now, and she swirled herself around to look at him. "What's this phone call I got from the school saying you left without permission?"

Before Nikki could answer though, Adriana let out a wail. "When Chrystan was coming down the steps, she saw me and pushed me down them. All because I came up behind her!"

Nikki sent an fuming glower in Adriana's path. Ted immediately grabbed her by the shoulders and turned her towards him again.

"What's wrong with you? Can't you ever be nice for once?"

Nikki seethed with anger. "I didn't push her down! She pushed *me*!"

Ted glared back. "Obviously she's on the ground crying, not you."

"She faked it! I'm just not a wimp!—"

"STOP! Just go. Leave! Go to Sophie's house or something."

Her thoughts were hazed and disoriented, but the punishment that Ted had forced upon her was no manner of torture. Nikki scuttled up the stairs in an almost skip-ish manner, while she heard Adriana whine, "But that's her friend!"

It was normal for Ted and her to fight like this. Although Nikki's face showed anger beyond imagination, inside she was gleaming. A spark had gone off in her soul. There was a new hope for the day. Finally there was someone she could talk to who would understand her completely.

She yanked on a thick sweatshirt to block out some of the rain—but not in any way that she wouldn't at least get a little wet. Nobody could stop her. She followed the orders completely by heading out in the ominous thunderstorm.

The rain. I feel so cool now. Was it just by chance that the rain felt so sickeningly cold on her steaming inside? *My forehead seemed so cold to me, but if I had a fever, then I should have felt hot. Why did I feel like I was boiling from the inside out, before? I think it should be the other way around. But I'm no doctor. Maybe I really* am *messed up.*

The surroundings were barely visible, but the fact that she was absolutely drenched with the never-ending stripes of rain and lightning around her made the scenery feel unreal and foreshadowing events that she didn't understand.

She took in a great breath. As the cool rain splooshed on her overworked and irritated body, she felt the mysterious fever trickle away. It was as though she had never felt an ounce of warmth in her body before. It felt good. It felt lovely to be free from that.

Nikki was undisturbed by the lack of homeliness the outside brought her, instead, she was entranced by the booms and the beautiful music the droplets played on the terrain. She felt more at home in the rain than she had ever felt with Ted.

Rainstorms are the best to just let go of everything that can or has hurt you. I just wish it were that easy for everything in life. I just hope Sophie won't mind me abruptly coming into her house. I never want to hurt her again like I did...

Sophie had been Nikki's friend since she had first moved into the house with just her dad and her sister, in first grade. It hadn't just been the divorce that had forced Nikki into her loss of self confidence. At that age, everybody hated Nikki. She had no friends, but when she went to the new house, she soon saw Sophie playing outside. Feeling self confident, but not used to the prospect of lying, Nikki went over to Sophie's house and made the strongest and biggest lies she ever made. Nikki, being the little child she was, convinced Sophie that she was magic. Sophie for some reason that Nikki can't fathom now, believed right away that Nikki was magic. The only thing Nikki remembered was the terrible look of anguish on Sophie's face when Nikki told her that she wasn't really magic. It was as if Sophie had found a great treasure that Nikki snatched back and buried again.

Nikki felt terrible for months afterwards; even today she still felt all the guilt and blame of those long months she had made a fool of herself and hurt the trust she had gained. Sophie had been the softhearted one, as she had forgiven her moments after Nikki told her. Even though Nikki thought Sophie would never trust her again, she soon found out that this had made them have a stronger friendship. Nikki felt it was odd to feel guilt over a lie that seemed so ridiculous, but they had both been so young, and the world seemed limitless and simple. Since then, Sophie and Nikki had been closer than ever; nothing could break their unending friendship. Not one person understood how they never fought.

By now, Sophie had been Nikki's friend for over seven years. They lived right across the street from each other. Nikki had made the journey into a five minute one.

Nevertheless, the alone time ended too soon as Nikki had made her way up the three stone steps of Sophie's neutral brown house.

Before Nikki even knocked on the door, Sophie was there, swinging the door ajar and giving Nikki a smile that, although huge, was barely visible in the downpour.

"Since when was a five second trip a five hour trip over here?" Sophie asked with a teasing smile, while Nikki stepped into the house. "Did your dad say, 'Go over to Sophie's because I don't know what to do with you?'" She put on a look that said, "I-know-everything-about-you-because-I'm-your-best-friend."

"It's like you read my mind!" Nikki smiled, genuinely amazed. *That's why I like you so much, Sophie, you always know exactly what I need to hear, even if it is words I've just heard.*

Nikki struggled with her tangling, long, wet hair while getting out of her waterlogged sweatshirt.

Sophie gave a shaky smile that was lucky enough to miss the view of Nikki. *Sophie* was a terrible liar. *Oh, if only you knew right now Chrystan.* She shook the miserable thoughts from her head and threw out quick words like a reel for a fishing line. "I'll get a towel."

Nikki gave her a thank you grin back, and she tried to run her fingers through her hair, which had become slightly wavy from the humidity of the air.

When Sophie had returned with a soft blanket-like wrap, Nikki wrapped her hair inside of it and they both ran up the stairs to Sophie's room.

"I have a lot to tell you," Nikki sighed.

"First thing is first, tomorrow is your birthday and I might not see you, so I'll give you what I got right now." Matter-of-factly, Sophie reached behind her book shelf. She pulled out something square bound in shiny red wrappings. When the box was uncovered from the paper,

Nikki discovered a silver necklace bundled in cotton. The pendant that hung from the beautifully twined material, was a deep glittering sapphire, Nikki's favorite color.

Nikki smiled. "Thanks so much Sophie. This is *so* gorgeous."

Sophie blushed back and looked down at the floor. "It's nothing really. I found it at this extremely old shop and knew you would like it. It really wasn't that much."

Nikki clutched the jewel tightly in her hands and looked at Sophie meaningfully.

"You have no idea how much this makes the rest of my day look horrible."

"Wow, and I thought thirteen was your lucky number. You haven't even turned it yet and you're already having bad luck!" Sophie kidded.

Nikki sighed. She held back the tears in her eyes as she looked to the ground.

Sophie instantly realized something was wrong, "So, aren't you going to tell me what happened today?"

Flashes of all the impossible events that had come to pass that day flittered through Nikki's mind.

All of a sudden, Sophie jumped back and tumbled off of the bed they had been sitting on.

"Um, what was that?" Nikki asked teasingly as Sophie came back to earth, with a dazed look in her eyes.

"Oh my gosh….um…. I totally forgot about this project for school I haven't even started on."

Nikki stared at her looking a little confused and disappointed. "Oh. So I guess you want me to go then?"

"No offense or anything but I think I better get started on it."

"That's fine. I guess I'll see you later Sophie."

When Nikki had gone out the door, Sophie thanked herself that she went to a different school, and that she wasn't as terrible as a liar as she thought.

I think that was the first time I ever went to Sophie's house and ended up feeling worse than before. Well, besides the obvious other time. I hope it's a good time to go home. I keep losing track of time.

IV

The rain had stopped, leaving things soggier, slimier, and shinier than they were before. An almost-full moon was glittering in the blackened sky. It was bright enough that even if the street lamps weren't on, you'd be able to see every house on the block. Happiness did not fill the air. It smelled like charcoal that had been hidden and now was burning in an ancient fireplace. *Why does the atmosphere smell so musty?*

It was almost amusing. The troubles that Nikki wanted to just spit out to Sophie were a tangled mess that wouldn't come out right. She knew that Sophie would have understood, so why couldn't Nikki talk about it when she had had the chance?

Dread filled her stomach as she realized tomorrow would be not only her birthday, but would be another day at school. She could just see Jasmine's face now. *I know I hurt her, but what's so wrong with me that she can't stop hating me? I never really did anything worse than that one year; some people have done much worse to her behind her back. I still don't understand that. Sure, she's pretty, but she's so mean to everybody. Why can't most of the other people see that in her? Even people she's hurt over and over still treat her like she's some form of royalty. It makes me sick.* Nikki's thoughts flickered over to her friend across the street.

It was weird that Sophie forgot about a project at the last minute. It's not like her to do something like that. Is the whole world falling apart or is it just me? Nikki shook her head in disgust. *I'm probably the one losing it.*

She hadn't realized she wasn't even halfway across the street.

I better boot it in gear. I'm already in enough trouble. I don't need grounding on top of it.

Thoughts shifting to Adriana, she remembered why the hostility was so high with her now. Adriana with no doubt blamed Nikki for the divorce. Of course, who else could she blame? Even Jasmine agreed with her... Everyone agreed with Jasmine; she was the most admired person in Nikki's school. The only ones who didn't see eye to eye with her were the only people in school who Nikki considered friends. Popularity was a joke to Nikki. If she had to act like Jasmine to get it, it wasn't worth it.

She had reached the front door. Quickly she slunk into the house and scurried into her bedroom making few noises besides the tiny tapings of her feet.

Once she had made sure that no one had noticed or seen her, she crept back out of her room to see what the time was. She did not have an accurate clock in her room.

Adriana and her dad were both asleep and, in fact, snoring quite loudly. Ignoring that she hadn't done any homework and her own project lay untouched, was of no concern to her right now. The clock was telling her that it was past eleven. No wonder she was exhausted. Nikki scuttled back to the door of her room again. Without even bothering to change into pajamas, she left her clothes on to fall into a sleep occupied by one peculiar dream.

V

Light poured on Nikki's face as she instantly woke up. She didn't lift her head. A bubbly fire-like feeling was continuously bursting in and out of her body. Her hands felt oddly the worst. They felt as though she had just put them deep in a campfire pit. Her head hurt almost as bad. It was worse than any headache she had ever undergone. With flares coming up and down her temples.

Despite the burning throughout, her hands and skin felt like ice to the touch. *This is so wrong. I know I must have some kind of strange disease that no one has ever had. It would figure.* She had told no one about her 'hot head.' It seemed too abnormal, which was a bad thing to be when your plan in life was to stay as unnoticed as possible.

The fact that she felt sick in only a fever-like way was not only taking space up in her mind. She had dreamt about that strange wolf creature and those hands that grabbed it back. She knew right there and then that she had definitely not imagined anything that happened the day before. However impossible it may seem, it had been there. Nothing could change that it had gone down. Or the fact that something was on top of her above her covers right now.

Despite the intense warmth, she sprang up to see a long box on top of her bed. *It almost reminds me of Sophie's wrappings on the present she gave me; it sort of has that same shimmering colors.* However, it was a crimson tint with a bright extravagant orange bow.

Unsure how to accept it, Nikki, like anyone else would think, thought that the present was from her father. She realized soon enough that the ribbon was not just means of decoration. A large paper was attached to the right hoop of the bow. Carefully, Nikki pushed the ribbon further undone. She tugged. The note easily slid off the thick bow.

Bewildered, Nikki unfolded the delicate paper. Soon her eyes grew wide.

My dearest Nikki,

All your life you've been kept from me, and I'm sure that right now you don't know who I am. When you were just born, a dark prince had a thirst of revenge for you. I can't exactly explain why right now, but just know this: there's a side of you that has just been exposed today, on your thirteenth birthday. You may have recently experienced some rather unusual events. If I am certain, you have the fire gift your father once had too. Which is where I'm getting to. When you were still in the hospital, two people took you from us, with our knowledge, to make sure that nothing would happen to you. They switched you with a baby that we knew was going to die anyway from crib death. You are thirteen now, finally a safe age since you get your powers. Another thing I'm getting to. Nikki dearest, that is your real name you know, you were born to be a Je Ne Sais Quoi, or a person who has powerful magic. You have the skills and the power in your blood. Keep safe, but soon you'll have to come home. Talk to your friend; she'll have all of the information you need. Also, if your head is getting extremely too hot, it is because your temperature is too high. Because you have to contain your fire heat in, your temperature rises and is very high naturally. That is also why your skin will feel extremely cold to you; all the heat is inside your body. So what you have to do is let the fire somehow get out, and then you will feel fine. By the way, your present is a highly unoriginal gift that Je Ne Sais Quoi families give their children on their 13th birthday. However, I'm sure you will find it very helpful and enjoyable.

 Goodbye until soon,

 Mum

 (P.S. There will always be someone watching you.)

VI

The air was dead silent for a very long time. Five, even ten days could have passed before Nikki even realized, or even begin to realize, that her mouth was wide open. It was definitely not what she was expecting, which was a simple note from her dad that said, "Happy birthday, here you go." No, it was not a simple note. It racked her brain. Made her forget everything she thought she knew. It made everything be what it wasn't. The worst part was: it felt right. Nikki had never felt like anything else in the world made more sense than what she had just read.

Eventually, she came out of her half trance. *Can't be true. Did Adriana somehow... ? But there's no way; she doesn't have an imagination like this. I guess there's only one way to find out if it's true.*

Nikki held her hand, palm up, in front of her. Concentrating ever so slightly, she felt her heat trickle down her spine to focus on nothing but her palm. In the place of the burning sensation, was a feeble, but glowing, red flame.

Oh my...

Nikki jumped back and lost her balance. She tumbled off of the bed. The flame disappeared in that instant, but the horrible heat was gone. No more fever. So was it true?

This is too hard for me to understand. How does this "person" expect me to believe that I just happened to be switched at birth and that she wants me to come back to wherever it is that she lives. This practical joke has gone over the top. It's probably just another prank set up by my friends. Maybe that's what they were trying to hide. It would so *be like them.*

But it wouldn't explain the fire. Okay...maybe I am some whack job psycho that has freaky powers or something. Nothing I can't hide. But if it was my friends, how would they know I had freaky powers? Ugh. My head hurts.

Her thoughts were put away then. A shout came from down the stairs. "Chrystan, you're going to be real late for school if you don't get ready and down here!" It was her dad. *Is he still normal? Does he know anything? No, probably not. Best to act dumb than make things confusing and terrible.*

Nikki was shaking with excitement. She got out of the bed and ran over to get dressed. She threw the letter on the ground, figuring it was nothing but a joke. The box caught her eye, with its shininess. Walking back over to her bed she lifted the red lid. For the second time that day, she got the shock of her life. Inside the box was a carefully cradled red and black broom. A broom. *How weird. This is getting to be too much to handle. Oh great, now I'm making puns.*

Nikki tucked the broom, still in its box, under her bed. Then she pulled on fresh clothes and sprinted down the steps. By now anyone else would have probably lost all of their right mind trying to not only figure out if this was all true, but also processing all of the information. She refused to admit to herself that she was Nikki. Kay had been right to ask her if she did believe in magic. Of course she did, but it's not like she was going to say that aloud for everyone to hear.

Nikki grabbed her bag and a quick snack for the road. Her sister and dad had apparently already left to go to school, which wasn't a surprise. On the couch was a white wrapped gift sitting abnormally misplaced.

Shaking her head, Nikki went out of the door, late for the second day in a row. *Going crazy. Absolutely crazy. There was never a note. You are not Nikki.* Nikki tried to convince herself. However, it was hopeless. Convincing yourself that you're not you is like getting caught cheating on a test and the teacher gives you an A anyways.

Soon enough, not just one head was visible, but two. Two girls: red and blond haired.

Kay was just the person Nikki wanted to see. Kay always knew everything that was going on around the world, not to mention the neighborhood. As for Michelle, it wasn't really the moment Nikki wanted to be harassed by Michelle's caring personality. Nevertheless, there was no way to go talk to Kay without having to talk to Michelle.

"Happy birthday, Chrystan!" Michelle greeted cheerfully. Nikki smiled weakly back, hating the attention and mad caring. *She didn't call me Nikki though. She's definitely not in on it. Unless she's just playing me.*

Kay added, "Yeah, happy thirteenth birthday." Then she came up close to Nikki and whispered into her ear so that Michelle couldn't hear, "Nikki."

Nikki stopped.

Michelle kept on walking, oblivious to what had been said. Kay stopped several feet in front of Nikki. She looked back. Wearily, she faced Nikki and said, "Are you coming." Her voice was dead even.

Nikki stared Kay down, deciding whether or not she was playing her. "Are you serious?" Nikki's voice was like a hot steel pipe plunged into icy water. It spelled anger, with a hint of confusion. Kay picked up on it right away.

Kay looked behind her. Michelle was nearly to the end of the block.

"I said Nikki. That is your name after all."

Kay swerved back to Michelle and started running after her.

Nikki stood flabbergasted at Kay's response. She would have never thought that Kay would pull a sort of joke like this. She thought it was maybe Breannen or someone. Kay never pulled jokes like that. She was always *so* serious. Then, how would Kay know and why would she play like this unless she knew that it was true. That *all* of it *was* true.

"Kay wait!"

Nikki sprinted after her.

Chapter Four

Explaining

I

"Hi," Nikki said once she had caught up with Kay.

"Hey. Um, didn't we already say hi to each other?" Kay gave a confused face. For a split second she let her guard down and showed that she was kidding. Nikki caught it right before it disappeared. Now Kay was *joking*? The world might have just exploded.

"I am *so* confused." Nikki shook her head. "Michelle, I need to have a quick talk with Kay. You can head on without us. We'll be right there."

Before Michelle could move, Nikki started dragging Kay off to the side of the walkway. "What do you need to talk about?" This time, Kay was genuinely confused. "You did get the letter right? And your 'gift'?" She used air quotes for the word gift as though it was a term she didn't like but fit pretty well compared to any other words she could think of.

"You have got to be kidding me. Do you expect me to believe that just because some letter shows up on my bed that I'm suddenly going to run away from home on some adventure? You know I'm not that type. How do you expect me to believe that this is all true?" The wind whistled through the trees. Nikki crossed her arms tightly to her chest.

"So you did get your gift?" Kay asked, ignoring Nikki's stubbornness.

"Gift as in a funky broom wrapped in paper you mean?"

"No. Nikki. I mean your 'power' gift."

"Stop calling me Nikki. That's not... How did you know about my thing."

Kay looked at Nikki at an odd angle. "Your *thing*?"

"Yes. This."

Nikki held out her hand. It would be a good time to do this anyways, she felt like her insides were going to melt from heat. Concentrating only slightly less than last time, Nikki's palms produced red flames that licked her fingers in her cupped hand.

Kay showed no surprise.

"Oh come on, don't tell me you don't think it's weird. My hands made fire! That's not exactly what I would label 'normal'!" She waved her lit hand in front of Kay's face.

"You have to come to my house this afternoon right after school," Kay stated simply. She showed no emotion, but when Nikki put on a face saying something along the lines, you-have-got-to-be-kidding-me, she smiled.

"We're making Michelle wait too long. Stop worrying. I'll explain everything."

Nikki let her fire die down.

They made their way towards where Michelle was snail-walking, impatiently waiting for them. When they had met up with her, Nikki's head was looking towards the ground examining the sidewalk's lines, while Kay's head was as bouncy and up-in-the-clouds as ever. Kay was very serious. But she was also very strange.

All through the walk to the school, Michelle kept giving Nikki and Kay hopeful glances, trying to guilt them into telling her what was going on. It reminded Nikki of a puppy that wanted food and would follow you everywhere until you gave into its pleas. Otherwise,

Michelle kept unusually quiet.

It's not like I don't want to tell you. Are you in on it too? It seems as though you're not. You would never believe me if I told you anyway. Then I'd have to give proof and other people might see. This isn't just hard for you, you know, Nikki thought. Her thoughts longed to be spoken.

It is always true though, that the more you dread a situation, the longer it continues. This moment was not an exception. It took ages for the gate of the school to even get close enough for them to see. It was foggy that morning; everything was covered in a grayish haze. Nikki felt chills run up her arms. Somehow, she could sense something wasn't right.

II

At the school, Breannen threw the glass doors open and each clanged against the white stone that made up the foundation walls. Her hair was wildly windswept as if she had been running all over. *I have to find her. Kay will know what to do. If I don't find her soon, James... He might... I don't even want to think it. Why does he always defend me? He knows that I can take care of myself! Look what he's gotten himself into. They might find out about him. What we are. You're looking down that path again, Breannen. Don't think about what can happen. Think about who you need to find to make sure it doesn't.*

The air was eerily quiet. The trees no longer whispered. The sky was blank and bleak.

Breannen's breath made spots of cold air appear. The world had gotten twenty degrees colder. It was an effect that Breannen was used to causing.

Shadows traced down alleyways she passed.

She found herself catching her breath more than once.

Fear danced in her body wildly.

There was barely enough time.

Breannen raced through the long grass fields that clung to the earth in heaps and intertwined the fences of the nearby cemetery gate. The school was almost impossible to see by now.

No time to waste. Ha. Very funny Breannen, you have almost all the time in the world. I just hope that he won't do anything stupid before I can find her. No, you were wrong, you don't have any more time. Nikki's now unaffected.

Run faster!

Her legs were pumping to inhuman speeds. Luckily her energy was sharp.

Voices filled the air before her. Breannen had found Nikki, Kay, and Michelle.

III

Kay reacted moments before Breannen ran towards them. With a soft gasp that gave her away, she made Nikki turn to see what Kay saw. Kay was starring straight ahead at a square that followed the patterns of the others sections in the sidewalk. Exactly three seconds later, Breannen appeared through the fog where Kay's eyes were glued.

"It was you!" Nikki whispered to Kay. "You gasped the same way right before I threw that flaming...football."

Kay turned towards her, face as blank as before.

Breannen was almost on top of them.

"You guys ... You have to come quick! At the school. The teachers can't stop it! James... He's fighting Jasmine!" Breannen tried to exclaim through tired lungs.

"No," Kay gasped, eyes burning through Breannen.

"What!" Nikki and Michelle questioned in unison.

"Come on, we have to go quick!" Breannen hollered, ignoring Kay's extreme look.

Kay took off like a rocket, flying through the fog and quickly disappearing.

Breannen, Michelle, who seemed to be running as if she was in slow motion, and Nikki, all took off after her. It was hard to find the school when it was blanketed with a snow white cloud of fog. It was even harder to find the track where James and Jasmine where fighting.

The vast illumination that lit the fields slowly exterminated every last puff of haze until the two outlines of James and Jasmine were clear. *James's hands should have at least a few nasty blisters on them by now.* Disbelief rang in her mind though as Nikki saw that the skin on his hands were completely unbroken.

But Breannen was right.

James took a low blow in the stomach from Jasmine. "That'll show you to not insult me!" She smiled viscously at him, pleased to see that he was slightly doubled over. James forced himself to stand up straight, but he didn't swing back at Jasmine.

Is he really asking for more of this? I would have at least smacked her, Nikki thought.

Out of nowhere, small crowd gathered around them, but a few of the teachers were trying to get James to "stop this fight or you'll be suspended." As far as Nikki could tell, Jasmine was the only one doing something. James had neither said anything nor hit back for as long as Nikki had been around.

Then a fatal punch was thrown.

In a blink of an eye, Jasmine's fist made contact with James's nose. No one could react faster than his face. Blood started gushing continuously like a fountain out of his nostrils. Blood poured on his t-shirt and trickled down his chin.

No! Come on James, fight back!

Rapidly, the flow slowed until it had come to an abrupt halt. The swelling of his nose, which had been the size of a plum, and rather the same color, minimized until it was entirely back to the way it was supposed to be. If everyone in the crowd hadn't known better, they would have thought that James had just dunk his shirt into a vat of deep crimson paint.

But they knew; everyone looked at him as though they'd never seen anything so strange in their life. Kay, Jasmine, and Breannen were the only ones who were faking their faces. Nikki looked at James then at Kay's knowing-face.

"He's one heck of a powerful healer." Kay murmured this to herself. Nikki's quick ears caught every word. Even though Nikki turned to stare at Kay, Kay's face remained uptight until she let Nikki get the few hints that were spelled on her raised eyebrows. "I'll tell you later," they read.

IV

"So let me get this straight, you know nothing about the letter and bizarre broom that appeared on my bed this morning?"

Begging silently that Breannen would just say this was all a hoax, Nikki tried to pry out information. "I don't know anything, except for what Kay told me," she insisted.

"What did Kay tell you?"

Breannen bit her lip. "Kay has to tell you herself. She didn't want me to tell you anything except that this is real, all real, so don't worry —for now."

"Somehow that doesn't make me feel any better," Nikki sighed.

Breannen grasped Nikki by the shoulders. Shaking her she cried in mock anger, "Don't worry about it!"

"Okay, okay," Nikki laughed.

"Art class is over you two," an annoyed voice advised them. "Better hurry up or lunch will be over by the time you get there." The art teacher shooed them out of her classroom, and closed the door without another word.

"She's right, we better go," Breannen agreed.

The two of them walked into together and went in a winding lunch line.

"I can't believe that James got sent to the office for harassing

Jasmine, and Jasmine just got a detention. She was the one with the punches and slams. What did James even say to her?"

Breannen shook her head angrily. "He didn't say anything; she just wanted to make a scene." She sounded disgusted. Nikki was too. It wasn't right for Jasmine to always get her way.

Breannen came to a absolute freeze when they both got out of the lunch line. *No!* Nikki screamed in her thoughts. She repeated it out loud, noisier than she wanted to.

"This can't be happening," Breannen whispered.

"There's no way I'm going to sit there," Nikki reminded her.

"There's no way you're going to leave me there by myself! We might as well go— there's nowhere else."

"Why did this have to happen?" Nikki wondered aloud.

Jasmine's table was the only one open.

Jasmine greeted them with a mischievous grin.

Nikki sat down at the one out of two only seats, and hid her face behind her thick brown hair. *You're right next to her, what are you going to do? You've spent forever trying to avoid her in every possible situation, well except yesterday. Don't look her in the eye—maybe she won't turn you to stone…*

The table sat in silence, Nikki forgetting her hunger, quietly fiddled with things on her plate. She made sure that nothing was splattered, smooshed, or made too much of a crunch when she touched things. She didn't want to lose control and ending up stabbing something that made a huge crunch that would make everyone at that table look right at her.

Her face burned in the cheeks. She knew that Jasmine was already watching her; waiting for her to do something that she could mock or make fun of. *Maybe if I pretend to eat and then race to the garbage, I can make a run for it. But that means leaving Breannen behind. I couldn't do that to her, especially since she might rip Jasmine's head off.*

She stayed there, and everything wasn't too bad until Jasmine crossed the line. "So, why do you hang out with *Chrystan* anyway, she's... I mean with the flaming football? What's next? Is she going to melt her tray?"

It wasn't the fact that she was being extremely rude, it was the fact that Jasmine said Chrystan in a way that implied she knew something. Like she knew that Kay said she was Nikki. Like she knew that Nikki was Nikki. Like she knew everything that Nikki didn't. It sent Nikki's teeth on edge. The look that Jasmine gave her when they caught each other's eyes. Jasmine would perpetually think that she was better than her. For once, Nikki was determined to prove her otherwise.

It was also the fact that Jasmine had noticed that there was something going on. Normal wasn't an option when you could make fire come out of your palms. *She's just trying to get to you. Calm down, this isn't helping anything. She's trying to push you over the edge... It's working.*

"No one loves you Chrystan. Face it. It'll only hurt more when you deny it to yourself."

White fire smeared her vision. Nikki tried to hold back everything she wanted to scream and just put Jasmine in her place. Her throat tightened up like she was going to cry. It was strange that the tears hadn't started. Her eyes had never been as dry.

Jasmine's eyes glittered with triumph and satisfaction, while Breannen had begun to stare wide-eyed at Nikki. Arms crossed, Jasmine whispered something into her friend's ear. She playfully swung her straight midnight-colored hair over her shoulder.

"Um, you might want to do something with your tray," Breannen whispered close to Nikki's ear. By now, Jasmine's friends were staring weirdly at her too.

She looked down at her tray, or actually, what *used* to be her tray. It was now nothing more than a pile of char-black food and half melted plastic where Nikki's hands had been gripping them tightly. A few staggering flames flicked upward for a few seconds longer before they died.

Nikki felt her face flush with embarrassment. *What is Jasmine, some kind of a future predictor?*

Nikki rushed over to the garbage can. *Nobody will miss this nasty tray anyway right?* She threw the gooey tray and the burnt food in the can without worrying about it. It wasn't exactly an easy task considering some of the plastic was melting into her hand. Then she signaled for Breannen to come with her. *We can't leave separate but we can leave together. And I thought I was weird. At least I don't know when someone is about to burn their tray into a pile of rubber-like goop.* Although Nikki couldn't deny to herself that what she had just done was entirely bizarre.

Breannen hastily made her way to Nikki. "*That,* was insanely cool." Nikki smiled at her.

V

"Come on, or my mom will get mad at me. I'm not supposed to be home late."

Kay and Nikki were walking at a faster pace than usual along the perfect road that ran to Kay's house. "Are you sure that this is all about you just trying to get home?" Nikki added nervously.

In truth, Kay seemed unnaturally tense and jumpy since they had left the school. "Yeah, I'm fine, I just feel like someone is following us."

"Really?" Nikki asked.

"Yeah sure, let's just hurry, okay?"

Something's definitely up. Kay would never be this tense. Nikki looked around her. The sky was cascading into a beautiful sunset that set the trees into an abyss of orange soda. It didn't feel to her as if someone was following them. Even so, Kay's words sent goose bumps on her arms.

Kay led the way up a small driveway.

"So, this is your house?" Nikki asked while she took in the surprisingly small but homey cottage.

Nikki was a little shocked that Kay's house looked practically normal, until she went inside and saw all of the impossible things Kay's house held. The house was tidy, but small and strange knick-knacks were placed in all areas. There were many things Nikki had never seen in her life. She felt at home in this house; it felt like she belonged. Kay flew up an ancient spiral staircase and into her mammoth-like bedroom, closing the door with a soft click. Nikki and Kay slumped down into her water bed.

"You have an amazing house," Nikki confirmed simply.

"Yeah well..."

A voice come calling from across the hall. "Kay! Do either you or your friend want a snack?" Nikki presumed it was Kay's mother calling up.

Nikki shook her head at Kay, "No mom! Thanks anyway."

"'Kay, Kay!" her mom yelled back.

Kay shook her head in awkwardness, "It's her favorite thing to say to me."

Nikki shook her head too, but for a different reason as a slight smile lifted her lips. "How did your mom know I was here? I didn't see her at all when we came in."

Kay seemed to have that same distractedness that Sophie had shone on her face the day before. Then she sighed and muttered something like, "I'm going to have to tell you anyway." She looked straight at Nikki, who was still trying to process what Kay had just said. "Well, to start out, it's all true. The letter is true, the fire power is true, the 'you're a magic wielder' part is true, your English mom is true, and the fact that we're all in danger is true."

Nikki put on a face that started out like a yes-I-understand, but ended up as an entirely confused expression. "What has that got to do with your mom knowing I'm here?"

Kay laughed a soft chuckle. "Did you think you were the only one that had some strange power? I have one because I'm a "witch," but no one of our type calls us that. And James, Breannen, Michelle, and Sophie also have gifts. But I don't think that Michelle has gotten hers though, because otherwise she would have know what we were talking about today." She looked at Nikki, who had a dazed expression on her face.

"*Sophie*? And Michelle—"

"Not yet for Michelle,"

"And Breannen and James? Are you *kidding* me? Hold up. Start at the way beginning before you totally lose me."

"Um, first tell me all that you know," Kay hesitated.

"My mom lives in England, I can make fire come out of my palms, I supposedly can fly on a broom, people are trying to protect me, someone wants to take revenge out on me, and you're suppose to tell me the rest. That's about it."

Kay sighed again, but kept her smile simple, and sincerely full of patience. "There's *a lot* more. But there's only so much I can tell you. I can tell you about your mom though."

Kay went on to tell about Ruby and skipped a few parts that she didn't know or really didn't want Nikki to know quite yet. Kay knew inside that Nikki had to find out some of it by herself.

"Your mom lives in a small section of England near the coast. The reason that you have a 'fire power' is because, along with the obvious spells as a part of your magic, everyone who is magical also gets one separate gift. A gift that is either rare or common among magic people."

"What's your gift then? You *are* magic right?"

"Yeah I'm magic, and my gift is to know things."

"Like predicting the future?"

"Sort of. Your mom can predict the future. I just sort of know things that no one else knows right before it happens. Which can get annoying."

"That's why your mom knew I was coming?"

"Yeah."

"Is your mom magic too?"

"She is. There's a lot of people in our area who are. That's because we're naturally attracted to each other. It's good and bad in a way."

"Which ways are those?"

"Well, if someone was looking for one of us, it would be hard to find the right one of us. Unless they already knew the one they were looking for or the one had something special about them that people usually wouldn't see. Likewise, if they were looking for us, they would know that the one person or many people they were looking for would, without a doubt, be in this area."

Nikki shook her head trying to make sense of it all. "So what you're saying is that it's not hard to find our sort as a group but it's hard to find an individual in our group?"

Kay nodded satisfied.

"Wait, wait, wait. How do *you* know *Sophie*?"

"Like I said, it's easy for me to know things and also pretty easy for me to find our sort. I knew who Sophie was because of my gift."

"What's Sophie's gift? Why didn't she just tell me what was going on?"

"How was Sophie supposed to know that you were going to be magic too? She only figured it out yesterday!"

"I thought you didn't know the future and..."

"Sophie's gift is mind reading. Probably, when you were thinking about your day yesterday, she saw it, and she probably got a little freaked out."

"Sophie's a mind reader? She's lied to me for so many things over the last week! Why couldn't she just tell me?" Nikki asked again.

"She couldn't! Don't you see? We have to keep this a secret. No one can know about us. It's extremely dangerous."

"Sophie's not thirteen! I thought you had to be that old before you got anything?"

"Usually that's the case, but with some people it's late or early, like Michelle's. Hers hasn't come yet but I know it will real soon."

Her thoughts flickered to the lie that she had once told Sophie about being magic. Had she really lied? Maybe that's why Sophie was so disappointed when Nikki admitted she wasn't magic. What if Nikki had subconsciously known?

"So Breannen, James and Michelle are one of us too?" Nikki asked.

"Yes. Breannen can do certain things with time. James is a healer."

"I heard you say that today. So can Breannen see the future?"

"No, why would she be able to do that?"

"You said she could do things with time."

"Not that sort of thing. She can make time stop for normal people. But for magic people like us, it doesn't."

"That's what happened when Breannen was fighting Jasmine, isn't it? It affected me at least a little because I didn't have my magic yet, right? She moved me away when I was in front of Jasmine so she wouldn't end up punching me."

"Exactly! I'm *so* glad you're getting this!"

"But Michelle doesn't have her gift and she was running with us when time stopped."

Kay thought about this for a few seconds. "Breannen may have restarted time by them. Michelle was moving really slow because time was catching up."

Nikki accepted the answer. "How do people like us get used to all of this?"

Kay shrugged. "I guess just after a while, people learn to acknowledge that they can't know everything that's happening. Maybe they'll just learn it later.

Nikki wasn't that easily persuaded to stop asking questions. "Do you know why I'm here instead of in England?"

Kay hesitated again. But truthfully she answered, "Not all of it."

"Is this *all* you guys have been hiding from me?" Nikki ran events and conversations through her mind that had picked up on her radar. "What about yesterday right before school? When James went up to Breannen and told her something? Were they really talking about wood?"

"Sort of. Breannen hadn't gotten her wand yet, so he asked her if she had tried to use her gift to find one yet."

"What?"

"When we get wands, somehow we have to use our power to get one. It can be very hard sometimes especially if you have a random gift. For me it was very easy. I just knew where to look. For Breannen, it has proven to be more difficult. She managed to tell me that yesterday she found out that she could go to any place anywhere. But only for about three seconds. She found an ancient piece of wood from an aloes tree in Egypt for her wand. She had heard of them from her text book."

"That's amazing! What can your mom and dad do then?"

"Well my dad can transform into any animal. My mom can read minds like Sophie."

"So Sophie's power isn't very unique?"

"Not really, neither is mine. Your mom can tell the future better than I ever will. She knew right when to send the letter, knew which baby to switch you with, and she knew that you would have the same power as your dad."

"Did he really have a gift like mine? Why didn't he write too?"

This time Kay hid her lies well, "I don't know much about him. Only your mom. But I know that fire is very unique, along with the other elements like winds, ice, water, an earth-moving or controlling power, and lightning."

"This is way too much to take in."

"There's so much more too, Nikki."

Nikki shook her head. "There's no way I'll ever get used to you calling me that. For now, just let me be 'her' or 'you', or 'no one.' It's hard enough for *me* to know who I am. I'll tell you when you can start calling me Nikki."

"You're going to have to get used to it once we get going."

"Going? Going where exactly?"

Kay shook her head. "Um to England of course! To your mother's house!"

Chapter Five

Pocket Watch

I

Garden's silhouette cast bleak shadows against the walls and fabrics of the castle whenever he passed by another cracked stained glass window. Attracting heat like a moth to flame, the glass showed the brilliant sun hovering above the many valleys that lay below it. Garden shook his head. *Such a wonderful day wasted as are many of the days that I could be helping others. But not today. I am in the place where I can do all that I can.*

His footsteps made clanking rhythms that caused most of the watchmen to become tense or nervous. Most of them had gained habits of paranoia by the frequent crashes that resulted from Colon's frustration. They stayed in the shadows of the hallway.

A few nodded at Garden uneasily. Feeling sorry for him was what others did. Was it not unfair that a man of olden age should have to face the most powerful magic weaver in the country? They did not know of Garden's power.

Before he was at the point where if he would turn back he would arouse suspicion, he swept over to the windows that shone bright, clear puddles of light on to the floor, and pulled out his wand. The white stick was nothing for a few seconds until Garden whispered the words clearer than any glass, "**Seloc**."

The elfin words worked, for the curtain shot forward together to make waves of black swirl around the glass. The light was gone. Some of the guards sighed in fear. Others took a breath of relief. It was unjust how it had to be this way; some of them had learned to like it though. Like it so well they couldn't see the light of day without withering in pain.

Garden sighed as well. *Not a single person should have to be sucked into Colon's lightless ways. Why are the young always the first to turn?*

He referred to the guards' gargoyle-like stature. Sunlight acted like poison, especially to the younger end of the watchmen.

Reluctantly, without showing an ounce of energy or emotion, he passed through dulled red curtains as though they were nothing but a thick fog. Beyond that was the **Door**. Lines and symbols swam around the black wood, as the many kings and queens of the past had their own portrayal of how their kingdoms were ruled. No new carvings had been etched into the wood for so long that the older scratches had become a little bit more than nothing but tiny bumps and unreadable patterns. It infuriated Garden to see such mastery of art wasted on a seventeen year old boy. *And his sister,* Garden reminded himself. *Bitterness has never ruled the kingdom for so long. I'll have to watch my own tongue for as long as I have time left to use it. Perhaps there will yet be a day when I walk into this room and find myself with the rightful king again.*

He pushed the door aside and was forced to look upon the room he loathed with such force.

Numerous drapes of fabric hung around the room, all of them different: torn and decaying; fresh, new, and crisp. Many extravagant designs played their games on the tips and brushes of pillows, ends of curtains, and more importantly the thin cape of Colon himself, back turned to Garden, probably speaking to another.

Black and red. Two colors that set this room apart from any other in the castle. The perfect colors for each other, but also for the individual who spent his days here. Two colors of death. Nothing but the sleek shadowy color of black mixed with the deathly rich shade of crimson, intertwining to make shades and tints of death. They weren't a very wholesome pair if you asked Garden.

Garden stood off to the side as Colon began to yell at the third person who shared the company of the room.

"It's almost time to get her, you know. I want you there and I don't care if that boy cousin of hers is there or not! If he is though, bring him too. He's done too much to let it slide. We might as well make the job easier," Colon yelled at Scarlet. He grabbed her by the chain necklace that bore a similar resemblance to the one he wore. "And don't you dare mess this one up, Scarlet," he snarled so close to her he could taste her fear. She ran then. He fingered the chain band he wore. It was the only thing keeping him and his helpless sister at age seventeen and eighteen forever, and also, the only thing left of his father.

It's amazing that Scarlet even follows his orders. She doesn't know what she's doing though, he has more control over her than she does over herself. I'm surprised with the gift he has. She's older than him. I'm astonished she doesn't hold that against him. Garden's thoughts swarmed in his head faster than a bee could chase.

It wasn't a very odd thing to hear yelling in this castle. Colon was constantly ordering his army and sister around to the point of exhaustion, for the people that is, not Colon. Most guards had never come into his bedroom chamber. The few who did often did not revisit their posts. The guards who were in lower rank, more of the younger ones, heard the yelling so often that the jumping had become a part of their job. They hardly felt fear anymore.

Hardly.

The yeller, and his crossed arms, stared down into the valley through a tinted window to see a few crumbling houses decaying on the yellow grassy fields. Abruptly, a realization came to him and his scowl turned into something like a twisted smirk.

"You're early Garden. That's unusual even for you."

"It is better to be early than late. I am, in fact, on time though."

As if on cue, the old grandfather clock that stood sideways and long forgotten, sang its song for the first time in thirteen years.

The boy's eyes darkened. His smile faded into a straight line. "I didn't ask for a smart mouth. Nor did I ask for any of your tricks." Colon's accent sang bitterly, but still in his chime-like voice.

How amazingly charming he would look and sound if evil did not constrict his heart. It runs through the family. The startlingly beautiful features but then, the wickedness. Always with gifts of torture too.

"Garden? Are you afraid to talk? You know your hypnotizing gift does not work on me. You are very lucky mine has the same effect on you, or we both would be in a very sticky situation."

Garden sighed. "I should feel very lucky and also very ill-omened."

Colon ignored his remark.

Garden's voice turned stern, "I believe our situation is that of the substance of stickiness anyways. Nevertheless, my time is limited here. Very soon I will have to go. There are many other souls that need help, and I will not waste my time playing."

Again, Colon's eyes clouded. They cleared when he sneered. "Another place to go? I should think not. Your place is here with me. No other place is in need of a pocket-watcher!"

Garden remained silent, only staring back into Colon's so-dark-brown-they-looked-black eyes.

"It's about time, am I right?" Colon suddenly whispered. "It must be getting close to the time? It has to be. I've waited too long for her to slip through my fingers again…" Colon trailed off, changing the subject. His mind was obviously hooked to other things.

Sighing again at Colon's impatient mind, Garden brushed back his glasses on his crooked nose. From an invisible indent in his green robes that covered his black shirt and pants, he cradled a golden pocket watch. Fantastic designs were impressed all over the linings; the chain was woven like a slim rope.

When he cracked it open, instead of the click normal watches gave, it gave a peculiar "*crisp*" sound as if it were a pop can being opened. He peered down at it uncertainly.

Don't tell me anything that I can't tell him. He knows that I can't lie to him. Tell me something abnormal but make it vague. Garden plead to the heirloom.

II

The minute hand spun out of control momentarily than stopped right on a particular symbol. "Right then," Garden whispered to it. He looked up at Colon who was eagerly waiting for what he would say.

Quite swiftly, Garden snapped the golden watch shut and thrust it into his pocket so he could look at Colon full in the face. "No Colon. I'm afraid that it is not time, at least not yet. She has just gotten her power, fire, and is just beginning to understand it. She's... quite vulnerable at the moment."

Colon raised his eyebrows. "So, fire is her ability." A smile spread across his lips. It was a bitter smile, full of hatred. "You have just found this talent out, am I right? A girl and the gift of fire. How much easier can this get?" Colon snickered a little to himself.

Garden immediately stepped in with determination blaring in his eyes. "Just because she is a young girl who has the uncanny gift of flames, does not mean that she is not strong. With the guidance of her friends and cousin, there certainly will be a problem for you to defeat her. Do *not* underestimate her." Garden turned his back to Colon at this point. Closing his eyes, he tried to concentrate. It was extremely tiring trying to explain things to young men who would never fully understand. Two young men in his life were too stubborn. The ironic situation of who they both were never caught him with seriousness.

Taken aback, Colon stood silent.

Garden started on his way again, unaware that Colon was just about to bring up another conversation.

"Wait. How are you now getting all this new information when you first told me you knew nothing more than that a person was going to come to my castle and try to dethrone me? Just yesterday I find out her cousin might be there to help her, and it took thirteen years to find out that she has the gift of fire. What *are* you playing at?" *Surely the old man must be playing games with me. I can't have spies here, not at this time anyway. I need to make sure he's on my side, it would be a terrible loss to lose such a powerful pocket-watcher. Besides, his information is so crucial for the sake of my kingdom.*

While Colon was deep in thought, Garden planned a well-thought out response to why his information was so hidden and in pieces while many pocket-watchers knew everything right away. *Lucky for me, Colon was not wise enough to trust anyone but myself. So fortunate for me to be able to play with his mind while he has no idea.*

Finally coming up with the right words, Garden spoke, "My watch does not know everything about the people and future it picks up on. As soon as it finds the target, it takes progressing time to collect all the information to repeat it to its master. It is not right to presume that a simple source of magic can produce such high expectations in little time. We will perhaps know even more tomorrow."

Colon smirked at this, fully satisfied with the answer that Garden gave. "Very well Garden, I knew I could trust you, and you've proven my reliance on you well." He stared back out the window this time towards the long river that ran like a spine along the grass fields. "Your king is very busy you know."

"However hard you may think of yourself as that, you'll never be one until fulfill your obligations," Garden whispered barely loud enough to be heard.

"Excuse me?" Colon had clearly heard something or everything that Garden had stated. Yet he asked what he had said anyway.

"With all due respect your highness," Garden had to fight to say the title, "you and I both know that you cannot become ruler until you prove yourself..."

"I know what I have to do!" Colon flared up. Garden was once again surprised that his gift hadn't been more reflected on his emotions. Then again, fate had chosen one of the worst for him anyway. Why give him more leverage?

It would be just Garden's luck that Colon would figure out what he was really up to.

Figuring it was wise to end the conversation for today, Garden started strolling towards the black doors again. It was then when a certain memory or perhaps a predicament flickered through his mind like a flash of light. He decided to choose his words carefully. One slip of the tongue at this point and it would certainly lead to death. Anything was possible in a room where death was lingering around the corner, waiting. It already hung on the walls. Besides, being killed or thrown out of the castle would not be so well on his part.

"By the way, your highness," Garden again bit his tongue, "the girl does not wish to steal your throne in any way."

Colon turned to Garden. Anger and frustration smoldered in his eyes. "What then does she plan to do? Or do you only know half of it *Garden*?" He spat out the last part with so much sarcasm that it was almost as though it were dripping off his lips, in a blood thirsty way.

Colon scowled at Garden. His eyebrows linked together into, what seemed like, never ending hatred.

"That's just it. She plans nothing. She knows nothing. Nothing about her past, or her future or even her present. She just has to come. That is the way it has to be. But she will be guided without a doubt, by her cousin."

"This cousin of hers is starting to get on my nerves," Colon said through gritted teeth.

Garden interrupted Colon from saying anything more. "Do not worry my prince, although he seems to know everything, he will not tell her of anything he sees unfit to tell. Which includes practically everything she would need to know to come to this castle and fight with the anger you fear she will. I don't think it is wise to let your mind wander over things like that boy."

"Do you know why he would try to come?" Colon asked while trying to calm himself down.

Garden threw a sharp look at Colon saying something along the lines of, I-really-shouldn't-have-to-explain-that-to-you.

Colon took the look with an eye roll and looked away. "The hatred we share with each other is strangely similar. We shall see if this boy is as strong as he thinks he is. Garden, go. Now. I will see you tomorrow. Same time, same place." Colon's naturally long sentences faded away like they usually did when it was near Garden's time to leave. Colon turned back towards the window again and stared down, thinking of his long gone father.

As solemn as ever, Garden bowed. For the second time today, which was more times than Garden had planned or wanted to, Garden tried to walk towards the black door and out of the horrid room before Colon could stop him again with any more comments.

Today, the prince seemed deep in thought, which was not unexpected, but at the moment, he seemed somewhere else. Garden could just see the black wheels of his mind clanking and whirring in Colon's head as he thought about Nikki's cousin. Their hatred was shockingly similar; Colon was right to have made such a suggestion.

III

Successfully moving past the onyx colored door, Garden saw the scared-stiff faces of the guards as they patrolled the hallways. Garden moved past them without a second glance.

They're so pitiful it's almost pathetic. Now let's see how Nicole is really doing, but this time, let's put it in further detail. Garden flicked open the watch again, this time the longer spinner wildly rocked back and forth until it stopped at a specific point once again. However, instead of acting like a normal watch and not moving after the spin, the glass surface turned murky and showed a shadowy image.

Looking around to see if anyone was spying on him, Garden closed the pocket heirloom and closed his eyes. *Just a bit more in the future please,* Garden plead to the pocket watch. When he opened it again to see a shaggy-haired boy looking down at the ground uncomfortably, Garden almost smiled. *Don't worry young Nicole, soon enough, you'll learn to trust him.*

A shadow crept along the wall. Unafraid, Garden snapped the watch closed with a sound that echoed through the corridor. A young woman snuck up behind him, tapping him lightly on the shoulder.

Without looking, Garden replied, "Ah, Alexandria."

The woman's lips sunk and her brows arched in confusion. "I didn't startle you, did I?" Alexandria swished her magenta colored robes back and forth while watching him react. She tried to pull up the brown comb that held her curls but they flopped, uncomfortably. Alex twirled one of the strands to her face and saw with dissatisfaction when she saw her blond shinning with streaks of dark brown.

"Ugh, do you see what all this darkness is doing to me? Evil does not settle well with elfin hair. I'm not giving up my curls for the side of malevolence—"

"Alexandria! *Okay,* I understand your troubles. Evil does *not* mix with goodness. Fear not young one. Time is coming soon enough for us both to depart this place and you will very well end up with your colors again."

Alex's shoulders relaxed from their tension and she moved towards the windows. "Why do the wise ones always get the calming gifts?" she muttered.

"Later perhaps I'll explain to you, but for now I think it to be wise myself for you to consider not opening those curtains."

Alex put on a face. "But it's not fair! It's not my fault if some of the guards turn to stone! Besides, I could do it without them knowing."

Garden stayed serious for the stone comment. Too bad she didn't know half of her comment was true, but he laughed softly at the last one. "I think it might seem the smallest amount anomalous if a rabbit or dog were pulling open a blind, do you think not?"

"The castle is not the only thing that needs light. I've only gotten caught once, and they barely even cared. The guards just ran off screaming—the young ones were the ones that saw me. Which reminds me of something I forgot to tell you yesterday. You should probably tell Colon when you see him that it would do good if he got new watchmen!"

Before Alex could continue, Garden cut across her words with his own. "Hush now Alexandria, you speak of too many subjects whenever we are around each other. Would you not rather hear of what I have found her gift to be? We both know I had some guesses and I was indeed right; she has the gift of fire just as her father had."

"The gift of flames? That's brilliant. It's so perfect for her, I know it!" Alex's smile widened, her heart relit. "She will have no problem —"

"Do not be so quick to judge. You and Colon both have that tendency. It is not only my watch that tells me her chances are horrendously remote. Although she may have her cousin with her, she has many things to learn in order to do what we all hope she will. Although it shocks me still that her cousin hasn't shown himself sooner. We all know what people are saying about him. Even with him, her abilities when she soon gets here will be undeveloped."

"Her cousin will teach her in time. I know he can do it, if anybody. Nicole is ready to learn. '*None have defeated him before.*' So what? Have we put our trust into the two children for more than eleven years to have it wasted?! Are you really so faithless that you have no trust in a girl and boy that are of their abilities? Garden, how could you even start to think for a moment—Colon has got to your head—"

"Alexandria! Alright. I think you have gotten your point across. I still have confidence in the young ones as much as I do in you. Do not worry for it is coming into place, apprentice."

Alex was staring at him as if she had never seen that side of him before. "What?"

"Do you not know of Colon's gift?"

"No I believe I don't. Should I know?"

"Not yet young one. You have much to learn yet, and I fear that you, like the two people we both have faith in, have little time to learn it all."

"So what are we going to do about it, Garden?"

"Alexandria, I think it may be time to get out that dusty book that is in the trunk beside your bed."

"Why?"

Chapter Six

Enemy and Visitor

I

Her mouth finally filled with enough wetness to gasp out a word.

"What?!" Nikki exclaimed, watching Kay's eyes wonder around the room. Kay numbly listened to the word that choked its way into the air.

This has to be a joke by now. How does she expect me just to leave? Maybe some of this is true, but this is too much to demand. And what a nerve this whole hoax has, to tell me that I have to leave the home I'm in. It would take so much faith in Kay to believe her. But I'm her friend I should have that… Why can't I believe her then?

"You and I both know what the letter said. You *have* to go. And don't you want to? Would you really want to stay here in a place with a family that you don't belong in? Don't you want to go to your real home?" Kay asked so many questions Nikki's head started spinning.

"I need proof; don't you get it?" Nikki snapped. "This is so hard for me to try to believe! I mean yeah my fire should be enough proof but how do I know what to do? How do I know *you* know what to do? Kay I—"

Nikki stopped then. Kay's questions had stung worse than

anything ever said to her face. As the hurt passed though, Nikki came to her senses. *You're smart. Be reasonable. Haven't you wanted something else? Another chance for a better life? But no, you've never asked for* this. *You know that you've never done anything that says brave or excessively strong. You're not exactly the hero image.* An important fact came to her mind to bring up.

"So am I going alone? I *really* don't think I could find my way alone around England," Nikki wondered aloud.

Kay responded to her earlier questions, trying to keep up patiently with Nikki's stressed out emotions. "Nikki, I don't have any more proof. This is something that you just have to believe. And no, you definitely are not going alone. Do you really think that I would tell you all of this just for you to leave us with no clue where to go? Wow, that would make me *such* a good friend."

Nikki stared at her, silently asking for more.

"Breannen, James, Sophie, Michelle—"

"But I thought you said that Michelle doesn't have her magic yet?"

"She doesn't, which makes things complicated. She'll be going of course, but we'll have to explain all of this to her too. Regardless, I am going and *you are too.*"

"That's a lot of people just to get me to one place."

"Would you rather go alone? I wouldn't. One of us is at least going so why not all? We're all your friends—magical friends at that. We're all in this as one. Plus a few extra numbers never hurt the balance. There's power in numbers, Nikki. Especially with our kind of people." Kay looked satisfied that she had gotten everything she could get out with one breath. Nikki however still looked like she was biting her tongue, trying to keep a question in and not bother Kay.

Kay caught her glance, and she moaned deeply to herself. "Go ahead. Why come here and not get all of the information you want?" Nikki was surprised there wasn't any sarcasm in Kay's voice.

"It's just that how do you expect us to make it to England fast? I mean even if we flew on a plane or took a boat, it would at least take a day, and that's just a approximation. And how would we get the money? The way you're talking sounds like we need to get there as soon as possible. "

"We do and we will."

"How though?"

"Nikki—"

"Give me some time to get used to that okay?" Nikki asked, referring to Kay calling her Nikki.

"*Okay*, **you** then, if you want to be that way. The fastest way to travel would be definitely on broom."

"On broom?" Nikki asked. "Considering that I've never ridden or even thought of flying on one before today, makes me even less comfortable doing that. Did you forget that I get chosen last for every single sport we do in P.E.?"

Kay rolled her eyes while a worried appearance grew on Nikki's face. "Don't worry. You have to trust me on this, but *every* magical human being has at least the tiniest bit of talent to ride a broom. Some more than others, and likewise of the opposite. But you *will* make it to England on a flying broom or so help me, may my knowing gift disappear forever!" Kay was getting intensely exasperated.

"Okay then. At least you think I can make it!" Nikki laughed at Kay's anger.

"Nikki—I mean, *you*... you have to leave. Sorry, but even my mom is getting a little bit frustrated that I haven't started my homework. I can tell." Kay gave her a small wink. "It's not that late, but your dad is probably going to get mad at you too if you don't start on your way. See you tomorrow then?"

"Yeah Kay. Or did you change your name too?"

Kay rolled her eyes, but smiled.

"I'll be going. See you." Nikki started out of the room and down the stairs.

"Goodbye sweetie! I'm going to see you again soon!" Kay's mom musically shouted while Nikki made her way out the door.

"Yeah," Nikki mumbled slowly barely above a whisper. A thought occurred to her that Kay's mother probably knew the moment when Kay said for her to go. Reading minds could easily get annoying though.

As Nikki stepped out the door, she stumbled into icy cold air and felt her breath nearly leave her. *It's never this cold this time of year. Why is it that suddenly it's as though the world is upside down, and that I feel like there's no one who can explain this to me in a way that I can feel totally sure who I am?*

Thank goodness that I was never the one that stood out in my life. Sure, I was weird, but I never was the one that everyone knew was different. But now I am. I have to face the fact. Just like Breannen said: this is real. All of it. I am Nikki. And whether or not I like it, I am who I am. Not many people get to change their name, let alone their life, so be thankful. I get a second chance. To do something.

The only thing that kept her worrying was a single thought that echoed in the crevice of every nook in her brain: What if she screw this chance up?

II

Nikki kept walking, eyes glued to the charcoal colored pavement. Absentmindedly, she wandered the sidewalks back to her house. Watching the surroundings get dimmer until streetlamps were shinning white mouse holes onto the pavement. An unexpected breeze shifted the leaves of the trees, and grass rustled wildly like they were in a sandstorm.

Nerves slightly breaking, the hair on the back of Nikki's neck stood straight up, reminding her of an angry cat. It snapped her attention back to reality, but not enough to know where she was. The startling breeze carried something with it, making the surroundings unfamiliar and shifty. The wind gave another sharp pull at Nikki. The breath-like stream of air exhaled on her skin, making it crawl with pins and needles.

Her hair flew into knots while she saw the scarcely discernible lamp posts flicker. Nikki held her breath. *Don't go out. Please, please. Don't go out lights.* With one more flicker the lights remained the same: lit and running. Nikki blew a breath of relief, and felt a calmness that she couldn't explain just as the wind died too. *So weird. Maybe it's a sign I should get home faster.*

She recognized that she hadn't moved a single step since the breeze had come. Nikki seemed to be rooted on the spot while she pondered about the horrific things that had started to occur around her out of nowhere. She broke into a run.

It's alright. Everything's fine now. Just keep going, she tried to assure herself.

While trying to see if anything had been affected—a car flipped over or even a few leaves fallen off a tree leaving a space bare—she tried to rationalize to herself. Anything to prove that what had just happened wasn't a hallucination. Something in the back of her mind kept gnawing at her. Something felt off about the way the wind was so silent. As thought it were waiting for the proper moment to attack. Her insides were constricted with fear that she couldn't explain. Yet, her scenery mislead her. She hadn't realized that she had stopped running again.

Trusting herself and not her instinct, Nikki took another stride forward.

This time, it was as if the whole process started happening again. But this time, it finished.

The street lamps died right there. A thick haze materialized and covered everything that Nikki was already having trouble seeing due to the howling wind that erupted from the sky.

The atmosphere was so thick, so eerie in an intangible darkness that if you put your finger right up to your nose and eyes, you would see nothing but black. The moon disappeared, the environs faded.

Out of the obscurity, a musty smell plundered. Like old furniture, moldy and grotesque, it entirely enveloped the air. It was getting hard to breathe. Nikki covered her mouth and nose while her eyes painfully watered as the rancid stench extended towards her. *Stay calm.* Nikki pleaded to herself. Was something or someone dying? She had never experienced anything like this. She was frozen in terror. She couldn't tell if she was standing or laying down on the pavement.

Her stomach dropped.

Something behind her caught her eye.

Nikki swirled around to the best of her capabilities to glimpse the black smoke swirl, and turn oil-like and gray. For a moment, the swooshing stopped. Everything stopped. Nikki tried to breathe, but the air felt tighter and tighter. Like it was contracting her lungs.

Feeling hopeless, Nikki failed to convince herself that whatever was there was there no longer. Her instinct had taken over. Survival was at the top of its list. Right in the middle of saying an argument to herself, something colossal leapt from the smog. It easily made a clearing for itself in the middle of the smog storm.

Landing on the smooth pavement, a beast easily the size of a large two-story house, shuttered its golden-glazed red scales that glimmered even though there obviously wasn't any light to reflect off of them. It had suck all of the light from the world.

Moving its mammoth, yet graceful feet, all of the creature's iridescent scales shimmered until a golden design seemed to almost entirely take over the crimson color. Maybe it *was* changing color; Nikki was too dazed by it to pay sharp attention.

Two plain bat-like wings struck and smote the air making the fog again turn murky and like a clouded glass ball. Fanned out, the wings expressed the beast's distress as it spotted Nikki in front of it. Yet the beast flickered in and out of her sight as the smoke swirled. Nikki only had every other second to be filled with terror. The other second was filled with emptiness.

Curling its lip to give a vicious growl, the dragon unfurled its blood stained teeth. *Please don't let that be the smell that's in the air,* Nikki screamed in her thoughts almost shocked that she was brave enough to think. She could only imagine the decaying flesh rotting on the teeth of that monster. A spike of fear raced through her veins. Her own flesh might be next.

III

Her heart was in her throat. The dragon opened his eyes to show the dazzling twinkle of his jade eyes. Part of the dragon's "eyebrow" took a sharp plummet toward the bridge of the snout. *Its angry.* If Nikki's thought had been out loud, it wouldn't have made it past her lips. Her mind was frozen as was her body.

You're wise to not make any movement while I'm here. Perhaps she'll take pity upon you... Or perhaps not.

Nikki put on a alarmed look. *Did that dragon actually* talk*? Calm down,* she ordered herself. What the dragon had said lead her to presume it wasn't going to be *his* job to kill her. What was going on?

She couldn't control the heavy heartbeat or the nauseated feeling she was becoming suddenly very aware of. *It doesn't matter if the dragon is longer than a football field, or that you have no idea what you are doing. Just keep a cool head, and keep your tongue quiet.*

Something told Nikki that this would only keep her alive for a few seconds longer.

What defense did she have? There were no items that could be used as a weapon. And her magic was too undiscovered to be used. Her mind was cotton in such a way that Nikki was pretty sure that if she even *had* known how to control her magic, it would have failed. Did this happen everyday for people like her?

Nikki was going to say no to that question.

This was not normal.

Even for **Je Ne Sais Quoi**…or whatever she was called.

The beast finally settled enough that Nikki realized something was going to happen. He folded his dull wings in and draped his arms over each other. In another instant, he was lowered to the ground with a thud.

A women, very disproportionably small compared to the beast, seemed to float down from the miniature saddle that had straps larger than the leather seat itself. The women looked depressed, amused, and frustrated, as oddly a combination as it seemed. Somehow, Nikki couldn't help but think that this woman had the same swagger as Jasmine. They seemed to be in the same league.

This didn't help her fear. Jasmine always won.

Her apparel consisted of a robe-like blouse cinched at the waist with a tight corset. Over her fire red hair, fluttered a cape so dark it camouflaged in and out of her background. Her skin-hugging boots crept up past her knees barely revealing the tight pants that were tucked inside of them. Kempt, waist long locks of hair were tucked behind her ears, draping over her shoulders, but her dark scarlet bangs concealed part of her face. She also looked extremely young, a couple years older than Nikki.

Why did her eyes seem like they knew everything then?

Awestruck at the mysterious girl's appearance, Nikki took a hesitant step backwards. Something like an electric shock of a thought kept screaming to run. Yet there was no way that Nikki would get away. That much was clear.

The girl was enthrallingly beautiful.

Nikki didn't trust her for a second.

"Oh no. You're not going anywhere this time. You got away from me once. I can't let that happen again." The last sentence was a mere whisper to herself. As though memories of the day were still fresh in her mind. The woman's voice was soothing like velvet, but still sent shudders running through Nikki.

Nikki failed to control her facial emotions. Her eyes bled with the fear her heart was pumping through her chest.

The woman's eyes grew softer for a split second, then as sharp as ever. "I get it. Do you not know who I am? Or is it just that you don't know who *you* are? Either way, I'm not letting you leave."

Nikki found the courage in her voice. "Who are you and why do you want me?"

She thought she knew the answer from the woman's smile. The ones who had been chasing her since she was born had finally found her.

The dragon behind the women gave a large growl that almost sounded like an irritated yawn.

"Do you really not know? Well then, I guess this makes this all the easier."

Nikki swore that somewhere around her she heard a twig crack, which in this situation, where every sound was amplified, sounded like a firework going off. The woman's head snapped in the direction Nikki thought she had heard the sound.

Confused, the woman focused back on Nikki.

Something made an echo along the smoke walls that sputtered like a shocked gasp, as the girl pulled out a thin gray branch. She grasped it in her hand at a odd angle.

"It's too bad magic has to be wasted to finish you off." The girl smirked, almost the same exact way that Jasmine had earlier.

Mouth faintly ajar, Nikki realized the girl was moving farther from her dragon.

Moving closer to her.

Nikki reversed, following the woman's pattern in walking, not caring if she ran into anything. When something began to prevent her from continuing to move farther, Nikki knew that she had to do something.

"Don't come closer, I'm warning you." Even Nikki could hear the shaking in her voice. No one had prepared her for something like this!

"Not a very brave one are you?" Scarlet sneered. "I was expecting someone with a few more ideas. After all, they took so much care to keep you safe. You'd think they'd train you better."

"That's what I was thinking…" Nikki muttered.

She was right on top of Nikki now. Nikki could see every intricate detail on the woman's porcelain face.

Nikki held out her hand defensively.

The woman's smile grew larger. "Not very prepared? That's okay, it just saves magic."

Nikki's forehead seared. Remembering her "gift" as Kay called it, she took in as much air as the surroundings would let. Her lungs screamed as the tar-like substance filled them. But Nikki needed to breathe to do this.

"**Malonane**—" The girl started but Nikki knew when to cut her off.

Sweat beading miraculously on her forehead in the freezing portal-like place, Nikki pushed herself farther than she ever had. Instead of the small red flames that had licked her palms before, bright purple and orange streams of burning lights, leapt outwards and surrounded the area. She heard the dragon roar in frustration, but it was a purr compared to the screaming in her ears. She wasn't yelling, yet the fire that she produced filled the air with a heavy warm shriek. With every spark that was lit, she seemed to find new energy. Soon it filled the street, the air, the night.

She had to close her eyes to concentrate and more importantly, not blind herself. The light was more than saving her, it was hope.

She couldn't even tell if the woman was there anymore. It no longer smelled; she couldn't tell if it was dark either. *Stop? Can I just stop anyway? I've never done my gift this huge before.*

But just as Nikki had thought about it, the firestorm shimmered and turned smaller and redder until Nikki was in the darkness of night. Covered in a thin layer of gray ashes too.

Her instinct had been right to stop. The dragon and its rider were gone. *Hopefully burned too*, Nikki snapped in her head bitterly.

IV

Nikki ran her fingers along her arms, brushing particles of cinders away. The last of the luminosity that had saved her life had died away. The clammy darkness that had come with the sky flyers, had seemed to trail after them as well. Now a friendly star-filled night replaced it, siding with the brightness of the streetlamps.

Nikki looked around at the familiar street. *Ha! If only I had known where I was.* Her mind was frazzled. She barely comprehended what she was doing as she stood up. Her energy was sky-high. She had never felt more powerful.

At that moment, a friendly face appeared out of the door to the house across from Nikki. Sophie ran out into the middle of the street where Nikki was.

"Are you okay? I'm so sorry. I should have told you about me and..." Sophie looked concerned at the amount of cinders on Nikki.

"Wondering why I'm covered in ashes?" Nikki asked in a slight daze.

Sophie nodded, then carried on. "That was the coolest gift I've ever seen, and being able to read peoples' thoughts, I've seen a lot of them. I almost had to look away. I couldn't believe that you'd have made something so powerful! No offense... I was reading your thoughts, because I could barely see you until you let your gift explode like that. You didn't look the least bit afraid until that end part. Your thoughts were really scaring me though—"

"Um, Sophie, can we please get out of the middle of the street so we don't have to end up being hit by some car or something?" By something, Nikki meant the dragon rider. Although, she had a feeling the woman wouldn't attack again right now.

"Yeah, here let me help you," Sophie absentmindedly helped Nikki wipe the soot off. "That was so amazing!" Sophie started gushing again. "I'm just so sorry that I didn't tell you I was magic. I was afraid you wouldn't understand or wouldn't believe me if I told you. But obviously I can tell you are now. No more secrets alright?" Sophie just kept going. "What the heck was that all about anyways?"

"A deranged woman attacked me on the back of her smog machine."

Sophie laughed.

Nikki smiled a little, happy that something felt right.

Nikki was surprised that she wasn't exhausted. She felt invigorated. Something else was surfacing too. Strength? Whatever it was, it sure beat the panic feeling that she had been getting since she set the football on fire.

"There's no way that I am going to let you go alone to your house. You could get killed there, and anyway, your friend… Kay is it? Well she called and asked if you were alright. At first I was like, what? Who are you? But then she like sighed and told me to look out my window. Is she magic too? Can she predict the future or something like that?"

"Yeah," Nikki agreed. "Something like that." Nikki enjoyed Sophie's rambling. It made her feel comfortable and normal if only for a moment.

"Anyway, so she told me to find some way to make you stay at my house. Then she hung up. She seemed kind of weird. Is she your friend at school or something?"

"Sophie!" Nikki laughed "Are you overexcited or have you been drinking too many energy drinks?"

Sophie pursed her lips. "I'll talk less," she promised, with a small guilty smile.

"Okay. Just don't you start calling me Nikki. I'm not ready for it."
"Nikki?"

"Oh gosh, well I guess you're in for a story when we get to your house. The only problem is that I don't know how I'm going to explain it to my dad." She barely understood it herself.

"Explain that you're staying at my house?" Sophie questioned.

"No, the fact that I'm not his daughter."

Sophie could tell that Nikki had a lot to tell her. "Let's go."

They walked across the street, and into Sophie's home. As they passed through the door, Sophie's older brother gave a questioning look at Sophie. "What is *she* doing here?" he asked.

"Nothing. Well, she's spending the night. It's a magic thing Andy. I gotta go tell Mom and Dad she's staying here."

"Oh." Andy looked depressed.

Is he not magic too? Nikki didn't even keep in mind that Sophie could hear her.

"No. He isn't." Sophie looked a little sad when she said it.

" Oh," Nikki said, slightly startled. "Are your parents?"

"Yes. Both my dad and my mom. It's been passed down for centuries. We still can't figure out what's wrong with him." She replied the last part in a teasing way, but Nikki could tell that Sophie still had a tint of seriousness in her bouncy voice.

"Let me talk to my mom and dad. I know that if I explain the situation, they'll understand. Good luck with *your* dad." Sophie passed over her phone and ran down the hallway just as her parents came out to ask her who she was talking to.

Nikki's heart was in her mouth this time as she heard the long stretching beeps of the phone trying to connect. A little while later, after a whole lot of persuading, Nikki finally convinced a reluctant father to let her stay at Sophie's.

"Thank you Dad."

Why did it sound so weird to call him dad now? All of a sudden, it was as though nothing made sense. Like she was dreaming of flying when she had never left the ground in real life. It was as though the pieces did not fit right and fate was trying to glue broken bits together. Wasn't this what fate wanted though?

Nikki's thought all the while were being read.

"Okay, just because I know that you can read my mind, doesn't mean that I want you to." Nikki teased. She had caught the focused look on Sophie's face as she sat on the sofa. "If I wanted you to know about it, wouldn't I have said it out loud?"

"Well, you're not telling your story, so I'm trying to figure it out. So far all I got is that your dad isn't your dad. But that really doesn't make any sense to me either. So, your dad gave into you staying here?"

"Sort of. I can feel trouble coming though. Anyway, it's not like I care if I'm in trouble anymore. According to Kay, we're leaving soon."

"Okay, now it's your turn to slow down. Please, start from the beginning."

Nikki took a deep breath. "Alright, here it goes."

V

Kay had called Nikki earlier that morning at Sophie's house saying that Breannen was going to meet up with Nikki on the way to school, and not Kay herself and Michelle. Right when Nikki got out of Sophie's house, Breannen was there.

"Kay thought it was best to have someone with you at all times. She couldn't be here herself...she and Michelle had an important conversation to have."

Nikki nodded.

"So we're cool right?" Breannen asked with worried eyes.

"Yeah, of course we are! Even if you lied to me, it was for a purpose right?"

"Yes, of course it was! And you already told your friend Sophie— or whatever—that she was coming too?"

"Yeah, according to Kay—our personal GPS—Sophie, *or whatever*, is coming with us. You've met her before, haven't you?"

"Probably. Anyway, doesn't it just feel like there's something that's going to happen today?"

"Oh no! Kay has gotten to you!" Nikki sarcastically stated.

They walked their familiar way to school. The air seemed light and peaceful for once.

"No, really!" Breannen insisted while she laughed.

"Um, sure okay. I'll humor you."

"Well, maybe I have been hanging with Kay too—"

Breannen sputtered to a stop in the middle of her sentence. A boy had just brushed passed her, and walked ahead of them. She fell silent, hiding her statement.

"Who's he?" Nikki whispered into Breannen's ear.

"I've never seen him in my life. Although…."

"Do you think he heard what we were saying? How long do you think he was behind us?"

"Not sure. But even if he did hear something, he wouldn't be able to tell or make out anything we were talking about right?"

"I don't know." Nikki bit her lip.

They watched carefully as the lanky boy ran his fingers through his thick auburn hair. He kept a pace steady to theirs, but slightly more graceful.

"Does he seem too old to come to this school?" Nikki asked.

"Maybe. But he has a backpack, so he must be going somewhere. He looks too young to be going anywhere else. He's too cute to be doing anything bad..."

"Breannen!" Nikki hissed. "He's right over there!"

As if on cue, the boy turned the slightest bit to catch the two girls out of the corner of his eyes. When he saw that they were looking at him too, he quickly looked away.

"Ohmygosh," Breannen murmured so fast that it sounded like one word. "He has blue eyes."

"Maybe he's going to be new at our school," Nikki suggested.

"I love guys who have the kind of shaggy hair like he does," Breannen dreamily stated while she flipped her hair.

"'Somebody likes him already," Nikki whispered, smirking.

"Shut up!" Breannen playfully shoved Nikki.

Nikki snickered.

They were soon at the school, following the boy all the way. When he turned up toward the stone steps, they both knew that Nikki's guess had been right.

Breannen stared lovingly after him as he walked up the stairs and into the nearly deserted school building. She saw several girls taking a quick interest in him as he walked by. This included Jasmine who was sitting on one of the steps as he briskly passed.

He turned to look at her briefly but his eyes shot away. Her face of disappointment gave humor to Nikki, but a thought soon came from all of his gazing. He had looked disappointed when he had turned away, his sharp features twisting.

Is he looking for someone? Nikki wondered. It sounded absolutely reasonable to her, considering everything that had happened in the last twenty-four hours. Breannen stood under the tree near the entrance, and Nikki followed.

Turning to see Breannen's face, she laughed out loud. "I wish you could see your face! You practically have little hearts racing above your head."

Breannen laughed too. "Did you see the shot down look he gave Jasmine? I bet that was the first boy to completely ignore her."

"How do you know that he just wasn't in a hurry? He could come right back out here and she'd be all over him."

"I saw his face. It was totally blank when he looked at her."

They both had a moment to laugh.

Before school had even started, the boy had come out again.

"Hi, I'm Jasmine. Are you new here?"

Nikki and Breannen both covered their mouths to stop from exploding with laughter. "Now, whose hanging with Kay too much?" Breannen mocked.

"I didn't think that Jasmine was really going to ambush him!"

"He looks so uncomfortable, should we do something?" Breannen wondered aloud.

"Nah, let him see what Jasmine can really be like." Nikki smiled mischievously.

Somehow, Jasmine had forced him to sit down with her on the marble stone steps. He kept looking away, making Nikki feel guilty. She also felt a little flutter. *He doesn't like her. I can tell. He could fit well with our group.*

"He looks like he'd rather be anywhere but there," Breannen sighed. "Is it just me or is he pretty darn close to perfect?"

"It's just you. You don't even know what he's like!"

Out of the blue, the boy's head snapped up, as if he had picked up on what Nikki had said. His eyes flicked her direction and stayed there.

At the same moment, the principal strutted out of the door.

"Everyone go inside. It's time for class to start, so we would like all of you students to head inside of the building and go to your classes."

This wasn't a normal thing for the principal to do.

Nikki sighed. *That's what the bell is for. It's three minutes to class anyway.* She wasn't sure how she knew that. She wore no watch.

Breannen and Nikki hesitated as the stampede of people bustled toward the entrance. The boy jumped up and grabbed the side of the steps just as everyone rushed by. As Nikki and Breannen started too and as they passed through the door, Nikki saw the principal pull the new boy aside. She heard the principal sputter, "Okay young man. Tell me exactly where you are from."

The boy sighed.

Breannen and Nikki turned to each other giving the same look.

Something was up.

"Let's go," Breannen dragged her away.

Sighing too, Nikki followed Breannen but they separated as Nikki headed into math.

"Now you sound like him," Breannen sarcastically remarked.

"Oh shut it…" Nikki rolled her eyes and slung her backpack further up her shoulder. "Trust me, he's no different than all the other idiot boys in this school. If anything, James could probably pass him up for a better person."

Breannen shook her head in defiance. "You're wrong about him. I can feel that there's something strange about him. It might be that he's like us—magic."

"Even if he is, that doesn't make him good. See you." The dragon rider flickered in Nikki's mind. No, not every magic wielder was good.

Nikki passed through the door. James looked up at her smiling, when she came in. She smiled back. *It's so lucky that he's not the one that can read minds. He would have known we were just talking about him and the fact that Breannen now has a crush on the new boy. I don't think James would have liked that too much.*

It had been about twenty minutes, but the announcements that usually started five minutes into class hadn't been made, the bells hadn't rung, and teachers were starting to stress. *What is going on? Why was the principal acting so strange around the boy?*

Finally, after the wasted amount of time, their Mr. Phillips gave up on waiting. "Alright everyone, pass in your papers from last week's take-home. Any questions? Come ask me after class."

Nikki passed her homework in with all of the other students while her mind wandered beyond the hallways and into the main office. *Is the boy in some sort of trouble? Is he really magic? What was he doing here if he was? Did he just come here to come here? Why now? There has to be a reason.* Fear gripped her as she thought that he might be coming here to attack her.

Mr. Phillips had his hand on the stack of papers while another student shared the other half, when Mr. Woodcut, the principal, burst through the math room door.

There was an awkward silence while the head of teachers stared down hard at the class with eagle eyes. Nikki tried to look around the man to see if there was any other company with him to explain why he had suddenly interrupted their normal day.

Then, she met the boy's eyes.

A shade darker than Jasmine's icy whitish blues, the boy's dark emotion-filled, sapphires were staring right into her wet-sand ones.

For a moment, that lasted only a second, they made complete eye contact. Then he turned away to look at the floor. But not the same way he had looked away from Jasmine. She could see the scrutiny displayed in his face as he concentrated at not looking anywhere but the ground.

"*Students!*" Woodcut barked so loud that Nikki jumped then turned scarlet as she broke her gaze at the boy too.

Everyone in the room who was already almost dead silent with just a few chatters in the back, became hushed to a point where the drop of a pencil would be amplified to a high level.

"This is our newest student who has transferred here. His name is Jake Sage."

Is this why he didn't make announcements? Nikki asked herself.

Sighing as if she were giving up a fight she couldn't win, she stared up at Jake again. For some reason, while his eyes were down at the floor, they seemed to have something screaming in them. She could tell how they looked from where she sat. While he stood just lankily a few inches taller Woodcut's plump body, Nikki wondered if he was just scared that Woodcut had just embarrassed him and he was a shy person, or if it was because Woodcut had said his name out loud.

That's ridiculous, why would he be afraid that someone had said his name? He doesn't look like the sort of person who would do...bad things.

Jake had a plain appearance. Light blue t-shirt and faded jeans. Yet, his face and stature were something to gaze at. She imagined he'd receive a hard time from some of the guys at her school, for stealing the longing looks of girls he would pass. His face was just good to look at.

"I want you all to show him how great of a school ours can be, so give him warm welcomes."

Then Woodcut left leaving Jake halfway through the door with everybody but Nikki watching the spot where Woodcut had been. It gave them an excuse to stare at Jake.

Mr. Phillips quickly saw a uncomfortable moment coming on. "Come in Jake, take a seat anywhere."

Hesitantly, Jake roamed around a few rows of seats, then sat down a chair behind James. Two chairs behind Nikki. Nikki didn't feel drawn to him in the same way as every girl in the room suddenly had. She was too scared that he might whip out another wand as the dragon rider had. Yet there was something else that bit at her.

Everyone was silent.

"Jake is it?" Nikki heard a guy beside Jake's seat whisper to him. "Where are you from since you transferred?"

Feeling the heat of everyone's eyes, but taking it calmly, Jake pronounced, "Europe."

Nikki jerked her head up at that moment. *Europe is close enough to England for me to be nervous....Could this just be by chance?*

James turned around to look from Jake then Nikki. He raised his eyebrows at nothing in particular, as far as Nikki could decipher.

"Wow, far away isn't it? What made you transfer?" Seeing this put Jake in a position where he even started blushing, the guy muttered something like, "Never mind," and went back to doodling bombs on his math assignment.

Math class didn't get very far that day. Nikki tried once to sneak another look at Jake, but once she realized that both James and Jake were looking right at her, she turned around faster than Woodcut had disappeared.

Just a few other girls kept nervously eyeing him too. They might not have been too eager to catch his glance because they knew that Jasmine was after him. It was a small school.

Right when the bell rang, Nikki scooped up her things and rushed out of the door before Mr. Phillips even said bye.

Strange girl. It's going to catch up to her one day. He pulled his thoughts elsewhere.

Nikki raced through the hallway, not caring if someone was trying to follow her. You can imagine the shock on her face when someone grabbed her shoulder.

She jumped.

James was there leaning against her locker, wheezing and huffing.

"Don't *do* that!" Nikki hissed.

"*You* don't do that! I have been chasing you through almost the whole building!"

"Okay sorry. I just got a little freaked out back there by Europe boy."

"He does seem kind of fruity, I don't know. I mean there are too many coincidences with you and him."

"I only spotted one—a Europe homeland—but still, the chances of that one are so tiny, it's stupid not to think about it."

"See you Nikki, gotta head in to English."

"Ugh, don't remind me about England and the language we use!" Nikki laughed.

James laughed too. "This time I won't be with you."

Nikki rolled her eyes. "I think I can make it."

"I don't know, with the way he was checking you out…"

Nikki turned ashen. "Don't even say that."

"I thought you'd be happy."

"I think the world's too insane for happiness right now…"

Nikki said her goodbye. Rushing through the hallway, she slipped through her second class's door. Then she had to stop her mouth from flying open as she saw who was there with her.

VI

"I'm serious, Michelle, all of the classes that I'm in, he's in. Jake is everywhere, and if he keeps this up, I'm going to have a very huge problem with a stalker on my hands."

"Calm down Nikki." Michelle looked tired and a twinge of confusion glinted in her eyes like a scar. She had obviously spent the morning with many explanations jamming in her head from Kay.

"I want to know what's going on. Kay can't give me all of the answers and I don't know who to ask."

"Go meet up with Breannen for free period, I've got lab on my hands." Michelle made a face. "Although maybe you could ask your stalker since he's from where you're born."

Nikki frowned, perplexed and irritated. "Bye."

She struggled to keep it together while she walked alone in the hallway. Until she spotted Breannen, she swore that if that boy was in another one of her classes, she might lose it. There were only two classes left. This one was the only one that mattered, because in the final class she would be by herself with Jasmine. Just what she needed.

"Hi! Is that boy in any of your classes? He's in absolutely none of mine."

"So far, he's been in every one of mine, and I now know that his name is Jake and he transferred from Europe and he doesn't talk much but when he does, he has a British accent that at first sent my spine twitching."

"Is that a good thing?"

"Mmmm.... I wouldn't say yes, because the only reason it does is because I got attacked yesterday by a woman who had the same accent. It's not exactly British. It's olden-like British. I can't explain it. But Jake has a very velvety voice. I was interested in how his voice would sound. But it kind of matches him perfectly."

"Now who has a crush?"

Nikki glared at her. "I do *not* have a crush on him. I just think he's strange and I'm sort of freaking out because if a creepy talking dragon bursts through our school, I think I might go insane." Nikki couldn't decide if she was serious or not.

"Why are you so talkative?"

"Because I had to keep quiet all day so he wouldn't notice me more than he already has."

"How was that?"

"He stared at me the whole day."

"Really? Maybe your good luck with having him in your class will make him come here!"

Soon the class had begun, without Jake. As Nikki blew a breath of relief, Breannen sighed with loneliness. "Don't be too upset, with my luck, he'll be walking home with us," Nikki whispered as she sat at a desk.

Breannen put on a sarcastic hopeful look. "I'm not that desperate."

Nikki mouthed the word "sure" under her breath as the teacher came in.

Social Studies was the only class that Nikki actually learned something in that day. She walked alone again to her doom class. For once she hoped the boy was in it. *I don't think I can take being with Jasmine the Pretty Princess, alone. At least if he is there, and he keeps starring at me like he has all day, she'll get jealous. Come on, please be there.*

When she walked into the door, her books felt twenty times heavier than they first were. He wasn't there. She got a lump in her throat. Only two seats were open. One in front of Jasmine and one behind. Blissfully content to the fact that there was absolutely no seat open beside her, she sat down behind. She'd have to stare at Jasmine's back all class period, but it was better than having Jasmine staring at her and doing who knows what.

Who's not here? she asked herself. Looking around, Nikki mentally recalled every person in the room. *No one extra. So whose chair is that?* There had always been an exact amount of chairs.

Then, he walked in. Seeming the slightest bit aggravated, Jake brushed back his reddish brown hair and muttered something under his breath when he saw what seat was open. Jasmine on the other hand, gave a outsized smile towards him. He tried to smile back but it ended up in a grimace.

Nikki shoved her face down into her hands and onto her desk, covered her head. She didn't want anyone to see or hear her small amused chortles. Surely, they would think her crazy.

Most of the class was eventless. Jake didn't turn around once, his back completely straight, while Jasmine kept trying to force him to turn around. Poking his back and whispering comments in his direction. A great deal of the time, Nikki had begun to feel a tiny bit sorry for him and eventually came to the conclusion that he definitely did *not* like Jasmine.

It was his turn to run out of the class as soon as the bell rang, and Jasmine and Nikki followed close behind. When Nikki had gotten out of the door she and Jasmine shared a confused look. Jake had disappeared instantly without any hallway but the single long narrow one to vanish to.

A girl came up to Jasmine and asked her something. Jasmine smiled, and began speaking quietly. Nikki started walking in the other direction but made out the words, "He disappeared without going anywhere."

Nikki glanced back to see that Jasmine's comment had caused a strange look from her friend, but she could feel her own face display just as much shock. Nikki left the hallway before Jasmine had realized she had been eavesdropping. It wasn't her fault if Jasmine had been talking loud enough for Nikki to hear.

Kay was waiting with Michelle and Breannen at the school entrance. "Hi. Gosh Kay, if you saw this boy coming and didn't tell me, you're going to die." Nikki notified her.

Breannen pointed to a spot behind Nikki and Nikki swirled around full blown ready to hit Jake with any blazes of flames she could. She could already feel the heat drain down into her fists. One wrong move and he would get a face full of flames.

Her madness drained out though as she saw Jake, but he was being closely tracked down by Jasmine. He was looking sharply at the ground as if he were trying to figure something out. Why was he always looking at the ground? It was as if he had something to hide. Jasmine was right behind him when his head snapped up as he passed Nikki's group, as if an alarm had gone off inside his head.

"Hello," Nikki heard Jasmine say to him.

Turning around so Jasmine couldn't see her face, Nikki concentrated so relentlessly she thought she could hear Jasmine's voice right beside her. Her eyes stretched out towards the track. Then further towards the graveyard.

"You're Jake right? I'm Jasmine. I'm really glad you came. Anyway, what made you decide to come here? To America I mean." She didn't wait for him to answer. "If that's too personal, you don't have to answer, but do you mind if I walk home with you?"

Nikki ground her teeth sharply together. Closing her eyes, she tried to picture what would happen if Jake said no. It wouldn't be pretty. And how could he? Jasmine was laying it on exceedingly thick.

What he said made her eyes snap open.

"No, I actually have to do something really important. I have to go, I really don't have much time today. Er, I really don't think you'd want to walk me home anyway. I probably don't live by you and..."

Nikki could hear the hidden words in his voice. *Does he have a place to live? Why isn't he falling for her? How can he resist when all of the other boys can't? Unless…*

Jasmine was left chewing on her lips as Jake left her. Tears stained her eyes.

Nikki felt pity towards her.

Nikki followed Kay and Michelle on their traditional path and towards the road that would lead them home. They were just passing the nearby cemetery.

Catching her breath, Kay murmured, "Nikki," just as footsteps approached them.

Jake was just behind them now.

Nikki didn't stopped. She closed her eyes. *Go away. Go away.*

Go away. She chanted in her head. It did not stop the silky accent from speaking behind her. He spoke with confidence.

"I need to speak with you. Alone and now."

Eyes shut tightly, Nikki brushed back the hair that hung in her face. She turned around and met him in the eyes. When what James had mentioned to her earlier clicked. They had the same color hair. Exactly, as if they... She had never met a person who had the same precise hair color. Until Jake.

It was too unusual of a color. Copper yet clear bits of red, yet light brown mixed with honey dark brown.

He could see she didn't plan on answering. He sighed. "Look, I know who you are. You're not Chrystan like people call you. Your name is Nikki."

Nikki's throat went absolutely bone-dry.

"We have to go, see you." Kay dragged Michelle away without even a glance back.

Feeling slightly sick, she answered, "My friends call me Nikki."

He gave her a look, and she instantly knew what he meant by it. She was hiding something, and he knew it.

"Who are you and what do you want? I already dealt with someone last night, so if you think you're going to get all murderous on me, good luck because I'm not afraid of someone three inches taller than me."

"So, I take it you are really Nikki?" Jake asked smirking. His eyes looked thirsty and excited.

"And who are you really, Harry Potter?"

Jake twisted one eyebrow up in confusion. "What?"

"What do you want?" Nikki asked again.

"Okay, if you really want the truth. It's a bit much. And you won't believe a single word, I swear."

"Don't swear, just speak." Her eyes were dripping with a promise of, *don't lie, I'll know.*

He caught it and grinned. "See, I knew it was you!" Seeing it brought no amusement to her he continued, "Anyway, okay, your mum sent me to watch you. After you got attacked yesterday, I rightly figured it was time to get you. Nikki, I'm your cousin, and I have to bring you back to England."

Nikki's face stayed blank for less than a moment. Her eyes narrowed. She didn't believe a word of this "Jake." "I'm sorry, you've got the wrong girl."

She turned and started walking away.

Jake stood discombobulated when all of a sudden, he realized what was happening. "You have got to be kidding me! Your mum and I both have been waiting for you for over twelve years! I've been watching you for over three days, I've seen you—you're magic and you're Nikki no matter how hard you deny it!"

"I'm *not*—wait, you've been *spying* on me? You were that idiot with that freakish creature in the bushes I saw on the way to school weren't you!?" Nikki was losing it. Shouting was not an option, but she was using it nevertheless.

"Er... Yes, but listen keep your voice do—"

"How dare you! I've never even met you. How do you expect me to believe some crazy whacko who comes out of nowhere and says he's my long lost cousin from England?! This is crazy, *you're* crazy! And I'm leaving."

"Do you want proof?" Jake's voice was quiet.

"Proof? Yes I want proof! If you are who you say you are, show me your "gift." You are magic, I figured that much out myself."

"My gift?" Jake turned a shade paler than he was before. He didn't move.

Nikki raised an eyebrow. "Maybe you're not even magic. Everyone who's magic has a gift. I'm going. See you, Crazy."

"But..." Jake grabbed her wrist.

Orange flames freed themselves from Nikki's palm and she saw Jake flinch back in pain as he let go and stared down at his extremely scalded hands.

"Bugger, girl! I know it's you!" He was practically pleading with her now.

"Don't touch me again," Nikki warned him so darkly, that he swore she could have made her fire gift kill him if she really wanted to.

Jake put his hands up defensively. "Alright, no contact, but—"

"No buts, I'm going."

Just before she spun around, Jake put on a wide eyed expression. But he was looking beyond her. It was too late to turn back, or to wonder what was going on.

Darkness.

Chapter Seven

Journey

I

The world came back with the feeling of a soft breeze tugging at Nikki's hair. *I hope this is proof enough for her,* came a sound that rattled inside of her head. It was not her own voice. "What did you say?" Nikki tried to ask, but her voice was lost before it could make it out of her mouth.

Her head felt like ten weights were piled on top of it, but strangely, she felt as though she could just start floating away. Her eyes were numb and heavy. Nikki didn't even know eyelids could be numb. Hers had found a way. When she tried to flicker them, her weight shifted and she could feel the sensation of slipping off of a glossy surface.

"Oh no you don't. You're not leaving. Especially from this height." This time Jake's voice rang sharp and clear to her ears. He sounded anxious. But Nikki felt from behind her the strong grasp of his hands pull until she was back up straight.

Nikki suddenly realized what she had heard when she first reached consciousness. *You could have told me that your gift was sharing thoughts with people. I would have probably believed you about everything else.* She directed her thoughts toward him, hoping that he would be able to hear her thoughts as well.

She jumped when she heard him groan loudly. Nikki presumed they were sitting on a broom since he had said "this high" and she could feel the breeze. She wasn't sure if she wanted to open her eyes, even to ask Jake what was wrong.

It seemed she had no choice… She flicked open her eyes.

Around her the air was quiet and dark. Far down below, Nikki could see people walking and driving cars.

It occurred to her that Jake's end of the broom seemed to be unbalanced and *he* seemed as though he were going to lose consciousness. Which didn't make sense to her at all.

Nikki turned her head to try and see what Jake was doing.

He was skidding further to one side, his eyes half closed in a strange daze.

Forgetting pain and discomfort, her mind began to reel in the split seconds she had. If only she hadn't been in the front. Her stomach tightened and a dry feeling got caught somewhere in her throat.

As Nikki's heart beat faster, she struggled to turn her body around to see what Jake's problem was. The more she saw of him, the more she found that he had dazed and entirely confused appearance displayed throughout his body.

Trusting without full reliance, she withdrew one hand off of the slick golden, broom handle and used the other hand to slap Jake.

He immediately came to, and she resumed her forward-facing position, thankful to have both hands on the broom again.

"Ouch! Why did you do that?"

"Because you were fainting, I owed you one anyway—you kidnapped me!"

"I did no such thing! I helped you! I am helping you now too—getting 'home.'" Nikki presumed by the way he said home that he was talking about her home a few blocks from where they were now.

"Why did I pass out? And why did *you* almost pass out?" Nikki asked. The last thing she needed right now was a cousin who had some sort of hereditary fainting habit.

"Jasmine spotted us while we were near the graveyard. Apparently, she's the jealous type, because she did one heck of an **enchantment** on you. And before you ask anything, yes she is magic. And yes, you should have known that. And for your final question, no I don't know why I just almost fainted. I didn't even realize I was fainting until you slapped me."

Nikki turned to give him a dirty look. Somehow, just the way he talked to her made her want to smack him again.

For a few moments she gave him an icy silence. Curiosity got the better of her.

"Do you have any ideas at all—why you just about fainted? Since you owe me an explanation?" she asked Jake.

"I have an assumption. But it probably isn't all that right."

"Tell me anyway while I'm on here."

"Fine. I don't have a gift. None whatsoever. Before you respond, let me finish. Either you somehow used magic without your wand— which is entirely possible just not very common especially since you just developed your magic—to not only talk to me in my mind, but also hear my thoughts, or you somehow have a split gift, which I *have* seen before. Have you ever read anyone else's mind? Wait, don't answer that yet." Nikki rolled her eyes. "Because I don't have a gift, the fact that you were making me somehow have one, as I heard you and you apparently heard me, might have accidentally, internally injured me somehow. Like, it stole my energy. Sapped it right out of my body. I wouldn't do it again just now to test it, considering we're several hundred meters above the ground, and you don't know how to fly, or save someone."

Nikki sent a glare ahead of her when he said that. "No, I haven't read anyone's mind before. But maybe I should do it again just so you'll fall off. I'm, glad you appreciate me saving your life." His words had stung her.

"Thank you. For saving my life." He sounded sincere.

"You're most definitely *not* welcome. Couldn't you have just poofed me home or something instead of getting all "magic broom" on me?"

"No, you don't understand magic yet. I haven't learned about "poofing" someone anywhere anyway." Jake seemed insulted by the fact that Nikki had called magic a "poof".

"Oh," Nikki said. "By the way, I believe you now."

"That's good. I hoped that I just didn't mess with your principal's memory for nothing."

"*What did you do?*" Nikki demanded.

"Just a simple age charm on his vision to think I was thirteen if he had any suspicions. Nothing extraordinary."

"How old *are* you then?"

Jake proudly announced, "Fifteen."

"And what, do you get a flying vacuum when you're fifteen?" Nikki laughed at her own humor.

"No." She could tell that Jake was confused.

Nikki changed the subject, "So, if you were the one in the bushes, what was that beautifully weird thing with you?"

"Arola."

"Okay. Is that what that sort of creature is called? I've never seen a creature like that and I've seen "magical" creatures in books and things."

Jake laughed. "Books? There's something funny. Never believe what books say. Especially ones written by people who aren't **Je Ne Sais Quoi** and think that they know all creatures of our kind. Ha! What a joke... But no, that's not what her species is called. She's a part of the **Drolgons**. They're a uncommon race and each one of them is unique. Depending on certain qualities and what abilities they have, they can be more wolf like or more dragon like. Arola is just her name."

"So, she's dragon and wolf? That's so strange. Where is she right now?"

Nikki turned to see Jake's face, and she saw him give her a crooked smile and his eyes flicker downward. She followed his gaze. They had lowered down quite a bit. Little more than a quarter mile below, the strange creature ran like lightning along the same path that they were taking.

"Is Arola your pet?" Nikki asked watching the white fur of the **Drolgon** stream beneath her.

"No. definitely not. She's my familiar. We're bonded. Everyone who's magic in our family gets one at a certain age. They have for centuries. Don't worry. You'll get one too." Jake read her mind without actually doing so.

"I have to get home," Nikki suddenly commented, her thoughts trailing to many things.

"Yes, I know. We'll probably head off to England tomorrow. We should arrive there before nightfall."

"No I mean— nightfall? On broom? Are you kidding me?"

"I have...special transportation planned. We will arrive by late evening."

"All right then. I meant that I have to go to the place that I've lived for the last thirteen years. I'm already in trouble I know it. Why add more when I have a great explanation that I just can't tell?"

"Right. I knew that. That's where we're going."

Jake somehow made the broom travel faster than it already had been and took a brusque nose-dive. Nikki held on to the golden handle for dear life. "Are you crazy?!" she screeched.

The motion immediately stopped and they were hovering about four feet off the ground. "Sorry. Forgot that you aren't the most audacious type." He gave her a smile.

Nikki jumped down off the broom just to prove that she wasn't spineless. Without looking at him, she turned to go.

"Before you leave though, I need to remind you of something. Let's face the facts, Nikki. You're no longer living in a child's picture book. Your life isn't going to be dulled down to numb the minds of frightened kids. This is going to be a journey. An adventure, if you will. With twists and turns around every corner. You'll never know what to expect now. Your whole life you've been living at a one year old level. We're dealing with a Shakespeare level now."

"Profound, are you?" Nikki inquired sarcastically. "What kind of life have *you* been living then to think that you're up to such incomprehensible trials?" She struggled to keep in the same I-know-big-words-and-can-use-them-together tone that Jake had held.

When he sighed and said nothing, she started walking again. She was right at her front door when she suddenly found another suitable thing to say. "I was and *never* will be the adventurous type."

She promptly slammed the door towards him.

The last thing she saw of him that day was the look on his face. Without meaning to, her thoughts melded with his. He was thinking about her, and the fact that he wished he could tell her something in her mind. She shut that frequency off before his thoughts could make hazy words. She'd had enough of British boys for today.

II

"Who were you talking to?" came a sudden voice behind her. In front of her was the devious smile Adriana always wore.

"I wasn't talking to anyone. Why are you looking at me like that?"

"No reason, but I guess you're crazy then if you're out there talkin' to yourself."

"I guess I am."

"Well then, I guess you won't need this box I found under your bed, 'cause crazy people don't get boxes."

Her words, although mostly complete nonsense, made Nikki stand at attention and stare at the red box with the bright orange bow in Adriana's hands.

"Give me that now."

"Or else what? You ain't gonna do nothing to me."

"Give it to me now." Nikki repeated.

"Or what?" Adriana demanded.

Flames bright purple, played delicately on the tips of Nikki's fingers, begging Adriana to continue. "What are you doing?" Adriana demanded, her lips quivered.

"Give me the box," Nikki requested simply. She let her ignition die out until it was her turn to smile at Adriana.

"I'm tellin' Daddy!" Adriana cried and took off. She dropped the box on her way up the stairs.

Shoot, shoot, shoot! Why am I so stupid? Can't I keep my magic to myself? Then again, I might be dead if I had done that.

Nikki heard angry voices from upstairs calling her name. She ignored them, despite her instinct of fighting back at what she thought was right. In an instant, she was glad she hadn't answered. A knock came at the front door.

Her first thought was, *Why didn't they use the doorbell?*

"Hi!" Sophie greeted her with a amiable beam.

"Um. Hi?"

"Did you really see a cute guy today and he told you he was magic and he took you on a broom ride? That's what you were thinking. Oh, and I knocked because I didn't want your dad to hear me."

Nikki shook her head blushing slightly. *What would Jake think if I told him I thought he was cute when I first saw him. Of course not as much as Breannen did, but still. I think I'm getting a little ridiculous. All this magic's getting to my head.*

Sophie nodded in agreement, apparently listening in on Nikki's thoughts. "It's definitely not right to think your cousin is attractive, but you didn't know. So you did go on a ride with him?"

"Yes. But only because apparently Jasmine got jealous while he was explaining things to me, and knocked me out with whatever magic she used. So Jake decided to just give me a lift home." Nikki shrugged it off. She didn't think it was a big deal, nor did she want other people to think it was. Especially Sophie. She knew better.

They heard a voice from the stairway. "Sophie? What are you doing here this late? Do your parents know you're here?" Nikki's "dad" had come down to ask Nikki why she didn't answer.

"Yeah, my folks know where I am. Can I stay for just a few minutes? I really just need to tell Ni— Chrystan some stuff real quick. Then I'll go."

"Well, alright."

Sophie had already read his thoughts of reluctance before he had said them, and she pulled Nikki down the steps of Nikki's basement before he could even say "Well ...".

Once they thought that they were alone, Sophie asked, "So, do you think that riding is cool?"

"Well, with Jake, it was terrifying. I was in front and he almost fainted on me—not literally on me, just almost left me alone on a broom." Nikki sent a flash of what happened in her mind. "But alone, I think I might be better. I still wouldn't really know what I was doing though."

"That's okay. I know that you can do it. Maybe you should practice some tonight. I mean, late at night, you can just kind of go for a ride by yourself when no one is watching."

"Or..."

"Shhh!" Sophie jumped up from her seat on the ground. "Someone's peeping in on our conversation," she whispered in an undertone.

They crept back up the steps of the cellar, barely making a squeak. "Okay," Nikki murmured. "I sure hope that no one is listening to what I'm about to say!" she shouted.

They heard footsteps from the other side of the door shuffling away. "All right, I think she's gone."

"Don't think so fast." Sophie shook her head.

Nikki moved towards the door. She placed her hand on the handle. It wouldn't budge a centimeter. "Evil, little... Always doing something... How can she even lock it from the outside?"

Sophie shrugged. "I guess it takes a malevolent mind to come up with locking us in by putting a couch against the door." Nikki couldn't tell if Sophie was being sarcastic. She rolled her eyes anyway.

Immobilizing, they both listened to the scoff on the other side. "Unlock the door now you little monster or I'll burn your toes off to the nub!" Nikki bellowed to the wood of the door.

The snickering stopped and Sophie made a face that looked like she approved of Nikki's idea. Nikki grimaced at her. "She's not going to open the door."

"I don't believe you! How would you do that?" Adriana commanded.

"Do you really want to know?" Nikki put on her best dark voice.

"Don't do it!" Adriana wailed.

Scraping noises filled the kitchen above the basement. Soon, Nikki and Sophie made their way out. They both weren't surprised to not see Adriana anywhere in sight.

"I'll see you tomorrow then?" Sophie asked as they made their way to the front door.

"No you won't," Ted declared as Adriana clutched him. "Chrystan is grounded for spending the night at your house when she hadn't asked first."

Too bad my name is Nikki. Chrystan can stay here and be grounded. I will go with Jake to England.

Sophie smiled a that's-the-spirit grin then took off in the dusk street.

Let Ted try to stop me. Or anyone for that matter. Nikki wondered what Jake would have thought about that comment. He probably would have laughed.

III

After a while of ignoring Ted while he yelled at her, Nikki scampered up the stairway and into her room.

"Should I pack then?" she asked herself, hardly believing that she would never see this house again. Until Jake had shown up and utterly confirmed everything that was so strange, Nikki had kept waiting for someone to just start laughing and say, "Ha! Got you! Go back home now and act like a regular person that nothing has happened to." She might have been depressed at that. Maybe not.

Why is Jake so serious? And does he really not have a gift, or is it something horrible he just wants to hide? Why didn't the letter say anything about him? Why didn't he come sooner? Where was he when I was getting attacked by that girl? Or was he the voice I heard? Nikki ran all of her questions through her head while digging in her closet for a big enough backpack. An older jean bag with a rusty crimson flower patched on the front, caught her eye. It was probably the best one she had.

She hurled it behind her and began thinking about what she would take. It all depended on what she would have—what she would have there, what she *should* take, what they would need. How was a thirteen year old girl suppose to know what kind of packings to take on something like this? She wasn't going for a hike in the mountains…

She prodded further into the burrow that was her wardrobe. A set of clothes for tomorrow—shirt, jeans and a sweatshirt, since it was suppose to rain and be quite frigid the next day—were laid out on the floor. Nikki shook her head. Why was it so hopeless? Why did she have to be so chicken… Jake was right, she hated thrills. She was officially a wimp.

If she had to choose whether or not to go on a quest to find a mom she had never known, she was almost sure she would have rather passed it up and stayed the same. Magic seemed to not be what it was supposed to be. Wasn't magic something wonderful and simple? That's what she had thought at least.

She set one other pair of pants into the bag along with two t-shirts. Nikki dropped a few more shirts in, along with three pairs of shorts.

Then she ran her finger along her bookshelf. *Which of these are true? Are all of them so much of a fantasy...or are they based on things magical people really have done or seen?* She clutched two of her favorites into her hand. *If these two are true, the world has gone completely insane. Then again, who wouldn't want to find out their hero is actually real?*

She tossed them into her bag. Nikki would have regretted it if she hadn't brought them.

She placed in her notebook of sketches and senseless ideas of writing she had come up with, along with a distinctive pen she had used for the entire thing. She couldn't leave those things behind. Adriana would get into them. It would be a waste.

Sighing, she flung herself unto her bed. What would happen to the things she didn't take? What would Ted do when he found out she was gone? Would he look for her, or presume that she would run away all along? Did he know something about how she wasn't his, or did he at least suspect it? She almost laughed with the irony as she looked down at herself. Her hair had flared out like auburn flames. The exact same hue as Jake's. Which was part of why she believed him. He was no practical joker. He was just sarcastic a lot. Nikki could sense he desperately needed her to come with him. She just didn't understand why.

Could I dig deeper into his thoughts, I wonder. Could I read what he had said yesterday or last week, or even memories from a year or more ago? Would reading them hurt him? Or even me?

The whole mind-reading idea seemed too complicated for just one person to share. *How does Sophie always deal with it?* She wondered if Sophie could just read the thoughts that she could hear while she was close to Nikki, or could dig and find memories earlier. Nikki was pretty sure that reading Jake's mind wasn't a split gift. It didn't feel the same as when she used her fire.

If only he were here right now. I'm so confused and when I was with him, not only did I feel safe, but he knew how to exactly explain things to me. I think that was what Kay lacked when she was trying to do the same. I don't really think he's all that good looking, partially because he seems like an idiot sometimes. But he's family. And he's still hiding something. I know it; I can feel it.

She moved up off of her cot-like bed. Placing her hand in her dresser, she pulled out a battered wallet. *Even though American money is useless in England, why not bring it? Maybe I can exchange it for pounds and notes or something like whatever they have.* She almost felt pleased to know some of their money names. Besides, you never knew when some freak incident would happen all of a sudden, and she'd need the American money. Not that she had that much to start off with, but it never hurt anything. In this case, Nikki couldn't help but feel a little unprepared.

Nikki tossed the wallet into the backpack. Besides a water bottle cradled in a portable icepack, her mp3, and a few more personal items she couldn't leave behind, there were few things she wanted to take with her. She felt like she was packing ridiculous things. But she would never come back here. She didn't want to leave it.

Before she knew it, it was one o'clock. Crazy as it seemed to her, three hours of packing didn't seem to be enough time to make sure that she had everything. Her mind was ecstatic as it raced through every picture of what had happened so far, making the rest of her completely charged. Not even a yawn had shattered her thoughts. Nor was there a heaviness to her eyelids.

Sophie came into her thoughts as she spread out on her cream colored carpet. *As scary as it may seem, I have to try to ride again if I'm ever going to make it to home. Might as well kill myself trying to fly than have that freaky dragon rider girl kill me in my shame. Wait, that might be backwards...*

She arose from her laying position.

Peeking out of her bedroom door, she heard nothing but the quiet snores of Ted. Nikki crawled out, regretfully landing on a Ghost Crack. Meaning to say, one of the many cracks along the hallway that Nikki always called Ghost Cracks because they seemed to be able to unnerve even a spirit from slumber. An echoing, "***FLEEEEK***!" made the walls of the hall shutter. *No!* She cringed.

Fortuitously, the Ghost Cracks remained silent the whole rest of the way down the passage and along the steps. It was only when Nikki got into the kitchen, she found her mistake. The box was nowhere in sight. Nowhere. Heart hammering, Nikki feverishly chased the hexagon-tile floor. No package. No box. No broom.

She exclaimed to herself in frustration.

With a dark pit in her stomach, she dashed back to the top of the staircase, all on the tips of her toes. *Where is it? Where could it have gone? It was right there. Adriana dropped it. Then Sophie showed, and Adriana came to bother us again. Then Ted came... You have got to be kidding me. It either has to be in Ted's room, or in Adriana's room, hidden. Why me?*

Mouth run dry and crusted with invisible film, Nikki pried open Ted's bedroom door. *There it is!* Nikki almost shouted in the tranquility of the night. A shadowed box as long and thin as the one Nikki had received rested on top of Ted's armoire. Of course, it was too tall to reach just on foot.

She grabbed a chair that Ted kept by the closet for reasons unknown. Placing it gently next to the side of the armoire, she scrambled onto it. Her feet jerked awkwardly to the right. *For goodness sake, he* had *to have a dang swivel chair?*

As the wild stool swayed, Nikki flailed her arm around, trying to catch the package in her palm. At last, the paper struck her skin. Meanwhile, the chair flew forward, lobbing Nikki backwards, until her skull cracked against the flooring.

Her thoughts were to jumbled to think even a cliché ouch.

Nikki quickly hushed herself to make sure everything was still at peace. Not a sound except for the sighs of sleep.

Gasping for breath, a sharp pain had sprung into the hand the package was held in. Brown paper. Not her shimmering birthday one. The thin tissue had ripped off leaving a round, sharp, jagged object tore from its lengthy box, in her clutches. That's what had gashed her hand. Her palm trickled a dark liquid on to the floor until she lifted her hand to examine it, and the blood started dripping down the rest of her arm.

Her stomach gave a lurk. Being squeamish wasn't the best way to act right now. *What is this thing?* Nikki asked herself. Tearing the paper fully off, she revealed a sharp piece of colorful glass. Just like the scales of the dragon that attacked her earlier, it glimmered in a way that didn't need light. "Wait a minute," she couldn't help whispering. "This *is* a scale." *I have to ask Jake about this. Would he even know though? Why is it here? Why would Ted have a scale like this?*

She shook it off. It wasn't worth getting caught right now. First, she had to find her broom. Then she had to find something to fix her hand.

It has to be in Adriana's room. There's no other option. Nikki pulled her hurt hand closer to her ribs, while with the other hand, she carefully slipped the scale into her jean pocket. She moved out of the door and into the hall, soon to meet the entranceway of Adriana's bedroom.

It instantly caught her eye. Only slightly hidden under the short bed of Adriana's, the parcel seemed to want to be found; the wrapping glittered against the shinning gem in her pocket that peeked out. Nikki snatched it up. "Don't touch my stuff," she mumbled to the sleeping body of her Adriana.

Nikki started out of the door and toward the light of her own bedroom. *I'll make it, there's no doubt that I can.* She clutched the box tightly in her hand while taking baby steps. *Almost there, come on!* "Oomph!" Nikki cried as she slipped on a large book sitting peacefully on the floor. Flinging out her hands to catch her, she didn't realize what a mistake that would be. Her bleeding hand and its partner caught the carpet just to spread drips of blood all over. Nikki flinched as Adriana moved.

Don't wake up. Nikki turned on her back to see what the girl was doing. Her eyes faced the wall and she took big breaths of sleep. Nikki sighed. "Any heavier sleep and an elephant could stomp around her room, and she wouldn't even stir."

She got up. Nikki walked through the door with a new confidence that she wouldn't get caught. She glanced at the clock hanging beside her doorway long enough to see that it was fifteen till two. "Got plenty of time."

She followed the door as it closed with her fingers, just in case it decided to squeak. The lock clicked happily as she pushed it. *Oh, Ted is going to kill me tomorrow if he finds out that I locked my door, let alone snuck out.* Ted never let them lock doors even though Adriana always did.

Slightly shaking and abashed, Nikki wondered how she was going to do this. *You can't do this. You've never ridden a broom before. There's no way you'll be able to do this.* But another voice in her ear was encouraging, *You know you can. Every magic person can. So what if you're not that good. It doesn't matter. All that matters is that you're good enough to get to England.* Nikki mused whether if that would be what Jake would have told her, or at least some of her friends.

She stumbled over to the window, numb. Grunting, she wrenched the window open until it had gone as stretched as it could. *What if I fall off? No one is here. No one's going to save you this time, Nikki.* She shocked herself by calling herself that. It wasn't that she didn't like the name, she found it to suit her much better than the name she thought had been hers. It was just the matter of getting used to it that bugged her. She stared down at her hand. *See what happens when you aren't careful? You're not made to go out there in the world and potentially kill yourself.* Knowing that she was just stalling time, she strode out into the hallway again and grabbed some gauze from the medical cabinet.

And I thought Ted was so weird for wanting a thing like gauze in the cupboard.

She fleetly moved back into her own room, and wrapped the white fabric over her wound. *Probably should have washed it first, but James, if he really can heal, might as well help me out tomorrow. So what's the point?*

She shuffled her feet back across the floor, just to nearly trip over the slim package still on her floor. Nikki was definitely getting frustrated. "How does anyone expect me to do this?" she exclaimed angrily at no one.

She knelt down and peeled the shimmering paper carefully away from the box. She tucked her hands in the underneath slits of its lid, and tugged it away.

IV

Nikki's mouth was slightly agape. It had a spotless, glossy coating over a black wood-like material. The broom was beautifully crafted. The black slowly faded into a crimson color near the bristles that were slicked together into a dark red tear drop. The whole broom was roughly as tall as Nikki. "This is amazing. To think I never wanted to ride one of these again. I wonder if they're custom made or something? That would probably explain why I was so uncomfortable on Jake's." She shook her head at the fact that she was talking to herself again.

Realizing she was delaying again, she moaned. *Just gotta make sure I can get through the window.* Nikki turned towards the glass and frame. It was a long drop of two stories, but if she somehow made it onto the overhang, just maybe she wouldn't die.

She took one step out the window, maneuvering her whole right leg through the hole where she had taken out the lining screen. Her foot found comfortable footing on the ledge. "Oh this is so dangerous... One more foot."

She pulled her head under the window.

Pulling her broom through, she grabbed the chipping paint of the top ridge to steady herself. Her left foot dangled nervously half way through the opening.

"*SLEEEK!*"

As her foot tried to meet its pair, the other slipped wildly to an angle. Her footing was lost, and her feet left the ledge. "No!" Nikki yelped as quietly as she could, but still in a very high pitch voice. Her fingers scraped against the air, grabbing nothing at the open window.

They finally caught the edge of the painted shelf.

Tearing at the chipping texture, Nikki panicked and dug her nails into the frame. *One chance. Got to get on my broom, or I'm bush kill,* Nikki thought as she pictured the spiky leaved bush below.

She began sliding the black handle through the hand that held it. *Don't slip, don't fall. You're fine...for the most part. Keep your cool.* Nikki could just image Jake laughing at her. Until only the very tip of the wood stayed clenched around in her hand, Nikki held for dear life in the darkness of a deadly windowsill.

Now what? she asked herself. The plan had seemed much more realistic in her head. *Let's hope that flying a broom isn't much more than thinking about doing it.*

She swung her leg over the top of her gift, losing the grip of the hand on the window above. Now, she swayed half on a broom, held by one hand that still had the stick in it.

"The things I get myself into."

She had yet to realize that she was no longer vertical, but almost laying straight horizontal to the wind. It blew a great breath at her and her hair quivered over her back. The hand she had on the handle was joined by the other. She stared at the scenery around her. Nikki lay her chin down on the stick of the broom making her legs dangle on either side. The broom seemed to know what it was doing more than Nikki. Or maybe it was just instinct.

The gift had been wider than she thought, giving it an almost bicycle feel while her jaw rested on a defiant dip that compared interestingly with the rest of the smooth surface.

I thought it would be terrifying. Which leads me to the conclusion again that all of the brooms are different and special for the magic people that ride them. Where would you buy a thing like this anyway? You don't see one of these in every Walmart. Do you have to be magic to make the broom magic, or could a normal person just grab this and fly off? I'll have to remember to ask someone that, sometime.

She let her hand glide on the ledge of the painted hinge of her window one more time, then slipped her hands away. Nikki lifted her head and held her two hands close to the rest of her, making her back stand taller instead of slouching. *Wonder how fast this could go.* She felt her side-swept bangs fly over her forehead to join her other hair, as the broom started to vibrate and increase in velocity.

"This is amazing," Nikki whispered to herself. *It's almost so comfortable that I could fall asleep on it right now.* The mentioning of sleep in her mind brought unwelcome feelings. *Maybe I should go back,* she thought as she sailed around her house in easy stroke laps. Her eyes were getting heavy. *I probably know all of the basics since they aren't that hard. I won't need much more than that, will I?*

The moon scraped the houses that Nikki gazed at, unseen as it moved closer to the other half of the world. The bitter autumn cold finally biting, Nikki flew towards her window.

Much quicker than the first time, Nikki maneuvered her way into the open gap. The sky was still a dark shade of cerulean, barely breaking dawn. Nikki groaned and collapsed on her bed, forgetting the window screen that lay forlorn on her carpet.

V

It was a too short period of time later when she had to wake up. *You're leaving, you're leaving,* came shouting in her head. Because of her "scared" half, she wanted to smack that voice and tell it to go to England instead. Another distant voice seemed foggier than both the ones in her head. It was also a man's voice. *Ted,* she sighed, stretching her arms like a cat.

Her eyes felt as though someone had put a heavy metal weight in a fire and then put it inside her eyelids. *Why was it such a bad idea to go out at night?* She asked herself rhetorically. *I think I found the answer. I've already been deprived of sleep several days this week, and if anyone expects me to learn anything—especially magic, I think I might pass out from exhaustion.*

Before anyone could say anything out loud again, Nikki shuffled up from her bed and pulled on clean clothes. While she brushed out her hair and pulled it into a lengthy, chaotic braid, Ted called up again. "Get down here or you'll be late! I don't want to hear anything about you from school today. If I do, you'll be in more trouble than you can imagine."

Nikki sighed. More and more every day it seemed like he acted less like her father and more like an annoying part of life she had to deal with. Adriana was a different story altogether.

She wasn't even worried about being late for school. *But what will people think when over four people who all hung out at some point or another disappear together? Are my friends' families coming with us? Do they even know what we're doing? How can they just leave them? It's different for me—I'm finding mine.*

She figured someone would do something, just to stop her from worrying about it.

Somewhere inside, she was still asking questions. She was pretty sure she'd have them for a long time. Months, years maybe. She was almost glad she hadn't been told about this earlier. What if she hadn't been able to read or even do math, and she had to go to England and she never went to school again? She shuddered as she thought of the answer.

Nikki didn't bothered to do anything about the bag she packed for the trip that was resting on her floor. She planned to write some sort of a note. It would be too cruel to say nothing. Her broom though was stuffed under her dresser—she thought it would be wise to switch positions especially since Adriana already knew that she had some sort of a secret box.

Running down the steps, Nikki nearly forgot about her breakfast. Like it mattered. Few things mattered now. Knowing who she was one of the few things that did. She ran faster than she ever had out of the door. Her school backpack was soon slung over her shoulders, while she searched for Kay in her speedy race to the school.

She wasn't the least bit surprised, not that she got too surprised at anything out of the ordinary anymore, to not see Kay anywhere as she neared the halfway point of her trip.

A face did appear like a thorn among roses though. Nikki came face to face with the very person she dreaded, yet strangely longed to run into. None other than Jasmine herself.

Without a doubt, Nikki would rather have one million Adrianas screaming and who knows what else at her than have one Jasmine to battle anything with. Jasmine *was* gorgeous. But what was the point if she had a venomous bite?

Now that Nikki knew that she was magic, and that Jasmine was also magic, the lines between them seemed to grow fatter a lot faster than they had ever. As though Jasmine had sensed Nikki's presence behind her, she swirled around, making her knee-high indigo skirt fan to the exact pattern of her coal-black hair.

"Oh. You. What are *you* doing here?"

"I appreciate your concern, Jasmine, but I always walk this way." Jasmine narrowed her eyes as she caught Nikki's dripping sarcasm.

"Don't snap your words at me, Chrystan... Or should I say Nicole? Jake may be fooled, but *you're* a fool if you ever think you can talk to me in that way."

"I didn't talk to you in any 'way.'"

"You'd better watch it, or do you want me to do the same thing I did to you yesterday?"

Fists clenched, intense purple and orange flames covered Nikki's whole hands. "Don't tempt me," she warned.

Jasmine laughed. "Oh I'm *so* scared. You really shouldn't give yourself away so easily. Now I know about you, but you haven't the faintest clue what my gift is. I guess that's the consequence for *you* being stupid—"

Nikki's eyes were blazed with the same blind vision she had had a few days before. Right into the cold pit of Jasmine's ice blue eyes, Nikki glared. Jasmine stared right back, with more assertion than Nikki could hold in her own eyes.

Staring into those eyes, Nikki knew what Jasmine's gift was, even before she could give it away. It was to bad she couldn't surprise Jasmine with her *own* medicine.

An interrupting chill crawled along Nikki's spine, making her lose more confidence that she had had. As her flames danced around her wrists, there was something else. Nikki struggled to keep claim of her fire. Like it was a battle to keep them going, and she wasn't winning.

Meanwhile, Jasmine had lost her attentiveness as well. Her eyes were no longer staring into Nikki's, but faintly off to the side.

Then, the unspeakable happened.

Jasmine's pupils dilated. Instead of the normal near turquoise color of her eyes, they turned darker at a rapid pace until they were so dark they were practically black.

Her mouth made a straight line and, since her eyes had turned so ebony, mixed with her emotionless face, she virtually looked demonic.

There was a flash of bright red light.

When Nikki looked again, Jasmine was now gone.

VI

For a moment, Nikki stood there, even lacking the ability to open her mouth and gape. Of all of the things that had happened to her so far in the past few days, at least they had been semi-rational. Except for this. For a moment, Nikki had thought she had done something to Jasmine. There was no way she would know how to do that though, even by accident. Her thoughts blurred for a moment, making her conscious to the fact that she felt faint. Instead she plunked herself down on the sidewalk.

She just sat there.

For a few moments.

All was still and silent. Even the destructive sounds of cars going by and anything moving, seemed to be on mute. In fact, there weren't any cars going by. No people. Nikki picked herself up, arms crossed tightly over each other.

Why does it feel like something's wrong? Like something worse or more weird than what just happened is about to happen? I can't let this...whatever just happened... stop me though. I have to get to school.

Her way to school was silent, yet she could feel it pulling her like a magnet. Nothing but a soft breeze made any movements. No humming came from houses she went by. Not a squeak came from trees that she had to come close to. Not a single living thing was near her the whole way. Until she passed by a car in the road and saw that the wheels looked almost suspended in air, she knew her guess had been a little more than right. Something was going on. Although part of her was glad the car's windows were up and very tinted, so she wouldn't have to see if there was an unmoving person in it. It would have freaked her out a little.

She sprinted towards the rest of the path that led her on her way. The school entrance was abnormally quiet as well. No one was outside, but Nikki wasn't too surprised at this. By this time, since she was so late, everyone should be in classes. Even then though, there should have been *some* noises coming from somewhere.

It nearly scared her to death when she heard a heart stopping clang sounding like barbed wire attacking a chalkboard.

Nikki was just about to run into the building, when Breannen literally flew out of the door. She rolled down the steps and landed about two feet away from where Nikki gawked, starring at her. "Don't just stare at me! We need you!" Breannen shouted, wrenching herself up.

Breannen loped back into the school, followed closely by Nikki.

"What's going—"

Nikki didn't have to ask the full question to find the answer. All around her, were almost a dozen men and women in eighteenth century-like clothes. They all wore black and had long flowing capes of the same color that closely followed their movements. James, Kay, and Breannen all had similar looking brown sticks raised that kept shooting out steady streams of light and colors. Occasionally, sparks of colors would also shoot out of their hands at someone as well. It was odd of her to think of it, but Kay's comment about wands suddenly hit her again. Her friends were using these "training wands." None of her friends were advanced enough to use magic yet without their wands. Somehow, this brought her a strange comfort.

Michelle was nowhere that Nikki could see, which confused her. In the other split second she had to think she remembered, *Michelle doesn't have her magic yet. If Breannen stopped time like I think she did, which would explain a lot, then she would be frozen in a way too, just like I was, sort of, a few days ago.*

Then, the real attraction came into view.

Right in the middle of it all, was the girl who had almost killed Nikki the other day and was attacking the boy who came a few days after her. She wielded a bright bulky sword.

Another clash filled the air, ringing in Nikki's ear.

Jake fought back with his own gold and ruby rapier.

By the looks of how they were fighting the woman must have been stronger.

Grinding his teeth, Jake was forced onto his knees, still pushing the force of his weapon against her.

"Shing!" their tools sang, as Jake managed to heave her off of him. "Is that your best Scarlet?" Jake called out viciously.

Scarlet swayed for a moment, they both took a second to breathe.

While Jake struggled up, she flung herself at him again and again, constantly banging aggressively against him until he fell to the floor once more.

"Come on," Kay hissed as she made another spell fly from her wand, "Don't stand there Nikki, help!"

Almost in despair, Nikki closed her eyes to concentrate. When she opened them, she felt her gift pump through her veins like a drug. She sent a tunnel of orange flames danced towards three of the black watchmen, knocking them to the ground.

Jake seemed to take a bit of a notice as they fell and turned towards the direction the flames had come from. Scarlet, the girl attacking him, took another split second to recover.

He almost smiled at Nikki's white and fearful expression, until the red headed woman threw her saber at him and slashed a large wound on his side. His hand flew towards it. Eyes slightly spinning, the ground met his head.

This time, it was James who looked up. Slightly shaking his head in disgust, he ran towards Jake and helped him up.

Scarlet wasn't giving anyone a chance to get healed.

Nikki darted after her cousin's fallen weapon, just as the red head swirled her own sword at Jake and James.

"CLISH!" rang the sparks as Nikki forced her weight into the golden sword that was protecting the three of them from a bloody death.

Heavier than she realized, the rapier grew laborious as she

strained her power against the woman. *To think that I would never have tried this a week ago.*

Scarlet must have thought it was getting too hard to keep up her constrain too, for she released the connection and backed up, to regain her footing.

"This is why you never tell anyone your real name if there are people who are looking to kill you." Jake's words were serious yet kidding while he got up, fully healed.

Nikki handed him his sword before he could even ask for it. Right after the girl attacked him again he called to Nikki, "Don't be so willing to not fight like this, I'll probably have to teach you what I know sooner or later."

She broke his connection this time and he stumbled back.

"You have horrible footing, Jacob," Scarlet laughed. "How do you expect to teach anyone?"

Jake ignored her and yelled at Nikki. "Go on, don't just stare at me. Help!"

James and Nikki took a quick glance at each other, then ran off in different directions.

As soon as he saw the tunnel of flames running across the room, Jake started again, swinging his saber wildly.

"She's not a very fast learner," Scarlet hissed at him.

"Faster than you were. How long did it take you to learn how to fight like this? Hundred years or so?"

Scarlet slid her sword at his arm, grazing it just so as Jake dodged.

"Bugger! See? You still can't kill me."

"Don't tempt me."

"Famous last lines."

"I don't like your cheekiness, boy."

Jake ran his fingers along the spiral lines of his sword handle.

"Foolish boy."

"*Pardon*? Now you're just being mean."

"Don't be daft, I'm pretty sure you deserve it."

Jake made a right uppercut to block her downward blow. "Get stuffed. What makes you so sure?"

"I'm sure you're worthy of it because you can't even think about scratching me up with your tooth-pick of a sword. You're strictly blocking."

"You sure 'bout that?" Jake heaved his weapon at her and ripped one of her heavy sashes that was wrapped along her shoulder.

"I knew you were too weak to hurt."

"So what if I don't hurt you? I can still *beat* you."

Meanwhile, Nikki and Kay were fighting side by side.

Kay sent a yellow light racing at a man.

"How do you know so many things already?" Nikki asked, sending a weaker fire channel towards a group of younger looking men and women.

"It's hard to explain while I'm fighting, remind me later."

"You're pretty confident that you're getting out of here alive," Nikki picked up, almost a bit smugly.

"Yup, saw this coming."

"How do you know that the future won't change?"

"Because you aren't willing for any of us to die." Kay said without looking, a small smile on her lips.

Nikki froze, looking at her with an odd expression.

"What do you mean?"

"Nothing."

It wasn't the time for conversations.

Nikki stared at Breannen, who was whipping her wand in a similar technique as Jake's sword. She took a swift look at James who was struggling. Nikki sent a twirling fire ball towards a person who was behind him, about to strike.

He noticed and turned to her.

"Thanks," he said only faint enough for her to hear.

A flash of memory from just a few minutes ago exploded in her mind. Of her holding back the dragon rider's sword with Jake's. Kay was right, she didn't want *anyone* to die. But wasn't it likely that someone would?

"Die" jabbed into her mind worse than any blade.

Had she realized before that she was going on an voyage where someone could actually die? She had never weighed that option before, yet it seemed very much a path that they might follow. Chills were sent all over her when she realized that she was putting everyone she cared for in jeopardy.

It didn't seem fair.

Her mind and body were petrified to the spot. She didn't even grasp that a woman had her wand right at her neck.

"That's right Beautiful, stay still while I blow your brains out."

"NO!" Jake shouted chucking his sword at the woman who was attacking Nikki.

The sword spun in the air towards her, acting as though pulled by a magical force and slashed the woman in the middle. Blood splattered as the woman fell to the ground, still alive.

The sword then swung back in one swift motion to Jake, acting like a boomerang. Nikki's mouth was agape.

"Pay attention Nikki! Don't get your bloody head blown off!" he bellowed at her.

He spun around back at Scarlet.

"Oh, I get it. You're only willing to hurt if someone else is on the line. I bet that makes you much more noble," Scarlet scoffed sarcastically.

Sparks flew again as he angrily flung himself at her.

"I do it because I've worked too hard to make sure she's safe to go and just let her be slaughtered by you."

"What *will* you do when I find a time when you can't help that feeble, powerless girl? She will die. Eventually."

"You keep. Your. Hands. Away. From. Us!" Jake roared, every word another reckless clang with the sword against her.

She paused for a moment, and Jake took the chance.

He cast himself toward her, giving her a nasty kick in the stomach, that sent her flying towards the lockers. She crumpled to the ground.

"You've hurt our family enough," Jake said, spitting blood out onto the floor.

Five watchmen were left.

They all saw Scarlet, briefly looked at one another, and took off towards the door, where Nikki could hear the disturbing sound of flapping leathery wings.

"Cowards," Jake muttered, wiping the remaining blood from his mouth. "Don't think you know this, but that was Scarlet, sister and slave of Colon. And I think you *do* know that she's the person who attacked you the other night." Jake kept his distance from her while he spoke.

Why does Jake seem so hesitantly towards me now? Is it because of the thought-sharing thing? I need to know more about that, test it more to see limitations, and ideas, maybe even to find out about that scale I found, if it's an early memory.

"You're a fool Jacob," someone whispered through clenched teeth. Jake swirled around to see Scarlet halfway up, touching the lockers. *"Goodbye,* Jacob, I'm sure I'll see you again." There was a flash of white light, and she was gone, along with the bodies of fallen soldiers.

Jake chewed on the end of his lip for a second, scowling at the spot Scarlet should have been. "Dang the fact that the necklace she wears protects her from dying."

VII

"What?" Breannen asked.

"She wears a necklace," Jake notified. He turned towards her, which made Breannen quickly blush and James glare in the other direction. "She and Colon have both worn one for the last century, which protects them from aging, dying, or even being wounded."

"What does the necklace look like?" Kay asked, while staring at Nikki.

Jake brought his glare, a little less fiercely, towards first Nikki then to Kay. "Why? Have you seen another one of those necklaces before?"

Kay responded calmly, "Well we couldn't tell, could we, if we didn't know what it looked like."

Jake again gave a questioning look towards Nikki.

She decided to take a chance. She closed her eyes just for a blink of an eye, then concentrated on Jake. Immediately, words came into her head that were not hers.

I swear, if I find out that somehow Scarlet found a way to get her one of those necklaces, I'm not sure if I'll strangle her, or thank her. A mental picture of a long silvery necklace with a green pendant popped into Nikki's mind. It bore a striking resemblance to Sophie's birthday gift. She could feel her mouth slightly come ajar.

"You *don't* have a necklace like that *do* you?" Jake asked.

"No." Nikki shut her mouth before any other lies could infect her. Why was it such a big deal to have a necklace that could save your life anyway?

"Well anyway, we have to get out of here now."

"Fine."

Nikki ran all of the way back to her house, not even stopping to think once. As soon as she got into her room, she tore off the birthday necklace that Sophie had given to her. "Sorry, but if Jake says you're bad, you're bad. He knows more than I do." She stuffed the chain down into the pocket of her backpack for her journey.

She took out instead, the scale.

"I need to find out more about *you* now."

She pushed it down into the pocket of her jeans. Then she took a look out of her window. Jake was running over to Sophie's. She tried to focus on his thoughts again.

Hope Sophie stayed home, Jake thought. *Really don't want to have to barge into another school.* She saw relief on his face when Sophie answered the door with her bag and a smile.

Nikki pulled herself out of Jake's head.

It was almost a suction cup reaction, that made her slightly dizzy. *Was that how Jake felt when I did it to him, or was it worse and different? I have to talk to him about this, and the scale, and the necklace. Right now though, he just seems to want to kill anyone who gets on his bad side—which, right now, is his only side. I better get out there before he comes in here.*

She looked around the room at the few things she didn't want or couldn't take with her. What personal possessions would await her in the future? She sat down and grabbed a piece of paper. She began to write a goodbye letter.

When she was finished, she raced down the stairs, two at a time.

"You got everything?" Jake asked, strangely more calm than the last time she heard him. Nikki walked out of the house with her backpack on her shoulder and her broom in her hand.

She shook her head yes.

"Good." Jake came up closer to her. "Also, I would appreciate it if you told me before you start going through things in my mind," he whispered in her ear.

Nikki looked straight ahead, blushing fervently.

He backed up a foot and said in a normal tone, "Maybe later we'll try to figure it all out, for now though, you should probably be worrying about where to find your wand. Then you can finally start learning some real magic. There's not a real decent tree for miles. Good luck."

He turned and walked away. Nikki watched him start tying unfamiliar objects to his broom.

"Well, what am I suppose to do?" Nikki asked, feeling deserted.

Jake looked up at Kay. He gave her a look.

Kay rolled her eyes, thumping his shoulder angrily as she passed him.

"Your cousin is a lazy bum, if you ask me."

Although Jake had heard what she said, Nikki bit her lip to stop her laughs. Jake seemed like the kind of person to get irritated by little things. It would make sense too, for Nikki was the same way.

Kay took Nikki's hand and dragged her to the backyard.

Behind a little shed, was a pile of burnt, forgotten wood. "Ever wonder how you could get a fifteen year old as a tour guide to England?"

Nikki smiled. "He really isn't that bad. Just has a hard outside is all. Why don't you trust him?"

"Probably because I haven't seen him at all. In the past, right now, or in the future. It's different for you to like him, you two are really similar."

"Whatever." Nikki took it almost offensively. "Anyway, we needed to see a giant pile of wood because?"

"It will be your wand."

"Okay then." Nikki had the urge to laugh.

"Because you have the ability of fire, your natural wand should start out as a piece of charred wood."

"What then, am I supposed to carve it or something?"

"Sometimes, and usually, people would, but considering we don't have a lot of time, and you have a different element gift, it will be easier to do it the other way."

"Which way is that?"

Kay glared at the black wood pile.

"Stick your hand anywhere in the pile. Somewhere inside of you, you should have the instinct to grab the right one. It should almost feel like a magnetic pull. The first pull you feel, drag your hand out, and the first stage of your wand should come out with you."

For a brief instant, Nikki stared at Kay slightly overwhelmed and terrified at the same time. *If this is the kind of things I have to remember to be great at magic, I might as well go back inside Ted's house and crawl under my covers.*

She shook off that feeling. *I have to prove Jake wrong. I can survive an adventure. I won't be afraid to step up to the challenge... maybe.*

Nikki stepped towards the wood pile and stuck her hand deep in the crusty ashes. Just as Kay had described, there was suddenly a pull. But it wasn't like a magnet one. While Nikki refused to let go of the smooth stick in her hand, her palm burned.

She refused to let it loose, forcing the stick out with her hand.

Getting down on her hands and knees, she brushed away the tiny fingers of other brambles and finally, hers was free.

Nikki caught the hint that Kay had no idea what happened. Only that it wasn't supposed to.

Nikki's hand had a thick layer of ash crust as she twiddled the stick between her fingers. "Go on, burn it," Kay ordered, only starring at the branch.

"Won't that just make it more black and charred?"

Kay rolled her eyes. "Gifts are magic, especially element ones. Your fire isn't just common lamplight."

Nikki shrugged, pretending she already knew that, but badly disguising it.

"Don't be afraid, Nikki, just do it."

"Afraid." The word offended Nikki. She wasn't afraid. Just a little nervous and intimidated. Why did everything that was magic have to be so mysterious? Why couldn't someone just say, "Here, I'll make the magic wand shop appear," and all they had to do was go inside and get one?

No. Everything had to be a million different orders all at once, to make your head spin, and dizzy. But no one who was used to it would understand.

Angry, Nikki clenched her teeth tightly and made purple flames shoot from her whole hand, engulfing the whole stick in one flame. The purple streamers were sent high above her wrist, almost two feet above them.

That's when Nikki fully understood the different colors of her gift. *When I was just playing, or putting out flames because I wanted to, they were red. When I was getting a little mad, they turned orange, when extremely mad, they turn purple, and when I totally just lose it, like with Scarlet, purple and orange. How strange that they would act according to my anger.*

She watched the purple die into a dull orange, finally into a maroon color, while the height decreased as well. Awestruck, Nikki realized that the charring stick was doing the exact opposite of what it should when fire was on it. Instead of singeing more, the twig did a slight dog-like shake and revealed a brown tinged gold wand.

"There," Kay said satisfied in a matter-of-factly tone. "That should be able to produce magic at your will and no one else's."

"Wait." Nikki just recalled something. "If you have to use your gift to find a wand, and Jake is the only one without a gift, how did he get a wand? Or doesn't he have one?"

"Magic people can do **enchantment**s without wands remember. The more years you have magic, the less you use your wand. Perhaps he just doesn't have one, or found another means of getting his wand that no one ever thought of before because they didn't need to. I don't know everything. You should ask him."

Nikki stared at the ground. "For some reason, he just acts strange around me, even after I found out who he was."

Nikki started to walk back up to the driveway when Kay caught her hand. Her eyes were wide, exposing her pale eyes. She wasn't looking at Nikki, instead, she stared at nothing. "Seeing something." Kay's voice was like a dead breeze. Her lips barely moved, but for some reason, Nikki could hear the raspy voice.

Almost as quick as it had happened, Kay looked at Nikki, calm and normal, dropping her hand. Nikki's face was alarmed.

"Not future predicting, knowing. It usually happens when someone asks me a question or brings up a topic that makes me start to think about it. I know why Jake is acting so strange."

"What is it then?"

"Part of the reason is a prince named Colon... He had a dad. Will Colon. It seems like everyone was attacking your family... Colon's dad was worse than he is. He knew something about Jake that no one else knew... Power or something. He decided to go after him, tried to kill him. But then something went wrong. I don't know how or when but Will Colon died. Now Colon is after revenge, even by means of killing you. People thought that the reason Jake doesn't have a gift is because he doesn't want to use it, they think it is some sort of a killing gift. Colon's dad was a very powerfully evil wizard. He might have been seeking Jake to try and figure out if his gift was what was rumored. Who knows what he would have done if he had made it to Jake…"

Although taken aback by the reasonable and quite scary explanation, Nikki had one question left. "But why would he be thinking about this now? He's just taking me home isn't he?"

Kay shrugged. "Don't ask me. It comes and it goes, my gift. Strangest one I've ever heard of."

"Great. Well, Jake is going to come hunting us down if we take too long, not that we're far or anything, so we better just go back up to where everyone else is."

Kay shook her head in agreement, at the ground.

Nikki ignored her, stubbornly walking up the grassy path towards Breannen.

"This is so exciting!" she declared, punching Nikki lightly on the shoulder. "I couldn't wait to get out of my dump of a home anyway. No one else in my family is magic. How weird do you think I was when I first started to freeze time? It's great though. You'll get used to the fact that everything seems to be going ten times faster than usual; it's just the life of a magic."

Nikki forced a smile.

VIII

The more she thought about the whole thing, the more it felt wrong. Something was going to happen and it wasn't going to be good. It also seemed like Jake was acting less like a cousin and more like a body guard. He was still keeping something from her. Why, was the question that was beyond her explanation.

Don't worry about it, Nikki surprised that she sounded like Breannen. *Don't let some stupid idiot prince rain on your parade. You're finding out who you are. Everything that you were. Isn't that enough to be happy?*

Jake saw her coming, giving her a warm smile.

He seems to have cooled down a lot.

Out of the blue, literally in this case, a small pigeon-like creature hovered in the air. It had come out of nowhere. A package, a bright cherry color in the shiny paper that everyone else seemed to have, was clutched tightly in the tiny bird's green claws. The strange purple bird seemed at least ten times smaller than the box. It was flying straight towards Nikki.

Jake blew out a great breath, as if he had been holding it forever. "Oh Garden, please tell me... The danger he puts us in," he muttered to himself.

Garden? Nikki wondered, wanting to send it towards Jake. She didn't want to have him faint or get hurt or anything though, especially in front of everyone before they left. She kept her thoughts hidden to everyone but Sophie, who couldn't help hearing them. Or could she? *You really have to learn more about your friends. Learn their limitations and things. You probably might want to learn your own limitations first though.*

Is Garden some sort of a magic term I haven't heard of? That would be weird.

Sophie nudged her and shrugged. Nikki swear that she almost

heard Sophie start to snicker though. Or someone. She decided to puck up the courage to ask.

"What's Garden?"

Jake bit his tongue to not offend her by laughing. "Not what: who. He's the person who helped you get away from England alive. Also, that's his bird."

"Oh." Nikki flushed. When even Jake was laughing at you, you knew that you should just shut your mouth.

"'S all right. You didn't know, don't beat yourself up over it. Although you might want to grab the package from her beak before she drops it on your head."

Nikki reached out to take hold of the bird's box. The bird let it fall into her fingers.

"Why would it be bad if he sent this to us?" Michelle asked, eyeing her broom nervously. It would probably be terrifying for her to even think about riding something that she barely believed in. After all of this though, and nearly fainting after they explained it all, how could she not believe it?

"Because. He's a spy for Colon, actually a spy for our side. It's not only dangerous because people could get after us, but also for him. He could lose his neck."

Michelle didn't need to ask Jake who Colon was. With this explanation, she figured it was best not to learn more.

The pigeon didn't fly away. It hovered over Nikki for a moment, flew past Sophie, and landed on Jake's shoulder. It obviously wasn't a stranger to him. "Fine then." He pulled out a slender piece of something green and handed it up to the bird's beak. When the pigeon decided to fly off again, he grumbled something that Nikki caught as, "Moocher."

"Um, why did you have that in your jeans?" Breannen asked, slightly giggling. James looked away grinding his teeth.

"Er..." Jake seemed to be deciding of something. "Later. Right now, we should just hurry this up."

"Right. I probably should put this away then?" Nikki wondered out loud referring to the gift.

"Yes. Later, like I said. Before some other watchmen come looking for us."

Jake pulled his head to the sky, as if dark cloaked men and women were going to start falling from the sky along with Scarlet's red haired head. It sent chills up Nikki's spine, which reminded her of something she had been itching to tell someone all day.

"Jasmine disappeared today. Before I was at school. She just was there and then she wasn't. Should we do something? Even if Colon's got her, being the evil witch she is, she doesn't deserve to die."

"If Colon had gotten you, she would have been happy enough to thank him and pay him to kill you," James whispered, afraid of his own words.

Kay shook her head in agreement. "James is right. We have no idea where she is. Even he does have her, there's nothing we can do that won't get us killed in the process."

Nikki bit her lip.

"Don't be afraid. Nothing will happen to her. Haven't you read the stories? The villains don't die until the heroes are about to," Jake nastily kid.

"That's not funny," Nikki snapped. "And I'm *not* afraid. She probably earned what's coming to her anyway. She almost killed me when I saw her. I could see it in her eyes."

"Great. Maybe we should just start going, before we have another conversation that takes time away from our daylight. We have to hurry, or we'll never make it by nightfall. We can talk on the way, or even when we get there. I have a foul feeling that Garden's bird was being followed."

They stared ahead at Sophie's house, not exactly knowing what to do about Jake's suggestions. "We've got nothing to lose, but all to gain," Sophie stated. "My mom and dad and brother might never see me again. But somehow I know they will."

Nikki felt a lump in her throat. Will there be a time when she might miss this house, Ted, and maybe even evil Adriana? She knew that someday it would hit her.

James came up behind her and patted her on the shoulder.

"Come on Nikki. It's fine. Nothing will happen to us. Everyone will be with their families in the end. There's no use feeling like you have committed some kind of a crime for bringing us with you. We want to help you; we're your friends."

James's words were soothing. Nikki smiled weakly. She felt determined. Determined to not let anything happen to anybody. That's when they knew it was time to leave.

A light filled their eyes, and all of them turned towards the driveway. Ted was driving up with Adriana.

"We have to go! Now, everyone!" Jake's voice rang loud and clear as the engine growled at the sight of them.

Uncertainty surrounded them, especially Michelle.

As they pushed off the ground, rising into the blue, cloudy air, the last thing Nikki saw of her old life was Ted's pale, shocked face and Adriana's mouth wide open at her.

They had been traveling for several minutes. The air was sweet and calm. Nikki's spirits were light and clear when Kay veered downward abruptly. Nikki's lungs suddenly tightened as she swerved back to see what was in front of her.

They were surrounded by heavy black cloaked watchmen on brooms.

Chapter Eight

Home

I

Nikki took a sharp intake.

Nowhere to go.

They were surrounded completely by black-covered watchmen. Right in front of the line sat a broom riding Scarlet, a "kill" expression glinted in her eyes.

"You're not getting anywhere this time boy. Nor will your dear girly. Don't think you can get rid of me that easily."

Jake glared intently at her. "Don't make me," he hissed through his clenched teeth.

"Do what? Cry home to your dead mum and dad? Good luck with that, Jacob."

"Go you guys. I'll catch up." Jake ground his teeth.

"Take them alone? Are you crazy? We're in this together!" Nikki was infuriated. There was no way Jake would survive attacking all of the guards and Scarlet, by himself.

"It's my duty to keep you safe! Go. *Now*."

She didn't understand what he was saying. His duty? They were *family*. She was the only one he had, it seemed like. She sat on her broom, not moving. Jake shot her a look that could kill. She pursed her lip.

Go—it'll be my fault if you die trying to get safely away. Go now, and I'll make it, I swear. Jake's voice rang in her head, even though he knew it would most likely hurt him.

Don't swear. Act. Nikki flew away like a bullet then wanting to rip her emotions out for being so weak, her friends carefully making their way behind her.

Scarlet snickered. "Brilliant idea, Jacob. Let's kill you so I can kill her easier. Then each of her friends will be next. I applaud you for your ingenuity."

Out of a leather scabbard at his side, Jake pulled out his golden handled sword, at the same time Scarlet pulled out hers.

In no time, the sparks were in the timing of the clish and clashes of the metal.

Standing up on his broom, Jake swung the saber around, as if his whole life had been dedicated to the art. His broom followed his movements like a loyal platform.

Scarlet mischievously egged him on, literally begging him towards the death she thought he deserved.

"This will show you not to murder a family member of royalty!"

She thrust her arm forward, slashing a deep gash in his arm.

Jake bit his lip. He refused to give scarlet the satisfaction of hearing him yell. "Still going on 'bout that are we? You have some priorities to work out." Jake joked, even though his arm was starting to burn.

"Look at you. All by yourself. You'll never make it out alive."

Jake pulled out his wand, sending a green light towards a hefty man who was closing in on him.

"I don't have to; I just have to make sure Nikki does."

"Doesn't it feel bad to know no one loves you?" Scarlet jeered, while his expression turned to that of shock.

"My life wasn't meant for love," Jake finally spat out. "It's so much more fun ripping people apart."

"Oh Jacob, you and I both know that you die at the sight of someone getting injured. I wonder how much it would take for you to get your girly to wear one of the necklaces."

"Would take everything I have and then some. Nothing is worth what it causes. Even death," Jake growled.

"What would it take to kill you right now? You're so weakened already, it's almost pitiful to watch. Poor Jacob. Failed your obligation. What would your parents say?"

"You shut it 'bout my parents. This is between *you* and *me*." He sent a blue stream towards a black-eyed women. She fell off of her broom.

He flinched and turned away as she hit the ground.

"Ha! What will Colon say when I bring him your lifeless body?"

"Nothing because it isn't going to happen."

"Mm hmm."

Suddenly, in a tight connection, he lost the gripping on his sword.

The rapier took a nosedive for Jake's face, until Scarlet caught it.

Both swords were pointed at his chest.

Jake whipped out his wand.

"It still is a mystery how you managed to get one of those."

"Some things are never solved, just put aside to ponder on later."

"What a fool you are Jacob."

"Somehow, I never understand why the people who call me a fool, are the fools themselves."

She jabbed the swords closer to his neck.

The other watchmen on the brooms grew closer, making a tight circle.

"I hope you know that I still have a wand." Jake spun it in his fingers to prove it.

"Not anymore," one of the guards hissed. He shot out a white blazing light. It shot Jake's hand, his wand flying out of it. A guardsman below him caught it with a grin.

Brilliant Jake, Jake thought.

Scarlet forced Jake to nearly lay down while still on his broom. He stretched out his hands—his last defense for magic. With a wave of Scarlet's thin fingers, his hands were bound with a thorn vine behind his back.

He inwardly cursed. "I'm not afraid of you, you know." Jake said. His heart was pounding, yet he still managed to talk confidently.

"No, but you're afraid of death. You don't have the spine to finish me off."

"Honestly, I don't." Jake's eyes widened for a moment, then he relaxed his expression.

Don't be stupid, he thought, but not necessarily to himself.

I don't have to be stupid to be able to help you, came a voice back to him.

"I may not have what it takes to crush you Scarlet. But she just might."

Scarlet turned around just in time to see Nikki rocketing by on her broom. She was alone.

Jake took the advantage.

He swung his leg around and socked Scarlet square in the jaw.

She lost her balance and nearly tumbled off of her own broom. Her hands caught the wood enough to get stable again.

"I'm shaking," Scarlet mocked. She wiped her cheek where Jake's boot had left a gash.

"You should be." Nikki tried to make her voice braver than she felt, succeeding in sounding as powerful as Jake had before. She felt her broom rock, but she was ready to copy Jake's moves. Nikki stood up high and tall on the rock solid surface of the broom. "I think I still owe you something from the first time we met."

Her palm itched to be used for the purpose her mind was begging. She gave into the will.

Great purple flames flew from her hands, scorching every inch of the soldiers around Jake and Scarlet.

Jake ducked his head down into his chest as best as he could manage. Massive waves of heat and ashes were flying from the molten power. Despite his **enchantment** of protection that he channeled through his wand-less power, he managed to get badly blistered hands. Nikki was more powerful than he had originally thought. Maybe this wouldn't be as difficult as he had anticipated. Scarlet stood up as well, unafraid and glaring at Nikki.

"Do you think we're playing a game, child?" Scarlet hollered above the flowing blaze, obviously not hurt.

"Blimey, sometimes I think she does," Jake muttered with a small curt smile. The vines had burned off, but he kept his hands back behind him.

Annoyed at his amusement, Scarlet sliced a cut on his shoulder.

The man who had stolen Jake's wand flew off in the other direction, the wand slipping from his grasp as he fled. Nikki caught it. By the time Nikki's anger had reached a point where she was tired of burning black clothes, she sat back down on the broom and soared back towards Jake.

"This isn't a game. Not anymore," Nikki commented, giving a glare to Scarlet.

"That's too bad, I was looking forward to beating you."

Not losing her hard stare at the red headed dragon rider, Nikki threw the retrieved wand at Jake, who snatched it midair, as she asked Scarlet, "How old are you? About one hundred or so because of that necklace?"

Although Jake was pleased she had come, he was at a loss to why Nikki was making conversation.

"What is it to you then if I am?" Scarlet demanded, her hair seeming to steam.

"Well it's just that we're thirteen and fifteen. You'd think that you'd be able to kill us by now."

Scarlet returned the two sabers to Jake's neck.

Nikki took a step back on her broom.

"Nowhere to go now, girly. Like I said before, a girl with a few more ideas would have been so much more useful for your side."

"She's not out of ideas yet," Jake insisted, reading Nikki's thoughts before she herself could process them.

Nikki looked at him with a desperately blank expression.

Scarlet smirked.

"While you two try to figure out whatever your *inspiring* plan is, allow me to finish off my job." Jake and her own sword drew closer to Jake, clipping a part of his neck. Blood trickled down his shirt. Jake didn't want to move, in fear that if he shot Scarlet with an **enchantment**, the swords would plunge into his throat.

Nikki flared up, shooting a wide purple fire ball at Scarlet's body.

The flame stopped close to an inch from Scarlet. The fire ball froze there, its tail wagging fervently, until finally it grew smaller and went out.

Scarlet rolled her eyes. She drew of the swords from Jake and pointed it and towards the gaping Nikki.

"Wasn't that just a *nifty* experiment? Again, I wonder if your childishness will come back and haunt you some day. This is no longer play time girly. You both are going to die. Slowly and mercilessly"

"You mean like your watchmen got charred?" Jake asked with a impish grin. All around them was no one. The charred guards had all fallen to the ground or fled.

Jake took a snappy look at Scarlet's broom, throwing the glance back to Nikki. *Get the message?* he whispered in her thoughts.

Nikki could already see that a conversation without Scarlet knowing that there was communication between the two of them, wasn't going to last very long. She was already giving them suspicious looks, one sword pointed at each of them.

I don't know how! Nikki whispered in her thoughts.

Jake took a deep breath looking, straight at Scarlet's hair. In the split second he knew they had left, he rushed thoughts of information into her mind. *You don't have to. You have to want it. Wands aren't needed to process magic, it's just a tool to help us. You already know how. You just have to do it. There's no magic words for the most powerful of spells. Words just sometimes help…*

Jake was slipping into unconsciousness fast.

Scarlet was beginning to catch on. "What are you playing at?" she ordered, pointing both the weapons at Nikki.

Nikki looked her straight in the eye.

I know I want it. Nikki outstretched her hand quickly.

A white shadowy vapor shot from her hand and hit Scarlet's broom.

"Stupid girl. You do magic, and you miss me!"

But it was Nikki who was smiling next.

Scarlet's broom began to drop, and drop rapidly. Her feet were glued to the wood, and as she struggled she gave a frustrated glare at Jake. The broom did a few wild turns as the broom became its own master. She did a few airborne summersaults, opening her mouth to say silent words. as if she was calling out to something beyond what they could see.

The rapier caught Nikki's attention. Just like before, but with her eyes being closed, she concentrated. Jake's sword spun madly in Scarlet's hand.

She almost refused to let it go, but the saber took a sharp pull and freed itself from her grip, and flew into Nikki's.

Nikki watched as Scarlet's broom refused to hold her anymore. It slipped from under her feet, and she just grasped it by her fingers.

A dark shape came flying under the red head. Followed closely by a trail of thick black smoke, Scarlet's dark dragon appeared and picked their enemy from the air like a fresh apple.

As soon as Scarlet was on the back of her beast, she thrust her head back towards Nikki and the half awake Jake. She was about to attack them when her pupils dilated and turned blacker than they were.

I'm in for it, she thought to herself.

She kicked her dragon, and turned in the other direction.

Scarlet screeched in despair, over the roaring of the monster she rode on.

She was gone in a black cloud.

II

The world was foggy and gray to Jake, as his head gave a sharp ache. He sat up on his broom only to see Nikki staring at him with a bored expression. "You were stupid for coming back," he whispered hoarsely.

"Your welcome." Nikki rolled her eyes at his I-want-to-do-this-alone comment. "We were only stupid for leaving you. Obviously you have a bigger ego than brain. You really thought you could take them all by yourself?"

Jake threw her a glare even though it gave his head pins and needles. "I would have found a way out of that. I still owe you one anyway, if that's what you're going after."

"Are you kidding me? Scarlet would have beheaded you if I hadn't shown up! I saved your life and you're not even grateful!"

"Fine! Thank you. You happy?"

Nikki just turned away and rode off.

"You know," Jake started, catching up with her. He wiped a drip of blood from his forehead as Nikki looked squeamishly at him. There was nothing he could do for now about his bloody shirt. James would probably refuse to heal him anyway, "you don't know the way to England. You'll probably end up in Asia or something. That's not very helpful."

"Aren't you still going to show us the way Mr. I-know-everything?" She was steaming.

"Okay listen. I'm sorry I've overreacted. Thank you. I'm just not used to people saving *me*."

Nikki seemed to ignore him, but as they approached the rest of them, her infuriation seemed to drain. James was looking at Jake's burnt hands with a look of justice. Breannen caught it and smacked James in the arm.

Fighting back a smile, Nikki resumed her post beside Michelle and Sophie. Sophie began whispering something excitedly to her. Jake sighed and brought himself to the front.

"I'm guessing that Scarlet had a reason for her retreat. Still, keep your eyes open. She's notorious for not following directions." Jake started flying in the lead.

The journey began slow, and raw cheeks and fingers brought discomfort to the group. All except Jake who had somehow during the hours, placed thin leather gloves over his skinned hands.

They were all quiet, which was a fine idea to Nikki. She kept her thoughts to herself, rather enjoying the idea that she was free. Once in a while, a whimpering groan would escape Michelle's mouth, just loud enough for Nikki to hear. She would try to turn towards her, but it just kept making Michelle nervous. Apparently, Michelle believed that she was going to fall off.

It wouldn't have been a problem for a while.

The ground was soft looking miles below with green grass that swayed comfortably. Long fields of dirt where corn and wheat shot up from the earth and stretched in areas as well, as they left their home state.

The terrain below became dull and dreary; they were all lucky that it didn't start raining. Until they started to pass cities, they were relatively close to the ground. "Go higher up," Jake commanded. He guided them straight up, nearly hitting one of the tall buildings.

An unsolved thought bubbled in Nikki's mind. She decided to ask Jake, even if it made him weary. It would probably serve him right. *Where's Arola?*

Jake almost laughed.

She's a fast runner. Far below, she follows our trail, unseen.

Jake remained silent after that.

I wonder if it gets easier and easier for him to talk and hear me?

Nikki wished she could experiment more without feeling the guilt of hurting the person whom she probably owed her life for traveling with her.

They passed an aging lake in Connecticut. Nikki could spot the harbors, as tired sail boats drifted in the Atlantic's waves. Her heart skipped a beat. They had been traveling much faster than she had thought; she had never been this far away from her home town either.

I set up an **enchantment** *to travel faster. Don't worry about it,* Jake answered her. She hadn't realized he was listening. She chose not to respond back.

Nikki had never seen the white sand of the rocky beach, the shells that were bigger than her fist, or the vast ocean waves splashing the air.

The lake was deserted.

They had all begun to hover their brooms over the icy looking waters. Scraping sounds of fingernails tightening over a broom filled the air as Michelle shook in fear. Everything was amplified in the quiet of the evening. Nikki wished she could ease Michelle's watery terrors, but her own fears, that she thought she had tossed behind her, were beginning to crawl back.

"Go down a bit. There's a shortcut."

Shortcut? Nikki wondered to herself. *Go lower? The wind will get the water all over us. Bet you'd enjoy that.*

Everyone else seemed as edgy as Nikki felt. Kay cast a petrified look at Breannen, who refused to look all the way terrified. "Can't be worse than a watchman," Kay whispered, voice hoarse from the fierce salty air.

Breannen shook her head in agreement, following Jake in a downward plummet. Nikki followed her. *At this point, it can't be worse than anything.* The rest of the group, a little less eager, began to follow. There wasn't much of a choice.

The blue waves shook in the winds. They towered over the crowd, even though they were at least ten feet from sea level, the waves sprayed a heavy mist at their faces. Soon all of them were drenched.

"What are we doing?" Nikki shouted at Jake, dodging a deep surf just to get soddened by another.

Jake looked back at her, laughing at Nikki's dripping hair that dangled feebly in her eyes. "Just trust me, I know where I'm going."

"You better."

Sophie rolled her eyes at Jake's unheard thoughts.

"You know, he can be real immature for being the supposed leader," Sophie said, trying to keep herself from getting as wet as Nikki had.

"I just hope some huge wave swallows *him* up this time," Nikki darkly muttered.

Jake seemed to be able to dodge everything the ocean threw at him. He kept his eyes glued to the waters below him as if searching for something in the chilling depths.

"What are you looking at?" Breannen called out when Jake froze.

Nikki zoomed up to the spot.

It was a spot stretching for about four yards, and at least three shades darker than every other drip of the ocean. "What is it?" James asked aloud.

"You have to trust me on this. It will seem like you're about to kill yourself, but it might be the only way that they don't know about."

Nikki found herself dazed at his words, not understanding them one bit. When Jake began backing up higher into the air though, at a slant towards the waters, she slowly began piecing his words together.

"Are you *crazy*?" she screamed.

The others looked at him with the same expression.

"Trust me," he yelled.

Then Jake plunged into the blue surface of the ocean.

III

"He's crazy!" Michelle squeaked.

"Are we really...?" Sophie began.

"I am. If he did it, then it's safe...although he did almost get unconscious before we got here. His brain might be a little messed up..." Nikki pulled her broom into the darkening sky. The sun made red, toddler-like finger paint streaks across the horizon.

"Are you sure about this?" James asked eyeing Nikki when she pointed her wooden handle towards the darkness.

"No!" she cried as she flew straight into the water.

The shock was unbelievably painful when her raw face met the blue Atlantic. She closed her eyes, afraid more than ever of death. She felt herself spinning and finally a warm breeze on her.

Nikki flicked open her eyes.

"I told you to trust me."

She was exactly as wet as she had been before she had plunged into the depths of the ocean. Jake was the same way several feet in front of her. She let out a breath she hadn't realized she'd been holding. Jake smiled.

They turned as a voice came from behind them.

"I really wasn't expecting diving into the ocean to be on the list of things I was going to do today. Flying, yes. Swimming, no," came Breannen, fresh from across the globe.

It took a while but eventually all of them were out of the water portal, nearly terrified to death at first. Michelle was oddly the least afraid one, explaining she had done worse than think she was going to drown.

Nikki still shuddered at the thought that she might have to do that again. She felt her gift almost seem to drain from her in there, and it was an alarming sensation. She felt cold and wet, slimy even, although she knew her clothes were now almost dry. Europe's winds drew heated currents on her face.

"Nikki," Jake called.

She looked up from her thoughts. Kay pulled a bit of seaweed from Nikki's hair.

"It's just a little further."

They rode for a minute before land came clearly into view.

A house, *her* house, lay comfortably on a cozy bank, sleeping on the grassy ocean's side. "Oh." Her speech fell away. The house was slanted in the tiniest bit to the right, while its three large, white-balcony-filled castle peaks poked from the fortress house. Although olden looking, the bleach white bricks held strong in a way that, without a doubt, looked magical.

Surrounding the house, was a misty looking stretch of trees. They seemed to never end. Instead they twisted around the back of the house as if they were protecting it from the now calm waves of the ocean.

The word home stung in her head. It felt strange there, as if it had been missing for a long time and finally sang its song. It hurt to think of this as her home, but for some strange reason, the word in this situation felt far from not feeling right.

She was home.

Home in England.

IV

It took a while to pry Nikki's mind away from just gaping at the house. It felt like a dream. So much that if she decided to get any closer, the dream would slip like sand through her fingers. By the time Jake had convinced her to come over to the shore that the side of the waters licked, and to get off her broom, she realized how numb and sore her body was. Her friends patiently waited, while taking their own turns, in admiring the house from several yards away and its expansiveness. There was a walkway that was made entirely of shells, that led off the beach.

Her mind was worse than applesauce mush. She couldn't think straight. Nikki knew she had to mentally prepare herself. Reality was hitting her hard.

"You can just sit for awhile. I know how it feels to be on that broom for a great deal of time," Jake explained, taking a seat himself. She saw that one of his deeper injuries was still brightly red.

She got up from the grass. "No. You have to do something about your wounds." James looked shamefully away as she gave him a heavy stare. Jake looked flustered, still awkward about having someone worried about him.

"Fine then. Your mum has troubled herself about you enough I think," Jake muttered, holding his arm as droplets of blood began to stain his shirt more.

He got up too, closely followed by Sophie and Michelle, who were worn out as well. The rest of them were already standing.

Jake led the way up the stone path to the front door. *The grass is so perfect. Magic no doubt,* Nikki thought. She glimpsed Sophie smiling at her. Her heart was thudding, and her skin tingled with excitement.

Jake passed a look back to Sophie, while she quickly read his thoughts. *Oh,* her mouth said silently. Kay's eyes widened and she moved backwards towards the edge of the water. Breannen and James were still talking at the water's edge while Michelle watched them as if she were interested in what they were saying.

Jake took a nervous look at Nikki, then chose to follow the rest of the seashell path. He and Nikki walked the way up to the house.

Jake knocked quietly on the wooden door.

Instantly, it was opened by a frail, pretty women. She had the same shade of hair as Nikki's, but small strands of silvery gray peppered her head lightly. The locks flourished past her waist. As soon as she saw Nikki, her bright green eyes glistened. Although she tried hard not to think it and even harder for Jake not to hear it, Nikki couldn't help but stop and wonder how it was a bit strange that the woman had seemed to be waiting for the door to knock.

How long she had been waiting.

Nikki flushed extremely red when Jake cocked his head while looking at her strange as if he had heard her.

Ruby then grabbed Nikki in a tight hug, while whispering in her ear, "I thought I'd never see you again," choking on the tears she was fighting back.

It's going to take some time to get used to, Nikki sent towards Jake. She numbly took the hug in, warmly hugging back.

He gave her an encouraging half smile. He could agree with that. Nikki brought something certainly new to his life.

When Ruby had sufficiently given the hug she thought her daughter deserved, she released herself and smiled at Jake, almost in an odd, lopsided way. "So nice of you to come home, Tomas dear."

As Ruby said this, Jake's face burned redder than Nikki thought a boy of his dignity could. He still kept a straight emotionless face though.

"No, Ms. Colon. My name's Jacob remember?"

Nikki had never heard Jake call himself Jacob before, thinking he preferred his nickname. *And why is he talking to Ruby like she's a five year old?* Nikki saw Ruby put on a face that looked not only half confused, but half angry.

Nikki shot Jake a look.

He ignored her, sighing.

At that moment, as if he knew something was coming, a head popped out from the opened part of the door. A girl probably a few years younger than Nikki brushed her long, thin silvery blond hair behind her ears. She was unnaturally skinny, but just by a touch.

The girl made contact with Nikki's eyes for little less than a minute, then ran off somewhere else. Her eyes were paler than any substance Nikki had ever seen; they seemed almost like liquid.

Now Nikki's mind almost bled with questions. Knowing she would feel terrible if she made Jake faint again, she kept them all swimming inside her head with nowhere to go.

Ruby quickly drew them inside.

Nikki sent a pathetic glance at her friends, who just shooed her in without worry. Jake and Nikki swayed in a silence once they had gotten inside, too long for it to still be a comfortable silence. Ruby smiled warmly at Nikki, then took her hand and began to guide her up a particularly long staircase.

"This is your room. I hope you like it. Prepared it just for you." Ruby showed Nikki the bright blue painted door of her room. "Suppose I ought to show your friends their rooms too, eh?" Ruby gave a quick smile to Nikki then hurried down the stairs.

"Here, I'll help you," came a voice a few feet away. Thinking the voice was talking to her, Nikki spun around.

The young girl Nikki saw earlier, had come up to Jake, stood up on her tiptoes, and began whispering something in his ear. He laughed, then looked up at Nikki, who rose one eyebrow.

"Come on, I know where she keeps them," the girl said. Jake followed her down the never-ending hallway and into a door off to the left.

Standing in the doorway, Nikki watched the girl come out a few minutes later. Without Jake.

She refused to look at the strange girl and instead opened the brass doorknob to her room. Her brow furrowed, as she wondered more and more about the world she was entering. Right now, nothing made sense, and Jake was too busy doing something to make any of it logical for her.

As she looked around the room though, her thoughts drained out faster than she thought possible.

The soft sheets and pillows of the fluffy-looking bed were the first thing that caught her eyes. They shone as blue as the door, if not brighter. The carpet her high tops twisted in was a bright maroon that seemed to sway like the grass of Africa. The lightning bolts and clouds that were literally swimming around the blue curtains of another door, led out to the balcony from which the ocean could be heard.

There were several more doors in the room. Nikki presumed that one of them was at least a closet. All of the doors were wood and red. She opened the closest one to the entrance, the closet. It had so much room that she knew there was no possible way to fill it. She wanted to walk into it, just to feel its opulence fill her, but she decided against it. She opened another door instead which was an intricately designed and decorated bathroom.

The rest of the doors she found were full of shelves. *What kind of a person would need this much room for all of the things she has?* The answer came from nowhere and it came immediately. *A magic one of course.*

There were also things besides the doors and the bed that caught her attention. A desk with many shelves for books and pens. A quill and ink sat on the top of that. Then there was a towering bookshelf filled with books she'd never heard of. Many of them were fat and looked as though they were excited someone had come to read them.

"This is the most amazing thing I've ever seen."

"Glad you're enjoying it." Jake stood in the doorway.

Nikki jumped at the sight of him. She barely recognized him.

Magic must have been used somewhere in the process between when he left and now. His hair was clean, wet and slicked back. His used-to-be-bloody parts of skin were unbroken and his natural pale glowed now. His old dirty clothes were replaced by a halfway tucked in white button-down shirt, a dark tank, and thick knee-high boots covering his brown pants. While Nikki's skin still had a thick layer of ocean and dirt, Jake was spotless, making her a feel a little less than comfortable.

She was pretty sure that if Breannen saw him, she would have fainted.

Nikki glared at him. "Ever heard of knocking?"

His face turned emotionless.

"But you *have* heard of ignoring, haven't you." It wasn't a question. "Where are the others?"

"In their rooms," Jake responded. Taking a step back.

Nikki realized what he was doing.

"Come on Jake. I've earned the right to an explanation." Nikki was extremely cross.

"What do you want to know?"

"Who is that girl? The one with the blond hair."

Jake sat down on her desk chair. "Sometimes when people like us can do powerful magic, they can do real strange and wonderful things. She's made of magic, Nikki. All magic, head to toe. Ruby considers her family."

"But why would she do that?"

"Don't you think she was lonely?"

"But what about her husband? What's his name? Is it Tomas? Why did she call you that then? And why were you talking to her like she was six?"

Jake furrowed his eyebrows together. "I can answer all of that. You won't like a bit of it, though," he said, drawing his voice grave. "Yes, your father's name is Tomas. He's not here. He'll never be here."

Nikki bit her lip. "Do you mean he's...?"

"Yes."

Nikki looked down at her toes, fighting tears caused by the fact that she'd never meet her real father. Jake put a hand on her shoulder. She swallowed the lump in her throat and wiped furiously at her traitor eyes.

"What about the other things?"

"You know that people were after you right?"

Nikki shook her head yes.

"The plan didn't work exactly as your mum and dad wanted it to. Sure the decoy baby wasn't a problem, but then they got your dad," Jake clenched his fist. "My uncle. Then they killed the baby. But your mum still had it. That spell was never meant to kill something that small when it could kill a bigger target."

"But Ruby isn't dead."

"Exactly. Because it didn't hit Ruby. It hit the baby. She just got the effects of being that close."

"What are the effects?"

"Madness."

"As in crazy?"

"Yes."

"But she didn't seem all that strange-acting until she thought you were Tomas," Nikki insisted.

"It's sort of like a half-crazy thing. But eventually...it could get worse. But, I don't want to sound so pessimistic or anything. Do you have any other questions?"

"Why is my last name the same name of the guy who went after you and me?"

"I really don't know that. Bet you'll find that out someday."

Nikki looked disappointed.

"What else?"

"How do you know all of this stuff?"

"Er...let's just say, I've just been through a lot of it."

"Where are your parents?"

"Colon's father, Will Colon, killed them."

"Did you kill Will?" Nikki knew it was a dangerous question to ask, yet she couldn't hold it in.

Jake looked at her for a long time, trying to read her, without reading her thoughts literally. "No," he finally stated. She couldn't tell if he was lying.

"I found this at my old house," Nikki said, pulling out the scale wrapped in brown tissue paper. Jake frowned at Nikki's blood spots, still splotching the wrappings. "I thought it looked like Scarlet's dragon's scale."

Jake handled it. "It does."

"But I found it in Ted's room. You know, my "foster" father per se. I don't know how it would have got there or why it was wrapped up."

"Neither do I." Jake saw Nikki peering at him from under her wildly messy hair. "What?"

"Well I was just wondering if somehow since you can read my thoughts, you'd be able to somehow pick out the memory of it, if I was around when Ted found it."

Jake glowered. "It's dangerous business dealing with peoples' minds and memories. In more than one case, appalling things have happened, revolting almost."

Nikki sighed. "Figured you say something like that."

Jake handed Nikki back the scale, gently brushing the tips of her fingers.

The lamp that was glowing brightly in the room shattered, both of their minds exploded full of a picture.

The light was bright and yellow. A little girl sat on the edge of a driveway, watching the colored cars go by. Her head was full of interest but her six year old mind could barely process all that was happening.

Another girl began walking down the street. As she passed the girl sitting, she stuck her tongue out and wished she lived somewhere else. Her hand scraped her package in her pocket, knowing what she had to do.

"Here," she cooed sweetly to the sitting girl the same age as her. The girl glared at her, wondering why she was doing this. "Go on, take it." The walking girl threw the wrapped present at her enemy, then ran off into the trees not too far ahead.

The girl sitting tore off the brown paper and found a red shinning scale. She ran her fingers along the sharp edges, pricking one, and it started to bleed. Tears welled up in her eyes. Quickly she ran back into her house, wondering why horrible things always occurred to her on her birthday.

V

Tears still welled in her mind as the memory faded into something darker.

The nightmare of the room full of shadowy curtains and the slicing blade dug deep into the two of their minds. "No," Nikki whispered out loud, as Jasmine filled her mind again. She tried to shove the nightmare away. It kept playing. It was worse the second time. Fear gripped at Nikki's heart.

Suddenly, she could feel Jake shove the memory of the dream away. The pictures in both of their minds disappeared, instead they were left in the darkness of Nikki's room.

Nikki was on the carpet.

Jake's mouth had found its way open in the process of the memories. The scale lay on the ground between them.

Both of them took heavy breaths.

"What was that? The last one. It didn't feel like the first," Jake asked, catching his beating heart back to its original pace. "What was going on? I couldn't tell."

Nikki brushed a stray hair from her face and looked away. "It was a dream. Nothing happened." In her mind though, the blades of the sword rang like an echo in her mind.

"Jasmine was the little girl who gave me that scale. I forgot about that. That probably triggered the dream I had... Don't ever do that again Jake."

"I warned you that memories are dangerous when shared."

"I didn't mean to share it."

He seemed restless. "People don't have dreams like that—that aren't real or have happened unless..." Jake gave her a funny look. "You *do* have a necklace like Scarlet's! You lied to me!"

Nikki shook her head, denying. "I didn't lie... I just didn't tell you otherwise."

"That's called lying! Do you even know what that kind of thing does? How in earth did you manage to find one?"

"Sophie said she found it in a shop! Besides, I left it at my house." She wished she weren't such a good liar. Her heart sank as Jake blew a breath of relief.

"As long as it's gone." Jake got up. "Well, now might be a good time to rest. Or. Open your birthday gifts."

Nikki refused to show her bewilderment at the plural noun, thinking she only had one gift—from the man named Garden. She just wanted Jake to go. He had such a split personality.

Right as he went out the door, he suddenly remembered something. They looked eye to eye, Nikki seeing how much her memories had drained him. "Bright and early tomorrow, we'll start training."

She didn't ask what training was, as she watched him leave and walk down the hall.

She decided to wash up.

As soon as she could only smell a small remaining hint of ocean on her skin and hair, she figured that was the best she could do. Sitting cross-legged on her bed, she pulled out the package from Garden.

The paper peeled away easier than melted butter, slithering to the floor while a thick, dog-eared book lay on her lap.

"Enchantments and All Other Practical **Je Ne Sais Quoi**," read the book cover.

She placed the book on a shelf beside her bed without looking. It landed on something that had a thin coating of glossy paper covering a large squishy surface of a gift.

It's probably from Jake. She hoped her guess was right. For some reason, she could only think that *he* would give her this gift, not anyone else.

She gently peeled off the delicate layer of paper. Underneath was a silky red material that was folded delicately. Nikki pulled the rest of it out to reveal a overflowing cloak that pooled on the floor. Just like her calm flames, it swayed and shimmered without the aid of a breeze. She found a slip of parchment under the long flowing present.

Thought you may like a gift to represent what we "English" people wore when you weren't here. This is what a normal magic girl would wear basically anywhere. Although, I added a few extra magical hints to it that you may find uncommon. I'll leave it up to you to figure them all out. Enjoy, and I hope you feel welcome here. I'll do my best to make sure you will always feel at home.

Jake

She smiled. Had she really thought that Jake had a split personality that was quite disturbing sometimes? Now more than ever, she felt the intensity of adventure pulsing through her veins.

Nikki got up from the cushiony bed and folded the cloak neatly to put it in the closet. She collapsed on the bed, full of mental and physical exhaustion, only to dream of the lurid things she had encountered that day.

VI

"Wake up, come on. I've got something for you to do!" Jake's voice was worse than nails on chalkboards, but maybe it was only because she was dreaming so deeply.

She swatted at him. "Not yet," Nikki mumbled.

"Fine then. See you."

She heard him shuffle away, slowly as if he was waiting for her to spring up.

Suddenly she heard the creek of a oil-needed door. *Wait a minute, my bedroom door doesn't do that.* She flew up. "What are you doing?" she demanded.

"Good. Didn't realize you got washed up and dressed for today."

He was sitting on the ledge of the balcony, feet dangling over the edge where there were no bars and railings.

"What do you want?" Nikki asked. Dragging herself up, she walked to the balcony doorway. She leaned against the white stone bars, smelling the ocean breeze twist her hair. It was still nighttime. The bright moon shone close as thousands of stars gazed down at them.

"Come on," Jake simply said, twisting his legs up over the edge.

With a sudden smile, he jumped off the ledge of the balcony.

He soared, silhouette skimming the air until he hit the ground three stories below. "Are you okay?!" Nikki screamed. He didn't move or say anything.

"JAKE!" Nikki screamed.

He didn't respond.

"Oh I can't believe I'm about to do this," she moaned.

Nikki leapt from the stone, feeling the sensation of flying, even just for a second. When she hit the soft grass, she realized her breath wasn't even taken. Nikki went on her knees, face towards the lush terrain.

Jake was above her then, standing and laughing. "So *that's* how I get you down. You know, you have an awful vulnerability."

"What's that?" Nikki asked, Jake getting on her last nerves. She jumped to her feet.

"That if someone's in danger, you put yourself in danger to save them. Even if *you* might get hurt."

"That's great to know. Why did you jump?"

Jake sighed. He brushed back his windswept hair just to have it flip back. "I hope you know that you may not always get the answers to things."

Nikki frowned. "Fine. Take me wherever you want me to."

"Good. We're going in there." Jake pointed towards the haze-surrounded forest.

"Sure. That seems *so* safe." Nikki crossed her arms and got up.

"It is when you're with me," Jake smiled almost sarcastically.

"Can I ask why we're going there or are you just going to throw more profound phrases at me?" It was her time to be sarcastic. They were already heading into the dark leaves.

Jake turned his head, giving her a grave look.

Nikki grew silent. *Acts like a mom more than Ruby.* She kept thick barriers over her mind, making sure Jake wouldn't hear any of it.

The woods were dense around them, but they followed a single beaten path. When they came across a clearing in the gloom, Jake stopped. Nikki hadn't noticed the backpack slung over his boney shoulder. He threw it off, and placed it on the matted forest floor. Reaching into the pack and struggling with something heavy, Jake finally pulled out a slender rapier, not unlike the one he had used with Scarlet, wrapped with reddish leather.

He tossed it softly on the ground.

Jake took a glance at her and then withdrew his own sword that was tied to a strap against his waist. Matted and wet as though it had been used many times in the same spot, the forest around them acted like a dangerous arena.

"Are you kidding me?" Nikki cried. "You would kill me if I started fighting you now!"

Jake rolled his eyes. "Don't be daft. I can't kill Scarlet, but I can kill you? You must really think I hate you."

"At least she was partly skilled. If I try to do a single thing, I bet I'll get sliced in half." She jumped back as Jake tried to pitch the wrapped sword at her. "Why me? Am I the only one you're going to train?"

"No. I let you rest. Your friends already got a chance to fight. But not with this sword. This sword, I saved specially for you."

"What am I supposed to do?" Nikki sighed. She knelt down and grasped the silver handle.

"First, unsheathe your weapon. Don't worry about getting hurt right now, I won't come at you hard."

Nikki slithered the extraordinarily light saber from its bed. The handle was sprinkled with a bluish dust that was surrounded by sapphires. She wasn't surprised that Jake had gotten her favorite color right. And she couldn't help a twitch in her lip as she admired the sword's picturesque qualities.

"I'll take it you like it," Jake said, smirking a bit as he looked up at her from his combat stance. He steadied his feet. "Go on, follow my posture."

Nikki did as he showed.

"Now, I'm going to come at you. Slowly, of course. Don't flinch and don't move. You're in a blocking move, so the only reason you would want to move is if I changed my attack position."

She nodded, gaining a strong shake of the head in disappointment by Jake. "I said don't move. It doesn't matter if you're ready; you'll never be ready."

He started jogging towards her. A few feet from her, he charged.

Nikki closed her eyes, waiting for the earsplitting clang.

It didn't come.

She flicked her eyes open.

He was an inch from her, breathing deeply. Jake sighed and dropped his weapon on the grass. "I can see you'll be a bit more of a trouble than those like Brea." Nikki presumed he meant Breannen.

Bet she liked you calling her that, she thought, forgetting her walls of protection.

She did actually. Although, I bet I could call her anything and she'd still like it. And anyways, she told me to call her that. Jake kept his expression fierce.

"Do you even get hurt when you hear me anymore?" Nikki almost wanted to take back the sentence. It sounded stupid when she said it out loud.

He responded anyways, "Sometimes. If I keep hearing you or start talking to you on purpose. But it seems to have reduced some what."

Jake reached up at her hands that were posed in the air, moving it slightly to the left. "Ever centimeter counts. One tiny movement off and you could end up one arm short. Literally—arm hacked off."

He could hear Nikki's heart racing like a frantic deer.

"For now, don't be afraid."

"Why are we doing this? Why is everyone saying 'for now'?"

Jake plopped down on the earthy surface.

"I didn't want to tell you yet."

"Tell me what?" Nikki asked sitting too.

"You have to train because we're headed to Colon's fortress."

"WHAT? Didn't you get me here to be *here*? Not to go get myself killed when you already tried so hard to keep me safe?" She jumped up.

"You don't have a choice."

Nikki gave a look as if daring him to say that again.

"I mean, this isn't a thing where you can just escape. They'll keep going at us until we do something. You were born to do this. Can't you feel it? You and I both. It isn't worth it at all if you just get yourself killed because you didn't train. If you stay here, you'll die. I'm going, and nothing anyone says can stop me. If I die, then I die. But I'm pretty sure your friends will be coming with me. Yes, they already know too," Jake had read her thoughts. "You have to learn this. If you go there you might die too. But we'll be with you—all the way. We *have* to go there to... to..." She knew the words 'kill him' were torturing him.

She could feel it; it was true. Something burned in her to fight. Nikki looked at the ground for a great while. When she caught a glint from a highlight on her sword. "I'll go with you." Her voice was no longer shaky. She was ready to learn.

Jake picked up his weapon again and posed for a swing.

VII

Training was more instinct than anything. You had to slow your mind to know when to hit, where to hit, or you'd *get* hit. Jake was proving to be good at striking. They went faster after several hours of defending. Jake's footwork for defense was completely messed up. He danced on his toes, while Nikki caught into the pattern quickly. Her steps become more graceful with every step. When the moon rose its highest in the dark sky, Jake switched it, and it was her time to start swinging. It was like he knew that she had it in her. Maybe in her blood. She could feel her fire burning, giving off an influence to just burn, and it was almost like it was, every time she let a spark fly off of her saber. Nikki refused to back down.

Jake was getting so into it one time, that he actually nicked her arm with the edge of his golden sword.

He looked mad at himself for a split second, but she eventually grazed his arm too. He was caught off guard then. She was frustrated that he was off balance. She gave him a moment to recompose himself. Before swinging once again.

The sun rose from the tips of the ocean's warm fingertips.

Drenched in cold sweat, they both barely realized that it was light out. From where they had been fighting all night, the moon was their lantern. "Ready to give up yet?" Jake asked gritting his teeth while forcing his sword into hers.

"Not quite." She was once again surprised at how strong he was. He didn't look like much more than a scrawny boy who was just a bit tall and thin for his age. She was more surprised though at his next remark.

"Fighting like this is in your blood you know," Jake hissed through the cracks of his teeth. His boots dug up dirt as he forced his rapier forward.

Nikki let her sword down. He tumbled forward onto the ground from the sudden let go of force.

"What the heck was that about?" he inquired. "I told you not to let your guard down for anything I say."

Nikki still couldn't tell if he had been lying about that statement or he had actually been telling the truth. "What do you mean, 'in my blood'?"

Jake shook his head and pulled himself up. "I mean, that you come from a long row of people who fought with swords. Medieval weapons are uncommon nowadays. Their use was more widespread though when others of our family members were alive. Just be glad that you have some passed down instinct and don't have to learn it all from scratch. Colon's family sword fights too."

She really didn't understand Jake's words much, but decided not to ask. He'd rather fight than be answering questions.

"You tired yet?" Jake grinned as they both tried to catch their stolen breath.

"Only if you are."

"I am. Your mum will get worried about us if we don't start heading back."

Nikki agreed. They started on the path to get back to the house. "Why would she worry? What kinds of animals live in these woods?"

Jake scoffed. "These are magical woods, Nick," Jake had seemed to take a liking in giving her a nickname like Breannen had given herself, "Animals are for humans. *Creatures* live in these woods. But I don't 'spect you'd know much of them. You wouldn't hear about **scrolts** too much in a fairy tale book."

"What are they?"

"Sort of like trolls, only smarter shape shifters that can mess with your paths."

"What do you mean mess—"

"Make you think that where you are going is the right way when it actually isn't."

They heard the sea before they saw it or the brilliantly white castle. "It's not actually a castle," Jake had explained to her earlier. "Made-by-magic houses don't count, even if they are grand. Colon's place, now there's a castle." He had seemed lost in thought when he told her that. As though Colon's castle meant more to him than he was letting on.

"Why is he prince? How old is he? Doesn't everyone hate him? And if they do, why don't they just overthrow him?" Nikki had wanted to ask. She had bit her tongue though. For now, it was just enough to know that she was going there, and it was final.

"Thank you by the way," Nikki stated, running through the brambly trees.

"For what?" Jake's face was suddenly solemn.

"Maybe you should just wait and see if you find out before I tell you."

Jake smiled a little bit.

It was foggy that day. Although there had just been a foggy day in Indiana, there was something different about the one here. More mysterious? Or was it more deadly?

"There's more than just training with swords, you know." Jake opened the door for her as they went into the house.

"What more is there?"

"Can you ever talk without asking a question?"

She remained silent. She had planned on saying a sarcastic, "Can you ever spend time with someone without changing your emotions every five seconds?" but that would have been a question, and it would have just proved his point.

"Training like I did when you were back with Scarlet."

Nikki threw her head back, "That was more like motivation. Are there words for some spells?"

"First of all, most of the 'spells' are called **enchantments**. Make sure you never say the word 'spell' around a sophisticated mage. He'd probably be so offended he'd suck the magic right out of you. Second of all, yes there are some with words. But a lot of **enchantments** and charms are dangerous. I'll explain later." Jake darted up the spiral steps and Nikki really didn't want to know what he was planning on doing.

A blond head popped out of a room. Startled, Nikki thought it was Breannen but was irritated when she saw that the hair was long and silvery.

"What were you doing?" Chrystal asked.

"I've been sword fighting in the forest." Nikki tried to sound dominant and egotistical, but only succeeded in making her voice quiver with tiredness.

"You look tired."

"Thanks for the memo."

The little girl loped down the steps as if they were puffy clouds. "You friend is nice."

"Which one?" Nikki asked as she made her way up the stairs. She dropped her act. There was too much innocence in this little girl. Chrystal followed her easily.

"The one with the glasses and knows stuff."

"Oh." *Why do the stairs have to be so long.*

"Jacob is nice too. He tells me secrets."

Nikki's sensors went off. "What kind of secrets?"

She looked like she was about to answer when they both heard a noise.

"What was that?" Nikki cried.

Chrystal shrugged.

Nikki flew down the staircase and into the kitchen where the banging crash seemed to have been coming from. No one was there and nothing was out of place. "What's going on?" Nikki pondered to herself. She searched the room with her eyes, seeing nothing, not even a speck of lint, out of line. Her eyes stopped at the door of the kitchen. It led outside. The door was slightly ajar. For some reason, it unnerved Nikki. She went over to it, and closed it tightly.

"Do you like puppies?" Chrystal asked as Nikki came back to the marble stairs.

"Um, I guess so?"

"I like little ones with lots of fur."

"So do I, I think."

"Do you think your friend James is sweet?"

"Only when he's not being annoying."

"Is he not annoying a lot?"

Nikki came to realize that Chrystal didn't have an accent like she herself didn't. "I suppose." Would she pick one up after being here a while? Did she even have one?

"I think he's very sweet."

"Good for you. Do you know what that crashing sound was?"

"No. It happens a lot. Jacob tells me that it's a **ghost crack**."

"What?" Nikki felt an odd alarm go off inside of her.

"Yes. Jacob tells me that there are cracks in this house because it is old. And when they open large enough, spirits come in."

Despite the difference in definitions, Nikki was still taken aback by what Jake called **ghost crack**s. Yet, she knew that something wasn't right about this situation. What was Jake hiding?

"Do these "**ghost cracks**" occur often?"

Chrystal shrugged again.

Nikki decided it was best to change the subject.

"What do you do around here?"

Chrystal smiled. "Jacob teaches me about things when he gets home from his school."

"Jake goes to school?"

"Everyone goes to school. His is special though."

"How so?"

"Its not only for magic people, but for..."

They were at the top of the steps.

"You should get some rest before Jacob decides to teach you **Je Ne Sais Quoi**." Chrystal said softly.

"I've heard that word so many times lately Doesn't that just mean something is mysterious?" She had heard that word when they were studying French culture.

"No. Well to regular people maybe. To us, magic folks that is, it means magic."

"Interesting word."

"Do you like that word?"

"Yeah I guess. I'll be going."

Nikki slipped into the blue door of hers. She washed up again and placed on a regular t-shirt and some shorts. Collapsing on her bed, Nikki fell into a sleep too shallow to receive a full and satisfying siesta.

VIII

Her world was a foggy place in her dreams. Full of shadows and murky shapes, as if her thoughts were confused at what to turn into. As her mind grew less numb, more darker solid shapes filled it. Until a voice filled her head.

"Nikki, Nikki! Wake up you lazy sleeper! Know you've been in the forest all night fighting and training, but it's time to do some more. This time, **Je Ne Sais Quoi.**"

The word rang like a bell in her head. She was too tired though to want to care about it. "No offense, but I really don't think I could make magic when I'm half asleep."

James groaned. "Come on or pretty boy will have my neck for not getting you."

"His name is Jake," Nikki whispered, as she sat up and glowered.

"Good, you're up. Let's go."

"Fine." Nikki's eyes felt heavy under the tiredness that swirled the room around. She got up and pulled on a gray sweatshirt.

"You good now?" James asked, teasing her at how lazily and half asleep she was doing things.

Nikki retorted, now awake. "Come on snappy, if you want it that way."

"Don't forget to grab the book Garden gave you."

"How did you know about that?"

James shrugged. "That's what Jake told me to tell you."

She sighed, muttering, "Never trust a boy who jumps off balconies." The book was in her hands as she let her mind creep and seep into the pages of the other books, wondering what they were.

They went out the door and down the stairs. "So where are we going?" Nikki wondered aloud to James. "And where are the others?"

"They're already there. And I really can't explain where we're going until we get there."

"Oh." She *really* had to stop asking questions.

They traveled further, through carpeted corridors that seemed to have the need for plain floors. Nikki still wondered if this was really a castle, even if Jake had said that it wasn't. James led her down a few twisting stairways until the walls grew darker as if they were in an unused basement.

"Have you ever wondered why you have such a big house for just three people?" James laughed.

"Um, I think there's four because of Jake, but yes."

"See? Just been a day and I already can't do math anymore!"

Nikki laughed. She had never had this much free time with her friends, never realized they might have been the humor needed under all of the darkness. *Or is that just James being James?* Nikki speculated.

They went deeper into the winding path of stone walls. The floor at the bottom was now cold and paved, making it seem more threatening than the other cozy looking ones. It was as though the person who made this house imagined everything perfectly for every room but when they got to the basement, or dungeons, they went blank and the creativity had died. Until they went into the room.

A double door was ahead of them. Large and golden colored, it stood out twice as much because of the dullness around it. "What do your rooms look like?" Nikki asked, her mind conjuring up wild ideas.

"Amazing, but they're all different. I liked yours the best though. If I had known I would have that much room for my things, I would have packed at a lot more than I had."

"They're big then."

"Yes."

"Have you seen Ruby anywhere?"

"No, but I think she went somewhere outside of the house though."

James pushed the door in, exposing the spacious, extensive, room. She presumed some sort of magic had to be used to make a room this big. It was probably taller than Scarlet's dragon—than the house itself! The ceiling, although you could barely see it clearly, was the most noticeable. A delicate chandelier dangled from ornate rafters while a wild and indistinguishable mural was painted on it.

A long table, stretched its wooden figure alongside the wall. The rest of Nikki's friends, and Jake stood there also.

"Look at you, James," Breannen called out. Her voice echoed off the mammoth walls. "You can actually wake someone up right!"

Nikki read his face. Trying to help, she said softly, "It's not Jake that's changed her. She's just more free now. You should know that, being her friend."

He twisted his lips into a contorted smile. "I know," he lied. James was jealous of something so ridiculous.

"Sure." Nikki gave up on the situation for now.

They came up to the others and Nikki placed the over-flowing book beside Jake. "Brilliant," he whispered to the cover, then turned to smile at her. "We're lucky Garden's on our side. I'm pretty sure that if he wasn't, we'd already be dead. You especially."

Nikki ignored him, without returning his beam, and leaned against the brightly colored walls. There was a purple, red, orange, blue and green wall, but each had the same swirl design on it. Since the ceiling and walls were full of colors, Nikki presumed that the carpet would be too, but it was a bleach white, a dangerous color. She knew that she would be dead without Garden's help. She also knew that her father wouldn't be.

How much magic had to be put into building a place like this? She pondered to herself for a while. When Jake started talking, she knew that she had better concentrate. Whether she liked him that great or not, wasn't the question; he would know if her head was in the clouds, and she needed to learn this.

"Magic takes energy as all of you know—"

Except me, the thought couldn't help but pop into her head.

"—and although some don't take words and others do, they all have different amounts of energy they take from you when you use them. All magic except for your gifts take this energy. Easy enough, when you use a gift, you receive energy to a point where if you use it so much, most **enchantment**s won't even cause you to feel drained—"

Which reminds me of when I saved Jake from Scarlet. I had used my gift a lot, and then magic. That must be what he's talking about. Did Nikki feel that much of an outcast that she didn't feel right to talk aloud, instead to leave her mind brimming with thoughts?

"You can use your gift too much as well, it won't harm you, but you'll get a bit high. Maybe faint."

Nikki remembered how insane she felt after using her gift so powerfully against Scarlet when she had first attacked.

"Now for a moment, use your gift, if you can at all, in any way possible. I want you to do this so that when we start to learn spells, you won't feel like you've just run a marathon—or several. I want you to get used to using your gift a lot. You'll use it more than anything else."

It took Nikki a minute to realize what Jake had told her to do. While James had started healing his (and other people's) minuscule scratches from sword fighting, Kay began to zone out and stare at the wall. Breannen did her gift and almost laughed at the frozen figure of Michelle; Michelle stood there paralyzed. Sophie stared straight at

Nikki reading what Nikki had just numbly thought. Until Jake glanced at her.

She couldn't decide if he was angry, frustrated, or confused. Nikki didn't really want to know, and soon she was lighting an annoyed red flame from her palm. She watched it for a while.

That was their first day of training.

IX

Several weeks passed. Nothing changed much. Nikki went out at night to sword fight and fell half asleep during her magic learning. Jake had told them about a few dangerous and off-limits **enchantment**s. **Lepra**, he had said, was an **enchantment** that broke possession. If a person possessed you, the charm would break it, but maybe just kill you in the process from the strain of too much energy. The third day, he had told them about **Malonanecra**, the death magic charm. When he had begun to say it, Nikki's memories twisted back to the first time she had seen Scarlet. Had she tried to use that **enchantment** on her? It seemed like it.

Nikki wondered why Jake would tell them so much about **enchantment**s they weren't supposed to use. With everyday, her fire became more normal. She was getting used to her strange and wonderful magic.

Then, the next three days, they practiced defensive and offensive charms until they knew enough to probably survive each other. It didn't seem enough. They would be facing people with years of training.

A few of them, like Kay and Breannen, already knew some **enchantment**s. A lot of them were useless from improper teachings, but it was still better than Michelle who still hadn't gotten her powers yet. Jake had even told her once that if she didn't get them soon, he wouldn't let her do anything but help them get in with a sword. It wasn't that she'd be useless, it was the fact that she was vulnerable.

They seemed to be there, endlessly training for forever.

Forever wasn't long enough.

Ruby told Nikki once and a while about Tomas, what had happened, and all about how he looked just like Jake. That was only when she remembered that he was actually dead though. Nikki often tried to avoid her. Not to hurt her, but because she didn't think she could take the fact that Ruby was part crazy.

Then forever slowly came to a halt.

A sunny yet foggy day in England about a month after arriving, Jake said he had to go into the forest for something, and that it would take a "bit." They didn't have magic practice that day; Nikki decided to search her room for the surprises that still awaited her. Knowing Jake, a bit could mean five minutes or ten hours, depending on which personality he was today.

Near mid-afternoon, she had settled down, and was reading a book that was extremely strange and well-written that she discovered on her book shelf. There were so many laws to magic. It wasn't free and it didn't come from nothing. The more Nikki read, the more questions she had. The more she learned, the more she believed that she was part of this magical realm.

When she finally looked up after reading the entire book including the three afterwards, she saw that the ocean touched the sun once again. But Jake, for all she could tell, was nowhere. It was still quiet in the house and she was sure that Jake would have come into her room to tell her about whatever he did. He was constantly barging into her room about things.

What if something happened to him? Nikki tried to brush the voice away. It came back stronger, *What if he got ambushed? It's been about a month, hasn't it? Not a single attack, seems kind of fishy? What if they were waiting in the forest just for him?*

By now, she had learned to trust her wise instinct.

Nikki began tightly lacing on the already skin-tight leather boots that Chrystal had apparently "found" somewhere, that fit her to a perfect degree. She sheathed her white sword, pocketed her wand, and took a deep breath. *You're not strong enough. Get the others perhaps? No,* she decided. *This is a job I can do.*

A red fabric glistened in a beckoning manner from the bed's shelf. Jake's gift to her, the cloak.

Yeah. I may not know all that it can do yet...or for that matter, anything that it can do, but I know that something will turn out right if I bring it.

She lifted the silky material from its lonesome spot and fastened the neckpiece around her. The hem was short enough to run in, but just long enough to hide her feet and body if she wanted to stand still. The hood was long enough to conceal her face. It attached neatly on her shoulder blades with a silver leaf clasp.

Wouldn't Jake have wanted me to wear this magical thing if I came after him? He doesn't want me to come after him, I know it, but it's a risk I'm willing to take.

The phrase Jake had said a while ago rang in her head, "That's your weakness: you're willing to sacrifice yourself to save your friends."

She sighed. They were dumb but truthful words.

She didn't want to risk it, but being in the position she was in, she wondered if she should take the necklace out of her bag. *No, it's too dangerous. You can do this without the help of dark magic.* With that thought, Nikki opened the door to the balcony. Stepping on the edge of the part with no railings, she took a shaky breath and jumped. Her cape fluttered behind her as her silhouette chased the twilight grass.

Chapter Nine

Running

I

She could feel her ankle crack stubbornly on the grass, which was so soft it provided no support. Pain flew through her body, but she had learned by now to not stop at pain. *Keep going.* She knew that this wouldn't slow her down too much if she had to run. Jake had caused her many twisted ankles in the last month.

The trees, that were already taller than she had ever imagined could be, seemed to stretch to no limit. Mist and thick shadows stretched along the dew-droplet grass. Although her heart was pounding, she knew that Jake was somewhere in the forest. She just knew it.

It was strange how the forest gave a path from the house to as far as the clearing. *Had someone made it that way or was it naturally made?* Nikki blocked her mind from getting fear-driven from thinking pointless questions.

What would Jake do when he saw her? What if he was in trouble? Why did it seem like he was always wanting to fight the battles for himself—like he was afraid someone else would get hurt. She knew that was how she felt as well, but if she had a choice to run and have all of those around her safe just as she was, she would choose that over attacking someone anytime.

Jake had said something about how he had trained to fight since he was little. He seemed endlessly skilled, but he had weaknesses just as well as she did. Worse than that, all of their enemies seemed to know them. Nikki could think of nothing worse, as she trampled over unbroken grass, than having an enemy know how to defeat you.

When she came to the clearing, she thought she would see him. Nikki had been sure he would be doing something or other, or just challenging the air to a sword duel. Jake seemed like the kind of person who would want to train to fight by himself.

Nikki didn't like the eeriness of the circular, treeless clearing. What if Jake wasn't in the woods at all, and she'd just end up as lost somewhere, waiting for someone to find her?

Jake had to be in there somewhere. She could feel he was somewhere that she couldn't see. Was it possible he was invisible? It seemed like he would have appeared to her by now if he was.

Jake was always tossing her trust out the window. Right when she thought that she might actually be able to rely on him, he proved that she couldn't believe *him*, or anyone else. Nikki almost wished that she had brought someone with her into the forest. She moved forward beyond the clearing, feeling the wet earth crunch and squish under her stiff boots. As she left the clearing, in the direction opposite from which she had come, the path became more narrow. The trees became less beautiful and more spindled. The forest seemed much darker when you were by yourself.

The wind was silent.

All noise was cut off.

When a bird's caw filled the nearly-full moon's air, she nearly jumped out of her skin. Nikki spotted the strange hawk-sized creature in a high branch of a tree.

Beak like a hook, the bird had more hair-like covering than feathers. The skin of its neck shone, gleaming white and gray. It turned its oval head in her direction. Caught her eye.

Her breath sucked in as she saw the features that were more dead than alive. A part of its flesh hung freshly from its skinny neck. Nothing but the glossy whites of the eyes remained.

She reached towards her sword, wondering if it would even work on such a creature.

Her lungs prepared for an automatic scream.

Right when her voice was running up her throat, an earth-covered hand came out of nowhere, covering her mouth. The other arm pulled her tightly back by the waist.

Fear rose higher in her chest, she struggled against the force that held her, but to no avail.

"Don't make a sound," a gentle voice whispered into her ear.

The decaying bird looked away.

"Come back into the clearing," he said softly. The familiar looking arms dragged her back into the foggy forest glade, where it roughly let her go to fall onto the grass.

"What are you doing here?" Jake demanded. "If you come and look for me every time I'm a little late, you're going to end up killing us both!"

"What was that thing?" Nikki asked, ignoring Jake's scolding deliberately.

"A rotting familiar. It belonged to Will Colon, Colon's dad. Colon probably sent it to find us. It can't see, nor can it go past the barrier between our walls—meaning, this clearing is safe. Ears like I've never seen though, on that one."

"*What*? What were you doing in here?"

"What were *you* doing in here?"

"Looking for you!"

"Well *I*, was..." Jake trailed off, looking towards the narrow pathway.

"Was what? Or are you just going to prove that I can't trust you. Again." Nikki shook her head angrily at Jake's pursed lips. "Why was it so decayed if it was alive?" she asked, changing the subject.

"Because Will is dead. Familiars can't go on that well without their masters."

"Alright then. What were you doing?"

"Partly scouting out the way. Partly..."

"What?" Nikki commanded.

"Well partly searching for Arola."

Nikki gave him a look of exasperation.

"Alright, alright, remember when you heard the crash in the kitchen?"

"Yes, but how did *you* know I knew about that?"

"Chrystal told me. But it's not a **ghost crack**."

"I figured that much, so what is it?"

"For the last probably year and a half, someone or something has tried to break the barriers of our boundaries and get in."

"Colon is doing this?"

"I don't know for sure, but there are no others who would. But recently, the attempts have gotten further. You can actually feel something is wrong. Things have changed where other things are at."

"But it wasn't that way when I heard it. I looked and nothing was changed."

"I don't know, maybe it was a fluke or something. But then, last night I saw someone when I looked out a window. Or something. I'm not sure if it was just a **scrolt** or something more like a unloving **shadow**. Either way, it has to be coming from Colon. Like I said before, we have to stop him or he'll never stop! He's been breaking into our boundaries, so that's why we have the right to do the same to his."

"But what if it wasn't him? That bird couldn't get through." She trying to reason with him, more than question.

"Only **scrolts** and **shadows** can break magical boundaries. But those creatures wouldn't do it unless under command. There's no one else who could break through, not even Colon's watchmen."

"I still don't understand what you were doing out here."

"Because after I saw it last night, I went looking for it. I spotted it between the borders. Then it saw *me* and disappeared under the ground."

"It *disappeared*?"

"Yes. So I desperately started to dig using magic, even took a few chunks out of the ground. If it was a **scrolt**, it wouldn't be very far down. In fact, just a few inches, and it would have been seen. They have thick leathery skin, but they can also shape shift. If it was a **shadow**, they can go on for miles under the earth without ever being seen or hurt. That's why I think it was a **shadow**. They can also shape shift. But **shadows** are made to be controlled, which makes it seem all the more likely that it's one of them. It definitely wasn't a person, and this wasn't a trick to fool me. Colon has an army of **shadows**..."

"*That's* what you've been doing today? Searching for a **shadow**?"

"Sort of." Jake looked sheepish, realizing how odd this sounded to Nikki.

"Why were you taking so long?"

"Because then I saw Valla, the bird. She can smell too, and let me tell you, if it had smelled the blood on my hands from the magic and digging, I would have died right then and there." He saw her face. "What? Don't believe me?"

"Yeah. I do. That's the sad part." She looked down at his hands. They were scarred and scratched from his frantic search.

"'Kay then let's go," Jake replied, ignoring the last comment.

She shook her head, disgusted with herself. She was more like him than she had given herself credit for. She had just done what he had: gone off to do something important, without telling anyone and wanted to do it alone.

"Be alert though." Jake said. Nikki realized he had a bow and arrow siding as a weapon with his sword at his waist. The quiver was strapped awkwardly to his back. He reached behind him to pull out one of the slim wooden shafts.

"Do you hear something?" Nikki asked wiping dirt hastily off her face. At least she was camouflaged.

"You can never be too careful. Where's your wand?" Jake inquired.

"I don't know. I had it—I brought it with me. I know I didn't lose it!"

Jake sighed and searched the ground with his eyes. "We'll have to go back through the barrier. Maybe it'll be there. Be thankful you can use magic without it now."

They walked past the clearing and into the outside lands of their boundaries. "What did you mean when you said you were looking for Arola?" Nikki inquired.

"She hasn't come yet, but don't worry. She's fine, I'd know if something happened to her."

Valla was gone without a hint of where she had even been. Jake shook his head as if to tell her it wasn't a good sign.

The path was empty. Shallow, leafless trees over grew each other. The grass was no longer soft, but a white wheat color. "It didn't help by digging," Jake whispered, lifting a branch from in front of him. "This ground is so full of magic that as soon as I took a moment to stop, it would start to fill in itself again. By now, I have no idea where the **shadow** even would be. That was another reason why I took so long."

Nikki shook her head, trying to force agreement from his words.

They couldn't find her wand. They searched along the intertwined tress and bushes with indistinguishable leaves and berries on them. "I don't remember going this way," she whispered as they passed a mossy boulder.

Alright, we'll head back. No matter what, we'll—"

A dagger flew millimeters from Jake's face, striking instead, a tree.

II

Their eyes widened.

"*Don't just stand there!*" Jake hissed.

Sending a arrow behind him, he took off behind Nikki's running feet.

Above them, they heard the caw of the lifeless bird. Valla. No doubt with company following it.

"Don't look back," Jake shouted. He shot another lean dart towards the dark trees. With a thud, it found a target.

They ran faster.

Soon, they tumbled into the clearing.

"Don't stop." Jake said urgently. "They might break through."

They continued sprinting. The cawing was still overhead. Nikki couldn't understand it. Her mind raced in the same pace her legs were. Thick roots blocked their way out of the mouth of the forest. She ran without even bothering to listen to what Jake was yelling from behind her. Like he knew more than her about running away...

Her feet slipped on the dewy wood pieces. Stumbling, she met the lush green grass of her house yard. Nikki heard the faint grunt of Jake falling next to her.

"Are you okay?" Jake asked, holding his hand out to help her up.

"I'm fine," she said crossly. She still took his offered hand as she got up. "They were using magic to make the vines and roots attack."

"I noticed. Doubt it was Scarlet that time though. I know she wouldn't have shot for the head, let alone missed me if she had."

She turned to him, about to argue, but froze. They heard the sounds of footsteps approaching from the house, but only paid attention to the fact of how awful both of them looked.

Nikki thought that Jake was filthy before. He was so covered in dirt now that you couldn't have figured out that he was pale-skinned, at all. She herself wore dirt in raccoon rings around her eyes and cheeks. The hair on their heads flew in all different directions, twigs and leaves in every other chunk.

Somewhere along the line of escaping the territory, Jake had got a long graze from his eye down to his neck, while Nikki had been severely scratched by trees down the length of her arms.

"What happened to you?" The small voice of Michelle's called out next to them. Jake and Nikki turned to also see Sophie.

"It's a long story," Nikki started. "But compared to the fact that we were looking for my wand and got attacked by a nearly-dead bird and knife thrower, none of the rest is important enough to tell."

Sophie's mouth slowly parted, although she was looking beyond them, into the shady trees. The wind wrestled through the branches unnerved. Despite the roar of the sudden current of air, a thick snap echoed through the forest.

"What is that?" Sophie whispered. Jake swerved, prepared to fight.

From the trees came the silvery-white slim figure of Arola. Something was in her mouth. Long and stick-like...

"My familiar," Jake told her, smiling as the debonair long haired animal grew closer. He bent down to tousle her fur.

"She's beautiful," Michelle enlightened.

"She is," Sophie agreed, carefully positioning herself down next to Jake and stoking the animal's ears.

You know, intelligence is more important to our breed than beauty, we take pride in being noble. Plus, it is a great honor to be scratched by a witch of your stance.

The three of the girls took a sharp intake, as Arola's thoughts filled their heads.

"She can...?" Nikki began.

"Yes," Jake answered, becoming accustom to Nikki's many questions. Arola gently placed her head in Nikki's palm, letting go of her wand that had been guarded in the creature's mouth.

"Thank you, but how can you hear her? How can *we* hear her?"

Her face was as shocked as her voice.

"It's in her nature, first of all, in her breed. They can talk to each other by doing that. I can hear though only because I'm bonded to her as a master. Before she was a familiar to me, I couldn't hear her no matter how hard she tried. You can hear her because she knows you by me." Jake smiled at the wolf like creature. Suddenly his face grew serious again. "But we have to prepare. Now. We have until morning, but then we have to leave."

"Why? Tell us *all* that happened." Sophie urged.

Nikki shot Jake a look then opened her mouth, but he cut across her words. "We don't have time to explain it all. The point is, we went over the borders of our land searching for Nikki's wand. We didn't find it but we got attacked by someone who I saw had the royal patch on his cloak. We have to leave. Their spy bird can already get through our boundaries."

"Alright," the two slightly confused girls agreed.

They made their way back up into the house. Nikki came close to Jake and whispered. "Why can she talk to you without hurting you? Jake, seriously, do you know *why* you don't have a gift?"

Jake turned stern as Arola strode beside him. "I don't know why I'm the only magic type who doesn't have a gift. It's *not* a killing gift, like people say, if you believe such rubbish. Arola is *supposed* to talk to me. Not like you when you mess with my mind. Stop asking me questions."

She couldn't tell if he was joking.

"By the way," Sophie called to them. "You guys look terrible." She and Michelle exchanged smirks.

"Won't the others be pleased when we tell them that we have to leave." Michelle yelled.

Nikki could tell that Michelle was being sarcastic.

"Why do you think that I can talk to you in your mind and you can see my memories? Why don't you consider this a gift?" Nikki asked as Michelle and Sophie hurried from the frothy air.

"First of all, it's not a gift because I can only hear *you*. And that's a **curse** in itself… I was born to fight your battles, to protect you. Maybe something sent some signal when I first heard you, and now, I can dig deeper in your mind to help you and hear you."

"You were born to protect me? But why?"

"I don't know, girl-who-asks-more-questions-than-she-should. Like I've said before, there are things that are unsolvable."

Nikki's eyebrows furrowed in annoyance.

"You're like a body guard—I hate it," she said.

Jake just walked ahead, up the stairs, and into his room. He was hurt by her words.

III

Dinner that night was very silent. Every night since they had arrived, each of them sat at an oversized table, while Ruby explained little things to Nikki as she sat by her. That evening, the air was crisp and hostile. Jake said nothing. Ruby was unusually quiet, as if she too could sense that something had gone wrong.

More and more, Nikki noticed that Ruby was a bit off her rocker. Jake had been right to say though, that she was only partly crazed. She seemed to be brilliantly minded. Very curious and loving. Was it only that she was a little edgy, that kept Nikki from really considering she was a great mother? She kept calling her Ruby, and even if he did know it was on accident, Jake kept giving her sharp looks. She couldn't help it though.

As they sat at the table, the rest of the group kept themselves completely quiet, fidgeting with their meal uncomfortably. Nikki had that same pit in her stomach. There wasn't a force in her that thought she was ready to go against forty guards and win. *Even with Jake,* she sighed, *there is a delicate chance that I might...*

Jake's head shot up and he made eye contact with her that they held. "I swear, I will not let anything happen to you. *Never* think that way again. A person with **Je Ne Sais Quoi** doesn't give up so easily. Especially our family," He had told her all of this in such a forceful tone that everyone at the table looked at them.

"I'm sorry," she muttered back.

Chrystal gave them each a hopeful smile.

She doesn't know what's going on, does she? Nikki sent it towards Jake.

No. I'd advise not to tell her unless the circumstances comes to no other option.

Does Ruby know?

No. His voice dragged for a second. Nikki watched as he shook his head quickly, trying to clear his head. *It's getting better,* he told her referring to reading her mind, *But once and a while, it really hits me.*

They cleared their plates. Nikki gazed out at the window by their sink. The sun was gone, replaced with a heavy moon. They were all washed up, clean and ready to go get dirty again. Nikki hadn't had time to pack yet. The others had all of their possessions already, ready for them to grab and go.

After the meal, Jake came up to her, his thick English-accented words ringing in her ear. "Go get your stuff and we'll all meet outside. Stop for nothing, talk to no one." He quickly passed her to get his things. His feet thudded as he went up the marble steps.

Nikki held the railing of the staircase as she thought.

"Nikki!" Kay had come up behind her. "Can I help you pack up your things?"

"Sure." Her mind felt frozen. She really didn't want to go, but a part of her was screaming, *This is a chance to actually do something!* "Let's go," Nikki's voice said with a new source of confidence.

They raced each other up. Nikki holding in the need to burn something. She could feel her head pounding, her throat as dry as a bone.

Into the blue-door room, swiping things off the floor they went. Nikki left behind little more than a few things than she had brought, she knew there was not a chance of her needing things like a pen.

"Your room's amazing," Kay smiled as she stuffed a pair of shorts into Nikki's bag.

For every thing she left out that she had brought from America, she put in one of the bizarre things that made up her room. Nikki knew that at least one of them had to be of some use to someone sometime.

When they looked around for another important piece to put into her bag, Nikki's eyes caught something shimmery on the shelf she hadn't seen before. "What's this?" she asked herself.

Kay shrugged in response.

She picked up item by its shiny leather covers. A very thick book. It was locked with an intricate key hole that wrapped itself around its bindings. "I've never seen this before. Why would someone have a book here with no key?"

Kay shrugged again. "I have to grab my packings now. Hope I helped you some."

"Thanks," Nikki declared to her.

Kay left and Nikki picked up the full bag from the walk in closet. There was something underneath it.

A pair of teal cargo pants were folded neatly; they had so many pockets, there were endless possibilities of what they could hold. Under that was a long sleeved shirt that cut off with a different fabric where a baggier t-shirt took its place. The shirt itself was deeply red and the sleeves were red and blue stripes in a horizontal pattern. A card was placed with care on top.

Dearest,

Although your silly cousin may not know it, I know that you are leaving. But it will not be forever, and I will let you go and give you my luck. Take these clothes I have made for you. They should fit well, and they are magic woven, making them terribly hard to rip. Good luck my dearest, safe travels, my **Je Ne Sais Quoi** *child.*

⌀ Ruby

She knew. Her eyes almost came into tears. How could she leave now? There was something in her though, growling and just wanting to beat the pulp out of someone. *I have to go. I won't cry. I'm not afraid anymore.*

She pulled on the new clothes and placed the scabbard holding her sword, at her side. Nikki pushed her wand into one of the deeper cargo pockets. On her back went the scarlet cape. Nikki pulled the pack on her back. *I'm ready.*

Nikki knew that everyone had put their brooms in their bag using a reducing **enchantment** to make it fit with little trouble. Nikki had always found that one "**enchantment**" to be interesting. She slipped her broom into the bag. As she looked in the mirror at herself, she realized that the clothes that she wore, fit perfectly.

Must be magic, she thought. *Thank you so much Ruby... Mom.* Thoughts poured out into her head.

"Wow, Ruby is really good with clothing. Don't you think so too?" Chrystal had appeared at the doorway.

"Yes. She's fantastic."

Then, the little girl caught sight of the bag Nikki was trying to keep hidden under her cloak. Nikki smoothed out her hair, uncomfortably.

"Are you going somewhere?" Chrystal asked, tears staining her cheeks. She began to fiddle with the pink bow that held up her silky hair.

Sometimes I wonder if she does *have a gift. Even if she already is made of magic. She has to be reading my mind somehow. Maybe that's one of the secrets Jake taught her. It would figure. That wouldn't be the first thing he had lied to me about.* Somehow though, Nikki couldn't bear to believe that Jake would lie that he didn't have the gift of mind reading.

"Yeah. I'm going somewhere."

"But you've only just gotten here!" Chrystal's voice stood high pitched and eerie against the silent night. It was getting deep into the moon's shift.

"It won't be safe for you or anyone if we stay here."

"You all are going? Why can't I come?"

"It's not your job. Someone has to watch over Ruby while we're gone. And yes, all of us are going."

"Why isn't it safe?"

Nikki suddenly realized how annoying it was when she asked so many questions. "People are after me and Jake. It won't be safe for him, you, or anyone of us until we do something. I'll be back. Soon. I promise. And when I come back, I'll stay longer than just a month and a few days."

"You swear?" Chrystal had come close. Her voice was like a soft bird chirp.

"I swear."

Nikki hoisted her bag on her shoulder. She left Chrystal in the room by herself.

She had bigger things to worry about than leaving.

IV

"Hey. Thought I told you to talk to no one," Jake frowned as he came out his room at the same time she did.

"Since when do I listen to you? Besides, it's not like I'm late. No later than you anyway."

Breannen and James came up beside Nikki. She presumed that the others were down and out the door. James gave a smirk at Nikki's comment. Obliviously, he still couldn't control his jealousy.

"Nice outfit," Breannen commented with a smile as she stroked the supple material of Nikki's red cloak.

"Thanks." Nikki's mind was teetering.

"It's almost morning. Oh and Nikki?" Jake asked as she held her foot midair the marble spiral steps. Would this be the last time she walked them?

"What?"

"Don't make promises to Chrystal. She'll take them too seriously. And by the way, don't swear. Act."

Nikki rolled her eyes and flew down the rest of the stairs at his corny play on her first words to him. *You'd think that you could be a little more serious when we're about to go on a quest to send ourselves into the mouth of death.*

Don't wear me out now, Nick, Jake sent to her. *You and I will have to be at the top of our game when we get out of the borders. We're our two strongest defense. And Colon knows we are.*

"Great," Nikki muttered, remembering Valla. "And maybe we can play a game of follow the leader while we're at it." Her voice was cold, her eyes were afraid. Breannen gave an encouraging smile as she passed her.

"Come on. We'll have to go into the forest again. There's no other way." Jake's voice had become as hard as hers had been.

She knew that she shouldn't argue with him when they needed to stick together, but she couldn't help the tension.

"There's not a chance Colon will not know we're after him at this moment. He would have called back anyone who was spying on us. He's going to need all the help he can get anyway. We'll be safe as far as I can tell from here until we get there."

"Michelle still hasn't gotten her magic yet," James reminded him.

"I know. There's nothing we can avoid now. She's strong enough. It'll be at least a two day journey. If we're lucky, she'll get it soon enough to teach her something."

"She's going to be an easy target!" Breannen cried out to him. "She's going to get hurt."

Nikki shook her head. "No she won't."

They were out the door then, greeted by the friendly face of Kay, Sophie, and Michelle. "Explain to me again, what other creatures are in the woods besides the **scrolts**?" Kay asked, taking Jake's side.

"Many. But the population is basically made up of them. Most of them are harmless." Jake raised his head to see the horizon and the sun's first peeks. "Especially during daylight."

"What kind of creatures are 'many' supposed to be?" Michelle whispered to Sophie.

Sophie put on her best freak-you-out-face. "The kind that make you see what they want you to see." Nikki saw Jake's face as she said that. Sophie wasn't that far off.

Into the forest the seven of them went.

A lot less frustrating than in the dark, the woods seemed calm and peaceful with few dead things. That was in their borders. Everything was alive in their walls. Flowers, animals, even magical looking bunnies hopped around as if they were in a picture book for a preschooler that was afraid of the dark.

As they approached the edges of the clearing, they saw exactly where their territory ended. Dead. Everything from trees to grass was a smoky gray or yellow color like they had been placed in a fireplace. The earth crunched stiffly under Nikki's feet. The wind whistled through her ear like it knew she didn't belong in this place.

She could feel Jake's tenseness. The bow and arrows were still strung across his back. "Don't be so stiff Nikki," Breannen kidded, coming close to her.

"Why don't any of you look suffocated? Doesn't this place give you chills?" Nikki's eyes connected with a corroding tree with a large slit coming to meet the ground off of it.

Nikki jumped. Eyes had appeared in the rotting hole. Large and like pieces of coal, they towered over her from at least ten feet. Breannen sucked in her breath, trying to stay calm. Emaciated fingers that looked like branches, swallowed the sun. Black fingernails at least a foot long came creeping into the light of day. When they hit a sun spot on the grass, the fingers fled into the trunk once again.

A hand grasped Nikki's wrist as the thought of running passed her mind. "Don't be so afraid. It's a wild **scrolt**, not under Colon's order, and won't come out here in the daylight." Jake seemed to enjoy the look displayed on her face. He let go of her hand.

Nikki's heart beat ferociously, she wished she could control her emotions better. "Why can't it come out?"

Kay answered her question. "It doesn't do well in sunlight. Even if it did want to hurt you, you'd have an awfully easy time getting away."

Nikki hurried up a bit, just as the eyes faded back into the darkness of the tree trunk. "She read up a bit while we were at the house," Jake said. *So did I,* Nikki wanted to retort. He wasn't looking at her. She'd never seen him so alert. Jake's eyes traced the pattern of the forest, she could just see the wheels of survival turning inside his head.

Nikki's fear drained away. *I can do this. Does every hero in the stories and real life always feel as afraid as I am? If so, why can we never see it? I wouldn't feel so weak and stupid now, then.*

Her mind must have not been guarded. As she slowed her steps to fall back by Sophie, she heard Sophie whisper, "Everyone here is just as afraid as you are. They're just better at hiding it than you." She said this delicately to let Nikki know she didn't mean it harshly. " Besides, you make everyone else feel like they're not the only ones. And yes, even Jake is afraid. He doesn't want anyone to get hurt either. Something tells me though that he knows we will anyway."

V

The sun soon hung low once again under the skeletal branches of the trees. Hot, sweaty, and extremely dehydrated, Nikki nearly collapsed right on the hard ground when Jake said to make camp before it got too dark.

"I understand," he smiled smoothly, glints of sympathy in his eyes. Jake pulled her back on her feet, and her feet grew wobbly. "You're not used to traveling like this. We'll be sure to take more breaks tomorrow."

James came up to her then and glowered for a while at Jake. He made sure his voice was low when he spoke to Nikki. "I swear, it's inhuman to be able to walk for as long as we have and not feel the slightest ounce of pain. Meaning to say, I think there's something weird with your cousin."

Nikki sighed. "Yeah, I got that message pretty quickly from you."

Jake didn't ask for help. Instead, he told everyone to just sit for a while. He tore his bag off his shoulders and pulled out a delicate looking, elephant-sized material that had slim beams folded under it. In a matter of a few seconds, Jake had magically put together a tent as big as a one story house.

Nikki could sense that James had tightened his lips, slightly jealous of what Jake could do. Annoyed, Nikki knocked into him. "You're turning green with envy. At least you have a gift."

When Jake turned around and smiled at her, she thought he was making fun of James silently. She ran her words through her head and realized that she had just the smallest trace of an accent in her voice. Maybe she was catching on. She thought about that for a second.

The tent was a battered old thing from the outside. On the inside though, it was homey. Nothing too out of the ordinary covered the inside of the tent. Inside they found seven sleeping bags, pillows of numerous amounts, and a small pantry up against the fabric wall.

"Amazing," Michelle smiled, pulling all of the tiredness out of her, replaced with a sincere body of excitement. Nikki was too amazed to speak. She had underestimated how well off they could be in the wilderness. She had never liked wildlife too much anyway.

Enough to want to sleep in it, she thought to herself. Sophie put her hand over her mouth to stop from showing signs of laughter.

"It's probably not what you're used to, but its warm, and well... not crunchy, so..."

"It's brilliant!" Breannen argued, defending the tent that she considered better than her old home in America.

"I'd rather not sleep where creatures of unknown species can crawl all over me anyway," Michelle shuddered.

Shadows of the dead trees crept along the sides of the fabric walls. Darkness had arrived. "Go on," Jake urged, "Get a good rest."

Nikki sat her bag down, watching everyone but herself and Jake grab a thick sleeping bag and pillow and roam aimlessly to a corner. She knew Jake better than this....

Jake set his bag down.

He didn't look like was ready yet to go to sleep.

Nikki read his thoughts without having to. Backing up slowly, she edged farther away from him.

"Oh no, *you're* coming with me." A roguish smile spread across his face.

Jake twirled his sword's sheath between his hand.

"I don't think I'll be able to concentrate while fighting when my legs feel like they've been through a wash machine."

"Are you going to get nervous and feel like your legs are jelly when you're about to fight Colon's soldiers?"

"Probably." Nikki answered truthfully.

"Such an open book. Then let's go. Let's fight. And prepare ourselves for your weak legs." Jake guided her outside of shelter.

Nikki took a deep breath., savoring the gleeful noise of her silver rapier being released.

A sword narrowly missed her arm, instead slamming into a thick, wilting tree a few inches from her

"What the heck do you think you're doing?!" Nikki screamed as Jake struggled to pull his sword from a tree.

Jake rolled his eyes. The trunk freed his saber. "I'll have you know that I missed on purpose."

Nikki eyes narrowed. "Oh yeah, and I'm sure you planned to hit the tree too."

Jake gave a short smirk.

Nikki made the first move. As her sapphire jeweled sword flew, sparks shuttered from their weapons. "You're getting good," Jake muttered through his teeth.

Nikki stayed quiet. She couldn't concentrate when she started talking as she fought. Jake was already pushing the pressure hard on their connection of metal. *How can he do this? Is it that much in his nature to fight that he can talk and still battle with ease and precision?*

She pulled her strength up, bringing a sharp cut towards the force he was pushing. Jake grit his teeth as the tip of the sword clipped his neck. Nikki regretted it until he took his revenge and snipped her shoulder.

Jake gave a half smile as Nikki's face turned to shock.

"That wasn't very nice." She threw her saber at him, clanging reunited itself with the air.

"A cut for a cut," Jake said, wiping a drip of blood with his hand.

"At least mine was an accident!" Nikki hissed.

"At least the one I did isn't near a place that could kill you."

"If you hadn't given some weight up, I wouldn't have cut you."

"I—" A sudden snap in the trees made Jake stop.

"So much for getting along," came a voice.

Nikki swirled around, sword ablaze, to face where the unfamiliar female voice had come from. Two people stood halfway between the trees. A girl with curly brown streaked blond hair and a red leather jacket over an elaborate dress stood with her hands on her hips. A tired man hung around behind her, holding his staff against the coarse ground.

Moving without fear towards them, the young woman walked with grace to where Nikki stood. She took Nikki's hand, shaking it warmly. "You've grown up so beautifully. It's so great to see you again!" Her voice was sweet, cheerful even, and it echoed oddly in the evilness of the woods.

"Again?" Nikki asked, giving Jake a confused glance.

He just grinned.

The man came walking over to them much slower, taking his

steps in even, easy strokes, which reminded Nikki strangely of the way she had taken her sword out. "Allow me to introduce myself and my apprentice who never seems to learn that reveling herself so easily can be a disadvantage of the extremes."

Nikki bit her lip. She wasn't sure if she should smile or be confused. A few more words from the man's mouth in that one sentence, and Nikki would have completely lost whatever he had said. Or meant.

"I'm your pocket-watcher, Garden, and this is my apprentice, Alexandria Selfthryth."

"I'm Elfin, of course," the woman added, much to the restraint of Garden. "But we're not here just for introductions."

"Shouldn't be here at all," Nikki heard Jake mutter. His eyes shifted away from the two figures. He no longer smiled.

What have you got to hide? Nikki wondered, carefully to herself though. She couldn't talk or ask anyone anything though, for at that moment, a thunderous cracking noise came from the other side of the forest.

Jake's hand flew back to his arrows, slithering one into the bow with startling alacrity. Garden was instantly at his side with a swiftness that could only come from without walking.

"Relax, Jacob, no one has followed us, and it is just Alexandria's Faester." Garden relaxed as Jake pulled his arrow back into the cloth pack over his shoulder.

Nikki felt her mouth come ajar, even though she knew that she should be used to the creatures of her world by now. A lean, majestic oddity clomped into the campsite's clearing. Talons grabbed at the ground on its scaly back feet, but in the front, paws with straight sharp nails clawed to them. A lion's tail swung playfully as it fluttered its feather wings, tossing its horse mane in the process. Seemingly tired, the beast slumped into a pile on the grass.

"Is that—" Nikki began.

Alex raced over to her side. A broad grin displayed on her lips.

"He's not a Gryphon nor a Pegasus. With a little of both of those fairy tale breeds that those humans have made-up, he's all **Siphonus**." The woman bent down and stroked the silky mane on Faester's head. "He's the last one of his type though. With all of the persecutions of his breed, he was lucky I was his familiar before he got killed too."

"Alexandria," Garden started, handing out a sharp look. "We didn't just come here to tell them of Faester's tale. We have our business here."

"No, not really," Jake said rudely. He still avoided the mage's eyes.

Alex interrupted Garden's unspoken words, "We do. You have to get to Colon within two days. He already has set up his crowning on All Hollows' Eve. If you don't make it in time,...."

"Halloween?!" Jake cried. His eyes flew into Alexandria's "And you mean he's found a—"

"Yes." Garden stepped in. "Now you must get there." He sent another look at Alex. She shook her head, understanding, and jumped on her strange creature's back. Garden had disappeared in his personal cloud of smoke. Soon, both of the visitors had vanished.

"What was with you?" Nikki asked. She watched Jake's expression try to pull off a confused one. She rolled her eyes. "Yeah, you're not fooling anyone with that look."

"I haven't the faintest idea what you're talking about."

"Then why did you keep looking away from Garden as he talked? Why were you so eager for them to leave?"

He crossed his arms. "Garden has a gift that counteracts Colon's. Colon gift is possession—haven't I told you that?" Jake watched Nikki's eyes widen in the fear she so clearly displayed.

"Anyway... No really Nick, it'll be fine, just trust me okay? At any rate, Garden has this gift that can influence you to do things or say things if you look into his eyes. Mostly, it's only a calming effect. His voice can also have that same ability but not as much. And Garden is practically the only person in the world that Colon doesn't affect.

Which comes in handy sometimes when Garden has to lie for our sake. But once Colon becomes king, it could all change. You and I, we wouldn't be here for very long. And let's just say that this won't be a very pleasant world to live in anyway."

"But what did you mean when Garden interrupted you? About 'He found something?'" Nikki covered her sword with its case, and watched Jake sit down on the brittle grass.

"Look, castle business is complicated. If you don't have to follow one rule of royalty, you have to follow another. Protocol."

"How do you always know so much about things?" Nikki asked in frustration.

Jake shrugged it off, but he wouldn't look into her eyes. "I don't know. But one of the more 'important' rules of The Code of Royalty is that in order to be king... or queen," Jake added after Nikki gave him a accusatory look, "you have to get a mate. Meaning to say, that Colon has found a person to stand by his side basically forever. And if we don't get there in time to stop the coronation, Colon will reign until the world ends, and I mean this quite literally, because he could single-handedly destroy the magical world as we know it!"

Nikki kept her straight face. "You know, that's a lot of pressure to lay on a thirteen-year-old girl's shoulders."

"At least you don't have to go in it alone," Jake reminded her. He had a bitter tone to his voice. As if he had some experience in doing something by himself. Nikki rolled her eyes at the ground. If there was one thing she couldn't stand, it was a guy who felt sorry for himself.

Nikki lifted her head. "Just curious, what is that girl's gift? Alexandria's?"

Jake smiled at the forest floor, picking himself up. "She's a strange one. What she does is turn into a dog or a rabbit. That's it. None of us really understand it."

"Like no one understands your 'nothing' gift?" Nikki knew she was pushing it, but she had let the words slip faster than she could catch them.

To her surprise, Jake just smirked at her with his deep blue eyes. "Yeah something like that."

She shook her head frowning. "You have such a split personality, it's not even funny."

With that, she slung her sword case's leather strap over her shoulder and pushed the flap up the tent to get inside. Leaving Jake, biting his lip and wanting to say something, outside.

Her excited body rebelled against the thoughts of sleep, but her mind was dead and frustrated. Soon, sleep came.

VI

The sound of someone fiddling loudly with something, made Nikki stir. There was no use now, she was awake. *Jake wants me to trust him, and I want him to trust me. But how can I trust him when I know that he keeps hiding things from me?* Her eyes starred into the darkness. When they adjusted, she sighed at the sight.

"What a surprise," Nikki muttered, as she saw Jake stuffing his things in his bag.

She was glad he didn't hear her, that he was on the other side of the tent. James was awake too. His anger and jealousy seemed all but drained out, showing while he nonchalantly talked to Jake. They even laughed a few times.

The two of them seemed to be the only two awake. Nikki wasn't surprised by that either. She sat up, ready to ignore anything that the boys would say or even if they glanced at her. Nikki pulled her hair up.

This is stupid. Deciding to just take the easy way out, she pulled off the sweater she had put on over the shirt her mother had given her. Nikki pushed up the shirt's sleeves.

It was cooler that day. However, with the constant walking, the only thing that would end up being chilled were her exposed ears. She put the cloak Jake had given to her, in her bag.

Twiddling the golden stick that was her wand, she placed the book that Garden had given her in her lap and flipped through the pages.

Although, the sun was barely over the horizon, she read on by a flame she had sent in a little magical orb of glass. "Go on," Nikki heard someone whisper from the other end of the room. She flicked her eyes up from the page.

James was gazing at her sheepishly. Jake nudged him.

Realizing that the voice had come from Jake, she let her eyes fall down again, angrily flicking the page over. *I can't believe James. I'm just a friend. Why can't he see like the rest of us... excluding Jake, that Breannen is madly in love with him. **Not** me. Besides, it's not right for my cousin to be egging my friend on, it's not in his place and* —

"You know, you're lucky that that book has a protection charm on it otherwise I'm pretty sure that you would have burned it to ashes by now." There was a defiant gleam in Jake's eyes as Nikki become conscious of the fact that furious flames licked the impenetrable force field, while her hands gripped the cover tightly.

Either James was smirking, laughing or gawking, although she couldn't tell because he hid his mouth with his hand.

Jake pressed his luck further, "I should be lucky you didn't throw a fire ball at us."

They both burst out laughing.

Nikki threw her book aside and stood up.

"That wasn't nice," Nikki yelled. She ran out of the tent and into the open air.

"Well that's just great." Another of the girls had woken up. Breannen. "You guys are idiots. While you're playing 'matchmaker for James,' Nikki could be out there right now getting ambushed." She looked around. "And what did you do to Kay and Michelle?"

James shrugged. "They were already gone someplace when I woke up. Ask Jake, he's been up for hours."

Breannen's eyes turned towards him, slightly widening as she took in the full blueness. Jake responded, "Kay told me that she was going for a walk with Michelle. There's a creek nearby. Nikki'll probably run into them there."

Breannen got up and brushed herself off. "Well, you can wait here and stay until Sophie wakes up. I'm going after them." She pulled on her worn tennis shoes. With a last look, Breannen threw an livid face at James and the boy who was suppose to be their leader.

VII

The crinkly sound of the grass swept over Nikki as she angrily strolled through the dead looking trees. Somehow, it just annoyed her more. *What am I doing? I'm better at magic and sword fighting, but I still know that I can't hurt anyone.* She ran her hand over the leather case her sword was in.

The silver handle left the cushion of the brown fabric. She loved that sound.

Nikki relaxed her mind, listening to the gurgle of the water nearby. She took a breath of the clean water that filled the air. Her sword was in her hand. Nikki closed her eyes, focusing her anger. Wildly, Nikki swung her body around. A thick branch from one of the shady trees cleanly fell to the forest floor.

Eyes still closed, a smile spread halfway across her face.

"There you are!" a voice behind her yelled. Breannen stomped forward from behind a dead tree. Her eyes caught the sword and the cleanly cut tree branch. "Nice swing."

"Thanks."

"Jake and James can be real jerks. But then again, I haven't known one guy yet who hasn't done at least something jerk-ish."

"And to think that you actually liked Jake," Nikki remarked, remembering Breannen's face when she first saw Jake. "Oh wait, you liked James too." Nikki beamed.

"Shut up," Breannen cried, playfully shoving Nikki.

"Hey, I'm holding a weapon!"

"You'd never hurt anyone."

Nikki looked at the ground. "I know, that's what I'm afraid of."

"Have you seen Kay or Michelle?" Breannen asked, changing the subject, aware that it was sensitive to Nikki.

"No. Why? I thought they were back at camp."

"Well apparently, they went by the creek."

"I can hear it from here. I think it's right over there."

They continued over and under the overflowing trees, few still alive, following the hum of the trickle. "I wonder why so many of the trees are dead? Would that prince, Colon, actually kill these?"

Nikki shrugged. "People get power crazy. It's not just me who's thinking he isn't just crazy though, right?"

Breannen took her turn to shrug. "I mean, if he was so powerful, he wouldn't send his sister to do his work. Unless, he's just a lazy bum."

"Ha ha," Nikki responded sarcastically.

"Why are you so worried? You're great at everything, including your gift."

"Thanks."

They reached the creek's trickling body. Kay was sitting with Michelle on a log, talking. "Hey, what you guys doing?" Breannen called out to them.

Kay just smiled, Michelle waving.

"Find out your gift yet?" Nikki asked as they walked up to their friends.

"No." Michelle kept her face from showing how upset she was. Her voice shook still.

"That's not good, Michelle." They stared at Nikki. "We have to make it there by the end of today, or it will be too late. He'll get crowned, then there's nothing we can do."

"How do you know?" Breannen asked, covering her gaping mouth with her hands.

"Two people who are on our side and are at Colon's castle, told us that in two days, he's going to get crowned. And if we don't stop him before, he'll virtually be unstoppable."

Michelle didn't seem convinced. "Oh come on. How could that guy be that more powerful if there's just a stupid crown on his head? If anything, he'll be so full of himself, he won't even be able to fight!"

Kay shook her head, her fingers placed on her temples. "You don't understand. On All Hallows' Eve, everyone who's magic gets more strength. The more powerful you were to start with, the more powerful you become when it's Halloween. Magic is based on rank unfortunately. If he gets crowned on Halloween, and we bust in, there's no doubt at least one of us would end up dead."

Nikki bit her lip. "We have to get there. Today if possible. It will be hard. And we'll all be real tired. But we have to suck it up; we have no other choice."

Kay shook her head in agreement.

Breannen's grinned in approval. "Spoken like a true leader," she said, knocking Nikki's shoulder.

"Thanks." Nikki felt her face flush. "We better go back to camp. Sophie'll probably be waking up soon."

Michelle nodded once. Her unusual silence had brought questions to Nikki's mind.

They started hiking back to their campsite, the first thing Nikki saw was James standing in front of the tent's flap. He didn't smile at Nikki, his eyes were serious. "Can I talk to you?"

"Sure," Nikki sighed, moving away from the group when James led her towards a leaning black tree.

"Look, I'm sorry for about earlier. I like you—I really do, but—"

"But you know I don't like you like that," Nikki continued when he had paused.

He stared at the crisp ground and shook his head.

"Listen, James, I like you too, but as a friend. There's nothing between us otherwise. It's too dangerous for me to have someone anyways right now." She grabbed his arm when he began to walk away. "But, Breannen is different. You like her and she likes you. *A lot.*"

He opened his mouth to say something.

"I know that you think she likes Jake. Except he'll never...return it, I guess. Trust me, I know him. You have to believe me when I say that she just has a crush on him. You guys are meant to be together."

They stared into each others eyes for a silent minute.

James nodded, a small but sincere smile on his face. Nikki turned and walked back towards the tent. As she came in, Breannen beamed and gave a small wink. "Thank you," she whispered.

"No problem," Nikki murmured back.

Jake's caught her eye once, but she ignored him, annoyed. *Come on Nick, you know I was just trying to help.*

She shot a glare at her. *Help? You call that helping? You have no idea what you were doing, nor did you care that Breannen likes him too, and I have no feelings for him. That's not help. That's irritating and stupid.*

Ouch, Jake said putting on a grimace. *No, I thought that maybe if you just gave him a chance, I didn't realize—*

No, you didn't think, *Jake. You didn't care for one minute that I might actually not want him. That someone else had their eyes on him and I didn't want to get in the way. Honestly Jake, sometimes you can be so like—*

An idiot brother you've never had, I know. I'm sorry.

Nikki looked up from her packing. Her eyes connected with his. *I forgive you.* She looked around the room, making sure that she hadn't missed something.

Sophie caught her eye, wide awake now and staring at her. She had woken a little bit ago, had started packing too. However now, her concentration wasn't anywhere but Nikki's eyes. "How are you doing that?"

Eyes wondered to Sophie and traced her path to Nikki. "Doing what?" Michelle asked.

Jake's face flushed as he realized what Sophie had meant.

Sophie's face was still blank; waiting for Nikki's response. "I thought Jake didn't have a gift. How could he...?"

Jake answered instead. "I don't know how. It kind of just happened. But I know it's not a gift. It's only her, and I know that it sort of drains my energy when I do it, and gifts don't do that. It's some sort of magic."

"I know it drains me too, so it can't be a split gift."

Only Sophie, Jake, and Nikki stood on the warm tent ground unconfused.

"What in the world are you guys talking about?" Kay asked.

Sophie replied, eyes not leaving Jake, "He was talking in her mind and she was answering in his. It was so weird when I could hear them it was like they were talking out loud, but in an echo—because they were both hearing each other. It was strange."

Michelle froze in her packing to look at Nikki and Jake.

Kay smiled. "Yeah it's probably just magic. Knew you two were weird though, so it's not much of a surprise."

Breannen started laughing.

"That's great," Michelle added. A hint of bitterness hid in her vocals.

"Come on," Jake urged. "We have to start a move on if we're ever going to get to the castle before Halloween."

"Why can't we just poof there like with the ocean?" Sophie asked.

"You kind of have to set that up, and agree on both ends where you are going to meet. Plus, I can't do that kind of magic alone. And no, you guys couldn't do it with me either. It still wouldn't be enough. No offense or anything." James smirked at Jake's words.

"None taken," scoffed James.

Soon, they were packed and went outside of the tent. Nikki wondered how Jake was going to fold the tent. Jake's eyes closed, his fingers twitching slightly as a soft purple color flickered between his fingers. The purple outstretched, and left his hand. Color invaded the bottom of the tent and soon, the massive shelter was the size of a matchbox.

"That's crazy magic," Nikki laughed, amazed. "You didn't even use a wand."

"I told you before Nick, wands just help our kind concentrate. The real magic forms when you need it, from you only. Without you, your wands are interestingly found pieces of wood."

The path to where they wanted to go got both more clear and less clear at the same time. Branches of trees didn't swing and catch their twigs of fingers on the group as much as they had, but there was no trail, so the path was stiff and bushes mocked their eagerness to push on.

It was only when the sun lay lazily in the sky and they followed the creek's trail, when something strange appeared in their path. A small, lopsided cottage with a sign posted on its roof, naming it to be the "Berlidge Inn."

Confused, Nikki turned to Jake. Why would he lead them to a castle whose woods held an inn? He just smiled at the brown little thing. She got even more taken aback.

"Nikki," Michelle startlingly began. "I found this necklace on the floor of the tent. Is it yours?" Had she not seen the inn or did she think that it was normal?

Nikki turned to see a necklace that gave not only her, but Jake, a lump in their throats. "Yes. That's mine." Nikki moved closer to Michelle, hand held out for the silver and sapphire necklace. Jake's eyes grew dark.

Michelle's hand wrapped around Nikki's. And at that moment, the world began to turn. An icy wet feeling draped along her arm. Nikki's head turned numb, feeling her fire dim. Her legs trembled and in that split second, try as she might, she couldn't fight the urge. Soon, her eyes went black, and darkness like velvet wrapped around her.

Chapter Ten

White Flags

I

The sun was clear in the room where Nikki's eyes fluttered. She couldn't understand how she would be in a *room*. Was it really all a dream, and she's just back in the world of Ted and Adriana? The room was unfamiliar though. A good sign.

Movement filled the room coming from her left. "Really, how come you always end up the one fainting?"

"I fainted? Why?" Her throat was sore, exposing rough sounds into the air. Nikki tried to get up.

"Well, Michelle got her gift. And it was about one of two things that makes you weaker. See that's the problem with having an element gift. Some are weaker than others and can't cope with the ones who have opposite gifts of them."

"You're confusing me again. Michelle got her magic? And her gift made me faint? I thought it was the necklace, the one you want to smash into a million pieces because you think it's 'bad?'"

Jake rolled his eyes and starred at the girl who was next to him. *Who is* she? Nikki asked Jake.

Jealous much? His eyes didn't leave the girl.

I'm curious, considering I don't know her and you're looking at her like—

"My name is Raisa," the curly headed girl said, extending her hand out for Nikki to shake. Her skin was extremely tan like a piece of caramel. Her long wavy, red hair held two small braids that had two auburn hawk feathers in them, as the rest of the hair swarmed around it.

Nikki took her hand, keeping a small smile on her face. The girl seemed to get the message and blushed. Raisa got up and left the room.

"Where are we?" Nikki asked. She was on a deep red couch.

"We're in Berlidge Inn. Now listen carefully or you might not catch everything." Nikki couldn't tell if he was being sarcastic or not. "Michelle has this water gift and it's hard to explain until you see it. The others are outside trying to teach her up with **enchantment**s..." Nikki couldn't help smirking at his wild accent. "...Raisa's dad works in the castle. It was the only way for them to keep their inn here. She helps her mum work here and believe it or not, they have people who come here more often than you'd think. We're not the first who have tried to stop Colon."

"Just the best," Nikki corrected as Jake helped her up. "Still one more question."

"Of course." That time it was obvious he was being sarcastic.

She ignored his rudeness. "How could Michelle just touch me and I end up fainting? Am I really that weak?"

"No. But when you first get gifts, they're more powerful, not to mention she didn't realize that she was hitting you with a great force of it, and the fact that it's practically Halloween. So no, you're not weak, just vulnerable to a few people's gifts."

"Who else am a vulnerable to?" Nikki cried. Jake was beginning to irritate her. How did he know *everything*?

"Jasmine."

"I'm vulnerable to Jasmine?"

"*No*! Her *gift*, Nikki!" He was obviously getting irritated too. Perhaps, they were all on edge.

"Which would be?"

"You should know this."

Nikki's mind traveled back to the time right before Jasmine disappeared. "Ice," she heard herself say.

"Exactly."

"How do you always know all of this?! I mean you know everything from Jasmine's gift to the fact that Alexandria can do only a little bit of shape shifting."

Jake spewed out more information. "Shape shifting isn't as easy as it sounds though. It's very complicated and takes a complex gift to even allow to turn into one other object. You have to picture your animal or thing perfectly or it'll turn out the way you imagined it— literally."

"Well that sounds like a terrible gift."

"Nah, it's only bad if you can turn into more than two or three things or if you're using magic to turn into something. Don't get me started on how many times people in magic history have made a fool of themselves by accidental transformations."

"Have *you* made a fool of yourself by doing shape shifting? You sound like you're saying all of this from a first hand experience."

Jake blushed. "Once, okay? The other time it was a second hand experience."

"What in the world happened that '*the Jake Sage*' messed up with his **enchantment** work?" Her words were sarcastic, but she knew that if she had said them any other way he would have not told her.

Apparently, Jake had done something extremely terrible. "You of all people are not going to find out." Jake smiled a bit, reassuring her that he was joking.

"I'm still confused. How could Michelle hurt me? And where did Jasmine go?"

"Michelle didn't mean to hurt you! Believe me you, she's already beating herself up for her accident. She never wants to use her gift again. But that's kind of impossible. And I don't know where Jasmine went. Maybe she's more mysterious than you think, or advanced. Either way, it doesn't matter. What really matters is us getting to Colon. Come on, let's go."

Jake pondered something for a moment. "By the way, I don't know how I get to know things, I just do. Maybe it's magic."

"Or maybe—"

"It's not a gift Nikki."

"Maybe you're just in denial."

He gave her a calm, yet fierce glare. "Haven't you just known things? You knew that I was magic when you first saw me. You knew what Jasmine's gift was without her even telling you. You knew that something was going on—"

"Okay! Alright. I get it."

"It's normal for our type to know things to at least some extent. Subconsciously, all of us are using magic, even if we don't know it. It's not a gift."

She was silent. She knew he was right.

They walked out the door of the room they were in. Jake spotted a slightly plump little woman who resembled in her facial features the girl who Jake seemed to like. "Thank you Rhyonnon. We'll pay you back someday"

"Dear, it wasn't that much trouble at all." The woman named Rhyonnon smiled warmly at Jake and let them through as she continued sweeping the floors.

"That was that girl's mother wasn't it?" Nikki asked when they were out of earshot.

Jake sighed. "Her name is Raisa. But yes it was." He continued to have the strange look on his face.

Nikki figured very quickly why the woman was acting so friendly when they were about to go meet their doom. "She doesn't know."

It wasn't a question.

"No."

"Where does she think we're going?"

"To Ruby."

"How could you lie like that?"

"You don't know Raisa's mum, okay? There's no way she would have let me or even you leave to go there if she found out. It's for the better, trust me for once will you?"

It was one of those times when Nikki saw that there was more to Jake than just the retriever and fighter he seemed. He'd had more than experiences, he seemed like he had a life before her. Like he really belonged to something but got sucked into her world just to risk his life for her. And how had she repaid him? For saving her life probably more than once?

She really couldn't think of it.

"I trust you," she finally said after chewing on her thoughts. What was it the look in his eyes that made her feel like he could persuade her to trust him? He just felt like a safe person to be around. Most of the time.

"What?" Jake asked as she continued to stare at him.

"Nothing."

"Then let's go out to the others. They've probably shoved enough information into Michelle by now." Jake led Nikki put into the perfect green lawn.

"Wow." It was all she could say. Every area they had been traveling on except the wide circle the inn was on, had been barren.

"Amazing how different just being evil can be, huh?" Jake walked beyond the green circle, and behind the cottage. It wasn't a surprise to Nikki at all that Raisa was there too. At least her other friends were out back as well.

Nikki couldn't decide how old Raisa was. Right when she looked about a year younger than Jake, she seemed to get so serious that it would be impossible to guess that she wasn't Jake's age. No wonder he liked her. She had the same split personality.

"Michelle will be a bit hesitant, but you should be alert as well. Let's practice before we leave."

"Does Raisa know that you're leaving?"

"Are you jealous?"

Nikki thought about it. Maybe she was. It didn't feel like jealousy. Just brooding anger that a girl like Raisa should have to know everything.

"I'm not jealous."

Jake didn't say anything.

I want to read his thoughts so bad but I'm pretty sure he'll need to be as strong as he can when we get to the castle. Besides, if Raisa and her gift of whatever figure out that I'm draining Jake's energy, she'd probably kill me. And it'd be just like Jake to let her. Okay, so maybe I am a little jealous. But why would I be? Jake's the most annoying, parent-like person I've ever met. I should be happy he's stopped caring about me for once.

Kay was the first to see her coming. Of course, her back was turned and she was fighting James in a friendly duel. "Nikki!"

"Huh?" James stumbled, his "**enchantment**" flying into a dead tree. He spotted Nikki, smiling sheepishly at his dense mistake.

"Hiah!" Breannen welcomed Nikki as she threw a spell that narrowly missed Sophie.

"Oh, we have so much work to do…" Jake muttered, running his hand through his hair.

"Don't think you realize it but Sophie was **reflecting**. That's why Breannen missed, Jake." Kay gave Jake a small smile.

Nikki only shook her head amazed at him. "Really? You'd give up on us that fast?"

She saw his face turn ashamed.

"Where's Michelle at?" Nikki asked.

He was thankful she was so forgiving. "Working with Raisa. And I wouldn't go over there right now."

"Why? Afraid I might rip your girlfriend's head off?"

Jake looked surprised. "No. I just thought that Michelle feel a little bit uncomfortable with you right now."

Nikki felt her face grow warm, and although it felt good, she disgracefully mumbled, "Oh."

"Now I really think you're jealous."

"Put your magic where your mouth is, and we'll see who you think is jealous then." Nikki flipped out her wand, watching Jake do the same. How interesting it was to see the curious expression that Raisa gave him when she had realized they were going to duel each other.

Nikki was interested to see how this would turn out as well.

II

By now, Nikki wasn't afraid of anything Jake threw at her. The old her was lost somewhere back in America. She knew she belonged here now, and as uncomfortable as it seemed to make Jake, she beat him too easy because of his unwillingness to hurt her.

It might be a little different now that Raisa was watching.

They positioned themselves within ten feet of each other.

A red light raced towards her.

Nikki leapt out of the way.

"Trying to impress someone? Or are you just taking frustration out?" Nikki called, sending a short line of flames dancing towards him from an outstretched hand.

"Neither," he lied. He pulled his wand sharply to the side, making the flames brush off into ciders onto the grass. "You like playing with fire too much," Jake scoffed.

"Hope you like light better." A thin stream of blue flared from her wand tip.

"Not by much." Jake sent another red light after her.

Much like the effect of little fireworks, the two lights crashed. Little sparks flew towards each of them.

"Oh, come on. How are you suppose to fight Colon when you can't even touch me? Give me your best shot."

Jake gave her expression reading something along the lines of, "Do you really want to see what I can do?" He sent a thick white blob of luminosity towards her.

Taken back, Nikki sent a defensive streak hurtling in the air.

As the two clashed, thin smoke flew.

The white **enchantment** still dashed forward.

"No way," Nikki heard herself gasp.

Her hands twitched with anticipation.

As fast as she could, she slipped her wand in her pocket. She would need two hands for this. Heavy tongues of fire burst from her palms. If she hadn't been caring, she wouldn't have seen Raisa's shocked expression.

It was Nikki's turn to stand amazed.

The white **enchantment** passed though the flames as if they were nothing but a sheet of air.

They were both left with the aftermath.

The speedy blaze hit Jake first. Guilt took her as she saw his unexpected figure fly backwards and land with a crash onto the ground. He didn't get up after the ground met his face.

Nikki didn't have time to think. The white glob hit her and she felt her body spin and crash into the ground.

She could feel her leg snap. Broken. But not for long. James came running to her, smiling as he placed his hand on her leg. She could feel a thin gash on her face disappear as well. "Thank you," she said. He put out a hand to help her up.

Nikki got up. As soon as she had though, she booked it towards the spot where Jake was lying. She had seen him fake being hurt, when he had jumped off of her balcony. He wasn't faking it. He hadn't moved. His face lay smooth on the ground. His eyes were closed. Part of his face was covered in smoke and ash. His hands and arms were blistered as far as there was skin.

Nikki rolled him over until he faced him.

"Jake?!" she squealed. "Come on, wake up! My gosh, my gosh! James!"

James came running. Tears were already spilled out of her eyes. "Do something!" she begged.

James placed his hand on Jake's limp shoulder. They blisters were soon gone. He was still unconscious. "Don't do this to me, Jacob!" Kay tried to hold her back. Nikki flew on top of him. She threw a hard slap on his face.

"That's not going to help anything," Breannen cried.

His eyes fluttered.

Jake slowly got up to see Nikki's tear stricken face. "Why are you crying? If I did that all the times you fainted, there's no way we'd be able to beat Colon."

She threw her arms around his neck.

Realization hit her. She tore her arms away and punched him in the shoulder as hard as she could. "I hate you!"

Sophie rolled her eyes. "Oh yeah, we can all tell that by the tears on your face. Honestly, you'd think you two were a couple."

Raisa raised one of her eyebrows at her.

"They're cousins," James assured as if he was glad himself that they were.

Nikki jumped up, angrily wiping her pathetic tears from her cheeks. "I'm serious. I hate you Jacob. Right when I start to hate you, you make something happen, and then I feel all guilty."

Jake smirked at her. "That's the beauty of family, Nick. But seriously, we need to leave now."

"Now?" Michelle asked. "You just fainted and now you want to rampage a castle?"

Jake got up too. "We don't have a choice. Besides, I'm fine, just a little shaken."

Nikki's arms were crossed. The confidence she once had was now nothing. She didn't believe that she couldn't beat Colon, only that she couldn't control herself if something went wrong. Whose job was it to deal with Colon? It now more than ever seemed like the easiest job in the world.

"We can do it." Was that her saying that?

Jake smiled at her. "If you can hurt me, you can hurt anyone."

III

Michelle didn't feel very strong. Nikki knew that Michelle probably felt like if anyone would hold up their operation and ruin it, it would be her. But Jake and Nikki both knew that it wasn't going to be Michelle that would be the problem.

Would it be Jake, who was already weak from their battle? Or would it be Nikki who knew that she couldn't hurt anyone too badly on purpose? The war between the two had ended. They both shared the similar feeling of defeat before the they had even entered the battle field.

They could hear the crunch of their feet echo along the hallow trees, and the final question came to them. It wasn't how they were going to get there. It was what they were going to do when they got there.

Nikki could feel the wheels of thought turning inside Jake's head as she walked beside him. There was nothing on anybody's shoulders, or hands, or even belts beside their weapons. They had left it at the inn, expecting to be back soon.

Finally, the little light bulb went off.

Jake had it.

"Alright, listen up," Jake started as they continued to walk. "This is what we'll do. When we arrive, if we haven't already spotted us, Michelle will distract the guards that will be standing out for watch. Don't make this plan permanent though, most likely, they *will* be expecting us. The rest of us will sneak in and when Michelle is sufficiently finished, she'll follow."

Michelle shook her head. "How on earth do you think that I'll be able to distract the guards?"

"You won't distract them—you'll get rid of them. Michelle, you'll have to get over the fact that your gift can hurt people sooner or later. Right now, we really need everyone. Even you." Jake seemed to be in the mood for motivational speeches.

"Do anything you can," Nikki encouraged. "It doesn't matter what you do, just get them out of the way. You'll be the strongest of all of us because you just got your gift. We need you."

"Besides," Kay started, "if you don't use your gift, then your body can't cope and you'll end up crazy."

"What?!" Michelle squealed.

The rest of the group, although quite shaken at the thought, were not surprised to hear her say something they didn't know.

"She's right," Jake agreed.

"That's awful!" declared James. "What if you have a real dreadful gift you'd have to—"

"Use it anyway, yes." Jake didn't look too pleased about the thought.

"Least you don't have to worry 'bout it at all, Jake." Breannen was the only one cheerful about attacking the castle.

There was an opening to the forest several yards in front of them. The battle would begin soon.

A twig cracked above them.

"Shush," Jake hushed to them.

They all spun in different directions, wands ready to attack. Nikki's eyes flew to the trees above her. A glassy gray eye caught her full in her view. "Jake," Nikki hissed between her clenched teeth.

Jake slowly turned towards her.

"Isn't that that Valla bird?" she whispered.

"I think they know we're here," Sophie murmured.

"What makes you think that?" James asked. The others still hadn't noticed the bird and its hideous features.

Nikki looked around the bird and saw the moving capes and bodies of people rushing towards them through the opening of the dead forest. Jake's eyes followed Kay's eye stream and widened.

"Listen to me," Jake said as calmly as he could, "on the count of three, start running. The opening will be big enough if we go together and quickly."

"Where?!" Michelle screeched as quietly as she could.

"In that direction," Jake pointed his wand slightly in front of him. "Don't stop."

"Why on the count of three? We're wasting time counting!" Nikki began to ask.

Just at that moment, a person with a scarf draped over their mouth flew from the trees above and landed behind them. "Three!" Jake yelled.

They all took off.

Brambles and traces of dead roots and branches scratched their feet. It seemed like they never had to run in a place where something wouldn't hurt them.

"I don't know if you know this," Nikki gasped angrily, as she clambered over a tall root, "but one and two generally come before three."

Jake didn't answer, his breath heavy. His eyes were glued straight forward, as if he were begging the ground to move faster under his feet.

There was no time to slip up. Breannen, Sophie and Kay were neck and neck with each others' speed. James was slightly in front of them, while Michelle was the opposite. Jake and Nikki were leading each other.

"Don't worry too much… We're almost there." Jake jumped high over a thick patch of wet grass that had been pleading him to slip.

What would happen next though? We have no choice. There's guards behind us, and guards in front of us. There's not a chance of us keeping to plan.

Without hearing her, Jake seemed to be thinking the exact same thing.

For the most part, the grass was dry and crunchy. When the atmosphere changed and the grass became suddenly tall and slippery, they had no say in the fact that they stumbled forward and toppled to the ground.

Nikki sprang up. She was wrong to have thought that her home was a castle after all. A beautiful yet threatening black fortress stood proudly before them. Her house was large. But by no means the size of this.

"There's no time for admiration!" Jake shouted at her.

A line of people had formed behind them.

"Go!" Kay shouted.

Before any of them could move from their frozen stance, more watchmen came pouring out of the palace entrance towards them. Scarlet, more bruised and scared than the last time they had seen her, was among them.

"Do *something*," Jake hollered, whipping out his wand and sending a sharp white flare towards a group of guards. "Most of them aren't going to be as powerful as us."

Nikki sent a red blaze of fire out of her palm to draw some of the attention from Jake away. Kay, James, Sophie, and Breannen quickly followed her lead.

Michelle was still frozen on the spot. "Come on Michelle," James called out, annoyed. He lay a swift punch into the man who was attacking him.

She finally snapped out of it. By then, it was too late.

A rough looking guard held a sword to her throat while roughly tying her hands together.

"No!" Breannen yelped, soaring across the battle field. A smart looking spell hit the watchman square in the chest.

The ropes half on Michelle's wrists slid off.

Michelle began to act.

Kay attacked a thin tall woman with a wand herself. When the unthinkable happened. The guard brutally grabbed hold of her arm, twisting her until Kay's back faced the woman. Her wand dropped.

"**Malonanecra**," the woman whispered.

Jake's head shot up. "No," his voice rang in Nikki's head. A purple light ran over Kay's body and her form crumpled to the ground.

Nikki saw Jake charge at the woman, full force slicing out his sword. The guard drew out her own saber, tossing it delicately along his. His face was hard, and his endless clashing against her weapon with that force hit Nikki hard. Nikki looked at Jake, not seeing Kay.

She knew something was wrong.

Realization hit her as she saw Kay's crumpled form.

Jake had the woman, sword at throat.

A thick slice of boomerang-like wind shot at her, and, unconscious, she fell to the ground. Nikki came running up to him, her hand still raised.

"You know what she did...?" His voice shook hard. Whether from adrenaline or fear, she couldn't tell.

Nikki nodded, tears betraying her vision.

Her throat was tight.

"Give in. Let them take us in. We don't have enough to lose another. They'll bind us with ropes, but we'll get away. And we'll be inside."

Nikki nodded again, thrusting her wand in her pocket. Would they search for it? Probably. Sophie read her thoughts.

"Stop," she whispered to James and Breannen. "Let them take us." She bit her lip. "Kay's been murdered."

Michelle followed them, willing to give up on her losing fight.

Scarlet eyed Jake suspiciously. Jake wasn't one to give up this easily.

A man was about to attack him.

"No!" The red head's voice ran loud and clear over the grass. "He's going with me." Scarlet raced down the grassy path towards

Nikki and Jake. "Giving up so soon, Jacob. Or does it just feel odd knowing that at least one of you won't be making it out of here alive?"

Jake held his silence.

She thrust his hands behind his back, constricting them. *Don't worry 'bout me, alright?* His voice called out to Nikki in her thoughts. Scarlet left the group while she half pulled, half dragged Jake into a different tunnel away from them. "Don't worry, Jacob," Scarlet growled. "Your little friends'll be fine as long as you behave." Scarlet turned towards a watchman, "Bind the rest." Jake and Scarlet disappeared into the chained tunnel door.

The yellow toothed guard that had fallen unconscious before, pulled Nikki's hands roughly behind her back as the other guards tied the rest of the group.

James wasn't as willing to give up. He thrust himself in opposite directions until the guard that was suppose to be tying him, gave in.

"Ah let me deal with it, you great lump," the yellow toothed watchman yelled, pushing the scrawny guard aside. Deep in his pocket, he pulled out a thin bottle of something. "Just picked up this 'ittle beauty from Garden's private stash this morning."

He uncorked the bottle draping his arm back and forth in front of James's face. James's eyes widened a second then he crumpled fell to the floor. "Go on then solider, round 'im up."

"No!" Nikki yelled. She feared James was dead too. Although she didn't think they would bind him if he was dead.

The guard tied his hands, and the rough one Nikki up by her bound hands. She struggled slightly. "Easy girly, you wouldn't want to end up like your 'ittle friend would ja?" She wasn't sure which friend the guard was referring to.

Soon the five of them were being dragged into another black steal door, carrying them farther and farther until the light of day seemed to have never existed. Her last view of the outside was of Kay's abandoned body.

The world around them was then gone.

IV

Scarlet threw Jake's body onto a cold slab of stone in the middle of the dim room.

"Don't you hate it sometimes that your parents put a **curse** on you to protect her? That you have no free will to say that her life goes before yours? What would your parents say now that they've realized that this task was far too hard for their Jacob to handle? I'm sure the girl's mother already figured that out when her nephew couldn't even think out how to get her daughter home at first."

"You shut it about my parents! They have nothing to do with you Scarlet."

"Oh that's right Jacob, you stand up for the dead. Soon you'll be standing up for more than just two. Tell me, was it her parents or your idiot parents that wanted to make sure you died before her?"

"Shut it Scarlet!"

"Or what Jacob? You have no wand." She fingered his stick between her fingers. "You don't have a gift. You're hands are bound with magic concealed ropes. No weapon. No family. You're nothing. How do you know she's not already dead?"

"I would know," Jake growled.

"How lovely. Colon will have fun with you. For now though," she bonded his roped hands to the table as if they were glued with his wand, "I think I'll pay a little visit to your girly. Nicole, is it? I hope you realized you never stood a chance."

"I'll stand a chance as long as I'm alive!"

"Don't you realize where you are!" Scarlet demanded. "It's over! You're *dead* already."

She left Jake.

Her mission had finally been accomplished.

V

The five of the others were thrown into a stone room with the chained door shut closely behind them. The ceiling was paneled with black, faded ropes.

"That didn't go well." Breannen had a heavy look of defeat on her face.

"Don't worry. I have a plan. But it'll only work if—"

The door came flying open. The red headed figure of Scarlet danced towards them.

She entered their cell, smile broadly on her face. "That was much easier than I would have hoped. All that trouble trying to capture you, and you walk right into our hands?"

Nikki glared at her, the only one to look her full in the face.

"I see that look of defeat on your faces. It should be worn more proudly, after all, you did make it into the castle." Scarlet laughed.

She traced her fingers around James's jaw line.

"You're a healer," Scarlet said, softer than Nikki had ever heard or thought possible for her voice to make.

James said nothing.

"It strikes me as odd how some of you have such powerful gifts. Yet you use them in such mediocre ways."

Still, no one said anything.

Realizing that she couldn't get a rise out of any of them she said, "Not a single one of you is to move, or that'll be four of you that might make it out of here."

Nikki recognized Jake's wand twiddling in her fingers. Her heart sank. None of the others had their wands either. Sticks poked out of Scarlet's pocket. *She* had their wands.

Sophie, listen to me, Nikki said in her mind. *I'm going to edge near Scarlet's pocket while she looks the other way. Distract her in some way that won't make her do something to you.*

Sophie didn't respond, only looked at Nikki quickly.

Her eyes flew up to the ceiling. Scarlet caught her gaze.

"What are you looking at?" she demanded. She stuffed Jake's wand against the other wood pieces in her pocket.

"Oh nothing," Sophie dragged on, giving enough time for Nikki to burn off the ropes that bound her hands. She knew as soon as the guards had tired her hands that the rope she had been given wasn't binding her magic. They weren't suppose to break free without Jake's signal, but Nikki feared the worst. Sophie looked at Scarlet. "It's just I thought the ropes on the ceiling were burning."

Nikki threw a skeptical look at her. It was lucky that just at that moment James woke from his slight comma from the rough soldier's bottle. His legs banged hard against the wall as he stirred, practically yelling as he woke.

Scarlet's gaze was directed towards the other side of the room where he was.

This gave Nikki just the right amount of time to throw a small flame at the ropes Sophie was looking at and thrust her hands behind her back again before Scarlet realized that they were untied.

Scarlet jumped a bit as she saw the flame spread.

Nikki's hands released the smallest amount of flames towards her ropes binding her legs. They cindered to a braking point.

Nikki lurched forward snatching not only her wand but everyone else's out of Scarlet's pocket. She grabbed the rails of the door and pried it open. "No!" Scarlet screeched. She grabbed Nikki's wrist.

Nikki sent flames up her arm.

Scarlet let go, as Breannen swung her legs and tripped her.

With a slam, Scarlet lost her grace and fell to the cold stone ground.

Nikki looked back once, at her friends. She slipped their wands through the bars. Their faces were determined and encouraging.

They'd take care of themselves.

She rushed out of the cell. Escaping into the castle.

VI

Jake struggled with the binding straps over his wrist. The soft glint of his and his cousin's swords peaked out of their leather casings and caught his eyes. They were thrown carelessly on two hooks near the room's entrance.

Come on, Jake, you're magic. Without your wand you are not useless. You've been telling Nikki that all month. Break through the stupid dang **enchantment**.

When he heard a sharp, "*Pink*," his head filled with involuntarily thoughts of freedom. They were crushed almost instantly. Before he had even the chance to move, the broken chain and ropes binding him made a crisp, "Slick!" No doubt were the binding magical clasps at least twice as strong as they were before.

Jake swore under his breath.

The first try to undo them already left him feeling light headed with pain. *How cliché-ish of Scarlet to use a charm that binds the ropes together again. Just my luck, it'd take something both sharp and magical to break them. Good guys aren't suppose to have this kind of trouble when they're in danger, are they?*

There was no time to think. It was only a matter of time before death had finally caught up to him. He could hear the slap of footsteps race down the hall towards the only door that was near.

The one that led to the room he was in.

VII

"I see three of you where's the other?" The snarling voice of Scarlet made Sophie, Michelle, and James jump. She couldn't let another person escape.

The red headed woman's attention had been drawn from the flame she had extinguished when Nikki had escaped. Now she couldn't find the short blond one.

"Here I am."

Scarlet swung around.

Just as her face caught in Breannen's outstretched, and flying, fists—her hands were still tied together.

Scarlet crumpled to the ground, knocked out cold.

"Man," Breannen sighed, "'Been wanting to do that since that evil cow got in here. Now then, is there anyway you guys can think of to get out of these ropes? The stupid guards apparently thought that only Jake would need magical ones."

James grinned. "Really I never understood why they took our wands away from us. I mean, honestly, they should know by now that people don't need wands to make magic."

He trained his eyes down to his palms for a second. With a sharp sound that filled the air, James pulled his freed hands forward revealing the rope in his hands. The girls beamed back at him.

"Let's just hope Nikki is going to be as well as we will," Sophie said, binding Scarlet tightly with her own ropes. They knew as soon as she woke up, she'd be able to get free. It would hold her off for a second longer though. And who knew how much that second would be worth it.

VIII

Nikki's footsteps followed the pattern of her tears on her face. Continuous. Deadly. What would Jake say to her now? What would her father or mother say if they could? Crying over the dead, something which could not be taken back. Kay's death had finally hit her heart.

Her heart hammered. She kept her wand by her side, wishing her other hand held the weapon of her sword. She had no idea where that was, having been ruthlessly torn into the castle and stripped of her weapons. Being lost in the castle probably wouldn't be the best way to start her rescue task. Nothing would or could stop her from completing her mission now. She couldn't fail.

The path she traveled was wide and barren. No one yet had gotten in her way. She liked it better that way. No one to hurt. It was raining hard outside. *Strange,* she thought, *It didn't look that cloudy out when we were out there.* The sky had been threatening rain for a few days now. Perhaps her mind had just been somewhere else whenever she looked at the sky. Yet, the rain seemed to motivate her beyond anything else.

Her path soon led to a gold painted door, arched slightly to bend to the wall's curve. It was then that she realized how loud her steps had sounded. Thunderous compared to the ticking of rain on the window.

Nikki's eyes flew to the doorknob-sized lock.

Too simple.

She didn't trust a regular **enchantment** to unlock the door. Instead, she sent her gift into the key hole. The flames slithered itself inside the hole in the security device, wrapping itself within the workings.

A satisfying click.

As she entered the room, she was looking into the worn eyes of Jake.

He could see the look in her eyes shine clear. "I'm afraid, I'm afraid!" they screamed. He wanted to smile. To show her that he knew that she was afraid and that she was not the bravest type, but that was okay, she was brave enough. He didn't think he could bear to lie to her at this moment. He was afraid she'd see the leaks in his smile.

She bit her lip in hesitation, her eyes wondering along the sides of the wall. "Swords...?" her voice trailed off.

"Won't work on these cuffs," Jake finished. His eyes were glued to the enchanted chains that tied his wrists and ankles.

"Why not?"

"Only something that is remarkably sharp and magical will most likely cut them at least long enough for me to move so we can get out of here."

"Right." Nikki was slightly amazed that even when they were in the pit of doom, Jake seemed to have enough breath and nerve to structure a huge sentence.

While she thought quietly to herself, a thought bashed into her head. Nikki reached inside her pocket and pulled out the jagged, almost glass-like object she had found in Ted's room.

"That's—"

"A thought you dug up yourself. The thing Jasmine gave me. I still don't understand it at all though; why would she give it to me? It looks exactly like a scale from Scarlet's dragon."

"Probably found it and just gave it to you to cut yourself like you ended up accidentally doing. And they're not exactly dragons you know," Jake started grinding his teeth when the chains constricted his circulation. "Regular dragons can't talk to you. Colon, without a doubt, would have trained them special. Mixed breeds, they are."

Nikki rolled her eyes. "I'm not even sure it's magic though."

"Loose ends and 'what ifs' really aren't going to help right now. How will you find out if you don't try?"

Nikki nodded. She closely bent down to Jake and grasped one of his wrists with one hand while her other hand began to lower down the glittering scale to the surface of the chains.

It took one slice for his right hand. Whether or not it was the fact that the scale was magically spell bound, Nikki had forced down a tight amount of pressure when she had cut. On the opposite side of the scale, a jagged edge caught her skin, and blood raced to meet the scar that had been healed by James from the same piece of glass-scale. The scar that she gave herself when she had fell off the swivel chair, reaching for the package she thought was her broom.

She ground her teeth from the pain, moving onto the next chain. So much had changed since that day.

The feet were the hardest. A thicker metal adjoined both of Jake's ankles. She made a face at his appalling looking trainers. His shoes were disgusting.

"Will you pay attention to where you're cutting!" Jake snapped.

"Sorry," she numbly mumbled.

Her heart pound furiously. The cut in her palm had become some what of a deep gash. "Here," Jake said, rubbing his wrist where she had grazed him accidentally. He cradled her hand for a moment, eyes squinting down harshly at the spot where blood gently gushed.

The flow stopped abruptly. Slowly, but definitely efficiently, the wound faded until about a minute later, it was nothing but a fine white lined mark. "Thanks. Which reminds me, here's your wand. Doesn't look like you need it much though."

"You'd be shocked." Jake gave a small, worn smile.

They stood there for a moment. The rain pinged louder than ever.

Nikki opened her mouth to speak.

But the door flew open.

"Knew I'd find you here." Scarlet, looking more sinister than ever, leaned against the side of the doorframe with a look of malevolent. "Sweet girly coming to the rescue. All I wonder is how you got him untied." A large seeping gash was cut on the side of her cheek. It had the same kind of look as a rope burn...

With a final slash, Nikki cut Jake's feet bind.

"With this," Nikki spat, drawing the glass-scale.

Scarlet's wide smile fizzled. "How do you have that?"

"I take it that it's important?" Jake pressed. "I just thought it was off your dragon."

"You have no ides the power that radiates from one of the beast's scales. There's only one person whom I gave that to. Hand it over you stupid girl."

Nikki had edged towards the wall all the while. "Don't think I will, thanks." She pulled the sword off the wall. Sliding the glinting scale in her pocket again, Nikki grasped the sword firmly between her two hands.

"Don't be thick now, girl. Jacob might just have to rescue you."

Scarlet slickly pulled one of the bulkiest swords Nikki had ever seen from a metal casing that was strapped to her back. "Afraid yet? Or are you just waiting for Jacob to step in?"

"I can take you myself," Nikki growled, lowering the sword so it pointed directly at Scarlet.

"Spectacular. Because your dear cousin will have to worry about the guards that followed me."

As she spoke, two things happened.

Jake flew towards his sword.

And three watchmen swung the door roughly aside.

Slightly diverted, Nikki barely noticed Scarlet's medieval saber swing savagely towards her middle.

She jumped back. The sword swung air, clipping nothing but the stone ground.

The guards charged towards Jake who had barely even got a steady grip on his rapier handle. The younger guard took a would-be futile strike, had he not tripped on a broken piece of chain.

His sword plunged into the stone table easily; no doubt made of onyx.

Jake twirled his weapon with grace, while a man jeered at him to attack. Jake took the call. The sword spun to scrape the man's middle.

But no blood came.

Instead, the sword ran right through the guards body as if he were not even there. "Surprised, eh?" the yellow toothed man mocked.

Jake's face when he had first seen his sword go through exposed his shocked eyes. Now his face was again hard. He pulled out his thin wand.

The guard stopped laughing.

"Don't be afraid of the magic 'e can do," said a guard next to the one Jake was going to send an **enchantment** at.

"That's right," Scarlet snapped, gritting her teeth as she put all the pressure she could on her sword that was locked with Nikki's. Nikki's footwork was too sturdy. "He couldn't hurt you if he wanted to."

Jake seemed deaf to their words. Nikki was too preoccupied to see any look on his face. Somehow, they had managed to get outside of the room Jake had been held in.

He shot a powerful **enchantment** towards a set of guards. They fell to the ground unmoving.

Scarlet turned towards him in shock.

While Nikki took the surprisingly poor sword fighter Scarlet to herself, Jake took on more than ten men and women together. More guards had joined the first few once they heard there were loose captives.

"You're as weak as your dear cousin Jacob, girl," Scarlet sneered.

"Look who's talking. Don't see you swinging a heavy blow towards my way either." Nikki gave Scarlet the same look the red head had given her.

Scarlet threw a loosely gripped swerve.

Nikki easily matched the strength of the weak attack, delicately swinging her sword in a small, vigorous circle.

Scarlet's weapon broke free of her hand, sending the saber crashing to the floor. Nikki drew her sword close, pinning the red head to the bricks.

Scarlet smiled.

Her body faded into the wall leaving nothing but a small faint black fog.

"What the bloody—?" Nikki began.

"Happens! Effects of the necklace! Little help here would be brilliant of course, or if you'd just rather enjoy the show—?" Jake gave a low blow to one of the figures that dissolved as his blade went through him.

Swearing loudly at his luck, Jake sent instead a silver light towards the man. The watchman flew backwards, and, to Nikki's disbelief, Jake also slammed into the wall behind him as if the spell had had some sort of an aftereffect.

"Come on, you ruddy well do something, Nick!"

Nikki opened her mouth to retort back to Jake's comment when a sudden burst of noise literally shattered her thoughts.

The building storm outside exploded against the windows.

The panes gave way reluctantly, and glass from the enormous windows splintered, littering shards on every square inch of the floor. Nikki felt her hands automatically shoot up to her face.

The awful sound of glass hitting others' fleshy tissue soon filled the storming night. The wind howled mightily and rain began to creep in by the buckets. Apparently some of the watchmen weren't **shadows**.

Jake still found the voice to roar over the weather. "SOMETHING A LITTLE LESS OUTSIDE WOULD BE A BIT MORE OF A HELP!"

Nikki shot him a filthy look. "OH, AS IF THAT WERE ME!" She drew her sword closer to herself as about ten men and women watchmen ran at her.

She shot out her arm, catching what would be one man's stomach. Just as Jake had done a little while ago, the sword plundered through the man as if he were common smoke. Of course he had to be a **shadow**.

He grabbed her sword hand.

Twisting her around, he caught her by the neck, her arm still in his grasp. His silver dagger cut delicately into her throat.

Gasping for air under the man's tight constriction, Nikki groped desperately for her pant pocket that held her wand. A sudden sickening feeling filled her. Was she always this stupid?

With the hand she had been using for searching, she grabbed at the guard's knife hand. Her brow furrowed in frustration; and a wild purple and orange flames illuminated the hallway.

The man holding her released. She could hear his footsteps back away, fallowed by several others. When Nikki opened her eyes, she found herself on the floor. **Shadows** apparently couldn't take the heat.

IX

"You 'kay?" Jake asked. He was tending to his scorched shirt sleeves but other than that, he seemed fine. He stopped to help her up. Catching her wondering glance he said in a matter-of-factly way, "Bit more prepared that time, is all."

"What was with those people? So afraid of fire yet swords went right through them?"

"Only some," Jake corrected. "I think you figured out that they were the **shadows**. They aren't structured like us. Like humans. They have structures of air so that ordinary objects can't strike, and often receive upper hand in man to man battle. Quiet especially with those who can use nothing but objects."

"Yeah," Nikki agreed with a shake of her head, reminding her that Jake was better with weapons of no magical powers. For probably the second time, she felt sorry that Jake still had energy taken when he used magic and had no way of receiving it because he had no gift.

It seemed to suck in the ripest moments.

Chapter Eleven

Fighting Instinct

I

"We need to keep going. Judging on the fact that Scarlet came after us, I suspect that the rest of our group got away. Perhaps they're even outside waiting—?" Jake trailed off, not sure what he was getting at.

"So what are we going to do?" Nikki asked. She kept up with the brisk walk, that Jake had begun right after the **shadow** guards had vanished. She was afraid they would come back.

"Surely you don't expect me and you just to leave? We came this far, we have to finish our job."

This made Nikki want to shudder. Why was Jake so keen to complete their horrendous task? His face was stone. "What's with you?" she finally demanded, grabbing hold of his shoulder.

"Listen to me, we'll never get another option, there's no turning back or it's your death we're talking about."

"And yours," Nikki added quietly. She liked it better when Jake wasn't so serious.

Jake nodded a moment later as if he had to think about whether or not he cared about being murdered. She could feel her heart start to race as they ran further.

"Oi! Nikki. Relax, alright?"

"You've got nerve to tell me that when you're the one who's shaking." Nikki could tell by his voice that he was just as scared as she was.

Jake didn't respond to this. "Follow me. It won't be much fun if we run into more guards, eh?"

Nikki began to go alongside him again.

The storm that had crept up on them was getting worse by every wasted second. Every once and a while a new window would break sending their already scathed hands flying to their faces again and again. Beyond that, most of the glass that had already caved in to the bend of the wind was allowing rain to seep through in impossible quantities. Everywhere they walked, the carpet seeped water up to their ankles.

Running wasn't too bad until they reached the edge of the carpet.

The whole tile floor was flooded. One wrong step and you'd land on your backside. Mist swirled around them as they teetered on the balls of their feet. In her frustration of her hair getting in her eyes, Nikki pulled the tie that held her hair up in a crazy crumpled bun. Her hair immediately fell limp with the amount of saturation it held. Her vision became slightly clearer than it had been when her hair was flying wildly.

"YOU DO KNOW WHERE YOU'RE GOING, RIGHT?" Nikki hollered over the scream of wind. The wind had died down for the while that they had just argued.

"YEAH... SORTA!"

When Nikki gave him a look that said something like 'what-the-heck-do-you-think-you're-doing-if-you-don't-know-your-way-around-the-castle,' he gave her back a look that made her keep her mouth shut.

They passed a narrow pathway just to come to another dead end. A staircase that led up and up in a spiral motion and made Nikki's eyes swim when she tried to look up at it, made her stop and demand an explanation for why they wouldn't go up it.

"Colon likes traps," Jake explained, as if he knew this because he had just gotten through with a pleasant chat with Colon himself, explaining how he set up little tricks just to mess with them.

Nikki knew by now that it was best not to comment.

"You know how when you watch movies on the box—"

Nikki presumed he meant the television.

"—that have 'scary' or 'haunted' castles in them, whenever the person who is not welcome in the castle tries to wonder up a spiral staircase, of course it folds in and buckles underneath their feet. I'm positive that Colon would think it would be a real laugh to see that happen to one of his enemies. Mental, his is."

"Riiight," Nikki said, making sure that she emphasized how sarcastic she was. "Any other way, then?"

"Well, I know for a fact that Colon's room is up top. He's too lazy to ever come down from his little tower so I think we got a fair shot of pinning him up there."

"Brilliant. And how do you expect us to get up there when we can't climb the stairs?!"

Jake gave her another look.

"I expect that that's not the only way. How could everyone else get up to his room then?"

"Maybe they sprouted wings and fluttered to the door up there?"

"Very funny. Really, can we stop making jokes and be serious?"

"Okay, okay, sorry. I'm just really nervous. I just keep waiting for another group of guards to pop up out of nowhere."

It was as though her words had brought them.

Ten guards came fizzling into view from the next hallway. It was at least twenty feet away, enough room to run. "Come on," Jake hissed impatiently, grabbing her wrist and pulling her along with him.

"Where are we going!?"

"No idea but we'll get there!" Jake continued to pull her until they disappeared behind a door. Frantically, Nikki looked around for anything to block the door. By a mantel, swords gleamed. They were as bulky as Scarlet's, and perfect for blocking a door.

"Good, good!" Jake encouraged her as she pushed the sword into the chains around the wooden door, hoping it would lock it tightly.

They were obviously in a weapons room. All around them medieval torture devices aligned the walls. A single candle sent the only light into the room. As it flickered, they caught sight of a figure. His shadow stretching high into the walls.

Jake and Nikki drew their swords close to themselves, prepared to do whatever they could.

"Hardly fair play, you two. Two against one? It would be easier for me to just surrender."

Nikki's mouth fell open and she felt her sword hand droop to her side. "Garden?" she heard her voice speak before she could stop it.

As Jake caught Garden's eyes, he suddenly seemed to be carrying a smug expression. How on earth Jake could even begin to feel smug at this moment was beyond her.

II

"Well of course dear child, do you think that you could have survived this far—lived from the wrath that Colon splits between the two of you —without the help of superiors?"

She bit back her tongue from stuttering or to make a remark.

"So," Jake began in a voice that was so casual that it seemed awkward at this moment. "Where's Alexandria?"

"I suspect that she is fighting off guards to your advantage. Quite unwise to bring them near here though I must say. And to lock yourselves into a room with no other entrance but the **Pool**? Very well thought through."

Just as Jake's calmness had been strange, Nikki could help but to stop her mouth from smiling at the man's sarcasm. If only she could understand all of it.

"But seeing as though you two have finally worked out

differences to work together—"

The sword blocked door was blown open. "Is a great improvement," Alexandria said, coming through it.

"This is great and all—having a big reunion, but shouldn't we really be finding a way up to Colon?" Nikki couldn't believe how calm everybody seemed to be.

Jake, who always seemed on the edge even when they weren't getting attacked by over a hundred soldiers, had pressed himself against the wall. His eyes were starring into nothing, appearing as though they were thinking; the way he twiddled his wand between his middle and index finger said otherwise though.

Alexandria had slaughtered perhaps over ten watchmen, yet she too was sitting contently in a small wooden chair and making small versions of stars shoot from her wand tip.

Garden was the only one paying any attention to Nikki, keeping his eyes carefully trained.

"Yes. Jacob," Garden started, pushing back his already slicked blackish gray hair. "I think it might be time to end your detour through the castle and make a stop in the place 'you lot ought to be.'" Nikki caught that Garden was trying to sound like Jake. He succeeded.

Jake pushed himself off the wall, studying a sword above him that resembled the one Scarlet had been using, as if weighing whether or not it would be useful in the near future. "Yeah, come on Nick."

He hadn't used her nickname in a while. It didn't feel like it was hers, nor that Jake should be using it at a time like this. Her thoughts scrambled rambunctiously.

"Calm gift?" Nikki asked, narrowing her eyes at Garden.

"Forgive me, for I have a selective memory, but I believe Jacob has told you? Nicole it's not a calming gift. I believe the word would be hypnotizing."

"You weren't even there when he told me... But why doesn't it effect me? Or does it?"

"In my office, as this is such the place, I like to keep a tranquility feel. I have found out though that those who are more stressed, as usually the ones who are older, find themselves locked within the calmness. Apparently the burden that you hold isn't great enough for you to feel the stress that others do."

Nikki longed to feel carefree. She bet it felt great. It made her blood want to boil when she saw Jake without a care in the world for those few moments until he had snapped out of it. *Would it be worse or better when you finally pull yourself together?* she thought to herself.

"Let's carry on, eh?" Alex asked, playfully grabbing the disoriented Jake by the sleeve of his shirt and steering him over to the red curtains that lined one side of the wall.

Nikki followed suit quickly. *It'd be worse*, she decided.

Jake came back to his senses only to laugh. "It's a wall."

"*With* a curtain," Nikki reminded him. She had to stop her laugh halfway after it came up her throat. She knew this probably wasn't the best time to kid.

"It's not just a curtain!" Alex exclaimed, extending her arm to show some unseen remarkableness.

"Behind it is the deep **Pool** that delivers you to any room in the castle. It holds the same magic Jacob set up in the ocean for you to get home. Perhaps just a touch stronger." Jake smiled with pride at Garden's words. It apparently took a strong bit of magic to make their ocean journey shorter than a few days.

"Great, let's go then." Jake now seemed anxious to get away from Garden.

"However there is a complication." Alex's face was no longer the light happy one they had seen earlier. Her expression was grave, ghostly almost. "It seems like Colon knew there was going to be no other way for you to get through to him except by means of the **Pool**. He had it heavily guarded with a spell that should be easily enough broken. But be warned, I don't trust what he did. It's too simple if you ask me."

"What do you mean?" Jake asked through narrowed eyes. "Alex, what did he do?"

"He made it impossible to go through. Unless...it's burned by magic."

Nikki's heart almost skipped a beat before Alex had finished what she was saying. Was that all? Piece of cake for her.

She took a step forwards.

Jake's hand shot up and caught her arm as she moved it up slowly. "She's right. Colon's smarter than this. No doubt he's cursed it somehow. Maybe you shouldn't do this?"

Nikki yanked her arm out of his grip. "I can do this. I know I can."

Jake backed up a bit to match Garden and Alexandria.

Nikki pulled her arm in the position again.

She could feel a small warmth spread through her, flowing gently from her palm. Then an ice like scrape ran through her body. She felt her energy trickle away as if she had been using magic that wasn't hers.

Once she felt her knees bend a tiny bit as if they felt like buckling. She flinched hard every time a new shard of pain rippled though her. She couldn't give up now though. The curtain was melting away like a popsicle. She pushed on, almost begging for it to stop.

And soon, it did.

When the last thread of the red curtain had cindered, Nikki forced her gift to stop. Although it seemed to have a mind for its own all of a sudden, it followed her command, if a little reluctantly.

Nikki felt her feet slip on the carpet of the ground as if it were black ice.

"Oh no you don't," Jake gasped through grinding teeth. He grabbed her sharply and pulled her up with a stubborn force.

"Th-thanks," Nikki stuttered. Her head was cluttered and seemed to be blocked from the rest of the world. She pulled out of his grip and felt the wall next to her slid to support her back.

Jake sunk to the floor as well. They needed to rest badly. Both of them were covered with scrapes from glass, worn from spell casting, cased with sweat mixed with water from the pouring rain. They both took a deep breath to keep calm.

Jake and her sat for probably thirty seconds. But it was long enough for them. They equally felt recharged enough to keep moving.

Nikki hadn't even looked to see what was beyond the curtain. She couldn't tell if Jake was just bored by what it held or he was also too preoccupied to have seen it too.

She leaned up against the wall and peered behind the corner.

"No doubt Colon put some sort of draining charm to reverse the effects of your gift on that curtain." Jake had sounded so matter-of-factly when he said this that for a split second, Nikki had thought he had been Garden. Come to think of it, Garden and his apprentice were nowhere in sight. "Where...?" Nikki started to ask, but the view that she saw swallowed up her breath.

In front of her was a diagonal tile room. A whole room. In the center of room were three limestone steps that led down into a stone, well-like pool. The pool—which was also lined with the same stone that led into it—was at least ten feet across but there was no visible end to the bottom as far as Nikki could see where she stood. When the third step ended, so did a sign for any kind of bottom, which greatly disturbed her.

"Is that the **Pool**?"

"Yeah, you 'member the ocean right? When we went right through it and landed near your house? This is like it but only for the castle. Not a spectacular place to swim."

"It looks like a well." Nikki slowly moved closer to the edge of the steps.

"Something along those lines," Jake said. He was bent down wrinkling the water with two of his fingers. The water swirling around his fingers turned from a pale blue to a dark violet in a quick swish.

"Well, what do we do now? And where did Garden and Alex go?"

"Dunno. But I know what we have to do. And so should you."

"We aren't going to dive in are we?" she whispered.

Jake didn't say anything, just stared at her for a minute.

"We are," Nikki answered quietly.

"What you'll want to do is think about where you want to go, in this case, just say upstairs near Colon's room. Trust me it'll be better if you don't go out and say 'his room'. You don't need a picture, just a word. Don't worry about drowning. If you think about it while you go in, you'll be out before you lose any breath." Jake got up.

After he caught her look he sighed. "After me I suppose." Shoving his sword back into his scabbard and his wand in his belt, he bent one leg forward. With his hands holding each other, he took a shallow, hasty breath and pushed off from the edge. Splashing very little, he entered with an almost perfect dive. The water turned a deep violet. Jake was gone.

Nikki was glad he went first; her dive would look pitiful compared to his. *Don't say Colon's bedroom. Say by Colon's bedroom.* It was hard to keep her thoughts on something she couldn't even imagine. She decided just to get it done with, losing time meant losing lives in this situation.

Go on, go, she encouraged herself. Her feet left the ledge and soon the icy waters were wrapped around her like velvet. She almost forgot to think. Her eyes flickered open and as she thought of upstairs, the water turned the purple it had earlier when Jake dived in and she soon closed her eyes to stop the water from making her dizzy. Each color that was around her faded into each other.

It happened fast. She opened her eyes to see herself laying soaking and dripping wet on the second step of a different **Pool**. At first, she was entirely confused. "Take a breath," she whispered to herself, forcing herself to stay calm and remember what had just happened. She could see barely anything ahead. A dark hallway with no other figure besides a small lantern hanging halfway into the next turn. She froze. Nikki's legs were still in the water and there was no way she could move without falling back in. Her feet were numb, but she could see clearly that they were stuck on part of a loose brick.

It was so perfect of Jake to disappear at that moment. Thinking about it made her stomach twist with panic. Had he gone without her? Was he just ahead? Or had he not even made it at all?

There was nothing ahead of her as far as she could tell. "Jake?" she whispered out. Her voice was hoarse and felt like sandpaper.

Jake came into view, drenched auburn hair clinging to his cheek bones. He had been just behind the corner. Rushing towards her, she could see he was just as soaking as she was. "Come on," he hissed, grabbing her hand and pulling her onto her feet. "I feel like I keep doing this. Is it just me?"

"No. I find myself in positions like this a lot."

"Right well, I suppose you want an explanation?"

"Of what?" Her eyes were focused on the turn in the hallway, waiting for any sign of a shadow to move against the wall. Nikki really didn't care that she was confused. She in fact hardly had noticed.

"Of the **Pool**?"

"Yeah. Why are we wet? And why did we land in another one? Should we have just plopped in the middle of the hallway? And what's to stop anyone from going the opposite way? From here down to Garden's study?"

"I really don't know why we're wet. I don't think we have too much time for explanations, but the **Pool** only works one way, you wouldn't be able to go back now—"

This made Nikki's face hot with embarrassment. She had thought that if she fell in, she'd be gone again.

"So no one but whoever goes in Garden's room can get through and use it. Oh, and why would you think that we'd just land in the middle of the hallway?"

Nikki shrugged. "You never know. Well *I* never know. You *always* know."

Jake smirked. "I've been around."

III

As Nikki rolled her eyes in mock disgust, the walls around them caught her eyes. There were wild windows displaying hideous pictures on them as they walked the rest of the corridor, but they were not broken so Nikki presumed that meant they were either protected by **enchantments** or else, just being stubborn to the wind.

"Lovely pictures," she commented, forgetting she was supposed to be annoyed at Jake.

"I know."

They turned the corner to see a red door. Striking the air in odd angles, chains draped around the wood frames and doorway. Jake made a sound with his tongue. "Not a very original way to lock a door is it? I was expecting so much more."

"I was expecting something like a sign posted on it saying, 'Come in at your own risk.' Why does everything pathway have to be blocked?"

"Because he had to make it hard somehow... Yet it's like he wants us to come."

The chains had creepily enough reminded her of fingers. If only that big rusty lock would open, so they could get through. She couldn't help wondering what Colon thought he was doing. They had already been through enough, was he too chicken to fight them or did he really think that they might give up?

Anger filling her, she threw her sword out at the chains. Despite the fact that they were rusty, they seemed to be doing their job well enough. Her sword clanged lifelessly against them and didn't break the lock.

Nikki desperately turned around searching the corridor for something that would be useful. She left Jake to stare at the lock pondering, alone.

Jake's sword jerked up and found its way into the lock. There was a soft hiss of a 'click' and the lock fell apart, leaving the chains to slither to the ground with it.

"What did you—how did you—?" Nikki sputtered, twirling around.

"You were being too forceful, all you had to do was unlock it."

"Too *forceful*? I'm not the one who just threw his five pound sword into a lock with all his might."

"It's too forceful when what you're doing doesn't work," Jake responded calmly. "Besides, after getting locked in rooms a fair amount of the time, you're able to figure out ways to get out of them."

Nikki shook her head. "You're ridiculous sometimes, did you know that?"

Jake didn't answer her at first. "Nikki, you ever wonder why I'm always so protective?"

Nikki was making her way through the red door when he said this and she stopped dead. "What?"

"I said, 'Do you ever wonder why I'm so protective over you all the time?'"

"Yeah, I do wonder." Why was he telling her this now?

"It's sort of hard to explain. But, my parents put a **curse**—which is an **enchantment** that can't be broken no matter what, as far as I know—on me right before you were born to make me protect you. It was their idea. But since they died soon after, I had nowhere to go but your mum's. I'm protective over you because I have no choice, not that I don't want to be. But the **curse** that's on me insures that if anyone between the two of us dies tonight, it'll be me."

Nikki, who had already backed up against the wall, slid down it slowly. "You have no choice?"

"No."

"But no one else is going to die." She didn't think she'd be able to cope if not only Kay died but Jake. He was annoying, but he was family-annoying.

"Don't be so sure. If I go, I want you to—"

"You're not going to go! You're not going to die!" Nikki yelled, getting so close to Jake that she could smell his strangely sweet-smelling breath.

"Nikki—"

"No, Jacob,"

Jake's face got all of a sudden, very solemn.

"You are *not* going to die." Nikki looked away then and continued to walk through the red door. After about ten steps, Jake followed her, his face still in the same darkness.

They didn't speak.

The red door led out into a corridor that was as dark and dank as the rest of them. As they continued to walk, there came a place where there was a small lantern, and a small sign, hanging above a fork in the path. One way was dark, like the rest of the corridors and the other was light, there were lanterns all along the path. She couldn't understand the words on the sign, but she knew what language it was in. Jake was reading the Elfin words fervently.

"You do know the way don't you?" Nikki asked quietly. She was beginning to fear that she had broke some invisible wall between the two of them and all of the friendship she had had melted away. But apparently, her guess had been wrong, or perhaps Jake was a better actor than she thought, because his voice was strong and clear.

"Sort of. You know that's Elfin on that sign, the language that most **enchantment**s with words are made up of. The binding influence that magical contracts are made of."

"I knew it was. But I can't read a single word."

"No worries, you'll learn magical contracts and elfin languages soon."

She shook her head. Trying to look as though she understood everything he had said was harder than it seemed.

"I know the language slightly, so there should be a way to translate it."

Jake got closer to the sign. The way the lantern illuminated it was almost disturbing to Nikki. She had never been a fan of horror. Something else was itching at her too. As Jake studied the wood plaque, a chill swept over her.

"Jake—" She began.

A window in the back corridor by the **Pool**, burst.

Voices filled the air. There were guards somewhere behind them.

She could hear another window smash.

"Jake!"

Jake was still concentrating on the sign, his eyes were wide and she could unmistakably see fear in them. "We don't have a lot of time!" She grabbed him by the shoulder and spun him to face her. "What does the sign say?" To her it was a bunch of letters mixed up. But maybe to Jake...

"We have to move," Jake agreed.

"Right, that's what I've been saying." She wheeled him around and pulled him towards the lantern lit path.

"No!" Jake's voice startled Nikki enough to let him go. "Only one can go each way. Don't worry about me. Go in the dark way, and I'll...meet you on the other side."

"It leads to the same place?"

"Yes."

There was that unsure edge to his voice, but there was no time to think. Nikki gave him a final glance and then disappeared in the dark hallway.

"THERE!" bellowed a voice behind Jake. A red faced guard that had a streak of blood running down his temple.

Jake raced in the lit way.

The guards ran forward too. "No," the blood streaked guard called out, arm outstretched. They stopped in their tracks. "He's gone." He smiled, and the others followed suit. "And he won't be coming back."

"What 'bout the girl?" one spoke out.

"You 'iget! Colon told us! There's not a chance 'bout her not be'n with him. He'll have taken her down there. Com'on." The leader guard with the stripe of blood, led them back towards the corridor.

Only one person can go through. And I know Jake knows something I don't. There's no way on earth that he would have told me to go down the path that leads to...wherever. He knows which way to go, I know he does. And if I end up right near Colon then what am I suppose to do without Jake? No. They have *to both lead out somehow. And Jake told me they did...*

She hated her mind. It was always wondering to places it shouldn't. Always reminding her that good things only happened to the good guys in *movies* or *books*. She wished it would shut up. Jake knew what he was doing.

She hoped.

IV

Her tunnel seemed to her to have the qualities of a sewage or drain pipe. The walls caved in at a circular angle. They got so narrow that she had to outstretch her hands to grip the sides making sure her feet wouldn't slip or trip. The ground, quite luckily, wasn't filled with water or anything undesirable. However, as her fingers brushed against the pipe-ish walls, a sticky ooze caught her fingers.

She was glad it was too dark to see. Once or twice, she felt thin legs crawl gently over the back of her hand. Her hand would catch on something stringy, webby. She only clenched her teeth tighter. There was no way Nikki could give up now.

Something crawled onto her foot. She shook it but she could still feel extra weight. Somehow in the trouble of getting whatever was on her shoe off, she pressed herself against the wall.

Which was a big mistake.

Trying to pry herself off the sticky sides, she felt whatever on her foot leave. Her hands caught the webs that covered her and she pulled them off as fast as she could. Shaking slightly, and her legs trembling under the pressure, Nikki moved forward.

She almost ran into it. Her hands were outstretched and caught a metal pole. A metal pole that led to other metal poles. Since she was practically blind in the darkness, it took a while to realize what it was. A ladder.

"Yes," she whispered softly to herself.

Her foot reached upward for the first step.

V

Jake's wand was out and ready. The lanterns above him were blindingly bright. *Guards gone. Colon's smart. Bet he thinks he's so amazing right now. Thinks he's going to get rid of us. Well if anything, one of us will make it out.*

There was no bitterness in his voice. He wasn't sure what he had brought himself into, but he knew that Colon always liked to push his captives to the limit. The lights shone blue against the white walls. "Be ready." He really wasn't talking to anyone in particular.

The pathway was long. Wide too. Every spec of the walls and floor was spotless, like he was in limbo. Jake kept walking. He was alert to the sides his path, along with where he stepped.

There was no turning back when he turned the corner the second time. Jake could no longer see where he had just walked, it was as though the walls had closed behind him. He could now figure out that he was in a room. Still painted white and brightly lit, it was a confusing scene. At the far end of the area was a twig-like ladder. Above it, there was a square cut out in the wall, where the ladder guided you up into another room. Jake jogged up to it. Stowing his wand in his pocket and his sword backing his sheath, he gripped the rusty rail.

As he gazed up, his teeth ground at the view.

Slowly, he put his foot up and moved forward.

VI

Her feet stuck to each step like glue. It was like the floor itself was begging her not to go forward. Her heart was about to pound right out of her chest. Fear gripped her throat, which was so dry now it was raw.

Nikki kept moving though, the thought of getting out of this retched place made her eager. And the promise she made Chrystal. She pulled her hand up again expecting to grip another dirty bar. Instead, she grasped nothing.

Her hand scraped for something to catch on. Meanwhile, her other arm had wrapped itself around the railing. Her feet had lost their space. For a moment, she was dangling fifteen feet in the air.

Her fingernails dug into the flooring on the landing above her. There was a space cut out. Finally, her feet found their place again and Nikki was able to sorely detach her aching arm from the rusty rail.

"Come on!" she cried out in desperation to herself. Her hand holding the ladder let go and reached to grip the ledge shared by the other hand.

When she had finally managed to pull herself to the ledge all the way, she lay on her back for a while, catching her stolen breath and silently congratulating herself for her efforts.

She turned over to see another door in front of her.

"More doors?"

Nikki got up quietly, and pulled out her sword again. She kept one hand free and did something she realized she should have done earlier. A sliver of flame outstretched about a foot off of her palm. *Sometimes, I just think I don't think at all. Of all people I should know when to use my gift.*

With her sword hand, she turned the delicate knob of the door until it opened. Thin spider webs stretched out with it. Nikki quickly burned them away. She slipped through the door.

Nikki was in front of a sheer, red veil. And beyond that, another door. Somehow though she knew this door was different. It had etches on it as far as she could tell. She could just feel the presence of people in the room behind the door. Colon had to be just on the other side. Nikki looked around her. So where was Jake? A few feet from her, another trap door was still latched…

VII

Jake climbed the ladder. He knew that it was coming. Above him in the square he had to fit into, it was pitch black. *Deceiving,* Jake thought, *tricking you into going into the tunnel that looked light and hopeful. My only question is what creature is worthy enough to make sure that no one makes it to Colon?*

He climbed up the last step, absorbing the last bit of light. When his legs swung from the square hole, the hole closed immediately, and he was trapped.

It was so dark that he barely knew where to move. He hadn't really realized he should have looked which way to go when he could still see three feet around him. Now it was just relying on instinct.

Jake got up. He began to walk forward, instantly regretting it. His foot found something under it, giving a large crunch. He winced. Just what he needed, whatever was in here to know where he was.

I hope I did the right thing when I didn't tell Nikki what the sign said completely. She would have freaked and I can just see her face. Sure the sign said one each tunnel, but anyone in their right mind would have stayed together. If I hadn't told her that, we probably both would be here. At least someone will make it through. Now just what did the sign mean when it said that no one would be able to make it out of here? What on earth could be in here that it can't attack in light?

Jake could think of a few. None of them were rather pleasant. He bent down and grabbed at the ground ahead of him as carefully as he could. A smooth object found its way into his reach hand he grabbed it pulling it as close to his face as he could.

He traced the thing with is hand and a cold realization came into view.

Bone.

The ground had to be littered with them. Everywhere Jake stepped, he had to do it lightly. It seemed there wasn't a square inch that wasn't covered with bone. And they were dry. So clean. There was nothing on them.

Jake's breathing got shallower. His sword was extended now, but there was nothing he could do if something grabbed him from an angle he couldn't cover.

There was a soft hiss and he spun around.

A thin fingernail was just barely visible about a foot away. Four more fingernails slowly come crawling into view. Like few creatures of magic, the fingernails defied light and dark and glimmered. Each one was longer than a foot.

Bony twig hands that were twice as long as the nails crept along the shadows. Jake had stopped breathing altogether. The thing had to be enormous. And it had to be able to see him. Jake took a step back. Now the thinnest arms he had ever seen were showing. They were dark, like tanned wood, but he could see them as though they shone like the moon.

"No. Y-You're a **scrolt**." His fear melted a way. There was no way a **scrolt** could have harmed anyone, let alone left a pile of bones.

Feet and limbs that matched the hands come into view with a long scratching dragging sound as the toenails scrapped across the floor.

Wild stringy hair was tied recklessly into a long ponytail while shreds of decaying fabric hung in clumps around the creature's body. It towered over Jake, who was quite tall himself, and its long pointed ears twitched. The **scrolt**'s eyes were like pieces of coal and its mouth revealed sharp fangs. A bit of drool rolled off of its mouth. Its body illuminated light around itself.

"**Scrolts** don't have fangs," Jake whispered softly to himself. So was it a **scrolt**?

The creature moved closer. Jake stayed where he was. His sword was up now. **Scrolts** were harmless. They don't attack humans... The sinister look on the **scrolt's** face said otherwise.

The creature lounged. Jake was taken aback.

The sharp long nails caught him by the neck and pushed him to the floor. White lights spread across his eyes. He couldn't breathe.

His sword had been knocked away.

Jake desperately grabbed at the floor trying to find anything to make the creature release.

Saliva dripped off the monster's chin and onto Jake's face.

He was lucky the thing was thin and bony. It was like a piano on top of him as it was.

A bone caught his hand.

There was no way he'd have enough strength to slam it into the monster.

His energy was fading as it was.

He could barely see.

Jake was holding his last breath.

A streak of red fizzled past his eyes.

There was a howl from the monster on top of him and he felt his lungs breathe air and his rib cage not feel crushed anymore.

A hand reached down towards him.

"What is this the third time I've saved your life, mister I-can-take-everything-on-my-own?" Nikki was grinning mockingly down at him.

"TURN AROUND!" Jake bellowed, making her jump.

Nikki twirled around sword ready. To her surprise, the creature was right behind her, and its skeletal flesh met her weapon with a clean slice that reminded her of the tree branch.

The thing crumpled to the floor, green blood trickling out of a corner in its mouth.

"And I thought you said **scrolts** were harmless." She had recognized its bony hands and black eyes.

"So did I. One that size doesn't usually take orders from people." Jake's voice was raspy. He took her outstretched hand when she gave it again. "How did you get here?" Jake was examining how severe the claw marks on him were. He scrambled around and finally found his sword.

"There was another trap door where I got out that didn't lead to Colon. I thought, 'I'm not leaving him and I'm pretty sure that there's something in there for Jake, the boy-who-doesn't-care-if-he-throws-his-life-away to deal with'. And I figured that Colon would probably give a door that leads to him in both paths to mess with you and he probably thought that you wouldn't make it out of this path. So I took it. And found you. Choking."

"Yeah thanks for that."

She shrugged. "You have a knack of finding danger just like me. It's like our job to rescue the other—and not like a **curse**. We're family. It's what we do."

"Yeah." he was clearly lost in thought.

"Going to stand there all day are you? Well I guess I'll just go back to Colon—"

Jake smiled at her then took the leading point. "This is where you went isn't it?"

The glowing of the **scrolt** was fading as they got farther away from it. Now everything was pitch black.

"Yes. Here this'll help a lot." Nikki outstretched her hand once again and a brilliantly bright orange flame fired out.

Jake stared at the flame and then turned away thinking. "Are you angry at something?"

Nikki didn't answer. She focused on narrowly avoiding a hanging spider that had decided to fall in front of her. Finally she gave in. "No. It's just frustrating to be me." She was expecting Jake to say something like he understood or ask why. When he didn't answer, she almost wanted to say her comment again. It wasn't like Jake to leave her hanging like this.

"I'm really sorry your friend Kay..." Jake started.

"I know you are. And you're her friend too." Together they climbed back up the trap door.

They came to the veil.

"You're ready?" Jake asked.

"I'll never be ready."

"You shouldn't, but—"

"But I have to be," she finished for him.

Jake nodded as he moved towards the veil. "No more tricks, Colon." He whispered it as though he knew there weren't, but there was also a pleading tone to his voice.

His hand outstretched to reach the veil and he slipped behind it. Nikki followed. She wondered what her friends were doing right now.

The door on the other side of the curtain was green. Etchings of names were delicately written in the door. Jake's fingers nimbly touched a name. Nikki didn't have time to see what the name was. Jake had already gripped the handle and was about to throw the door open.

It struck her odd that Colon had tried so hard with guards and traps and when they finally got to the door, it would open so easily. What kind of a trick was this? Everything was so easy, except for the **scrolt** a bit. Was it possible that Colon could have wanted them to make it here...?

The door opened with ease.

"Be ready." Jake held his sword up high.

Nikki shifted her sword in her hand. Her tension wasn't easing.

They walked in.

There was no way on earth she could have predicted what lay in that room. A man was sitting in a chair, smugly ignoring the fact that Jake and herself were there, as he wrote something down on a piece of paper. Once he was done, he laid his little feather pen down and got up.

Nikki held back a gasp.

Even though Jake had touched the fact that Colon was young and only seventeen, it was still a big shock. His cheek bones were hollowed and his hair was blond and wavy, hanging in clumps all along his face.

There was no way to ignore the fact that he was dashingly handsome. His eyes were as dark as night, and his clothes were extremely old-fashioned, which seemed to give him even more of a mysterious and gorgeous look.

If she had just seen him somewhere, there was no way she could have considered that he had an evil bone. Jake and her knew better though.

He was the first thing that caught her eye. On a rather large cushion next to Colon's very extraordinary throne, was a creature with body angles that seemed to defy reality. It was black, and snake-like, yet had the features of a komodo dragon. Its nails were sharp and were just a few inches smaller than the **scrolt**'s. It was wingless and was missing one of its hind legs and an eye.

The good eye was a black slit, while the rest of the entire eye was red. Its forked tongue flickered in and out, glaring at her and clicking its menacing nails.

Nikki really didn't want to take her eyes off the creature that looked big enough to swallow her whole, but Jake nudged her and jerked his head towards the other side of Colon's chair.

She didn't know how she could have missed it.

How could she have not seen this first?

How?

Nikki could feel the anger boil inside of her, her hands became tightly clenched over her rapier. Whatever fire that had settled inside of her before that moment, roared inside of her until her palms seared with pain.

The girl in front of her swung back her black hair.

Jasmine had been found.

Chapter Twelve

Colon and Jasmine

I

"Surprised?" Jasmine whispered, but in the large room, her voice echoed so it was like she was right next to Nikki.

"Yes," Jake and Nikki said at the same time.

"You shouldn't be," Colon replied just as quietly as Jasmine. His voice was like honey.

For a second they just starred at each other.

"This is just pathetic," Jasmine began to sneer. "A fifteen-year-old and his pitiable, inexperienced thirteen-year-old cousin! I'm shaking in my skin."

"You're thirteen too, and if I remember, you're the one who wanted Jake all to yourself when he came!" Nikki growled back.

Jake shook his head at her.

She couldn't understand why he wasn't being so defensive, like he usually was. Why wasn't he spitting something awful back at Jasmine?

Jasmine blushed at her words.

Colon interrupted. "I see you got past my **scrolt**. It was specially bred. Now tell me, which one of you had to fight it?"

Jake took a breath.

"Knew it. There was no way you would have let your dear cousin fight a **scrolt**. Once again Jacob, you have proven yourself as acting like the hero."

"*I* didn't fight it." Why was he acting so calm. Jake's breathing was even. Nikki wanted so badly to get inside his head.

"No?" Colon looked shocked. "Have you run away from your problems this time like the ruddy coward you are?"

Jake gave Nikki a look, giving her silent instructions. How quickly Colon twisted their words. He seemed a master at it.

"*I* did," she spoke out. "And it's dead."

Jasmine laughed at this. "*You?* You're a nobody. I bet you don't even know how to use that sword in your hand."

Where was this conversation going? This was not how Nikki thought things would be. They were having a discussion like they were old friends catching up. In a venomous sort of way... She had been sure that the fighting was going to happen as soon as they got in. Perhaps Colon was not what he had not seemed.

"I've been practicing for months at my fighting and **Je Ne Sais Quoi**. You have no chance with me." Jasmine had gotten up. She reached behind her gold chair and grabbed an odd looking sword that was still in its sheath.

"Don't worry dear, I'll take care of the boy and you just take care of his worthless caddie." Colon smiled into Jasmine's eyes and did something that made Nikki want to hurl. He drew close to Jasmine, and kissed her deeply. There was something disturbing about their relationship.

"I'll freeze her heart," Jasmine whispered to Colon as he smiled. At that, she pulled out her sword and gently placed her hand on the blade. Ice froze all around the steels.

Jasmine strutted down the steps that stood between herself and her enemies.

She turned to Nikki and said, "You're probably wondering why

I'm here. Colon asked me to marry him so he could rightly become king. He wanted someone who hated you as much as he did."

Nikki shoved her wand inside her pocket. *Get ready Nikki, your dream is just about to come true,* Nikki bitterly thought while she positioned her sword so it sat comfortably in her hand. She caught Jake's mind-reading expression searching her questioningly.

She saw his face suddenly realize what she was talking about, but before he could react, Colon shot a streaming light at him that barely missed his face.

He sent a I-am-pathetic glance at Nikki but she was already swinging away, and the endless clanking echoed through the room.

Jake caught where the flash went out of the corner of his eye. The white blaze struck a wall and took out a huge chunk the size of a car. Colon's hand steamed from the **enchantment**'s force.

Although he tried to hold it back, he did it anyway: Jake gulped.

What am I getting myself into? he wondered.

Quickly he sent spirals of **enchantment**s bouncing and flying and twittering, none of them coming near Colon. Every time Jake got a good aim, Colon with his controlling power, would make him miss.

Jake flinched hard every time. The suffering on his face spelled out pain.

He held back his scream. Instead, he let it loose in his mind. In his mind, his thoughts were nearly choking in screams. In turn, it made Nikki lose her concentration over worry and ideas of something worse was happening. She heard every thought flickered in his mind. She couldn't force him out of her head. It was as if the room amplified all of their powers.

A spell narrowly missed Nikki.

Figuring the color out, she guessed it had to from Jake.

Watch it will you? She couldn't help her thoughts reach out to him.

I'm sorry. He's better at his gift than I've seen anyone in a long time. Stupid idiot—

His voice was caught up and fear struck her stomach. It must have been just the fact that Colon was controlling him again. She felt comfort in the fact that Colon couldn't hear them.

Sounds of everything the swords hit, that obviously weren't yet flesh, also consumed everyone's attention. Nikki and Jasmine's swords were evenly met. Each was holding each other's power with as much strength and will as the person wanted to live. For both of them that amount was great.

"It's a pity that Jake's related to you," Jasmine finally called. "I actually thought he had potential."

"Potential for what? Your slave? Jake isn't that stupid."

She could feel Jake's annoyed glare at the back of her neck. *That stupid...!*

That was when a dark red spark finally collided with someone.

Nikki twirled around to see Jake up against a wall. His head banged deep in the bricks. Her concentration swayed dramatically. But as he moved, her frustration flew high above where it was before.

Nikki took a wild swipe.

Sparks flew.

The ice on Jasmine's blade acted as a separate protection, making it harder for Nikki to give a direct hit on it, but it made a clang and colorful sparks all the same.

"You'll never win." Jasmine ground her teeth.

"We'll see."

Nikki slammed her sword down. She thrust herself back up into a straight position and threw her sword with two hands angrily at the blue ice; it swung powerfully like a baseball bat.

She was surprised she could talk aloud, even more surprised that she could send messages to Jake through her mind without getting sidetracked.

Jasmine dodged away at the last swipe Nikki gave.

Nikki's sword swung aimlessly as her footing became unbalanced. Until it found a target.

Wall.

II

"No, no, no!" she cried out in anguish, tugging helplessly.

Jake had not yet noticed. He himself had just gotten struck—again. When he shook his head and the dust of concrete fluttered off, he saw the distress signals Nikki was sending out.

There was no time to help; an angry black haired girl was just about to strike...

"No! Look out!"

Nikki whirled around just in time.

Jasmine hurled herself at Nikki.

"CLASK!" The sound of metal splitting air.

"Eek!" Nikki chirped as she lurched out of the way.

A little too late. The sword grazed her arm roughly. Nikki gripped at her arm tightly.

Jasmine ran her fingers over her ice blade, wiping the blood and concrete. As she did, more ice grew onto the blade. She flung her weapon again.

Nikki ducked more towards her sword this time, praying her plan would work.

"Crack!" Jasmine hit the wall right above where Nikki's rapier was. Her sapphire sword slithered out.

Nikki lunged and caught it by the silver handle.

She nearly jumped out of her skin when Jake's eyes opened wide and he shouted, "NIKKI!"

Nikki whirled around just in time to see the ice blade hurtling towards her once again.

She slammed her own sword with as much force as she could muster.

The ice blade shattered into nothing more than mini ice cubes. Jasmine's sword became nothing but a dull handle and a bit of edged steel.

Colon this time was distracted. His eyes flickered from Jake to Nikki for a moment, then he closed them.

Jake's wand fell to the floor.

And so did he.

His eyes were closed too, and he was gripping at the floor, scraping it with his fingernails as if he were trying to peel off the cement. Jake writhed. His face was twisted up in pain.

A smile grew on Colon's face.

"What are you doing!" Nikki cried. Her heart was beginning to pound. Jake didn't look like he could take much more of this.

"His gift," Jasmine stated satisfied. Her smile scared Nikki worse than Jake's pain.

She pulled her mind into his, immediately pulling out. He was screaming, but he refused to let it out.

This was the other part of Colon's gift? He *could* control people. But into pain too.

She had to act.

Nikki knew the forbidden spell Jake had told her about a long while ago. *Just do it. Jake doesn't deserve to die. Do the* **enchantment lepra***. You'll be fine.* Her head seemed so much more sure than her heart.

There was no choice.

She whipped out her wand.

A single word flooded her mind as soon as she did.

No.

It was Jake. He *must* know what she was planning on doing.

He didn't want her to. She put her wand away to mislead him. But she didn't need a wand to do this.

He had told her that he was going to die. There was no way she was going to let it happen when she could have done something... She could hear Jake's rattling breaths.

There was so little time left. So *why* was she still thinking?

"**Lepra**!" She screamed, allowing her energy into her magic.

It didn't feel half as good as she had made the **enchantment** sound. She could feel her energy leaving her. So much. But Jake had stopped writhing.

And Colon had opened his eyes to glare at her.

Jake's eyes were open now. He was breathing hard. But breathing. That's what she was concerned about.

Nikki's knees sunk to the floor. She could feel her body sink in and out of consciousness, but she fought until she could at least keep her eyes open.

Jake had gotten up, wand pointed sharply at Colon, who was still staring at Nikki with a new-born hatred. Jake had told her so long ago that **lepra** would protect a person from being possessed for at least twenty-four hours.

Jake held up his wand, words teetering on his lips. It would be for Nikki, whatever he would do. She deserved to use that **enchantment** on someone worthier than him, in Jake's eyes.

Do it! Do it fast! Nikki chanted him on.

Jake still didn't move even as the seconds blurred and got slower.

Colon smiled. He said something so soft that Nikki couldn't hear him.

But both he and Jake seemed to be doing nothing. For a moment. Then, thick smog had wrapped around the room. Nikki instantly was forced to remember that one night when she had first encountered Scarlet.

No one could see anything.

They just stood there.

An odd smell invaded the room. Nikki felt her nose wrinkle up without meaning to. *What is going...* she started asking Jake in her thoughts, but the haze was beginning to clear. When the fog had entirely disappeared, so had someone else.

Colon.

III

"NO!" Jasmine screeched. She flung herself towards Jake, new ice blade ready.

He jumped back in surprise. He dodged the blade by millimeters to spare.

Jasmine continually thrust and slashed air. No matter what she hit, she didn't care.

"YOU KILLED HIM! YOU EVIL, SELF-CENTERED... WHAT DID YOU DO?! I'M GOING TO KILL YOU!"

Although Jake's mind was absolutely clear of every thought but survival at that moment, Nikki picked up by his expression that he was just as clueless about the fog as she herself was.

Jasmine seemed not to notice.

He ducked a high-blow and near beheading.

She kept swinging.

Jake kept dodging.

By now, she had finally grazed his arms in several places. Although a few were bleeding quite heavily, he kept his reaction speed the same.

Suddenly, with a change of plans, Jasmine ran at Nikki.

Nikki was too weak to move an inch anywhere.

They say it happens in slow motion. That your life flashes before you eyes. With her, there was no time to think, no time to breathe, and certainly no time for thirteen years worth of memories to flow through her mind. With a long swoosh sound, the blade had been plunged into her. Nikki's face illuminated shock and surprise.

Jasmine's face was triumphant. As she slithered the blade out, a wide sneer covered her burden-viewed face.

Jake's eyes widened.

His heart was pounding. How could he have let this happened? He was sworn—**cursed** to protect her!

He ran forward towards Jasmine with all his strength, swiping Nikki's abandoned sword up.

There was no way he would back down.

Adrenalin filled him.

Something had to be done.

Nikki was fading.

He grit his teeth as the swords made sparks fly.

That's when a movement caught his eye. The giant lizard like creature had gotten up from is throne and was slithering towards them. Without a doubt, Colon would not have possessed his familiar to attack Jasmine, but he had a pit in his stomach that he might just be off that small protected list.

The window at the far corner of the room shattered. Faester, Alexandria's familiar flew in and landed in front of the beast.

Jake went back to the fight with Jasmine as his own Arola leapt majestically off Faester's back.

"You do realize she'll die before you can help her?" Jasmine's face shone triumphed but there was something hidden in the paleness of her skin.

"I didn't do anything to your Colon."

Jasmine laughed uneasily. "You think this is about him? I would have done that to Chrystan even if Colon had already killed you."

"It is *Nikki*," Jake said struggling with the weight Jasmine was putting down on her sword against his.

"She'll never be anything once I'm done with her. You failed, Jake. And now I'll finish you."

There was no doubting that Jasmine had been practicing day and night.

Jake's knees bucked from underneath him.

Her sword bowed closer to his neck. This was a risk. But he was so close to Nikki, and something had to be done. His one hand slipped off the golden handle on his sword.

Jake's fingers extended towards Nikki until it hurt to stretch any further. Jasmine pressed harder on the sword. For a moment, Jake's hand on the sword almost slipped. His attentiveness almost slipped.

His fingers rearranged on the gripping. *Please let this work. I'm not a healer and I don't have enough energy, but I* can't *let her die.*

He felt the familiar feeling of energy leaving him as a sickly green color faded from his outstretched palm towards Nikki, and the blood puddle that surrounded her...

His heart started beating again when she moved. He wasn't quite sure what the **curse** would do to him if Nikki died. As it was, he had never experienced it, so how should he know? He forced Jasmine off of him.

He ducked a swing and sent his own.

He wasn't planning to hurt Jasmine. The fact that he wanted revenge just pumped thick flowing blood through his veins to make him twice as strong as he would be if he was fighting any other opposing person.

There was a wild growl from the other side on the room. The giant lizard creature angrily grabbed at Faester. Colon's creature now had several large and gaping wounds that spilled bodily fluids along where it swept.

It frustrated him that the thing wasn't dead. What a jolt of pain it would give Colon if his familiar dropped cold onto the ground. Jake had always had little mercy for lizards.

He saw Nikki's head slowly turn a bit his way. *Her ears have got to be ringing with the endless sound of metal,* he thought.

Another shriek from the lizard.

This one was different though. The sound of talons scathing hardheartedly filled the air. Jake turned with enough time to see that the giant beast was a foot behind him. He threw himself to the side. He hooked his sword with Jasmine's, in effect pulling her too.

It was one thing to let her get hurt, another to get run over by a creature of the lizard's stature. Jasmine smiled. She heaved ruthlessly, dragging Jake's sword towards her.

She tugged again, and the swords came unhooked.

Jake tried to stumble backwards.

Instead, he lost his horrible footing and plunged the sword forward.

Right into Jasmine.

She crumpled to the floor. He had hit just the right spot.

Jasmine was dead.

"Jake?" Nikki's voice wasn't hoarse. It was crisp, and clear and fresh, like she had forgotten how to use it for a long time, and was savoring the words.

Jake's face grew hot, rushing over to her. "I told you not to save me."

"What are you talking about?" Nikki had gotten up, and although there was a splitting pain at first, it faded and she was able to sit up with eventual comfort.

"When Colon was possessing me—"

Nikki almost flinched. It was such a harsh word to her. Couldn't he just use 'control?'

"—I told you not to save me. I told you before that I was going to die."

"But then who would have saved me after you died? You would die, then it would leave me with Jasmine *and* Colon, so I would have died anyway. I saved us both by saving you."

Jake opened his mouth to retort. But it was a battle he'd rather lose. His face darkened at the sight of Jasmine's body.

"It wasn't your fault, so don't go blaming yourself for it," Nikki quickly said. "There's no use. She's gone."

"You almost were too."

She paused. There was still a puddle of blood—her blood—on the wooden floor of the castle.

"We have to go," Jake stated, absentmindedly in the middle of her thoughts. He looked so stressed. There was something going on. He seemed to read her mind, for all she knew, he could be. "We need to get you out of here before that healing spell wears off. It was weak because I wasn't strong enough."

A thought like a lightning bolt struck her in the head. "What happens when the spell wears off?"

"It was temporary."

That didn't answer her.

Now he was definitely avoiding her gaze. He was uncomfortable; there had to be a problem.

A dry lump landed in Nikki's throat. *Was* she going to make it? She looked down at where Jasmine had struck her, out of the corner of her eye so that Jake wouldn't see it.

He was busy retying his sword to his waist, his fingers trembling. "Listen, it was stupid of me to use that spell, especially in the condition I was in. I didn't do it properly. And now, it's going to wear off."

"Can't you just do it again?" They were walking outside of Colon's room. There was nothing left for them to do.

"Would *you* be able to do **lepra** on me again?"

Nikki bit her lip. "No."

"They take about the same amount of energy."

"Does it take as much energy to hurt a person as it takes to save a person, because so far all the awful spells—"

"**Enchantment**s," Jake reminded her curtly. They rushed down a flight of stairs.

"*Enchantments*, that can kill you are the ones where you're saving someone else."

"No."

"Why not? That's so unfair!"

They were by the **Pool,** a different one than they had entered Colon's chamber from. Jake was in such a hurry, and Nikki was getting more terrified as the second went by. How many did she have left?

"Because. If a person is going to die because of a wound or

something, and you use an **enchantment** to save them, you're messing with the laws of nature, and you can pay for it with your own life."

"That's awful."

"It's the way it is."

Jake took a step in. "Ready?" he called out to her. "Think of Garden's study."

She shook her head yes. She liked the sensation of being in the **Pool**, it was just the momentary sense of drowning that started her fear going.

He took a dive and the water changed its color again.

Jake was gone.

Nikki took her breath. It was hard; for some reason, she was feeling really lightheaded. The cool water spread through her, as her ungraceful dive hit the surface.

The lavender color swirled around her, and Nikki's eyelids came together. She didn't feel like feeling sick.

Her arms were locked to each other when she opened her eyes again. She was sopping wet again and Jake's face was screwed up in a contorted expression of worry. It was awfully cold in Garden's room.

Nikki waved a soft flame around her arms and numb legs as they began walking again. Jake did the same, but from the tip of his wand. She could tell the flame was barely alive, and more than ever, she was sorry for him that he didn't have a gift.

There was a strange coldness creeping up along her side, but she pushed the feeling away, and was beginning to feel nauseous.

Nikki took the lead. She couldn't help noticing how loud their footsteps were. They made a hard "Pitter slap, pitter slap," on the rough slab of pavement. It had become several times more slipperier as the rain had become more serious.

Somehow, the swerving tunnels eventually took them to the dungeons where Sophie, James, Breannen, and Michelle would be if they didn't do what Jake had requested. Which was abandon them. Nikki didn't think they would.

Jake pushed the door roughly aside to greet four expectant faces.

"Scarlet got away, there was nothing we could do she just—"

"Fizzled out into in wall!" Breannen finished for James.

"It's fine," Jake said out of breath. "She caught up to us but she's gone for now, now that Colon has left."

"Colon *left*?" Sophie asked in disbelief. "You didn't finish him off, and he just chickened out and *left*?"

"Yes," Nikki assured. "And Jasmine is gone too. Forever."

The look on her friends faces displayed every question from, "Jasmine's here?" to "You mean she's dead?"

Nikki didn't want to explain, and she wondered why she hadn't let them come with her to find Jake in the first place. Colon would probably be dead by now if she had, and she wouldn't have to worry about being on the line of exile.

An icy feeling was spreading through her and it took her about a minute to realize that she wasn't just getting chills. Her side ached and the throw-up feeling she had earlier seemed to double. There was a throb in her temples.

And then, Nikki crumpled to the floor.

Chapter Thirteen

Savior

I

The voices Nikki heard seemed to be yelling through a thick fog.

"I'm not going to lose anyone else." The voice sounded like James but there was a sharp crack in the vocals.

"Why can't you heal her?!" That was Jake. She had never heard him so frustrated.

"It only works from the outside in! I can't heal inside wounds!"

Jake's voice got quiet. "She would have died."

"She hasn't fainted yet, Jake. She's not dead. We *can* save her." Nikki thought that was Sophie.

She could imagine Breannen biting her lip. Breannen had always hated it when she had nothing to say in an argument or agreed with both sides.

Nikki didn't know what Michelle would be doing. She was probably scared to death.

Nikki could feel her body being lifted up. She couldn't imagine why until she heard Jake's voice again. "We have to take her to Garden and Alexandria. They'll know what to do."

Jake had to be carrying her. He was the only one who was strong enough. Her friends hadn't met Garden. They'd have to trust Jake on this.

"Don't give up on me yet. I've been stupid, but you deserve to live more than one month in your new life." Jake invaded her mind.

Nikki was glad he had, even though she felt Jake have to shift her in his arms because he was using his energy.

She sent him two easy words that would at least bring his pessimistic hopes up. *I won't.*

Jake's foot tripped slightly. She was becoming somewhat of a burden. There was nothing Nikki could do for him though, as much as she wanted to. She was physically paralyzed.

The others followed quietly. She wish she could read their minds too, or at least ask Jake about what their faces were, but he was wearing out already from the little conversation they had had.

You're lucky you're pretty light.

His attempt to start a conversation flared up anger in her so that for a second, she thought that she could feel her flame again. It was gone just as fast.

Stop talking to me, you need to save your strength.

Jake was quiet after that.

They had arrived at Garden's room that also held the **Pool**.

"We're here," Jake called out.

He laid Nikki gently on the ground and opened the door with a immense shove of his elbow.

Nikki could feel the coldness creep up into her neck, constricting her lungs. It was painful, but she swallowed her voice.

She felt her body being lifted again by Jake—she presumed it was Jake—and she could hear the steady footsteps of her friends behind her.

She could tell Jake almost dropped her.

"He's not here?"

Strangely enough, Sophie had said it. Probably from reading Jake's mind.

"No." Nikki could imagine Jake's face, full of solemn worry.

"What do we do now?" Breannen whispered. She was afraid that if she spoke too loud, her voice would crack in pain.

"We have to find him."

"There's no way," James argued. "This castle is huge and this Garden guy could be anywhere!"

Jake started leaving the room, Nikki still in his arms. The others were in front of him. His heart started pumping as his brain egged him to look back. He didn't want to, disappointment would only strangle his heart; Garden was his only chance.

But he did.

And at a thick wooden desk, was a man. Who hadn't been there three seconds ago. "Garden," Jake said, his voice full of peace and relief.

"Ah, Jacob, right on time as usual."

Jake raised an eyebrow. "As usual?"

"He has a point Garden, usually he's quite too late." A pretty young woman with blond hair had come up as sudden as her master. "However, in this case, you should be glad you made it in time." Alexandria's eyes trailed down to Nikki in Jake's arms.

"I know. She needs help, Garden, I know you can do something!"

The rest of the group seemed to have melted away. Michelle especially seemed uncomfortable in this situation. What could they do anyway? Jake was the one, who if anything, could help. They were no longer important.

"I cannot."

Jake's face went dark as Garden stated those words. "Can't or *won't*?" He didn't want his voice to sound as sharp and hurt as he had displayed it, nevertheless, it had.

The air had gone from tense, to nerve-racking and painful.

Alex's face was emotionless.

"Won't." Garden stated simply.

Jake ground his teeth. "She will die."

"I won't because... Michelle has to."

"What?!" Michelle, Breannen, and Jake said together. Sophie's, who had read his mind a few seconds before he had said that, mouth just gaped widely open. James was too taken back to respond.

"Me?" Michelle asked with a shaking finger pointing to herself. "I can't save her. I don't know what to do...I'll mess it up...I..."

"Come this way," Garden beckoned, waving his hand towards her to come hither. Michelle took a few steps forward. Jake gave her a look of comfort as she passed. His look was also nerve-racking

"In this cupboard, are several potions and medical magical cures. One will save Nikki according to her gift. Several will kill or even make her sickness worse. She has ice poisoning right now. And since neither Jacob nor James have the energy or are able to save her, I'm afraid it comes down to you."

"And where are you going that you can't save her?" Jake demanded.

A crashing sound come from behind them as the final window broke. There were guards not far behind it. A rushing wind blew through the room, turning everyone of the group's attention to the back's large brass door that was wide open.

The doors, with a sudden sweeping motion, closed with a heavy slam. Jake turned and saw what he had expected. Garden and Alexandria had vanished once again.

Although there was something he had not expected though. Ahead of him were a few steps where the cabinet and Michelle were standing. There was now a clear wall. It was as though the rest of the group was looking through distorted glass.

Michelle was just barely visible on the other side. Jake could hardly believe how unfair Garden was playing. That he was playing a game at all.

He gently laid Nikki down on the floor. Her body was as cold as the ice that had pierced her. Jake ran up to the wall, slamming his fists thickly against the solid wall. "Michelle?! Michelle, can you hear me?!"

Michelle walked a bit closer to the glass but made no faces or gestures that she could hear him. "She can't hear us," Jake whispered quietly.

"I can hear *her*, you know." Sophie's hands held high on her hips, stared with glaring eyes at Jake. "You give up way to easily. There must have been a reason that Garden would have done this. You trust him, so trust what he's doing. This is a test for Michelle—"

"We don't have time for tests—" Jake started, at a thin whisper. He was clearly in shock that Sophie would stand up to him like this.

"—and although *you* may think that Michelle can't do this, she came with us. She's Nikki's friend. And you should trust her. Because Nikki does." Sophie pursed her lip.

Jake had nothing to say. But he nodded in agreement.

II

Michelle was scared to death. If it was up to her, or anyone for that matter, she would have not chosen herself to save Nikki. She couldn't be trusted. She knew she might screw things up. And this time, there was no way to fix them if she did.

It was awful the pressure she was in.

Her heart raced, but nevertheless, she forced herself to walk forward towards the cabinet of medical needs. It was bright gold in color, and coming from the inside was both sweet smelling scents and foul scents all jumbled together. She wished more than ever that she had the spine of her friends.

Who in their right mind would pick her anyway? she thought.

She grasped the brass handle of the cupboard tightly, taking care not to make it squeak as she opened it. Nikki was counting on her, and she was worried about a squeak that the door might make. If that tripped her up, what would the vast size of the cabinet do?

As Michelle pulled the door ajar and peered inside, she almost felt so lightheaded, she thought she was going to faint. There were hundreds—no *millions*—of glasses of liquid. Now all she had to do was find the right one.

Dust filled her mouth, nose, and eyes, making them tearful. She wanted to cry too. And that just made it worse.

Every size, shape and color of both the glasses and the fluids lie in the case. How in the world was she suppose to know which one? Jake had never talked once about magical remedies, she had thought they didn't existed. Plus, she was inexperienced. But the world just *had* to rely on her.

She took a small green one off a shelf in front of her. Uncorking it, she wafted. Michelle's nose wrinkled and she quickly stuffed the bottle back on the shelf, capped again.

If only they were labeled.

Her mind racked.

What would seem like a medicine that Nikki would take for a wound like this? Jake had mumbled something about her being ice cold, so maybe something that would heat up her fire?

This was such a stupid job!

There was no time to back down either.

III

Jake saw a familiar looking potion through his side of the glass. It was a red bottle, very thick, at about ear level to Michelle. He had always hated potions, partly because of his incapability to make them, and also the fact that they were unreliable and unpredictable.

All he could hope for was that Michelle bothered to look up. He knew that potion, the only one that he found himself interested in (which he blamed on his **curse**) as a potion for those of a fire gift to be cured by all wounds and internal damages. He also spotted several ones he had just come to know through his years of living. Several of which Michelle seemed to be picking up...

Would she pick the right one?

His heart was racing faster than it ever had.

He could feel his own heart faltering.

If Nikki died—the one person he was sworn to protect—he was almost positive that he would die too.

A life for a life.

A life for failing to protect.

He shot a look at Nikki.

Had she paled even more in the last thirty seconds?

Hurry Michelle.

IV

Michelle rummaged faster, squinting at the vastness of the cabinet. It just wasn't fair. A sudden glint caught her eye, making her turn her head a bit to the left.

There was a bottle wrapped in slender, golden glass flames. Inside was a crystal-like blue liquid. It felt like it had already been five years as she searched, and every color was standing out to her in the case. But the glint this potion gave off surprised her, throwing her attention off everything else.

Michelle picked it up. Right behind it was another glass, this one was skinny, surrounded with miniature icicles that gathered around it like stones to a castle. This one had a glinting golden and red swirling liquid in it.

She picked that one up too.

She could feel the time slipping away.

Michelle felt her eyes training hard on the two potions. Something was seriously wrong. Either something had gone wrong within the two potions from being inside the cabinet for who knows how long, or they had been rigged. Perhaps Garden knew that Michelle would figure it out.

Garden wouldn't have done that though, would he? She knew he wanted to test her, but this was just cruel. She had seen tricks; throwing eggs at peoples' houses, or joy-buzzing them from a shocker in your hand as they shake it. This was no laughing matter. No game of hide and seek. This was real life. Yet Garden was acting like this was some sort of a sick joke.

Michelle had made up her mind.

V

Jake saw Michelle pick up the right bottle and another that looked as though it were death itself. Until he saw her do the worst thing he thought she could possibly do, he thought she was doing fine. That was when she put the right bottle down and started walking towards the wall with the bottle shaped like ice, that he knew would do the opposite of what they wanted to do for Nikki.

Michelle passed through the wall of mirror-like substance easily, and ran towards Nikki faster than he had ever seen her run. He himself made a break towards her, praying that he would make it before she tipped even a drop down Nikki's throat. Jake wondered why his **curse's** protection mode hadn't settled in.

Nikki was in danger, yet the fact that the **curse** usually gave him a feeling ten times stronger than adrenaline, hadn't come to his senses yet.

Which was odd.

He saw her uncork the bottle as she ran, making sure that not a drip spilled out. She was so close, he had to stop her. Why did she have to come out of the glass wall so far from him? She was less than a few feet away.

"Michelle! No! wait!"

The others had finally noticed the urgency in Jake's movements and voice. His face told all they needed to hear.

But Michelle wasn't listening.

She was at Nikki's side now and spilled a few drops of a

substance that looked like a liquid sunrise into Nikki's mouth.

"NO! MICHELLE! YOU'RE GOING TO KILL HER!" He knew that Garden was foolish to pick Michelle.

He was by her side in an instant, his hand brushing Nikki's cheeks. They were warm. Her eyes flickered open, and as her fingernails dug into the cement around her, trying to lift herself up, large flames licked the ground around her. Flames more powerful than he had ever seen her do subconsciously.

Jake let out a hand, despite the fact that he might get burned. Nikki took it with a smile and let him pull her up. "Power in numbers. That's what Kay told me. I saw her…when I was unconscious…"

Jake sent a desperately thankful look at Michelle. "You'd be surprised what people can live through. Even if they die. They don't really." Jake had added words to her spoken thoughts. It lit her inside with more heat and fire than she had ever felt. It felt good to be her. For once.

Jake then did something she could never imagine him doing. He wrapped his arms around her. "I really didn't want to lose you. Not just because of the stupid **curse**."

Michelle smiled brightly as Jake let Nikki go.

"I knew you would do well," came a sudden voice from on top of the few stairs. Garden.

"What are you talking about? We all nearly got killed. And we didn't even accomplish our task. The best thing that happened to us was that we didn't lose three people in one night." Jake stuffed his sword back in its scabbard.

"You gained everything, including more trust in each other."

"But—" Nikki started.

"No one expects anyone to kill Colon in a night. No was has been able to kill anyone in his family, except when his family turned on each other, for the last two hundred years. But, no one has gotten as far as you all have since then. He won't be crowning tonight. For a while. You have taken care of Jasmine, rather brutally might add."

Jake blushed hard with anger.

"But all the same, he will be in mourn for some time, and yes you both will be seeking revenge on each other. And you will get your chance. For now though, go home, rest, and you two... you six will meet each other again. I can promise you on my pocket watch that he will not strike within a year. Kay's body has been transported to your mother's house Nicole. Oh, and the guards have been taken care of. At least for the moment."

Jake nodded.

"We need to leave," Jake said to the group.

They started walking towards the door. A final door that lead to safety.

"You know, I would have probably killed Nick for picking the wrong potion." It was a calmer time. When nicknames were again used. Especially by Jake.

"That's probably why Garden picked Michelle. For some reason, he knew that she wouldn't be tricked." Breannen was finally glad she could get her voice out without being afraid of what the answer would be.

"Yeah," James agreed. He had found his voice too.

They had somehow made it outside again. The morning dawn was just breaking through the last of the fading storm clouds. Nikki had never fully appreciated the fact that the sun was warm, full of hope, and nothing short of beautiful.

Jake, she wanted to talk to him about something. Something she wanted to start now, but without the interested gaze of her fellows.

I know what you're about to ask, Nick. But I just couldn't do it. I'm just not a killer. When I was there, and I had the huge chance to just kill Colon, but I knew that if I did, I couldn't forgive myself. I just couldn't. I don't think I'm meant to, as strange as it sounds. Before he disappeared, he promised me that he would see me again, and that next time, I should be more prepared.

Nikki bit her lip. It was something that had itched at her insides all through the night. *The way I was chanting at you, encouraging you to do it... I wonder what I would have done in your place. If I were you.*

Jake had been staring at the sun rise but suddenly turned to her with a glare that was not just full of anger, but pleading. *Don't think that way, you're not a killer either. I've been inside your head, I know.*

Relief flooded into her as Jake said these words to her inside her head. They were closer now. More than they had ever been. And it was just because of what happened that night.

Nikki, Jake, and the rest of the friends picked up the rest of their abandoned things at the Berlidge Inn, and headed towards the looming forest. But they were together. Something Nikki hoped they would stay for a long time. If they had made it this far.

"Jake?"

"Yes?"

"I heard Kay. When I was almost dead. She's okay."

Jake nodded thoughtfully. "I don't doubt that. She died fighting beside people she loved. We've been through a lot."

They walked silently for the rest of the way.

Nikki smiled softly to herself. *Yeah*, she thought. *I'm definitely not the adventurous type.*

Jake grinned.

CPSIA information can be obtained at www.ICGtesting.com
Printed in the USA
BVOW061815070312

284662BV00001B/33/P